BOOKS BY C.E. POVERMAN

NOVELS

Susan
Solomon's Daughter
My Father in Dreams
On the Edge

SHORT STORY COLLECTIONS

The Black Velvet Girl
Skin

ON THE EDGE

C.E. POVERMAN

St. Martin's Paperbacks

Published by arrangement with The Ontario Review Press

ON THE EDGE

Copyright © 1997 by C.E. Poverman.
Cover photograph by Matt Lambert/Tony Stone.

Library of Congress Catalog Card Number: 96-35491

ISBN: 0-312-97089-7

Printed in the United States of America

Ontario Review Press hardcover edition published 1997
St. Martin's Paperbacks edition/September 1999

St. Martin's Paperbacks are published by St. Martin's Press, 175 Fifth Avenue, New York, NY 10010.

10 9 8 7 6 5 4 3 2 1

For John Murphy—Friends

Thanks to Richard Oseran for friendship and timely advice.
And to Linda, for everything.

ON THE EDGE

FRANK TIPPED HIS head back into the shower, but the hangover stayed with him. Once more he thought of the California State Bar Exam—he'd have to take the monster again. The notice had come to the office yesterday. Before that, Christ, he hadn't had a drink in what? Weeks? Maybe even a couple of months—probably not since the last time Karen had warned him. It had been a tightrope walk, but he'd managed. There'd been a few beers and a vodka or two; yeah, a toke here or there. But it had been more or less under control until yesterday when he'd spotted the envelope on his desk and felt a sense of dread clenching his stomach as he opened it. Afterward, he'd tried to stay with his work—a trip to the sixth floor at the Hall of Justice to see one of his defendants, a couple of subpoenas to serve—but with a ton more left to do, he'd drifted into a corner bar in the Upper Haight just to be alone and slow down over a beer, which had turned into a second, and then a couple of vodkas, and then it had gotten blurry. . . .

Frank turned the water from hot to lukewarm. The problem wasn't the exam, itself. It was that he couldn't get far enough ahead to stop running his business full time. He had finished law school five years ago, started to study for the bar, run out of money, and been forced to put off the bar to go to work. A mentor of his in the Public Defender's office had found him something with a private investigator. A year later, he'd gone out on his own. He'd been on the run ever since, always with the urgent sense that he had to get back to taking the bar. Several months ago, still scrambling, still not ahead, he'd registered for the exam, anyway. Frank had studied nights, evenings, in-between, always on the run, always jammed with cases. He'd still only failed by a few points.

He turned the shower from lukewarm to cold, felt his neck and temples tighten and pound. Hadn't the law always just been there for him? Even before his father lay in the hospital saying, "I'm not telling you to do it. Just give it serious consideration. It's a strong connection to the community, it's a way to make a living, all of *that*, but more, it's the way to help the underdog, Frank—the guy who's getting stepped on." By then, the skin on his father's face was thin, almost translucent, his voice an echo of the voice Frank had always known. Then his father had started talking softly, almost privately, about Catholicism as a way of believing in yourself: "Don't turn your back on it, Frank, it's not about priests and masses, that's only the outer appearance." Later, they had all come to seem one thing to Frank, practicing law, Catholicism, believing in yourself, something about his father in that hospital bed.

Frank gulped several mouthfuls of the cold water. The nausea pooled into a return of last night's nightmare. Driving. Some other time in his life. Something horrible waiting for him, the road and desert stretching away endlessly to the horizon; some place he had to be and was not getting to in time, his father's presence close.

Frank turned off the water, stepped onto the mat, and starting to dry himself, thrust his head into the space between the open window and sill, which swirled with plummeting steam. He took a deep breath. He pushed open the bathroom door and peered into the kitchen. Listened for Karen. Called. Called again. He could tell by the silence that Karen was gone already. Gone and pissed. She'd left her anger and reproach in the silence. Her back to him as she'd made coffee. Hungover and shaky, he'd ducked into the bathroom. That was all he could do.

The last time he'd slid, Karen had said, "I can't—I won't—live under the threat of whatever this thing is." Frank understood her feelings. Hey, he'd been okay. He was okay. He really wasn't drinking. And Karen was grateful for his effort, but whether he drank or not, she still claimed his behavior had grown increasingly erratic; she said she felt things eating at him; once she had used the terrible phrase "dry drunk" somewhere in a conversation, and said, "If things don't somehow smooth out, I'll do whatever I have to do. . . ." She hadn't finished the sentence. Lately she had taken it into her head that he needed professional help. Ominous euphemism: professional help.

Karen, Frank thought, liked to dramatize things. And things eating at him? Anyone Frank knew who wasn't a half-wit had things eating at him.

Okay, he'd fallen yesterday, he was wrong, he was sick this morning and paying for it. He dried himself, stepped out of the bathroom, and turned on "Good Morning America," ignored it, set water on to boil. Naked but for a large, ridiculous diamond pinky ring—real diamond—he'd found on the bottom of a swimming pool years ago, he ground coffee beans. He was about to start working on his list for the day when he noticed the red light flashing on the answering machine. He played it back.

"Mr. August, this is Aram Melikian's office. Please call Mr. Melikian as soon as possible. It's 8:20 now. Thank you." The machine beeped. Frank glanced at the clock. 8:30.

Aram hadn't called or spoken to him in months. In fact, Aram had just started avoiding him; Frank had asked around, what was the word, was it something he'd done? but lawyers, public defenders, guys who knew Melikian just said, that's the way he is, man, brilliant, moody, unpredictable, the best, but when he decides to hang you out there for a while, you hang out there. Just forget it. He'll come around. Still, it had bothered Frank.

Relieved that Aram had finally called him, he said, "Turn me on, turn me off, what am I here?" He pulled on a pair of slacks, thongs, a T-shirt, and yanked a long-billed fishing hat on his damp hair. The hat was silver, said Kino Bay, Mexico in red script, and had a blue marlin leaping on the front. He sifted the ground coffee into a cone, filled it with boiling water.

He poured coffee, debated toast, fought back nausea. Stood in the middle of the kitchen, hat on backward, hair damp and drying, cool air coming in the kitchen window. He was fifteen pounds overweight, hungover, thirty-four, had too much to do, and after all was said and done, still had to pass the bar exam. Though his face was a little heavy, he had clean, handsome features—the almost che-

rubic hero's profile of a young Paul Hornung—tight curly
blond hair, and traces of a wounded boy's vulnerability
and bravado, which surfaced as charm—sweetness—and
which belied an arbitrary temper, deep suspicion, and calculation. His eyes changed from light green to something
smokey—chameleon eyes. Almost six-three, he had a
thick, powerful chest, legs so heavily muscled he had to
buy his pants big to get a fit, and considering his build, he
had smallish, almost delicate feet.

He wasn't quite ready for Aram. He didn't have a feel
or instinct for what he could want, how to deal with him.
Why now after all of these months? He stepped to the
window, peered out across the rooftops, breathed the cool
morning air. In the distance, he could see the Bay, the
lightstandards from Candlestick, the big cranes out at
Hunters Point.

He turned when he heard the mailman on the porch.
Wandered through the dark interior of the old Victorian
house, down the long narrow hallway; he picked up the
Chronicle off the mat, took in the mail. A large, padded
envelope in Karen's handwriting. Self-addressed and
stamped. He looked at the return address: Meg Kessler,
New American Makers, San Francisco. He squeezed the
package, felt a cassette inside. Months ago Karen had sent
something to Kessler, who curated video art for an annual
collection to be shown on public television and in Opera
Plaza, all with fanfare. Karen had been hoping and waiting
for this. "Please don't let a self-addressed, brown envelope
come back." But here it was.

Feeling badly for her, Frank shook his head, then considered hiding it for a day or two just so he wouldn't have
to go through whatever craziness would come out of this.
He dropped the mail on the kitchen table, set the envelope
aside, and glanced at the sports page to see how the Giants
were doing. Three games back. He called Melikian's office, gave his name. His secretary said, "He's on another
line. Can you hold, Mr. August?"

"I don't know, can I? We're all formality today, Velma. You know you can call me Frank."

"It should only be a minute."

He didn't reply and she put him on hold. He leafed through his notes and files, stared at "Good Morning America," turned the sound down, stood and paced.

Aram came on. "Francis Ignatius August!" He was in his expansive, affable mood. Frank didn't know which way to jump. Decided to play it cool, funny.

"Ya voy, qué pasa, Señor Melikian?" he said in a thick Hispanic accent.

Aram laughed. "Frank, how've you been?"

"Be bad. What's happenin'?"

Aram laughed again. "I've got something for you. Just came in. Jesus, can you hold a second?" The phone went silent. Frank thought, good, whatever slight Melikian had imagined, or had taken place, Melikian's resolved it, it's over, we can start working again. He came back on. "I've got a client who specifically requested you as his investigator. You been hanging around with the wrong people, or do you just have a fabulous reputation?"

"Both."

"Fabulous reputation? Client's name is Ray Buchanan. You know the guy?"

Frank suddenly went blank, as if he'd been struck. "I know him a little."

"You don't sound thrilled. From where, if I might ask?"

"Oh, here and there, Aram. He's a friend of a friend, seen him at a party, in a restaurant, that kind of thing. I don't really know him."

"Well, you must have made a great impression—the old charm—because he wants you for his investigator. We've had a long standing arrangement that if he ever got into any kind of trouble, he'd call me and I'd step in." Frank was surprised. He'd known that Ray had someone, but he hadn't known it was Melikian. There were all kinds of things he'd never known about Ray. Or Melikian, for that fact. ''From the few times I've talked to him, I think he's a good guy. He's not a hood or greaseball. He could be anyone at a dinner party. He's good looking. Respectable. Plays a lot of tennis, supposed to be very good.'' There was a pause. ''You there, Frank?''

''You want me to play tennis with him? I'm listening.''

''The DEA busted him last night. They've got him on the sixth floor at the Hall. Can you get down to the jail and talk to him? The grand jury meets this afternoon so I'm expecting the indictment soon. I don't know what we've got. He called me at six this morning. It doesn't sound great for him, but we'll do something. Three other guys were busted with him. I've got it written down here . . . wait . . . Jack Adams. Guy named Sam Coleman. A Dean Miller. You heard of these guys?''

Frank hesitated. ''No. What happened?''

''Find out the details. I've got to run. Just interview him and report to me. Do the thing you're good at, which is getting people to tell you more than they thought they would. Find out how he was busted, what money he saw, what drugs, where things went. You know the drill. Calm him down. Tell him help is on the way. Call me this afternoon, we'll pick it up. Where'd you say you knew him from?''

''A party. A friend in common. Nothing. I don't really know him.''

''Well, he wants you for his investigator. He's allegedly one of the bigger dealers in the Golden West.''

Christ, Aram was a great lawyer, he'd taught Frank a lot, but when would he ever stop talking like that on a telephone. Well, what the fuck did Aram care? One way or the other, he got his money, and what was another dope case to him, except fifty thousand up front. First, last and always the thing that juiced Melikian was his murder defendants looking at the death penalty and him in front of a jury where he could be in total control. That was what he loved. Control.

"Gotta run. Call me after three. Heard you took the bar last time?"

"Yeah, sure did."

"How'd you do?"

"Haven't heard yet."

"I'm gone. Talk to you later."

"Aram. Probably much too early, but anything about it in the paper?"

"Not this morning's *Chronicle*. Talk to you."

Melikian hung up. Frank looked at the receiver and moving slowly, hung up. He spotted an old snapshot of his father on the bulletin board. It had been taken in army boot camp. WWII. His father at attention, rifle on his shoulder, shadow falling to his side. His father wearing a brimmed hat, eyes ahead.

He straightened. Blank and queasy with adrenalin and hangover. Ray. He wandered down the dark hallway to the front of the house. Looked out the window to see if Kramer was home. Glanced up and down the narrow street. No car. He wanted to talk to someone he could trust. Maybe Kramer. Momentarily, Frank remained motionless and, strangely, almost terrified to turn around. Whether it was the hangover, the nightmares, the sudden news of Ray, or some combination, a terrible presence seemed to have emerged and filled the house. He forced himself to turn and face an empty room.

Frank climbed the stairs to the second floor and dug out a laundered shirt, remained looking at the opened drawer. Yesterday, he'd reminded himself to check the drawer before he moved anything. He carefully pulled out the four remaining drawers, the topmost one being a catchall—mementoes, coins, snapshots, letters, film, a broken watch, what have you. He was sure Karen had been going through his things again. What was she looking for? He thought she'd started this about six months ago. Exasperated, uneasy—was it him? her? nothing at all?—he shook his head, went on dressing, dropping things as he did so, all of the time trying to imagine Ray on the sixth floor of the Hall of Justice.

But shirt half buttoned, he sank down on the sofa and stared out the window and around the bedroom. It was the attic space of the old Victorian which he had converted, first gutting, then insulating, furring and sheetrocking it, putting in a bathroom, and big north-facing skylight. The deal was that if he bought the place, all of his expenses and labor went against the price of the house. If he bought the place. . . . He sighed. Not now. Probably not ever. One phone call and that was gone. He stood. From the large back window, he had a clear open view across the clutter of rooftops from the back of Holly Park to the Bay. He sighed, groomed and watered a plant. Glanced at one of Karen's beautiful black and white prints. That was what she should be doing: her still photography. People loved her prints. Galleries sold them. But no, she had to do something marginal, unmarketable: video art. Part of him loved her for her refusal to play by the rules, part was exasperated. Frank went back down to the kitchen and called his office.

Gloria answered. Cool English accent. She was a tall, elegant strawberry blond from London. Somehow, with seemingly no excess motion at all, she kept the office under control, kept the books, and frequently did cases. She could get anything out of anyone. Where Frank would have hit a stone wall, the male to male trip, men blabbed-boasted-flirted their heads off to her. Talked. In deference to his need for Gloria, he always paid her first whenever money came in.

"Morning, Ms. It's me. Any messages?"

"The phone's been ringing off the hook."

They ran through several messages, and then Frank said, "Gloria, you're going to have to cover for me. Something's just come up which blows the day apart. I've got a witness coming in at ten . . ."

"Hector Sanchez."

"Right, Sanchez. Let John interview Sanchez. He knows the case."

Gloria hesitated. "I don't know if we can count on John."

"Why not?"

"He just called to say he's not coming in until noon."

"Christ, he was supposed to be in at nine! Please call him back and get him in now. We've got a dozen cases, we've got lawyers screaming for reports, we have to locate and interview witnesses, we've got twenty-three subpoenas to serve, I'm supposed to meet with the Public Defender at noon . . ."

"John says he has to settle something with his wife and that he can't be in before noon. He wants to be paid by noon."

"Jesus, Gloria."

"Frank, I'm only giving you the message. He says you owe him $3,000 for cases. He won't work until he's been paid."

"How am I supposed to pay him if the courts and lawyers don't pay me? I haven't been paid myself. He knows that!"

"I'm just relaying the message, Frank."

"Okay, Gloria. See what you can do. He's got to work. He knows I'll pay him. I'm overwhelmed by this show of loyalty. Why's he squeezing me? I'll check back with you around eleven."

"I'll do what I can. What's the case, Frank?"

"What case?"

"The one that's just come up?"

"Loose lips sink ships. We'll talk. Gotta run."

He hung up. Glanced at his watch. If only the goddamned courts and lawyers would pay him when they finished a case, he could run his business and wouldn't have to hassle with money. They waited, lawyers didn't file their vouchers, or they said they'd gotten judges' signatures for court ordered funds when they hadn't; lawyers finished cases, they got paid, they went on vacations, but they didn't pay him. Pay you when we get back . . . whatever. Christ, what if John wouldn't work? Did he really owe him three grand? When had it gotten to be that much? Kramer . . . Maybe Kramer would pinch-hit. He'd go talk to Kramer—quick, just for a second. . . . John, what an incredible turkey to pull this now.

In fact, Frank had a deep and abiding respect for John, particularly after a case he'd handled a year ago. The City had sued one of the last gay bathhouses, claiming that its clients weren't complying with the ordinance to wear condoms. The bathhouse had denied the charges. John had gone in several times to see. Wearing literally nothing more than a towel, John, who was what one might call an extremely heterosexual male, had steered through whatever sexual hazards he'd had to and written a twenty-page report full of references to the Caucasian male who entered room six, fellated a black male, who then rolled over . . . pages of it. Not once had he seen a condom. This in the midst of the AIDS epidemic. The report had been the ammunition the City had needed to win the case. Frank had been amazed at John's nerve and cool. John said laconically, "Well, okay, Frank, I literally gave you more than the shirt off my back. Give me a raise." And Frank had. But pulling this money thing today . . . ?

Frank looked down at himself. Shirt out, tie askew. He tucked in his shirt, knotted his tie, pulled on his jacket. It kept coming to him. Ray. A wave of panic rose. He stared at the kitchen table. A hollow queasiness—both hunger and a repulsion for food—went through him, and breaking into a sweat, he took a deep breath. He ran a glass of cold water, drank most of it, took a couple of vitamin B tablets. Spotted Karen's video. He picked it up and looked around the kitchen. Hide it? Just for a day or two? He heard a key rattling in the front door and froze. The door pushed open. Karen. What was she doing back now? He shoved the Chronicle over the padded mailer. She followed the movement of his hand, but didn't say anything.

"Thought you'd gone to work?"

"I did. Got there and realized I'd forgotten the designs, Jeanette's in a terrible mood this morning, and when I forgot the layouts, she blew up. I didn't say a word, just ran out the door. How're you feeling?"

"Been better."

She looked at him, but didn't answer. She was slim, with wide-spaced, gray eyes, hair so black it was like an animal's coat, a raven's feather. After they'd been married a couple of years, a single blaze of white had appeared at the left temple. She had debated dying it, but a girlfriend said, "My God, it's beautiful, no way!" It reminded Frank of an animal's breed mark coming in, though it remained indecipherable to him. It *was* startling, and she was beautiful, with a jogger's tight fitness—compulsivity and narcissism—which had peaked over to a look of strain around the eyes and mouth.

"Really have to go, I'm already late." He leaned over to kiss her, a conciliatory kiss, she turned her cheek to receive the kiss cooly, gave him a steady gaze which annoyed him because it tried to imply and elicit all sorts of things—a little psycho fishing expedition—and suppressing his sudden irritation—alright, I had a few drinks and came home late last night, I made a mistake—he took a step toward the door.

"Be late?"

"Not too late."

"Should we meet for dinner?"

"I'll call you this afternoon."

"And make a date?"

"Sure, let's make a date, Karen."

"And then call me back every two hours until midnight . . ."

"I'm sorry . . . the last few months have been impossible . . . You know I've got to find people, witnesses, whoever, serve subpoenas when I can catch people—which is when they don't expect it."

She looked at him questioningly, slid back the *Chronicle*, and saw her video. She flushed, went pale. "Is this what you were trying to hide when I came in?"

"I wasn't trying to hide anything. I checked out the first section, tossed it on the table, and was on my way."

"Everyone believes you. You can con everyone in the world, but me, Frankie. That's why you stay with me. I suppose you were trying to do me a favor by hiding this, right?"

She sank down into the kitchen chair, her eyes suddenly going soft, sad, glassy. She opened the manilla envelope, removed her video. A note fell out with it. Slash of green ink:

Dear Karen Bainbridge:
   I know and admire some of your other work. The producer and I went back and forth on these, which I liked a good deal, but finally, we didn't think either were quite right for this year's format. Please send us something next year.

                                   Sincerely,
                                   Meg Kessler

Besides the recognition and the pleasure of having her work shown to the public, Frank knew she'd hoped it would lead to a grant, which translated into time to get new work going. Frank put his hand on her shoulder. She went to the refrigerator and poured herself a glass of juice.

"They kept it three months."

Frank sighed and said softly, "I'm sorry, Karen."

"Why talk softly and pretend you care? If you really cared, you wouldn't stay out half the night, come home drunk like you did last night. Sloppy. Falling over things. Mumbling like some incoherent beast. I'll just make a date to go to the movies with Susan.

"I can't tell if it's this work that's changed you—ruined you. I ask myself all the time. You look so nervous today. You're cold, you're suspicious, you're irrational, half the time I don't know what you're up to . . . Christ, you look at me like I'm an enemy. Everything I'm saying just freaks you out. I understand how it is . . . I really do . . . you're overworked, lawyers run you to death, you're as smart as these guys, you just about do the case for half of them, all the legwork, and get paid a third of what they get; you're angry and resentful . . .''

''You act like it's my fault when the lawyer calls two days before, find my witness, then he's screaming where's his statement, I go to his house twenty times, six in the morning, six at night, eleven at night, he's never there. . . . Look, Karen, I'm sorry about last night. I really am. I don't know exactly how it happened. I didn't plan it. I regret it. I'm sorry if I hurt you.''

She stood with her arms crossed; something went out of her.

''When are you going to hear on the bar exam? Should be any day now.''

''Haven't heard yet.''

''I know you really didn't get time to study, but I have a feeling you passed. Once you pass, the pressure will be off . . . you'll get out of investigation, have some time, get some money and breathing room. We'll be better.''

She turned and looked out the window. Mused. ''Lately I've been wondering if the qualities which make you so impossible are what make you good at what you do . . . You love to provoke people, you're suspicious, a charming con man . . . secretive, sometimes, I think, for the sake of it.'' She picked up her video. ''I'm just saying I don't know anymore, Frank.''

''I'll see you tonight. Make it eight. Call you this afternoon. Karen, what were they? *Kiss? Glasses?*'' She nodded. ''I loved them.''

She glanced at him. ''Don't. Please. I know you're trying to make me feel better, but I also know what you think of video art.''

He picked up his files and camera and stepped out of the kitchen.

''Did you feed the cats?''

''No, I thought you did.''

He moved quickly, heard her open the door and call in a high musical voice which made him love her, "Sally . . . Joe . . ." He turned and looked back to see Karen's silhouette against the silvery blue backlight of the high kitchen window. She extended her arms. Sally, the Siamese, gathered in a crouch, and meowing, deep, throaty, turned-on and musical, leapt.

Outside, Frank stood on the porch, put on his sunglasses, and stepped into the narrow sloping street. He could only hope Gloria would find some way of covering the morning. And now where the hell was his car? No recollection at all of driving home last night, parking. He walked slowly down toward the corner, turned and walked back up the block. Found the car parked in a yellow zone near the corner, half sticking out into the street. He walked around the metallic, mauve 70 Cadillac Coupe de Ville. One of his defendants had given it to him before going to jail for five years. Told Frank he was the only one who'd cared or tried for him in his defense. The glove box was twisted from where the Feds had pried it open in a search and seizure. They could have just asked for the key, but that would have been too easy. He looked at the car. Nice going, August, he said out loud. Really, amazing that someone hadn't creamed the back of it.

He tossed the files and camera on the seat, threw his street maps on the floor, started the car. It stalled. He started it again, revved the engine. John wanted to be paid at noon, where was he going to come up with three grand? Maybe John would take $500, they'd been through this three months ago, big fight, lots of growling and posturing. John had walked out, they'd finally settled it; he knew there was going to be another big go-round. When had it become 3000 bucks? Christ, he had no choice, he'd better stop in now and see if Kramer would work. He checked his watch and was amazed to see that only half an hour had gone by since Melikian had called. It was nine o'clock. Just nine o'clock. Well, one thing for sure; Ray wasn't going anywhere. He drove quickly down to Kramer's, which was right across the street from his own house, spotted June balancing two grocery bags, and Zachary, who was kneeling in the gutter to examine a broken lightbulb.

June closed the car door with her elbow, kneeled to support the slipping bag. Tall, athletic blond. Frank double-parked, got out and took the bags. "Thanks, you're sweet, Frank."

Frank reached into his pocket and pulled out a piece of gum.

"Zack, can you handle some gum, dude-san." Frank followed June up the stairs, checked out her legs and ass as they fumbled the key into the lock. "One kid later, still looks good from the south side." June rolled her eyes, did a half wiggle, feigned ga-ga dumb blondness. Zack stood beside him, waiting for his gum.

"Gum, Frank . . ."

"In the house, dude. This be called friendly coercion, my man." Frank followed June into the front hall, walked the bags into the kitchen. Gave Zack his gum. "Thank you and please, these are the words which open any door with ease. Check it out, dude." Frank looked into the dining room. Kramer's word processor and notes on the table. A snapshot of several other journalists and Kramer in Nicaragua. Two of them, he knew, had been killed since.

"He hasn't gotten back yet."

Frank rolled his eyes. "Surfing?"

"There was a huge storm three days ago and it's big now. He went out just before sunrise."

"Christ almighty, 39 years old and out surfing in a wet suit. Believe that? Hey, anybody worth a shit's a little crazy, I guess."

"This isn't as bad as waiting for him to come back from Nicaragua."

Frank shrugged. "Dude's always been crazy. You knew it when you married him."

June half bowed her knee in a mock curtsy, smiled insipidly. "And I'm the good WASP ceramics teacher who stays at home so he can try to become white bread and picket fences like everyone else. How about a Dr. Pepper and a fresh mayonnaise sandwich on Tip Top bread?''

"What it is, June, my help's staging a coup today and I need Kramer to work. Can he lay off Commander Zero and the rest of the boys for a few days and help me?''

"Actually, that's an article about survivors of torture from Bolivia and Uruguay.''

"Whatever.''

"You'll have to ask him when he gets back.''

Frank browsed over Steve's desk, silently read, " 'The corpses looked reproachful . . . ' No wonder he's out surfing. I hope he can sell this. If he can't sell it, it's a waste of time.''

"*Mother Jones* wants it.''

"Good. Look can you have Kramer call the office when he gets in? I've got a dozen cases with lawyers screaming for reports. Really. It's a disaster.''

Zack chewed his gum and pushed a kitchen chair over to the counter. He climbed up and fiddled with the answering machine. The message filled the kitchen: "Hi, we can't come to the phone right now . . .'' The machine played: ". . . Anybody home? Stevie? June?''

Halfway down the hall, Frank stopped. Turned. A stunned, sickening feeling overtook him as he listened to his voice, slurred, faraway, coming into the room.

"Nobody home?'' There were fumbling sounds. Loud music in the background. ". . . Stevie, I fucked the bar . . . missed by just a few points . . . hey, if six were nine . . . Kramer, Karen's going to be pissed, wants me to get out there and start making some real money. Anybody there?''

Frank stood motionless. A fine sweat rose across his back and chest, his hairline. "What time was that call, June?''

"Last night. Late.''

"I have no recollection. Nothing. Blank. I don't even know where I was when I called you.''

June put her hand on his shoulder. "You okay, Frank? You don't look good." June pushed Frank toward a chair.

"Gotta go."

She brought him a glass of water and an Alka-Seltzer. He drank it. "It's okay, Frank." She looked at him, said half jokingly, "You give it all to your friends, the good, the crazy . . . your friends know that. Steve knows. Maybe it's a special trust."

"Tell me something. Is Kramer cold?"

"Absolutely: ice."

"I mean, can you trust a guy who can just turn around and completely stop drinking—stop anything—literally overnight. Wouldn't you think his basic nature was cold? Cold at heart."

"Yeah, Steve's a cold guy." She started reminding Frank of all the times they'd helped each other. She said softly, reproachfully, affectionately, "Shame on you, Frank."

Frank stood suddenly. "Gotta run!"

"Want to come for dinner tonight, you and Karen?"

"I don't speak for Karen. She's an independent entity. Frank August, Karen Bainbridge, husband and wife. You'll have to ask her."

Zack punched the play button again.

". . . anybody home? Stevie? June?"

"Zack!" June turned. "Stop it! Please! I'll try to reach her, maybe look for you both at dinner."

"I'll call you this afternoon, but I'm really jammed. Thanks." He turned. "Maybe you can talk to Karen before she goes back to work. She just got her video returned from some self-important curator." He put his hand on the front doorknob. He yanked open the door. "Tell Stevie I need him." Frank put out his palm. "Five, Slick."

Zack slapped his hand. Frank turned and jogged down the steps, saying to the street, "First, I want a kid, and Karen doesn't, then she wants a kid—her biological clock, you know—and I don't . . ."

He started the car, shot down the narrow street, some

asshole, as always, double-parked at the corner, he whipped out, another coming around the corner, he swerved, honked. Hit the brakes. Kramer. "Kramer, you asshole! Nice driving."

Kramer in a white Toyota pickup, surfboard caked with wax and sand in the back, music loud. Elvis Costello boiled out of the cab. Kramer's long hair was tangled and tufted with salt water, flakes of dried salt all over his face. He wore a faded Amazing Spiderman T-shirt, his gray eyes bloodshot.

"How was it?"

"Gnarly, dude," he shouted in a feigned fey voice. "Amazingly big. There was a monster storm offshore a few days ago. It was a little scary."

"So why do it?"

"Why do anything? We're all just going to die, right?"

They were shouting over the music which Kramer had no intention of turning down.

"I gotta go. Work for me later! I'm jammed."

"Can't."

"Can't. Then fuck you! I'm serious!"

"I'll call you."

"Back up!"

"No! You back up! I'm not backing out into that traffic. Hey! Frank. Sorry about the bar. You'll get it next time."

"If there ever is a next time. I should be like Aram Melikian, have a rich father. Jesus." Frank nodded, glanced behind him, put it in reverse. Stuck his head out the window again. "Don't tell Karen. She doesn't know yet. Tell June not to mention it, either. Karen had high hopes—me in a suit in a glossy office. Me full of self-respect or some such. I just need another few days to think it over, figure out the best way to break it to her."

Kramer waved back and nodded. Frank backed up the length of the street, Kramer shot by him as Frank Y-turned at the intersection. Now that Frank was alone, it came at him, Ray, the Hall of Justice, and his stomach rolled hard. He shot down the back streets, hit the traffic on Mission, everything sliding across the front seat as he turned, files and camera falling onto the floor. Mission Street. Salsa bars, crowded sidewalks, streets choked with cars, buses, Mexican restaurants, Latino movie theaters with their melodramatic, larger-than-life posters of impassioned lovers, gangsters, the low tangle of MUNI wires overhead, the streets filled with blowing paper, the gutters dirty, blacks and cholos at the graffiti-covered walls of the BART stations, crowded bus stops, the thud-thud-thud of a bass blaster, cholos cool taking it all in, suspenders, pants, sneakers, T-shirts, shirts with a single button buttoned, wind blowing shirts open. Frank stopped at a light. Smell of freshly ground beans coming out of a coffee shop.

At the Bank of America on Mission and Van Ness, he hopped out and walked to the bank machine. A muscular black in a tanktop stood under the windy portico, giant tape blasting, stoned face, rap music. Frank punched out his balance, worse than he thought, where'd the money gone? withdrew two hundred dollars. Stepped into a drug store. Pall Malls for Ray. Back outside, warmth of morning sun, chill of bay breeze funneling up Market. He slid into traffic, found himself slipping and sliding on the track behind a MUNI.

Momentarily, he felt himself drawn back into the recall of his voice on the answering machine. Music in the background. Where was he? His office? A bar? A queasy wall of darkness. Something not there. That's what Bobbie DuChan had been saying for two years: Didn't remember. Crackhead. Daytime hot prowls. They pick Bobbie up for burglary, take him to a local station. Within twenty minutes, he confesses to a murder. What murder? Cops go back up to a house and find a body. When she visits him in jail, Bobbie tells his wife, "I don't remember killing anybody. I don't remember making a confession. All I know is I went to the store yesterday and now I'm in jail."

As his court-appointed investigator, hired by the Public Defender's office, what did Frank believe about Bobby's blackout? Frank in various combinations of a little part of

me does and a little part of me doesn't, didn't know. He
wandered into an inconclusiveness: Kramer's answering
machine playing his voice back out of a wall of darkness.

As he pulled into the parking lot at the Hall of Justice, he
said in the deep voice of a cartoon explorer, "I come to
the land of shvartzer," didn't find himself particularly
amusing; Frank grabbed his briefcase, clipboard and yellow legal pad, was halfway across the lot before he
stopped, returned to the car. In the front seat, he quickly
went through his pockets, something he'd taught himself
to do before entering the jail. The jail was run by the
Sheriff's Department and had tight security—lockdowns
twice a day and so on. Christ, they didn't even allow
stamps to be brought in—there might be a hit of acid in
the glue on the back. He dropped the Pall Malls on the
seat. Pens and pencils, keys, change, film, batteries. He
opened a pack of Pall Malls, took out a few, rolled up two
hundred dollars in twenties into several tight rolls, and put
them into the pack, placed it in his breast pocket, put the
other pack in his side pocket.

Inside, he walked around the metal detector, showing
his ID to the cop, who nodded, and walked into the Hall
of Justice. Crowds of people. Attorneys talking to clients,
families, people reading the directories, people waiting for
the elevators, uniformed cops, undercover agents, narcs,
public defenders, lawyers, witnesses, clients on their way
to the courtrooms. When he'd first started interning here
six years ago, he hadn't known anything, who did what,
that the sheriffs ran the game cards for the prisoners, nothing. He looked over, saw an elevator closing, Aram Melikian, they spotted each other, Aram called, waved: ". . .
talk later . . ." The doors closed.

Another set of elevator doors opened, Frank tucked his
briefcase under his arm, squeezed in, a crowd of attorneys,
blacks and Hispanics, mostly women and their kids. The
overpowering perfume of the Latina women, the close
smell of someone's scalp beneath his chin. They rode up

several floors, attorneys getting on and off, cops; he rode up to the sixth floor. The elevator opened into a large cell with a locked door on one side and a small chest-high opening on the other. A sheriff's deputy sat at a window facing the opening. Frank took out his ID, thrust his arm through the opening to the window. The deputy took the ID, studied his face, nodded. Though Frank had been up here hundreds of times before, he'd never felt like this— heart pounding, nervous. He stepped out of the cell, slammed the door behind him with a loud clang. A second deputy looked up.

"Hey, Frank, how ya doin'."

"Tim . . . I'm okay. How's it goin'?"

Frank turned to sign in. There was an enormous echoing clamor of voices, shouting, TV's, radio . . . The smell of men in confinement, stale food, Pine-Sol, sweat, laundry soap, all swept up around him.

"Who you here for?"

"Ray Buchanan. Believe he was brought in last night. We have a contact visit. Aram Melikian is his attorney."

They walked side by side down to Post 8, and the deputy sent a bailiff into the cell block. Frank stood behind the line painted on the floor and waited. A black trustee, in a lime-green jumpsuit, swept the floor with a push-broom. Another mopped. Frank noticed the tears tattooed at the corner of his eye. The Mexican Mafia gang members tattooed a tear for each year of jail time. He looked young, but there was already a chain of tears. Tim waited a moment.

"Giants lost last night. Dodgers killed them."

"Saw that."

"No bullpen. They're not going to make it without a bullpen."

Frank couldn't think in the clamor. He was watching Ray walking toward him down the center of the cell block. He was wearing the loose orange jumpsuit of a prisoner. Frank and Ray looked at each other through the bars and Frank nodded. His heart was pounding, part of him felt as though it were himself in the orange uniform walking toward himself behind the bars. He made an effort. The first thing, the most important thing, was to stay cool, calm, help Ray believe it was okay, find out what was going on.

Frank had always admired Ray. He had an aura, and the things Frank had always admired were still with him in orange prisoner's uniform behind the bars of the cell block. He was tall and lithe, a bit like Kramer, only taller, with an erect, easy good posture, almost the kind of posture which graduates of military academies kept through life. He had a self-possessed dignity—it was something about the quiet, attentive look in his eye, something relaxed and good humored about his mouth. He had blue eyes, a Roman nose, thick, straight black hair, and small, fine features. His face was tan and unlined, though he was in his mid-thirties, the same age as Frank. There had always been something of a mystery about him, something unreadable to Frank. Perhaps it was because of what he did. Or the way he went about doing it. Frank thought if he'd been a lawyer, surgeon, or physicist, though, he still would have had that intangible, unreadable quality. This fascinated Frank. Ray stopped beside the deputy as he unlocked the cell block door, and then Ray came through.

Tim had returned and was walking back to his post at the security window. "I hear they're making a three-way trade for pitchers with the Padres."

"We'll see," Frank said.

"It's a long season, but it'll be a lot longer without some pitching, that's all I've gotta say."

Frank nodded. The accompanying deputy stepped into an office. Frank led Ray back down the hallway; the black and Mexican trustees watching them, they stepped into another narrow corridor. A sign said: NO PRISONER WILL HAVE OVER $30.00. On the left, there was a succession of several doors, each with a window at about head height. Frank looked into the first—occupied; he looked into the next. He nodded to Ray, who stepped into the room. A single table, two wooden chairs. The room was the size of

a small bathroom. Another sign said: DO NOT GIVE
ANYTHING TO INMATES. Ray turned, walked to the
far wall, and turned again with his back against the wall.
Frank stepped in and pulled the door closed behind him,
put his briefcase and pad on the table. He faced Ray. "Is
there anyone behind me in the window?"

Ray looked past Frank. "No."

Frank stepped towards Ray, gave him a quick hug.
"Ray, man." Stepped back. "You okay?" Frank looked
at Ray's face. There was a dark bruise on one side of his
chin. "What happened there?"

Ray felt his chin, considered. "I think I got that when
they pushed me down to the floor. Cement floor." Ray
shook his head and rubbed the bruise.

Frank dug the cigarettes out of his pockets and put them
on the table. "This one's open.".

"I've just about quit."

"Yeah, well you've started again. There are two hundred dollars in twenties rolled up inside with the cigarettes.
Put it in your pocket. Never know. And cigarettes are good
to have inside."

Ray took the pack with his cuffed hands, put it in his
chest pocket. "Thanks, Frank."

"Jesus, Ray . . ." They looked at each other and shook
their heads. "Let's sit down."

They sat in the wooden chairs on either side of the
table. "All I know is Aram Melikian called me an hour
ago and said they had you—DEA busted you last night."

Ray nodded. "That's about all I know myself. I haven't
slept."

"Tell me what happened."

"Can I smoke in here?"

"I don't know. Light up and if they don't dig it, they'll
let you know."

"Forget it, I just about quit anyway." Frank took out
a yellow pad and pen. "You were almost out, I was going
to get out for good."

Frank glanced around the room, looked into the window

in the door, which remained empty. "What happened, Ray? Let's start with the arrest. Who arrested you?"

"A guy named Enrique Hernandez. Pretty proud of it. Wanted me to know."

"When he busted you, did he Mirandize you, you know, read you your rights, you have the right to remain silent and so on . . ."

"Yeah, he did. Twice."

"Okay. After he did that, did you say anything? Anything at all?"

"Nothing. I just asked to call my attorney."

"And nothing else?"

Ray hesitated. He looked down at his handcuffs, pulled the links out taut. "Nothing."

"Okay, good. Did they try to get you to say anything else? Because after you ask for an attorney, they have to back off. If you tell them you've got nothing to say, they can ask you again in a little while—you know, you want to say something now."

"No, they didn't do that."

"And you didn't say anything. Volunteer anything, try to explain, whatever?" Frank couldn't think of anyone less likely to volunteer information, but he was going to ask. And watch Ray's face. Ray was the most closemouthed person he'd ever known.

Ray slowly tightened the links. "Nothing. They took me over here, I called Melikian, nothing else. You're the first person I'm talking to."

"Okay, Ray, good enough."

They lost their momentum. Ray took out a cigarette, fumbled, and placed the unlit cigarette in his mouth. Frank reached in his pocket for a match. Ray shook his head, no. He said in a hushed voice, "Can we talk in here?"

"Who knows? Maybe there's no safe place to talk anywhere. Talk quick, soft and low . . ."

Ray eyes were trancelike, alert, and bright with exhaustion. "I've been lying in there all night just playing it all backward, and a while ago, it kind of came to me, this has to go back to Richie Davis's computer. Has to. Remember Richie? Remember that night you called me?"

Jesus, how could Frank forget? He nodded grimly. That night. What was there to say? He'd seen Richie in his nightmares since. They—Ray, Frank—had been to a party at his place, a huge house up on Parnassus Heights. Richie Davis had been in the grass business like Ray, but then after a few years, he'd decided to get into coke, heroin, all of it, and so Ray had stopped dealing with him. Ray didn't deal other stuff—just grass. By the ton. He and Richie had parted ways. Then it had been in the papers. Richie Davis murdered.

Frank knew from the newspaper that investigators had found the paraphernalia of a major drug dealer in his house. Scales. Money. Counting machines. Also, a big league art collection. And, it was mentioned, they'd found that Davis had put his entire business, records and transactions, on computer disks in an elaborate secret code. That was one mistake. A second mistake—for Richie Davis—was getting murdered. The papers hadn't said much else, as Frank recalled, but that was enough. When that piece of information appeared in the paper, Richie Davis murdered, computer disks found, anyone who had ever known Davis got nervous.

But that had been what, a year ago? and from what Frank had been able to observe, Ray had always been exceedingly careful. He knew his suppliers. He'd always known his suppliers. He never bought from people he didn't know. He never sold to people he didn't know. Unlike Richie Davis, who might have put his whole business on computer disks, Ray never wrote anything down. He had a photographic memory, and kept everything in his head—names, dates, money in, money out, money owed. In eleven years, he'd rarely written down a name, a telephone number, a location, a plane reservation, nothing. And he'd never made a mistake. Or at least a mistake he couldn't get out of. Ray went to make his deals with money and no weapons. Incredible. But that was Ray. He bought good dope, sold it at a good price, and that was all. No one had ever laid a hand on him. Not here. Not in Mexico. Not in South America. Not in Thailand. At least, he had always come back in one piece.

Ray stared, eyes distant with fatigue, shock, a night of trying to figure out what had happened. "It's got to go back to Richie Davis's computer. My name must have been on a disk from when Richie was in the grass business. I supplied him for a while. And from the moment you called me about Richie, I was on the lookout. The paper said the cops were sending the disks off to Washington to have them deciphered—they were supposed to be in some kind of weird code. If they were decoded, they had names: Richie's clients, suppliers, amounts, all of it."

"And you think they put you under surveillance after that?"

"I don't know. Yeah, sure. I mean, if I was on his disks. If they were decoded. I've always acted on the premise that I was being watched, even before the Davis thing. I know that maybe six months after Richie's murder, people contacted Sammy. They wanted to buy some weed—a couple of tons. Sammy said they were friends of clients. I said forget it, friends of clients weren't clients. At least, not after the Davis murder. The same people contacted Sammy a few months later. Tried to buy from us again. Sammy really thought they looked okay. But I kept thinking of Richie Davis and those computer disks and said, 'Forget it.' "

Frank was thoughtful. "So, what? The DEA got Sammy's name from the disks and was trying to get him— or both of you—to sell to them?"

Ray smoothed the cigarette between his cuffed hands. "I don't know who they were. Never had any idea."

Frank decided not to bring up what he was thinking just now: that maybe the DEA had gotten only Sammy's name off the disk, turned him, pulled Ray's name out of him, and tried to follow through to get to Ray. Ray studied Frank's face, shook his head. "It couldn't be Sammy. And

anyway, last night, no one was trying to buy from us—
we were doing the buying.''

But Frank thought about Sammy a moment more. Wiry,
very white, intense, with a Nixon five o'clock shadow,
round, tortoise-shell glasses, mustache, an overly firm hand
shake, like a skinny guy who'd been told by his father
back in high school in a man-to-man talk you always *shake*
someone's hand and look him straight in the eye. That was
Sammy, along with smarts about money, and a deep voice.
Coming out of this skinny guy, it cracked Frank up. He
lived with his girlfriend in Noe Valley, wore Oxford shirts,
gray slacks, looked like a Silicone Valley M.B.A. nerd.
Sammy?

Frank said, ''I didn't say it was Sammy. Maybe it was
just DEA surveillance. You said yourself you thought your
name came out of Richie's computer. If you were under
DEA surveillance, maybe you brought the DEA to your
buy last night.''

Ray shook his head hard. ''The computer starts it, but
it's somebody.'' Maybe Frank's face didn't show anything. ''It's got to be somebody. It's not just a computer
disk. Somebody did something.''

A wave of hangover nausea went through Frank, and
he broke into a light sweat. He licked his lips. He desperately wanted a glass of cold water, but didn't want to get
up and leave Ray alone in here. A deputy glanced in the
window, Ray turned. Frank turned. The deputy disappeared. They remained silent.

''It's okay, Ray, go ahead. What happened last night?
Who was with you?''

''Jack Adams. And Sammy.''

''No one else?''

''No one.''

Frank wiped his forehead. ''Sammy I can understand.
Jack . . .'' He recalled Ray and Jack as having been almost
inseparable the last year or two. Tennis. And Jack lived
not too far away from Ray in Mill Valley. ''What'd you
tell me? He's some kind of developer, right?''

"Jack puts together big real estate scenarios, malls, condos, planned communities. Some of them he's proud of, some of them he's not." Ray turned the unlit cigarette over between his fingers. "He's my tennis partner. We've been playing doubles in Masters tournaments. You've met Jack, haven't you?"

"Oh, yeah, that time I was over in Marin serving a subpoena, I swung by, there you are, the middle of the afternoon, tennis whites, Marin Tennis and Racquet Club, living the life of leisure. How could I forget that, me working, you guys in tennis whites. He's a blond guy, right? preppie looking. Born to play tennis at a country club, something like that."

"He's got the good looks, but he's got heart. He's a player."

Frank had sat down in a lawn chair and watched the two of them play. Shirts drenched with sweat, they were just finishing up a set, and Frank could see they were evenly matched, both very good, serves exploding, hard, fast and low, both of them covering the whole court; they had the shots, backhands, forehands. Afterward, they'd come off the court together, and Ray had introduced them. Frank remembered Jack's racquet palm callused, forearms glistening with sweat and blond hair, both players deeply tanned. Ray smiled and said, "This guy's got the moves."

He'd smiled, touched Ray's racket with his, nodded at Frank and walked quickly across the lawn. Frank watched him get into a new white Mercedes and drive out of the parking lot with its Mercedes and Porsches and BMW's. The hard, clean rhythm of tennis balls filled the air. From somewhere, a woman laughed, soft, intimate. It was one of those beautiful California summer afternoons, the sky high and blue, the grass dried to a golden white on the hillsides, each flower, each petal catching the sunlight, illuminated, outlined in a way which made Frank faintly melancholy. It was the kind of day you could feel the sun moving over your head, feel the earth turning in space, sense how limited your time was.

Now Frank bounced his pencil on his yellow pad. "Yeah, sure I remember Jack. Tennis whites. Matching white Mercedes. Malls, huh? What were you guys doing last night?"

"Just business, Frank."

"You *and* Jack?"

Ray glanced at the handcuffs. "I was squeezed. I hadn't been able to do anything for a while."

"A few months, right?"

"Longer, eight months, I know when and why it began. I took a big loss, and from then on it was hard to move. I could feel them out there. The zero tolerance thing. It was a hard squeeze."

Frank lowered his voice. "I wanted to get my money out a while back, you said, 'Leave it with me a few more months, I'll double it again, then we'll both get out for good—just walk away.' You remember saying that a few months ago?"

Ray extended his legs under the table, slid down in his chair. He shrugged. "Some things had happened, Frank, some big things. And I was still really bugged by the way Sarah Anne had left."

Frank took a breath when Ray said Sarah Anne's name. The white of her neck when her hair fell forward that afternoon in La Traviata. "When did she leave?"

"September 18th. Last fall. Almost nine months ago."

"Where'd she go?"

"No idea. She wouldn't tell me. Three years, she's with me, then one day it's I can't be with you, I'm sorry . . ."

They'd been living together. Frank had no idea where he'd met her. One day she'd just been there with Ray. Things were great for a while. They always were. Frank recalled Karen and himself, others before Karen. Beginnings. The best. But then Sarah Anne had gradually started complaining to Ray about the way he would just disappear. Why didn't he ever leave forwarding addresses or phone numbers? Why couldn't he let her know when he'd be back? Where exactly did he go? Why, if he was an importer, was it so necessary just to drop out of sight for weeks? Why didn't she ever meet any of his clients, and finally, why, if there weren't other women, couldn't he take her with him—she loved to travel?

As Ray had said to Frank a few months ago after he'd drunk a little too much. "Look, it finally got to be a problem. I had to tell her something. Sarah Anne is smart. I mean, I think she had put it together. I looked at it this way. If I tell her something, I minimize it, keep it under control. Better that than let her imagination work overtime. But if she's figured it out, and I don't tell her something, and she decides to leave, maybe she'll leave pissed and then who knows what she'll think or who she'll talk to. I know it sounds weird, but I figured it was my best chance at that moment—to tell her something.

"I made myself out to be a kind of schlepper. That there was a Mr. Big out there and when he whistled, I had to fetch. That it was set up so that I couldn't just walk away—it was business—but I told her I would be getting out of it soon."

He'd told her that what he did wasn't really harmful—who knew, maybe they'd legalize things anyway. Look at prohibition. It hadn't worked, either. And he didn't have anything to do with hard stuff. No one got hurt. It wasn't the movies. It was a business. He couldn't go into details, but she'd be amazed at the people who had their money in this—really amazed: doctors, lawyers, architects, stockbrokers, everyone. Which was true. It was what people wanted. He did nothing more than make arrangements. He was an entrepreneur. She heard him out.

Ray said, "When I finished, she turned away from me and cried. She said, 'I think it would have been better if you told me you'd been fucking another woman.' Can you believe that? Another woman? I was stunned. I told her if I didn't do it, someone else would because it was there to be taken and people wanted it. I said to her, 'I never saw you walk out of a party where they were smoking a joint.' She didn't want to hear it. You know, double standard on everything. As long as people don't have to know the dirty little details. Sarah was no different.

"After two weeks of her coming and going at all hours of the day and night, sometimes crying, sometimes staying out for two or three days at a time, she never would tell me where—'Why should I, Ray? I'll do what I want now'—she came in about three in the morning. 'You said everyone had their money in this—doctors, lawyers, whoever. Which ones?' She wanted me to name names. She started running down everyone we knew. Does so and so have money in this? Does she? How about him? What am I going to say, Frank? She couldn't believe anyone or anything anymore. She looked crazy. When I wouldn't give her names, she left in her car.

"She came back an hour later, she was totally different. She'd been frantic. Now she was," Ray shrugged, "maybe resigned. She said she was afraid of me. She said, you've been two people. I said, no, I'm the same person I always was, the exact same person. Some things I kept to myself. Everyone keeps some things to themselves. Have you told me everything about yourself? She wouldn't answer. Frank, I told her I was protecting her by not letting her know. She wouldn't stop shaking her head and wouldn't answer."

Ray said, "I leveled with her to keep her from leaving and she left anyway." He'd shrugged. Frank remembered the way Ray had been drinking the night he told him this, sometime back last winter. Now Frank couldn't help but think about Sarah Anne. She wasn't really beautiful, but once you saw her, you didn't forget her. One of her eyes was slightly tipped askew, a face where if you'd taken either half and mirrored it, you'd have a new person, unrecognizable from the whole. She had lightly pocked skin from adolescent acne, thick straight brown hair off her shoulders which had a weight and swayed when she moved. And she had a smell—thick, of hair, perfume, skin—that, and something else in her presence, which always hit Frank hard. People noticed her. Once they'd been in a restaurant—Ray, Frank, Sarah Anne—and she had excused herself from the table. They'd watched her walk across the room. Beautiful legs. Frank and Ray glanced at each other, aware that the tables had quieted. People seemed to be holding their breath in some awareness of her movement and presence.

Ray smoothed the cigarette and said, "I can't decide what bugged me most about her leaving—that maybe I misjudged the situation and told her some things that could hurt me—or, that she couldn't see past them."

All Frank could think of was a tall glass of ice water. He swallowed. "So she left and you and Jack were kind of hanging out."

"Jack had this custody battle dragging on down in some place—Leucadia. That's where his ex was living. Bitch to hear him tell it. Jack would show me pictures of his seven-year-old kid who she wouldn't let him see. Named him Jett after James Dean in *Giant*." Ray shrugged. "He missed his kid. Jack and I were playing tennis, drinking a little too much. Not a great time. Sarah Anne gone, my business jammed." Ray took a deep breath, puffed his cheeks, let it out. "One night we're drinking together and Jack says, 'I want to talk about something.'

"Jack has this business opportunity. He doesn't like this, but he's in trouble. He's overextended. Some properties he's invested in have gone south on him. His wife is killing him with this divorce. Lawyers' fees are killing him. He's got to have money to stay afloat. It's very serious. He wants his kid."

Ray pushed himself up in his chair. "Frank, this is this, that is that, but Jack has the opportunity to do a buy ... It's weed. Good weed. A couple of tons. He can buy it one day, turn it over the next and double his money. But he's short. He's got people who can move the weight, the whole thing. All he needs is more cash to make the buy."

"What had you told Jack about yourself?"

"That I was an art dealer, importer-exporter. Actually, after one of my trips, I brought Jack some pre-Columbian figures, another time, some rugs. He dug them. Had them around his house. I knew that was never in question to Jack, what I did. I had artifacts around the house, books, rugs. Jack saw the house and cars, knew there was money there."

"What'd you say?"

"I just thanked him. I said I'd like to help, but my money was tied up. Jack's a developer who's going to do a one-night stand. Amateur hour. A lot of ways to get burned. I just said no. Politely."

"What'd he say?"

"He was just nervous. Hey, I told him, do what you have to do, I understand. I don't talk."

Frank said, "You don't think it's a weird coincidence, you're a big player and he comes to you?"

"Of course, my first thought. But look, Jack takes big money risks. Some of it's not going to turn out, no matter how good you are. Look at some of our money people, Frank. A lawyer, a banker . . . remember, a couple of years back, Sammy brought in a money guy, a stockbroker, who was margined out. Cover red ink quick or go down the tubes. Jack wasn't the problem for me; it's all the people he was going to be coming into contact with. You don't do this in a vacuum. I just didn't know who he'd be dealing with. That bugged me. I let it go. I thought I'd watch and see what happened to him.

"A few more weeks went by and things were still jammed for me and so I asked Jack, 'How's business?' Jack said, 'I want to show you something.' We got up and walked out of the bar, walked across the parking lot to Jack's car. Jack unlocked his trunk and opened his attaché case. Must have been $200,000 in cash. Some people were walking toward me. I said, 'Close the fucking trunk, Jack.' "

Ray shrugged. "I said, 'When it comes your way again, I might be able to contact some people who can raise the money next time you go around. Give me some time.' "

"And what did Jack say?"

"Terrifying way to make money. Hoped not to do it again. That's where we left it until a few weeks, maybe a month, something went by and Jack said he thought he had something coming up he couldn't pass on. He said I could come in as a money partner."

"How much?"

"Each of us bring a million."

Frank drew a deep breath. Ray said, "Hey, I know, but I was sinking. Jack had rented a truck. The idea was we'd go to a warehouse, exchange the two million in cash for two tons of weed. All we had to do was buy it and take it to a safe house a few miles away, run the truck into a closed garage and leave it there, we'd never have to touch the stuff again and we'd have our money a few hours later. I told Jack I'd have to come to the buy to see the weight. Jack said that was okay, we'd meet his contact, check out the weed together. If things looked good, you know, I'd go ahead and call my partner—Sammy, and he'd bring the money. If not, I was getting out. I told Jack that's the way I wanted to do it—no offense, it was just business.

"Jack tells me how the contact, a guy named Dean Miller, wants the money put together—you know, so many stacks of fifties, so many stacks of hundreds, put it in a case. Very professional. I put together the money and put Sammy at the other end of a phone and told him not to do anything until I called. I'd bring a cellular phone to the warehouse. If I didn't call him in half an hour, he was to take the money and beat it. The warehouse was somewhere in south San Francisco." Ray put the unlit cigarette to his lips. "Frank, give me a light."

Frank reached into this pocket and lit the cigarette. Ray inhaled, blew the smoke out. Followed its slow drift in the closed room.

Ray said, "There's not much more to say, Frank. Jack and I went to the warehouse, Jack in his Mercedes, me driving the truck—eleven-thirty last night. The guy comes. Dean Miller. Nondescript. Medium height, build. White guy. He's got a truck, a friend, I don't even remember his name—Garcia, maybe. Miller was nervous, you know. He'd never seen me before and Jack's telling him I'm alright. He keeps looking me over. I said I wanted to check out the weed and he said fine, no problem. He opens the back of the truck, there's the weed stacked inside. He says do whatever you want. I check it out. It's high quality. I thought it was good weight for a good price. I said, 'Let's go ahead,' I called Sammy. Sammy was five minutes away in a motel room.''

Ray stood, took a step, leaned against the wall, hands holding the burning cigarette.

"Sammy comes into the warehouse with the money, Jack goes to his car, gets his suitcase, we put the two suitcases on the tailgate of Miller's truck, open them, and Jack goes through his money. This is this, that is that. Miller says, 'Wait, these are hundreds?' Goes through a whole big thing. They get it cleared up. He turns to me. I've got the money in bundles of ten thousand and twenty thousand. I show Miller. He looks at me confused, does the same thing. He says, wait a second, this row is ten thousand in hundreds? I say, no, this row is ten thousand in fifties, that row is twenty thousand in hundreds.''

Frank spaced it out for a moment. A couple of years ago he'd been on another big dope case and something about this seemed vaguely familiar.

"Anyway, we finish that, Miller says, 'Okay, money looks fine.' Jack and I look at each other. Okay? Okay. We load the bails of weed from their truck to our truck. Thirty-five pound bails. It takes a while.

"Miller says to Jack and me, 'Our organization can get you whatever you want, weed, coke, heroin—you guys interested in coke and heroin? Jack looks at me like are you interested, maybe like he wants to say yes, but he's not sure what I'll think. I shake my head no. You know, Frank, I've always been a grass dealer. I don't deal anything that hurts people. Miller says, 'Well whatever you're interested in, we can get it, just let us know when you're ready or if you change your minds on the coke or heroin.'

For me, this is a one-shot deal until I can get my own game working again. We shake hands. Miller seems to have calmed down a little, and Garcia is just kind of following his lead.

"It's time to go. I'm walking back to our truck and next thing I know there are thirty guys pouring in the doors in combat fatigues, their faces are blackened, they've got M-16's, big handguns, they threw all of us down on the floor, I had no idea who they were, I thought it was a rip-off, murder, I saw our bodies in pools of blood, black and white pictures in the *Chronicle*, then some guy with a big mustache is frisking me spread-eagled on the floor, one of these guys stood on my back like he'd shot a lion, he was hooting, I mean it, he was crowing like a rooster, they handcuff me and pull me up, read me my rights, Frank, I'm telling you, they were high, hooting, pumped, they were dancing, high fives . . . I mean, I was just doing business, but it was really a personal thing to these guys. I think it was a couple of SWAT teams—it was dumber than television. Dumb, but I was never so fucking scared in my life."

Ray fell silent. Frank was trying to take it all in. Then the thing which had jogged his memory from the earlier dope case came back. Frank said, "He asked two or three times about the money like that? The confusion with the rows?"

Ray nodded. Frank wrote, DEA? Videotaped the bust? and circled it.

"In the car, all the way over here—Jack and Sammy and Dean are in different cars, last thing I see of the three of them, they've got M-16's jammed against their heads, they're being thrown into cars—I'm alone with the big mustache, Hernandez—he and the other guy who was with him during the bust are talking. From what they were saying, I got the idea he was an agent who'd just been transferred up from Texas and didn't know his way around. You know, where are the good restaurants? The mustache—he tells me he's Enrique Hernandez—kept saying,

'Why don't you ask Ray, Ray likes to eat in good restaurants, with all that money, Ray would know. Ray, what about it, can you recommend any good five star restaurants?' I didn't say anything. They kept it up. 'How do you think you and Jack are going to like the tennis courts where you're headed, Ray? How about the pussy? They tell me that after a couple of years, you can't even tell the difference between a boy and a girl. You don't even remember. Think you're gonna be a pitcher or a catcher? Couple of good looking studs like you and Jack, never can tell which way you're going to go. Someone's gonna like those blue eyes and tight ass. And look at Jack with that curly blond hair. Oh, man, someone's really going to like Jack's curly blond hair.' He kept it up. He was trying to get to me, make me start talking. Finally, I said, 'Hey, they pay you to make the bust. Congratulations. They pay you overtime to break balls?' Hernandez just looks at me. 'That's it.' '' Ray shrugged. They looked at each other and fell silent. Again, a deputy's face appeared, disappeared in the window. ''It was like he knew me and Jack and Sammy and had some kind of grudge against us. Hey, to me, it was never anything personal.''

Frank nodded, but he was thinking of the million in cash. Thinking about money in piles. How Ray used to joke that the worst part of this whole thing isn't the risks, but counting the money. It was so endlessly boring. At the end of counting, your hands were filthy—money was literally filthy. Ray had gotten a money counting machine. Like Richie Davis.

Absently, Frank said, ''What'd you say you guys drove over in?''

''Where?''

''To the buy?''

''I drove the truck. Jack drove his Mercedes.'' Frank shook his head at the thought of the car. Ray said, ''Yeah, they got that Mercedes along with everything else. After last night, the Mercedes is the least of it, though Jack loved that car.''

When Ray said "everything else," Frank realized the rest, that the cops had to have been standing by with search warrants, and once they'd made the bust, they'd most likely sent teams into the different houses, and in the case of Jack, also his office, and just torn their places apart. They loved to tear a place to pieces. It was their message. Next would follow the IRS, the confiscation of property, the whole dreary scenario.

Frank said, "Anyone at home last night?"

"Marla—woman I've been seeing last couple of months. Left her sleeping on the sofa. I never told her anything about anything. But she's got to be wondering why I didn't come home. Maybe you can give her a call for me and tell her . . ." Ray faded. "Just tell her I'll talk to her. I'll be the one to explain. Say there are some real reasons and not to worry, it'll work out. I'll tell her." Ray drifted. "I guess now it won't matter what I tell her."

Frank thought of how it must have been for her with the DEA kicking in the door in the middle of the night, but didn't say anything.

Ray said, "You trusted me, Frank. Eleven years. And I blew it. Two hundred thousand would have been yours eventually. I told you that if you let me keep it in one more time, I'd double it for you. I knew you were going to get out. And I lost it."

Frank couldn't say anything. He was thinking of a friend who had taken his money out in time. The rules were any money lost in a bust was gone; Frank had always left all of his in. He finally managed to say, "I trust you. Something happened. Beside what the DEA got, you still have your money, the money you saved?"

Ray nodded. "It's hidden." He shook his head. "It was almost over for both of us. We were going to top out."

Neither of them looked convinced. Frank was sure he'd let his money make the last run. With the money, he would have had time to study for the bar—really study. Once he'd passed, he could set up a practice. But Ray had said, leave it in one more time, I'll double it for you.

Frank said, "You always joked, you took the risks, we made the money, you'd take the fall." Though Frank remembered the last few times he'd said that, Ray said it with a variety of undertones: somewhat reproachfully, ironically, though always with a sense of humor. Ray was too cool to have complained. Anyway, Frank knew that Ray loved the risks and highs of pulling it off and might not ever have been able to quit. He wasn't sure what to think about himself.

Ray didn't say anything. Frank said, "I think we have some things going for us. You have no priors. You weren't carrying a weapon when they busted you. They'll help."

Ray nodded. He seemed preoccupied, perplexed, as though in talking to Frank, he was working toward some conclusion. Frank thought about Ray's house being under surveillance. If that had been so, they had photographed everyone going and coming to the house, run their plates. Frank's car. No doubt he'd gone into the DEA computer.

Frank took a breath, thought there wasn't much more either of them could do now—he could see from Ray's eyes that he was exhausted—and decided to explain a few procedural things to Ray. That someone from Pretrial Services would come and interview him, ask him where he lived, how long, what ties he had with the community, and so on, and then, based on this information, and whatever indictment the grand jury came back with, they would make a recommendation for bond. There'd be an arraignment. Bond would be set. If there was to be a bond. Everything considered, if Frank were a magistrate and he were looking at someone like Ray, he'd consider him a flight risk. He thought about explaining more, but decided that was enough for now.

Frank stood. Ray pushed himself upright away from the wall. Frank said, "I know it's a zoo in there, but try to get some sleep. I'll be back."

Frank picked up his briefcase and yellow pad. Ray reached over with his two cuffed hands and took Frank's shoulder. "Frank. I made a mistake. One mistake in eleven years. I let the things slip that had always made it work. Got sloppy. Maybe it was the way I read—or misread—Sarah Anne. Maybe I drank a little too much, started feeling sorry for myself. But someone had to have informed on one or all of us—Sammy, Jack, Dean Miller, me, I just don't know. I'm real tired. I can't think straight now. Somewhere between Richie Davis's computer and now, someone got information and put us in that warehouse last night. I don't care what else you do, I want you to find out who it was and how this thing went together." Frank studied Ray's face. Ray held his shoulder with his two cuffed hands. "Frank . . ."

Frank put his hand on Ray's hand. "We've got other things to do now, Ray."

"Remember, I took the risks, I'm taking the fall. I want to know who it was." Ray let go of Frank's shoulder. "There's money in it for you, Frank, when you can tell me. I've always taken care of business for you. You take care of business for me, now."

Frank nodded. Ray would cool down and forget this. He pushed open the door, moved back for Ray, who stepped into the hall. They squeezed between the legs and backs of the prisoners talking on phones at the window in the narrow corridor. The deputy came. "I'll be back, Ray."

Ray nodded. He had on his unreadable, distant face, his easy, upright good posture. The deputy unlocked the cell block door and Frank watched him lead Ray inside, relock the door, and take him into the cell block. Ray, shoulders back, didn't turn to look at Frank as he walked through the clamor. The cell door was buzzed open, Frank stepped into the cage, slammed the door, the elevator came, and Frank rode down to the lobby.

He gulped tepid water at a fountain until he gasped, took a deep breath, gulped more water. He wiped his mouth. As he walked through the crowd, Frank remembered meeting Sarah Anne—it must have been just a few days before she'd left Ray for good. He'd been looking for a witness in North Beach, he'd stopped in at La Traviata for an espresso, just thinking of going, when he'd looked up to see her. Coming in out of the late afternoon sun into the low light, she was momentarily blinded and seemed to be looking into a void. He raised his hand, she looked over, and off balance, trailing her fingertips along the swoop of barstool backrests, she walked over. Still that dancer's tight pelvic walk. The beautiful legs. He noticed the bartender at the other end pick up her presence. Close, Frank caught her thick smell of skin, hair, some body perfume which always tightened his chest.

She sat beside him. She ordered a drink, they tried a little small talk, but something wasn't working. Everything she said seemed out of rhythm, the words and phrases to have the wrong weight. In town for the day? Yeah, nothing special, maybe see a friend later. Anyone Frank knew? She seemed startled. No. Frank tried to pull something back with a joke. Anyone he should know? Anyone he'd wanted to know? Not sure what to do with any of it, she shook her head too hard. Her beautiful hair cut in that even line off her shoulders hung forward and hid most of her face. Frank noticed her neck, smooth and white, an open softness between the top of her dress and where her hair fell and parted at the back of her head, and Frank took a breath. He'd never noticed a woman's neck in quite this way. He wanted to lay his hand gently across the untanned white skin. He couldn't imagine beyond that—to cup her neck—caressing it, nothing more. Just to feel her neck. He looked away, took a swallow of his espresso. So how was Ray? Ray? She glanced at him. You mean, Ray, the art dealer? Ray the importer? Her eyes moved over his face and he knew something was up and blanked his expression. Ray, the tennis player, Frank said. Her eyes looked into him and said: *You knew. Did you know? You knew.* He read she was on to something, but she wasn't quite sure what it was he knew or how much. She said, "You tell me, Frank. How's Ray?"

Frank thought, this is just really great. What's happening?

She said, "Ray's not the person I thought he was. Are you?"

Frank shrugged. "Who knows? Who's anyone? Who do you think I am? Do I have to play this to sit here with you and have a drink?"

She didn't answer, but he felt her leg against his, and she put her hand on his knee. She said, "I always thought you were a good guy. Funny. Heart on the sleeve." There was affection, but craziness in it, and her hand on his knee, her thick smell, and the edge in her voice, put a tightness into his stomach and made Frank not care about any of the things he knew he should care about. She turned and looked at him steadily and then she said quietly, "Finish your drink, Frank, and then walk me to my car."

Frank couldn't move. Her command had excited him, but he didn't want to respond to a command; she stood. Suddenly, she seemed to understand his impasse, understand everything, and it was as if he could only watch himself with her. She took his arm and led him and he dropped some money on the bar as he went. She drove to a duplex in the Upper Haight. It was like he couldn't stop himself, he was sleepwalking to see what would happen next, he was thinking, I can't do this with her; he followed her up the front steps. He understood she was through talking, that as part of whatever emotional arrhythmia was going on in her, she didn't need to talk, that words were finished with her, or she had finished with words. They had not spoken since the bar.

She opened the door, he followed her in, the hallway was dark, she pressed her back against the door, then she reached for him, pulled him to her, it was rushing at him beyond the constraints of friendships, obligations, loyalties, she reached down and pulled her dress up to her waist, they slid down the door unable to stop moving against each other, and when they were done, tangled, still half-dressed, she tipped her head back against the door and said, should

I open the door, Frank? Should we let them see us?

He didn't answer. She repeated the last thing he'd said in the bar, who's anyone? But really, he didn't have the feeling she was talking to him. She said, It doesn't matter, I'll do what I want. She started kissing him again.

She'd left Ray shortly after that. Now Frank understood. Ray had told her his real occupation just before he'd run into her at La Traviata. That now put it together for Frank. He had felt a mixture of regret and guilt, but then said to himself that it was something which was so weird and singular, that it couldn't be helped. Almost like a car accident or something falling on you. He'd shrugged it off. He was sorry, but he hadn't gone looking for it. They were through with each other, anyway—Ray and Sarah Anne. As Frank walked across the Hall of Justice lobby, he realized that given the way she'd been, she could have gone anywhere, told anyone anything, gone to the Feds, set things in motion she couldn't even imagine.

"August . . . August like the month." He heard a voice behind him and instinctively froze. "A. U. G. U. S. T.," this last a good imitation of the way he spelled his name for clients, strangers, official business.

Frank turned. Farrell stood about five strides away, not coming closer, not walking away. Hands on his hips, he had on a nondescript suit. Mid-fifties, skin the texture of a cut raw potato, and blue eyes which were so pale they were almost white. He shook his head at Frank. "Frankie, you walked right past me. Never said a word. Very rude. A thousand miles away. And coming from the sixth floor. August, I make my living reading people and I must ask you, Frankie, who's up there on the sixth floor and what kinds of funny little houses are you building now?"

This, of course, in reference to the Tyrone Mayfield case, where they'd met. Farrell had been chief investigator, Frank a court appointed investigator for the P.D.'s office. A black junkie, Mayfield, had robbed an ice cream store. He'd held a customer and countergirl at gunpoint while he'd emptied the register. A third woman came out behind him, and he whirled, shot her, got away. A year later Tyrone's girlfriend dimed him. The case had languished around the P.D.'s office: hopeless case.

In desperation, Frank got an architect to draw up floor plans of the store, found out from the two witnesses where everyone stood, and made a discovery. The old woman who got killed was sitting behind where the defendant stood; she was hidden from his view by a partially closed door. When she heard Tyrone, she pushed the door open. Without knowing who was at his back, he whirled and fired at the sound of her moving. A mitigating factor. Frank recommends to the Public Defender, some kid without a clue, that whatever else, they do not want the jurors to go down and actually see the layout of the store; it will remind them of their childhoods, their kids, make them feel too much sympathy for the dead woman. Instead, Frank spends weeks building a scale model of the place.

The second day of the trial he wheels this thing in on a dolly and sets it up in front of the jury. He remembers the look of astonishment on the Prosecutor's face; he sees Dennis Farrell shaking his head. The Public Defender shows the jury where everyone was standing, how the door hid the woman from view; the jury buys it. The defendant is convicted of second degree murder. Afterward, the jury foreman said to Frank, "Until we saw the model, we thought it was first degree murder; the model saved the defendant's life."

Leaving the courtroom, Farrell had walked over to Frank and just stared at him with those overexposed eyes. But a few days later Farrell passed him and said, "Hey, it was a good piece of work, you rude turkey, the doll house."

Now Farrell looked at Frank. "You know, I've got a kid your age. Still a wise-ass. Just like you." They were on the level of cautious, friendly banter, and Frank played along. Farrell reminded him of his uncles. In his heart, he knew Farrell inside out, suspected that Farrell knew him. Long ago, he'd learned the hustle, learned how to play to

Farrell, it was part of Saint John's—wear a tie and jacket, yes sir, no sir, fuck up and get punished, shine the fathers and brothers on, get along, play the game, Catholic boy's prep school. He smiled at Farrell. Frank was gratified by Farrell's friendliness, and if Frank reminded him of his wise-ass kid, that was cool, but he had no illusions; he knew that down the road, he'd try to use Farrell, Farrell would try to use him.

Frank smiled a neutral smile. Farrell looked Frank over. "Frankie, still not wearing a piece?" He shook his head. "Bad for business. You private guys, you know, your clients expect it, everyone watches TV, you've got to give 'em maximum theater, check it out, see what they're wearing on TV these days, you know, those oversized handguns . . ."

"I always thought wearing a piece was a low class act—you know, the real heavies use attorneys, not guns—but I'll remember that. What're you up to, Dennis?"

"Testifying in the Jenkins case. Jenkins murdered—we'll say allegedly murdered until the trial's over and we have a conviction—a nine-year-old girl."

"Oh, yeah, read about it. You the main guy for the People?"

"Yes, sir, Mr. August, one of 'em."

"Good luck, hey, I've gotta run."

Frank turned. "Frank . . ." Farrell called him. Farrell looked at him with those pale eyes. He smiled. "What's up on the sixth floor this morning?"

"Just some P.D.'s office, felony slop. Court appointed. Twenty-five bucks an hour instead of forty-five." Frank tucked his briefcase under his arm.

Farrell said, "Walked right by me. It's got you thinking pretty hard for twenty-five bucks an hour." Frank smiled, waved, and suddenly queasy from his hangover, walked through the lobby. Just Farrell playing games. Like his uncles. As he crossed the parking lot, an unmarked white car came straight at him quickly. Frank stepped back, spotted the driver, a lieutenant he knew from narcotics. The lieutenant sped up, brushed by Frank, and gave him the finger. Frank restrained himself from returning the gesture—hey, okay, Frank defended the creeps he busted. So what? Someone had to. It was all a game.

Frank drove from the Hall of Justice parking lot, down Bryant, turned up Third toward Market, transients, street people, runaway kids filtering in and out of the back streets, the area known as the wine country because of the winos and derelicts. John would be at the office at noon, and then they'd do a money scene. He didn't know how long he'd be able to hold him off with promises.

The bar exam. Failed by what? a few points. Christ. Money was the difference. There was nothing Aram Melikian did in front of a jury that he couldn't do. Just that Melikian had a father who had put him through college and law school; he'd driven a new Jag as an undergraduate, he'd never had to work for anyone painting, plumbing, hustling. A couple of years clerking, then straight to the P.D.'s office, then out on his own. Money greasing the way. Time to study. So what? He wasn't Melikian, and the bottom line was that Frank wasn't going to be a member of the bar soon. The light changed and he stepped on it.

Someone honked behind him. He sped up, then hit the brakes as a car came out of a parking garage. Both cars stopped, bumpers almost touching. "Hey, fuck you, fuck me," he said out loud. He leaned on his horn, pulled around, drove erratically, blindly for several blocks. He hadn't said that in years. Fuck you, fuck me. His father's voice.

Spring, his last year at St. John's. History class. Cropped graying hair, silver wire-rimmed glasses. Brother Malcolm. That Jesuit look. Four years of it. Medium height. Never raised his voice, but never gave an inch, either. Each senior to have done a year-long project. Frank's a Roman trireme. He researched everything, the sails, the provisions, the crew capacity, all of it. He spent months building the model. Finished in late May.

Brother Malcolm walked slowly along the display table looking at the different projects. As he came to Frank's, he stood still for a long time. Hands on knees, he'd leaned forward and peered into the rigging. He picked up one of the carved figures—a sheep—replaced it. Then he turned, "Mister August, is this your project?"

"Yes, sir."

"Did you build this ship yourself?"

"Yes, sir."

Brother Malcolm crossed his arms. "You did not build this ship yourself."

"I beg your pardon, sir."

"I said you did not build this ship yourself. You could not have."

"Why not, sir?"

"Because it is too good. It belongs in a museum. Your lie outdid you. Who built it?"

"I built it." Frank stared at Brother Malcolm. "You don't believe me?"

"I don't believe you, Mister August." Frank rose from his seat and walked to the front of the room, around Brother Malcolm, and over to the table, raised his fist, and brought it down on the ship. He did it two or three times more, hard, fast, picked up the hull and cracked it hard against the edge of the table.

At home, his father was in the living room. As he saw him, Frank didn't let his face show anything. His father was big, six-five. He'd lied about his age and joined the Army when he'd been sixteen, landed at Normandy on D day at seventeen, fought his way through Europe to VE day; Frank had always been aware that his father had something which allowed him to survive what many other men hadn't. His father said, "I received a phone call from Father Principal Conlan about you just as I was leaving the office . . . let's go in here." His father pointed toward the den. He sat at his desk, the chair pushed back against the wall. "Frank, Father Conlan mentioned an incident in

Brother Malcolm's class. I want your side of it."

Talking to his father, he often felt his words squeeze into an airlessness in his chest. Frank shrugged. Suddenly his story disappeared. "Brother Malcolm came into the room, inspected my project, asked me if I'd built it myself. I told him yes. He asked me a couple of times. I told him I'd built it. He told me I hadn't."

"Why?"

"He said it was too good, that I couldn't have."

"What then?"

Frank shook his head. The unexplainable part. Better to get it over quickly. "I smashed the boat." Frank shrugged. He looked at his father. "I don't know why. He just didn't believe me." It was too big to explain, the sense of outrage; Brother Malcolm asked for the truth, Frank gave him the truth, the truth had been what? denied? refused?

Frank's father said, "Frank, you know something? When it's fuck you, it's fuck me, know what I mean?" Frank didn't dare say anything. "Brother Malcolm was wrong, no doubt. But you've gotta play the game."

Frank repeated it now as he drove. You've gotta play the game. His father had maintained a general law practice and Frank recalled that there were always people stopping by the house for help; his father took them aside and, speaking softly, comforted them, took care of them. A Democrat, he had run for City Council with a supporting coalition of working class and ethnic groups, won a term, and his vote had swung a number of important, hotly contested issues—a major one being to stop a highway corridor from cutting through their neighborhood and destroying its character and peace and quiet. But then the money people had targeted him, stopped the nonsense and defeated him with their candidate. The corridor had started construction within the year.

His defeat had echoed that of his Congressman's some fifteen years earlier, when his father had been the secretary to Congressman Pierce of New Mexico. Up for a third term, the Congressman's blue collar support had been heavily eroded by a big money Republican campaign. A large number of his staff had defected, but Frank's father had stayed to the end. On leaving office, Pierce had made a Congressional speech thanking and praising Francis August, Senior. A framed copy of the Congressional Record entitled, In Praise of Loyalty, hung on his wall. You've gotta play the game. But whatever his father and Pierce had—courage, charm, idealism—it had not been enough. Money had defeated them both.

He glanced in the rearview mirror, and took a hard right, the files sliding across his front seat and spilling onto the floor. He watched the dumb trolley full of tourists clatter through an intersection. He could feel the sharp thickening of dread through his stomach and chest. In praise of loyalty. The Congressional Record. Frank wondered if there was such a thing as loyalty—or even if that word could be applied once the prosecution started its squeeze. If it hadn't happened already, the DEA case agent was going to start pressuring for names. He'd have Jack and Ray and Dean Miller, Sammy, taken from their cells and brought into interrogation rooms. The agent—Hernandez, whoever he really was—would say, "Ray, here's what we've got on you." He'd run it down. He'd say, "There it is. The grand jury meets this afternoon and will hear this and indict you in five minutes. Conspiracy to transport, buy, sell, distribute. You're dead. We're going to convict you and bury you. But hey, it's not too late, maybe you can help yourself. Give me some names—where does your money come from, who supplies you, who distributes for you. Help me, I'll help you. Be a hero and don't talk to me and I'll recommend to the judge that he buries you in some maximum security shithole for twenty years. Go ahead, think it over, but don't be a schmuck."

According to Ray, after Richie Davis gets murdered, names come out of his computer. Maybe. And among others maybe Frank has turned up in a surveillance photograph coming or going to his house. "Ray, who's this?

Don't know him? We know him, we've run his plates, Frank August, that's not the question. Who's he to you?" First time he's asked, maybe Ray says, "He's nothing to me. Lots of people came and went from my house." Fine. He's no one. We'll bury you, Ray. But the ninth or tenth time they ask Ray, what's he going to keep saying? "Frank's the maid. He comes in on Tuesday and Thursday, wears a tutu, and Lemon Pledges the dining room table." And if Ray had nothing to say, maybe it would be Sammy. Or that other guy, Dean Miller. And what about Jack Adams? Jack was an amateur, if anyone was going to panic, it would be Jack Adams. Be realistic. If it was himself looking at heavy jail time and being asked for a few names, or to follow through after a buy to set up his connections, what would Frank do? He had no idea, but in dozens of cases, he'd seen friends turn state's evidence, plea bargain, and set up and testify against friends, lovers testify against lovers. He could feel the thickening of dread in him; he'd asked if Hernandez had questioned him anymore after Mirandizing him, and Ray had hesitated and pulled on his handcuffs; he'd kept his eyes down, hadn't he?

Frank was suddenly so thirsty he could barely swallow. Tight emptiness in the mouth. He again started looking for a parking space; he saw something flicker in his rearview mirror, glint of light, the slow movement of a funeral procession pulling away from a curb and starting through an intersection, black hearse, globes of headlights white in the daylight, he turned and looked behind him, nothing there but some schmuck in a delivery van with his lights on, Frank hit his brakes as he spotted a space.

Inside the cafe, he sat at an empty table near the front window. A waitress came, and he ordered a large Coke and then drank half a glass of water, loosened his tie and top button. He checked the notes on his yellow pad. Jack Adams. Sammy. Sarah Anne. Part of him was in an interrogation room, Brother Malcolm, without the least doubt or humility or sense that he might be wrong, Frank's sudden rage, had it been Brother Malcolm's self-righteousness? that he wouldn't know the truth from a lie? fuck you, fuck me, Brother Malcolm, never a word of apology, he'd graduated a year after his class as punishment for something he'd never done, a bad year between himself and his father, the Coke came and Frank took several deep loud swallows, wiped the sweat from his forehead, drank, and calling the waitress, ordered another, felt the tension in his muscles giving way, the weight in his shoulders and middle, the fatigue in his legs, became aware that his body was completely exhausted, he slumped down into his chair, he was loosing momentum, he felt suddenly as though he'd been up for hours, that he'd been running hard on pavement, not just for hours, but days, he slid the ice around in his mouth, years, he'd been running for years, his body felt battered, he took a deep breath, another, he might not be able to get out of this chair, he noticed the space between the table and the wall, the morning sun slanting in, several green plants in the corner, broad leafed dieffenbachia, fern, this spring Karen and he hadn't planted a garden, first year, or had it been last year, too? he saw the back yard, empty, when they'd first been married, each year, they'd planted gardens, he'd taught her how, he and his father used to do this together, plant big gardens, Karen had loved it, he'd had a dump truck bring in several cubic yards of good soil, spent a day rototilling, mixing good soil and fertilizer, and then planted corn, tomatoes, squash, zucchini, sunflowers, melons, by late July you could walk into the flowers and corn, they were so tall, you could hide, Karen had loved it, she'd walk into the flowers and laugh, Frank, Frank, he'd wander into the corn and sunflowers, hug her, unbelievable, she'd say, she'd show everyone the garden, Frank, did this, what a trip, look at this, she'd laugh; no garden, nothing this year, or had it been last year, too? blurred, he wanted to slide out of the chair onto the floor, stretch out, turn on his side, just sleep, sleep indefinitely, his father being turned on his side by two orderlies, Frank heard him groan, saw a bubble slowly rise in an i.v., cancer, his father told him from his hospital bed, in three months, I won't be here anymore, I'll be dead, and then he and his father had cried, first time he'd seen his father cry, there was no one else in the room, he sensed his father was not crying out of fear of death or self-pity, but because they would not get to finish what they'd started, his other brothers were too young really to understand what was happening, over the next few months, Frank sat with his father, sometimes Frank could only cry, sometimes they sat and talked quietly, his father said, nothing was right for me until you were born; and once, speaking of his younger brothers and sister, he said, you're all they will ever really know or remember of me . . . and he'd turned and looked at Frank and gone on looking at Frank. And yet another afternoon his father came out of a long silence, opened his eyes, and said quietly, Catholicism . . . being a Catholic, Frank, the ritual, the Gospel, all of it?— Frank nodded—look beyond that, it's really a complicated system to get a person to believe in himself and keep on believing in himself. He looked at Frank. Understand? Surprised, Frank nodded. Remember that, Frank, when things get tough.

His father would lie there with his eyes closed and when Frank thought he was asleep, he'd say, Frank . . . Frank . . . are you there? And Frank would nod or reach out and take his father's hand. I'm here, Dad. And his father would nod, open his eyes, look at Frank, close his eyes. I'm here, Dad. I'll be here for you, no matter what. When his father closed his eyes, Frank could look at him and see with horror how the cancer was eating him, how his body was slowly starting to disappear beneath the sheet, the big muscles in his arms growing slack, drawing down to the bone, the bones of his skull starting to surface through the skin. When his father's breath would thicken into sleep, Frank would stand at the window, look out across the glare of Albuquerque toward the desert, look up into the blue sky. In a few weeks, he would be going back to Las Cruces, New Mexico State, a four hour drive. Not that far. Close, really. Close enough. His father knew he was going, wanted him to go. Go, Frank. I'll be back, Dad. I'll be here for you. His father nodded. I know you will. You'll be here. Though neither said anymore, each knew Frank was saying, I'll be here by your side when it's time for you to die. And though the thought terrified Frank, it was the one thing Frank knew he had to do, wanted to do.

Frank felt a wave of hollow nervousness, called the waitress, ordered scrambled eggs and another Coke. He ate the eggs tentatively, one bite, a second, then he ate quickly, grateful for the food, that he could eat something at last. He took several bites of toast and felt himself dampen with sweat, pushed the plate away, saw the long coffin resting on the catafalque, the coffin draped with a large American flag before the altar, he'd been shocked by its weightlessness as he'd helped slide it out of the hearse, two bishops came for the funeral, one from Albuquerque, one from Phoenix, Knights of Columbus were ushers, the cathedral was full of people, family, friends, his father had been eulogized by the bishops as a man who had always given to the community, as a man who knew who he was, a father, a Catholic, an American, sitting next to his mother at the front of the church, Frank had to put the funeral program away, each time he'd look at the picture of his father, he'd begin to cry . . . Frank stood suddenly, held up his arm for the waitress, check.

In the men's room, he rinsed his face, swirl of cold water, faraway whisper in the drain monologuing out of Kramer's answering machine, ". . . anybody home . . ." The voice rose out of a wall of darkness, music faint in the background. He straightened and looked at himself in the mirror, water dripping from his chin onto his shirt, heard himself say to his father, "I'll be there." The desert glaring white, a shivering heat mirage balanced far ahead where the road met the white horizon, the maze and careen of long hospital corridors, Frank felt an empty blankness numb him. He dried his face. Yesterday Ray had been out, there'd been money; today Ray was in jail, the money was gone.

A few steps down the long-narrow staircase, Frank stopped and looked at his office door. Open. He listened. He heard Gloria politely put someone on hold, take the other call. He was half hoping Gloria had been able to smooth things over with John, make the problem go away. He descended the remaining stairs quickly and stepped into the office. Starting just inside the door, there was a ten foot long strip of paper taped to the wall: a time line documenting the FBI's prosecution of a murder last year. It covered several years and had cryptic notes—pieces of evidence, phone calls made, receipts, etc.—at different junctures. Frank had been the investigator for the defense, which had won.

He shifted his load of files, nodded at John slumped in a director's chair. Behind him, a ficus was losing leaves. Sometimes Gloria watered. Sometimes Gloria stopped watering. The ficus went on losing leaves. There were a couple of large furnace ducts overhead, which Frank had painted bright pink and which made the room look invaded by some lunatic contraption out of Dr. Seuss. One of Kramer's surfboards, caked with wax and ingrained sand, rested on the ducts. Kramer. Was anyone ever there when you needed him? Though Frank had offered to store the board in the space, he now decided he'd call Kramer and tell him to get his surfboard the hell out of his office. His business wasn't a joke.

Two voices came down the sidewalk outside, rapping loud, laughing. One of them ran a stick over the grating on the frosted windows at sidewalk level. Here and there, a stereo, bookshelves, a sofa, a picture of his father; Frank's Juris Doctor, framed; a large color picture of Karen smiling; a bulletin board with out-of-focus shots of friends—Karen, June, Kramer, himself—all with their arms around each other laughing; a lumpish reproduction of Rodin's *The Kiss* on his desk; and a fake bottle of spilled ink with a black enamel, metal puddle which he had placed on a finished print of Karen's to freak her out. Taken in, she had screamed at the sight, and then, discovering it was a joke, alternately gone on laughing and screaming at Frank, telling him it wasn't funny, but then laughing, for two days.

Gloria sat at Frank's desk, phone cradled against her ear and shoulder. She was writing on a pad already covered with messages. He took a handful of messages and looked at John, who was leafing through a magazine. "What's the password, Slick?"

"I give up, Frank, what is it?"

"I dunno, thought you knew. That's why I asked you. Fellatio? Smegma?"

John said, "Both. Neither. Heard on the bar exam yet?"

Frank shook his head, nope, Giordano could be such a schmuck, heard on the bar exam? He's here to get paid and asks something like that, Jesus, never pay him now, though, really, Frank did like Giordano. He could talk to people. Slip and slide. His bathhouse number had been a real piece of work. On a daily basis, he could go into the project, talk to blood, get their confidence, cross the street, rap with kick-ass construction workers, blend in. He had certain compunctions, and he sometimes gave up too soon, but he could do the dance. He was smart and had a memory for detail. He was a good-looking Italian from Queens—six feet, straight black hair flecked with gray, who'd once scored forty-two points in a high school basketball game. Two high school guards, they'd gone at it one on one in the playground, and Giordano'd been tough. They had gone to the same local law school, which was mainly for students who'd had other careers and were still working while they were making a career change into law. Practical. John was just finishing, turning forty, had been a plumber, before that, a radical hippie, antiwar activist, lived in a commune in Berkeley—his father had thrown him out of the house for his long hair and politics when he'd been eighteen; it was the whole thing, hair, dope, Vietnam. Most of his idealism was gone, though a kind of

quirky contentiousness remained, and he was in the middle
of a messy and vindictive divorce. He was going to take
the bar exam in the next few months and was trying to get
enough money together to take time off and study.

"Gloria said you've been to the jail this morning on a
new case—good one?"

"That Gloria. Loose lips sink ships. Good case? Ask
me no questions, I'll tell you no lies." Gloria smiled as
she went on talking. He shook his head. "That Gloria.
Gloria, you just talk my business to anyone who happens
by in here, Ms?" Gloria nodded, went on writing.

He crossed the room, put his case files, briefcase, camera on the corner of the desk. Turned away. The files
started to slide. John and Frank lunged and caught them,
came up with their faces almost touching. Frank closed his
eyes and puckered his lips. "Oh . . ." Frank said in a fey
voice. "Will it happen like this?" Frank piled up the case
files, pushed them to the back of the shelf. "Be right with
you, John, really and honest true."

He went over to the ficus, felt the soil, dry, and swept
up the leaves with his hands. "Hey, it's attention to detail
that makes the difference, we're trying to run a business
here." He dumped several handfuls of leaves in a basket,
went around the room straightening up.

Gloria hung up the phone. "It's been absolutely crazy
this morning."

"Care to talk about it, " Frank said in her English accent.

"Well, for one thing, Karen has called three times."

"Three times? Any message emerge through it all?"
Frank raised an eyebrow which meant go ahead.

"I don't really know, Frank, I'm sorry to say. She just
seemed to talk. I think she's worried about you. Wanted
you to call her at work as soon as you get in."

"Am I in?"

"Your call."

"Did you cover those appointments this morning?"

"I did, Frank. All of them."

"Gnarly. Excellent." Gloria stood, giving Frank his swivel chair, and crossed to her own desk.

"You're a talent, Gloria. Really." Frank sat down, scanned the telephone messages, rocked back in his swivel chair, eyed Kramer's surfboard overhead, its long graceful curves, said to John, "What'd ya think of a guy who can stop drinking overnight? One day you drank together. Next day, he won't touch the stuff. Never takes another drink. Someone you should trust?"

"Who?" John followed Frank's eyes up to the board. "Kramer?"

"What's the difference? Anyone. One day this, the next day that. Someone you trust? Or not trust?" John shrugged.

Frank shrugged, "Yeah, you tell me."

"Trust for what?"

"I asked the question. Not trust for what. Just trust. You tell me. Yes or no?"

John shrugged, tuned the stereo to KJAZ. Frank followed the jazz into an abstraction. What a morning. Nightmares. Hangover. Melikian's call. Karen. Ray. Farrell in the Hall. Frank saw the model of the ice cream store in front of the jury. Tyrone Mayfield. He'd gotten away, would have gotten away with the holdup and killing, but his girlfriend dimed him six months later, bitch dialed 88-CRIME, the police went out with arrest and search warrants, Mayfield, the dumb fuck, still had the piece right there in the closet. Gun matches the slugs, the two witnesses ID him, testify, his girlfriend testifies in court looking him right in the eye the whole time. Frank swung upright in his swivel chair.

"Gloria . . ." She was on another call. "Gloria, can you please put it on hold."

She looked over at him. "Take this down. Sarah Anne Gillette." He carefully spelled it out for her. "Yeah, Gillette like the razor. Got it?" She nodded. "Good, run a skip trace on her in the next few days. Last known address was . . ." Frank looked up Ray's address in Mill Valley, gave it to Gloria. "That's about nine months old for her, but if there's Postal Forwarding, they should still have the new address." Ray knew there was a snitch. Sarah Anne leaves, no one knows where, nine months later, Ray's on the sixth floor, it was too simple, too obvious, how could Ray have ever just come out and talked to her? that just wasn't Ray, he knew better. . . . "If the guy at the P.O. gets lazy on you, tell him you know he's got the books going back two or three years, make him dig it out, make noises about the Freedom of Information Act, whatever. Do it all. Voter registration. I'll fill in some of the details, but please get started." He made a note on a pad: Sarah Anne. "Let's see if Sarah Anne Gillette is still in California and if we can find her."

He peeked at John. Okay, now the money game. "John, coffee?" John nodded. "Sugar? Cream?"

"Black. Three years black."

"I assume nothing. All of us are unique and wonderful. Maybe you'd had a revelation during the night. Like Kramer. Sugar and cream. Assume: Ass. U. Me. Want to get your own?"

"Yeah, rather than listen to this."

"Oh, listen to him, Italian and proud. Stay put, Homes." Frank stood. "Everyone's got such a hard on. Gloria, did they have Gillette blades in England. Yes? No?" She went on taking notes on something. "See, Gloria knows how to concentrate. You could learn from her, John."

Frank went upstairs, poured two coffees, stepped out on the second floor deck. The sun's warmth deepened in his skin, his eyelids closed under the weight; he felt that something which had once been broken and patched had been broken again this morning. Something which had been in motion for years had come to a stop; he wanted to lie down and sleep; faraway, the sound of traffic rose up the street like distant surf, abstracted into a voice. Frank listened, opened his eyes, rubbed them hard. Inside, he took a deep swallow of the hot coffee, refilled the cup.

He returned to his desk, placed a cup in front of John. He looked across the globular reproduction of Rodin's *The Kiss*. "Sorry to keep you waiting. Very hectic, I'm jammed. This must be success. Gloria, been to lunch?"

"Not yet."

"Anytime you're ready. I'll cover the phones. Go ahead. You've got ten minutes. Take twelve if you really must, Go for a walk in the park."

"Very sweet of you, Frank."

"If you're happy, I'm happy. That's what my buddy Kramer says. I never know if he means it or not. Go ahead. Did I tell you to run a skip trace on Sarah Anne Gillette? Yes, I did. Didn't I?"

"You did."

Frank fell silent. "John Giordano, how might I help you today? Let's share."

John took a swallow of his coffee, shifted in his seat and said almost apologetically, "Frank, I've got to get paid now. Today. I know you're hassled, but I owe money, people are pissed off at me, it's one thing after another."

Frank heard him out, then leaned forward. "John, I know I owe you money. I want to pay you. I will pay you; all I want right now is just a little more time."

John ran his fingers through his hair. "You've stalled me for three weeks. I can't work and not be paid. I have to be paid. I've got to pay my landlord. I mean, hey, we're not kids, this is embarrassing. It makes me look like a bum, a schmuck. I explain to the landlord I work. He says then you should have money. I say, yeah, but you don't work for Frank August."

"Thanks, John."

"Well, come on! He gave me until next Monday—five days. He's pissed. You can understand that."

"I've always paid you, haven't I?"

"Yeah, sure. . . . Christ, Frank, I don't want to be unreasonable, but my wife is going nuts, she's already crazy, says I've got to give her some money for Annie's tuition, which is only fair, I've got to pay my lawyer . . . Frank."

"Okay, John, I'm telling you I understand, but I don't have it today. How much do you absolutely need this second, this minute?"

"You owe me three grand. I need the three. All of it. Really. Today."

"This minute? This very second? Not some today? Some tomorrow?"

"To-day, Frank," John said with sudden temper. "Last time we did this, you stalled me around for weeks. And now, it's the same deal."

"You got paid, too. Hey, you need a law class, contracts, torts, you ask me, no problem, I tailor your work so you can take your classes. Did we work it out?"

"Yeah, and I appreciate that, Frank. I really do. I couldn't have finished law school without that kind of consideration from you."

"I mean, you need slack, I cut you slack."

"And I appreciate it."

Frank turned his palms up. "So. Hey. All I'm saying is I'm jammed, I need some slack now, too. Cut me some slack, John."

John took a deep breath, looked at the floor. "Frank, I've given you slack. Weeks of it."

Frank pulled a checkbook out of his top drawer and wrote a check for three hundred dollars and pushed it over to John. John picked it up, looked at it. Shook his head, no.

"I'll get the rest to you within a week."

"Frank . . ."

"Trust me. Can you trust me?"

"It's not a question of trusting you. I know sooner or later you'll pay. I'm at the end of the line. You're using me, Frank."

"Hey, you want to talk about money, go talk to Aram Melikian about money."

"What's Aram Melikian got to do with it?"

"I mean, you think I'm using you, Aram Melikian

knows how to use people, dude-san. No, really, man, listen and learn, Aram, taught me about money, he pulls in a case, hires me as the investigator, People vs. Delaney, big murder case. I do all the legwork, hours of digging, figure the whole case out for him. I send him a bill for eight thousand dollars which is really doing him a favor, no padded hours, no time for cappuccinos, ball games. Aramie sends me six thousand dollars and a note saying we'll discuss the other two thousand smackers. I come in for a conference, he's not saying I've padded my hours, but my bill is high, he's got his felon client to protect, too, yenta, yenta. He writes me out a check for another two hundred, end of discussion." He came to a stop. "Hey, he gets to do that to me because he's a lawyer, and I'm an investigator and the money always goes through him. I can give you a list of twenty lawyers that owe me bread—ten, fifteen grand. The courts owe me another eight." He shrugged. "My point here is you're pissed at me, I want to pay you, I'm making it, but where is it? You know they do this to us."

Frank swiveled his chair. "I'll be right back." Frank took the stairs, arrived breathless at the top. The carpeted second floor. Calm. Tranquility in the beautiful law offices. The receptionist. "Mail come yet, Connie?" She sorted, handed him several envelopes. He went through them quickly, opened one. Two hundred dollars.

Downstairs, Frank held up the check. "Two bills. I'm making it over to you. That plus the other three hundred is five bills, John." Frank sat, endorsed and slid the check over to John. John placed it in his chest pocket. "Give me until the end of the week for the rest. I'm jammed. I need you to do People vs. Evans. They're going to trial next week. Work for me this afternoon. I'm doing what I can. You know that, John."

John remained slumped and silent in the director's chair. He followed the prosecution's time line on the wall, then said, "I'm not leaving here and I'm not working until I get paid all of it. This is one time, Frank, one time, when

no matter what your good reasons or how you lay it out,
no matter how charming, how funny, I'm going to get what
I came for."

Frank rocked back in his swivel chair, looked at John,
who avoided his gaze. Frank went with the soft slip of jazz
from the speakers in the corner, rocked, his chair squeaking, rocked, rocked, felt something go cold in him. He
spun the Rolodex, quickly dialed all of a number but the
last digit, spoke into the dead phone, first the secretary,
then the lawyer, a few pleasantries, question about partial
payment, you can, thanks, man, we'll get together, go
ahead and take your other call, we'll set something up for
lunch. Frank hung up. He spun in his chair. John looked
at him. Frank smiled. "Michael Lassetter himself of Lassetter and Eisenstein. Twenty-five hundred dollars in the
mail this afternoon. Be here tomorrow, Friday at the latest."

John remained silent. Frank said, "What, want me to
have him send a courier over with the check?" He shook
his head, pulled out the checkbook and wrote a check for
twenty-five hundred dollars. "Don't cash it for two days,
there it is, it's all over, let's work. No?"

John didn't answer. He didn't take the check. Frank
pushed the check toward John with the certainty that by
the time John cashed the check—two, three days at the
most—Frank would have covered it somehow. "Here.
John. Take it. What do you want?" Frank stood, pulled
his pants pockets inside out.

Kramer appeared from the dim hallway, leaned against
the door frame, not in, not out. The phone rang. Gloria
picked up. "Good morning, August and Associates . . ."

Gloria put it on hold. "Karen."

Frank shook his head vigorously, no, not now. Gloria
went back on the line. "Karen, he's just stepped out. He
went to move his car. No, he really is not here." Gloria's
tone went chilly English, a quality for which he loved her.
"I beg your pardon, I have absolutely no reason to lie to
you. I'll have him call you the moment he gets in."

John shook his head at Frank's endless on-going problems with Karen. Frank looked back at Kramer, who chewed a large wad of gum quickly and nervously, the gum making soft spitting noises as he popped it. His hair was a wild knotted tangle. He wore jeans and the Amazing Spiderman T-shirt. Frank felt he'd had more of a handle on Kramer before he'd stopped drinking. Now, with this raw nervous edge, he seemed unpredictable, often, just plain unreadable.

He reached over, took a file, and pointing out the door, he nodded to Kramer. They went down the hall to a vacant conference room. "Steve, I'm jammed. Look, just read this file. Police reports, transcripts from the preliminary hearing. Keep track of your time—I'll pay you ten, no, twelve-fifty an hour."

Already sorting through the file, Kramer said, "Later you'll say it was ten an hour."

Moved by his showing up to work, Frank said, "Kramer, I've got to talk to you later." Kramer looked up. "Some weird shit's happening. I've got to talk to someone I can trust, see if I can get a handle on it. It's just going around in my head."

Kramer said, "Okay, Frank. We'll talk. Come to dinner."

"I have to talk to you alone."

"We'll eat and walk in the neighborhood."

"Thanks for coming, Steve. I'm serious. I'll remember this. When you need me down the road, I'll be there. Hey, this case is going to take you into the project. Hunters Point. Indian territory. Can you deal with that?"

Kramer nodded, went on reading. Frank walked back down the dim hall. Frank looked at John. "Are you working or not, Mister Giordano?"

"Pay me and I'm working."

"I did what I could. It's on the desk. Pick it up." John didn't move. Frank said, "Okay. I don't have time for this anymore. I really don't. If you're not working and you're not leaving, make yourself comfortable." He went to the closet, pulled out a pillow, and threw it on the sofa. "Here, I'm a caring person. I've slept there plenty of times. Does it look like you're in for a long one?" He opened his drawer and pulled out a bent toothbrush, threw it on the desk. "If you change your mind, Gloria will give you your assignment."

Frank indicated the sofa for John, sat at his desk, and started returning calls. After a while, he went to the closet and took out a white shirt and clipboard and went back down the hall. Kramer was just finishing the file. "Steve, here, wear the shirt and carry the clipboard in the project, it'll make you look like a social worker. The heavies will still be sleeping it off now, but watch out for the dogs. Blood got these wild fucking dogs to protect themselves from each other. Dobermans. German Shepherds. I tell you, I talked to a narc who blew away some shvartzer's dog the other day, was going right for his throat."

Kramer stood, took off his T-shirt, and put on the shirt, tucked it in. "Here's the case, Steve. My guy, Curtis Bledsoe, is in for assault, rape, sodomy, you name it. His story is he goes picks up this bitch, Ashanti Showers, it's mutual consent all the way. I think she's a toss-up—you know, a coke whore, she fucks for coke. Maybe she is. Maybe she isn't. But if we can make her a whore, the prosecution's case goes into the dumper. Ain't got no rape charges standing up anywhere in the USA on a nigger bitch whore. You understand, Steve, ain't my point of view here. We're talking your basic racist American juror. Unfortunately for Ashanti, we're not on her side." Frank shrugged. "Make her a whore, Kramer, and Curtis Bledsoe, my dumb, self-righteous defendant won't have to go to trial."

Kramer sighed. "Bledsoe, is he guilty? Did he do it?"

"Who knows? Says not. Probably is. We're all guilty of something, Slick. I'm not judge and jury. And that's not even a question here."

Kramer looked blank. Frank patted him on the arm. "Steve, whatever you do, don't misrepresent yourself to anyone who you think may testify. Tell them you want them to tell the truth. When the prosecutor gets them up on the stand and asks what the investigator told them, they'll say, 'He told me to tell the truth.' That brings juries to their knees. They can't resist it.''

Kramer took the file, a yellow pad, a pen and started for the door. Frank said, "Keep track of your mileage." Kramer nodded. As he went up the stairs, Frank said, "Steve, hold on. Listen to me. If anything feels wrong in the project, anything at all, just get the fuck out of there. You've got good instincts. Listen to them. I don't want you to die while you were doing me a favor and getting paid ten bucks an hour. Last time I was in there, the fuckers threw rocks and bottles. I got out. Barely.''

"You said twelve-fifty twenty minutes ago." Kramer laughed and went up the stairs.

As Frank stepped back into the office, John stood, picked up the check, folded it once, and put it in his chest pocket. He walked by Frank without looking at him, "I'll work, but the check better be good, Frank, or this is it.''

"Wait two days, John, it'll be good," he said, knowing he'd get it covered somehow.

John went up the stairs, and Frank sank into his chair. He drifted with the jazz, two days to cover the check, though if push came to shove, he could always tell John he'd deposited it Friday afternoon, but it hadn't covered, run the check through again on Monday, which would give him the weekend, an extra two days, he'd have the money for sure on Monday, it was all just a bluff, they bluffed, he bluffed, the lawyers bluffed, the defendants bluffed, the prosecution bluffed, somehow it all kicked over, another day. He glanced at the picture of his father with his right hand buried in his suit pocket, swiveled in his chair, became aware of Gloria.

"What? I like my employees to speak out."

"I believe, Frank, that Lassetter paid you the twenty-five hundred a month ago."

"Gloria, I never called him. I figured you knew what I was up to. What could I do? John staged a little coup. But look, if he walks now the whole thing falls apart and no one gets anything and then where are we? The bottom line is they keep coming in, then John gets something, I'm here when he needs me. So today I stretched things a little, everyone saves face, I'll make good on the check, and in the meantime, we live to fight another day—John's wife, his landlord, everyone. I'll cover it. Go ahead, Gloria, break for lunch, I'll cover here."

She nodded and stood. "You alright, Frank?"

He looked at her. She was always so calm. He could almost love her. He put the thought out of his mind. "I'm okay."

As she walked by, he pretended to make a grab for her, she slapped his hand, and they laughed. She closed the door behind her. He should probably call Melikian's office, schmooze Aram along a little. It was all swimming around in his head, anyway, drawing the line between what Ray had said today on the sixth floor, his case, and Frank's connection to the whole business, where Ray's story started and stopped, and Frank's began. In Ray's best interests, he should remove himself from the case. The case was four hours old for him, and it was making him crazy.

He'd reached the door, when remembering Karen, he went back to his desk. He dialed her work number. Busy. Fine. He could say he had tried, but of course that wouldn't do it. He'd have to reach her. He knew how their conversation would go. It would start with another apology about last night, or an attempt to say something conciliatory, but somehow escalate from there.

. He pressed the redial. Still busy. Return her call and hassle now? Or don't return her call and go around later? He tried her number once more, this time got through. She had just left for a late lunch. Yeah, where . . . And who? He thought of checking out a couple of restaurants in her work neighborhood to see who she was with. Hell with it. Frank said, "Can you tell her that Frank called and will call back. And please make sure she gets the message."

Relieved, disappointed, he hung up. At least he'd covered himself.

He took a last look around, and met the bemused, unreadable gaze of his father. The picture had been taken in the early Fifties. His father stood surrounded by eight sprinters—they'd just won a city-wide track championship. The day before, the head judge had called his hundred man second at the finish line when two other judges and their stopwatches had him first. In the following argument, Frank's father had plunged his hand through a window and required over thirty stitches, which was why his right hand was in his suit jacket pocket—to hide the bandage. His father. Explosive. Charming. Unpredictable.

"Hey, Dad, I just failed the bar exam." Frank picked up the framed photograph. "But love me anyway, okay? Please. No, I didn't think you would. Well, that's okay. I love you. Trying, anyway." Frank debated, then gently placed the picture in his middle desk drawer.

Outside, he locked the door, then paused trying to make a list, decide which things first. He placed one foot on the first step and stopped. Screw the list. It was time to go to the library.

In the reference section, Frank found the index to the *Chronicle* and carried the thick book over to a table—the squeal of the chair as he sat raked his nerves. Someone coughed and hawked behind him. Frank hesitated. Davis had been murdered when? a year ago? He flipped through the index and within a short time, spotted a headline: *Parnassus Heights Man Murdered—Wealth of Art and Drugs Found at Site*. He flipped forward, but there was no follow-up. Frank noted the date on a pad, went over to the reference librarian, who took his driver's license and set him up at a table with several spools of microfilm and a viewing machine. Focussing, Frank rolled the film forward. Parnassus Heights. . . . A wave of old terror momentarily surfaced in Frank. Richie Davis upside down. . . . Surprised, Frank took a deep breath and fought back the memory. Just read the article, Frank. He read a couple of paragraphs and stopped. Dennis Farrell, Chief Homicide Investigator. He'd forgotten that. What kinds of funny little houses are you building now, Frankie?

Frank took another deep breath and went on reading. Richie Davis, bludgeoned, strangled, stabbed. Money—fifty-six thousand dollars—found beside the body. One hundred thousand dollars worth of drugs in the house—the investigators wouldn't say what kinds of drugs. And a treasure trove of Buddhist art. Museum quality. In fact, the article went on to say, Davis was a high figure in the Buddhist religion and neither his family or friends had any idea there had been another side to him—that he dealt drugs or handled large amounts of money. The article did mention investigators finding computer disks, Ray was right about that. Extremely right. And it said that the disks seemed to be in some kind of bizarre code; they were being sent off to specialists in cryptography in Washington, D.C. Ray was right about that, too. Right, but Ray still found himself on the sixth floor today. Maybe it wasn't all about being right, but being right in time or at the right moment or . . . Frank couldn't stay with the thought. Just that something was wrong and it was too late. That much he knew for sure.

The article went on to mention that there was no evidence of forced entry which suggested that Mr. Davis knew his assailant or assailants. Nothing appeared to have been taken—robbery was being ruled out as a motive. With fifty-six thousand dollars left beside the body and one hundred thousand dollars worth of drugs, one might safely assume that. Frank took a deep breath. As of now there were no suspects. The article ended by saying that Farrell and his team of investigators were being assisted by agents from the Internal Revenue Service and the Drug Enforcement Agency and that the investigation was continuing. That's all there was. The killer or killers, Frank knew, had never been caught.

Frank sat back, closed his eyes, and stopped fighting

the memory. Let it come. He'd met Richie once. He'd
come from work, rendezvoused with Ray for dinner, then
followed Ray in his car. No preamble from Ray, of course,
who when where, but come to a party, a friend of mine.
That was it. Ray's control trip, Ray's game. Okay. Up and
down the street outside the house, a lot of pretty cars—
BMW's, Mercedes, Jags. . . . Inside, twenty rooms. A
house full of people. Glossy people. A lot of beautiful
women. Everyone was very juiced on something, and after
a few minutes, Frank recognized what it was, that there'd
been a big score, and it was all raining down—money,
drugs, and most of all, a sense of triumph, someone had
gotten away with something big. Ray's parties had often
felt that way. Frank realized now that the person or persons
who had killed Davis might have been at the party, though
try as he might, he hadn't ever been able to recall a single
face. Ray had pointed out Richie after they'd come in, Ray
and Richie in the course of things had shaken hands, and
Ray had introduced Frank. Frank had the sense of a guy
who was mildly amused by everything going on around
him, but also kept himself very distant. Frank couldn't decide if it was because he had no real connection to anything or that he felt nothing could touch him. He just
seemed somewhere else. He was drinking Perrier from a
champagne glass. Cool.

The house was fantastic. It appeared to have been built
in the late twenties and had beautiful picture-hanging and
floor moldings, doors, wainscotting, windowsills, and, as
Frank had worked on places like this, he noticed how perfectly it had been painted. From the front rooms, there had
been wonderful views of the city lights spread below.
Throughout the house, there had been Buddhist artifacts—
Japanese and Chinese Buddhas, several waist-high
bronzes; another one, life size, black marble polished
smooth, each with his faint, distant smile. In some rooms,
Tibetan mandalas. In a well-appointed den, there had been
a MacIntosh computer on a desk. Frank had wandered. The
rooms, the house, the artifacts, all said money. Real

money. As it turned out, Frank hadn't been wrong. But somehow, Richie Davis had been very wrong about something. He wished he'd paid more attention to Davis that night.

Anyway, Frank had been here and there, a little walking around, a few toots of this, a toke of that, a few drinks, the women were starting to glow, and take on that wonderful secret life where everything was infinitely promising and possible and magical—a laugh, a gesture, the fall of hair on a shoulder—and Frank had rolled with it, but somehow the mood had a bottom, and Frank could sense the bottom, or perhaps there wasn't enough illusion left in it or him that night, and then, too, Karen, he knew, was home and he felt thin on excuses. He and Ray had left about the same time, going their separate ways, and then driving past his office, he'd gone in to pick up several case files, had sat down to organize them, had started reading a grand jury transcript in preparation for a preliminary hearing the next day, and dozed off. He'd awakened on the sofa to a deep silence, the beginnings of a hangover, and then, standing up, the sudden realization that he didn't have his wallet. He searched his office. His car. No wallet. Jesus, his credit cards. He remembered having the wallet with Ray at dinner. He had to have lost it at Richie's, possibly slumping down on that living room sofa. He glanced at his watch. 3:30. The party would probably still be going on. He debated. He knew Karen wouldn't be too happy about this, but he'd been out half the night, anyway, more than he'd intended, and whatever the damage, it had already been done.

Bleary-eyed, he'd driven back to Richie's, slowly winding up the deserted streets of the Heights until he recognized the house. Surprised not to see any cars, he pulled over. Almost four. Maybe better to come back tomorrow. He looked up at the house. Lights were on. Well, if he didn't get the wallet now, he'd have to make the trip again tomorrow. He got out of the car, walked through the thick hedge surrounding the front walk. He stopped, listened—

not a sound—and then continued up to the heavy front door. He was about to raise his hand to knock lightly when he noticed the front door ajar. He hesitated, pushed it open, called softly. "Richie? Richie? Anyone home?" He stepped into the front hall. All of the lights were on. "Hello? This is Frank August, Ray's friend—we met earlier?" He listened. He walked into the living room. No one. The smiling bronze Buddhas. Beyond, the enchanting view of the Bay, the Golden Gate Bridge, faraway, as if in a dream or fairy tale.

He turned, walked down the hall, calling softly, suddenly uncomfortable. He thought that it might be better—instead of going farther—to head back into the living room and feel into the cushions of the living room sofa for his wallet, but then if Richie suddenly walked out, that wouldn't look too good, either. Still, if he kept walking down the hall, this could end up as one of those scenes where he walked in on Richie making love to two transvestites, the neighbor's Jack Russell terrier, the maid, and a parrot named Oscar. . . .

Something lightly slapped him, Frank recoiled, in front of him, he raised his eyes, something hanging upside down from a beam, swaying from where he'd hit it, blood dripped slowly out of a hole, Frank staggered backward, froze, heart pounding, took it in as if a series of snapshots or slides, each erupting frozen out of the darkness which was pounding in him, a man? a man's body? naked, but no sex, just a huge gash; the thud within Frank's head, a man, cock cut off, something in his mouth, or where his mouth had been, but his face, there was little face left, ears cut off, nose, eyes gouged, bloody teeth snarling in a grimace. There was not a place on his body which had not been carved. Whoever had done this had taken his or their time. Below him, a huge pool of black blood. Placed around the pool, stacks of cash. Then, as if a single giddy spontaneous afterthought, a handful of flung cash floated and congealed in the blood.

Frank staggered backward down the hall, stumbling,

whimpering, gasping, fell backward out the front door, down the walk, stood doubled over, hands on knees, gasping. . . . He stumbled back toward the front door, where he wiped haphazardly around the door-pull with his shirttails. He made himself step back inside, stumbled toward the living room sofa, pull back the cushions, amazing, there was his fucking wallet, the only physical thing that could tie him to this house, holding it in his hands, he bolted, next thing he was in his car, gasping, panting, driving, tires squealing as he sped down from the Heights. . . .

Sometime later, somewhere, car pulled up at a wild angle beside a gas station phone booth, engine running, Frank fumbled coins into the phone. After an infinite number of rings, Ray answered.

"You know who this is? You recognize my voice? Just yes or no?"

"Yes."

"I can't talk now. I can't think. I'm scared. Something's going on. The place we were tonight. It's the worst thing that could happen. Get me?"

"Yes."

"It's a monster. I don't know if it's an isolated incident or if it will spread out to reach you. Hang up, get out of your house, break your routine. Call me at my office later. We'll meet somewhere. I'll tell you what I saw."

"Uh huh."

"I'm hanging up. Hang up."

And Ray had hung up. Still stumbling, Frank had fallen back into his car. In the rearview mirror, a large mark on his forehead. He leaned forward. Dried blood. Blood where something, the hand? he'd walked into the body, yeah, the hand, had lightly slapped him. Frank rubbed at it furiously, spat on his hands, rubbed, slammed the car into drive, drove.

Though Frank routinely looked at crime scene photos, pictures of his defendants' victims after autopsies by the Coroner, the monstrousness, the sadism of Richie's murder was beyond them. Later, when he thought back to those moments, he recalled the house as tilted; the floor under his feet made him feel as if he were skidding and scrambling to remain upright against a steep and precipitous incline which shifted unpredictably with each step.

Frank sat up, pushed himself forward in his chair. He saw now that Richie's murder had been the beginning of where Ray was today. He just didn't know how. Apparently, neither did Dennis Farrell. But one thing Frank did understand. Whoever had done it had been sending a message to make all of Davis's associates feel their proximity and power. They'd gotten the message.

Frank began to scroll forward, the articles blurring as they slid by—murders, rapes, assaults; many he recalled. Some he had helped investigate and defend. What was he looking for? Periodically, he stopped to rest his eyes and stave off dizziness. This was a great thing to be doing on a hangover. He scanned until the names and incidents started to bleed together; he was well past a short article before something registered and he ran the film backward: *Trawler Seized off California Coast. Twenty Tons of High Quality Thai Marijuana. Intercepted by the U.S. Coast Guard.* Frank checked the date. October 25th. Eight months ago. He paused. This morning, Ray had mentioned losing big in the pipeline. Frank had thought, what, three, five tons at most? Twenty tons! This had to have been Ray's tonnage. This was exactly the way he brought it in. Christ, how big had he gotten? Twenty tons lost, Ray had never said a word, and the times he'd seen Ray, Frank hadn't been able to read any major changes. Frank sat there with a feeling of misgiving, irritation, and then realized that what bothered him most was that he hadn't had any idea. Not that Ray hadn't told him. That was right. But that he, Frank, hadn't read it—things were getting by him.

He stood, returned the microfilm to the reference librarian, and walked out of the library. He took a deep breath of fresh air and looked across at City Hall, wondering vaguely about Richie Davis—fifty-six thousand dollars beside the body, the smooth bronze and marble Buddhas with their mysterious beautiful faces throughout the house. For weeks after seeing the money scattered beneath Richie in the huge black pool of blood, Frank hadn't been able to handle paper money without sudden flashbacks. Several times someone had handed him cash and he'd seen the currency black with blood. Once, as a clerk had started to count back his change, he'd taken back his extended hand in frozen confusion and Karen had just looked at him. He'd awakened from nightmares, and Karen had held him and said: "Jesus, Frank, what in God's name is it? Talk to me." What could he tell her? "There are so many things I feel you keeping from me, Frank." There was just nothing he could say. Impossible. And all of it contributed to Karen's feelings that Frank was erratic, that he was losing it, that maybe they just weren't going to make it together.

Muddling Richie and the disks, Ray and Sarah Anne, Karen and himself, Frank started down the library steps. Then he realized he'd find a way to approach Farrell. Ask him about the disks. Some pretext to ask if Sammy and Ray were on them. And if they were, then there it was: Ray had brought the DEA after him and brought down Jack, Sammy, Dean Miller, all of them. If the DEA had put Ray and Sammy under surveillance, there was no snitch. He'd have to get something out of Farrell.

Frank walked over to the newspaper dispenser, dropped in change. The *Examiner*. About now, according to Melikian, the grand jury would be hearing the case agent, Hernandez, presenting his evidence. Frank leafed quickly through the paper, but there was nothing about the bust yet.

As he placed the paper under his arm, a woman turned the corner and a vortex of wind lifted her skirt—she pushed it down with both hands—but not before Frank had seen her black panties and felt a stab of desire. Making love to Sarah Anne in that dark hallway. Lying on the floor. Should we open the door, Frank? Who's anyone?

Frank stopped. She'd left in September. Ray's boat was taken in October.

A little breathless, he walked toward his car. He remembered running windsprints for basketball back in high school. He'd been able to run all day. Reaching his car, Frank realized it had been a long time ago. He hesitated, then walked on toward a bar. Inside, a corner stool, familiar darkness. When the bartender placed the beer in front of him, Frank looked at it for a long time. Here it was. One beer. One ounce of alcohol. This was the big deal, the subject of all the talk, or when there was no talk, the pregnant pauses, charged silences, searching glances, nuanced undertones between himself and Karen. Yesterday afternoon it had led to trouble. A blackout. Frank took a sip of the beer. Another. He slowly drank half the glass, felt soothed, and then he stood, watched the foam settle and walked out. He could take it or leave it.

Frank drove south down Mission, wind blowing newspapers, plastic bags, burger wrappers. He was driving fast. He wanted to be home at eight just to prove to Karen that he could be, would be. Braked for a red light at Mission and Twenty-fifth. Crowds still gathered at bus stops and the BART station, blacks and Chicanos in hightops listening to salsa, rap, rock and roll. Here and there, ugly graffiti spray-painted on the stone caught his eye. Angela & Tito. Fuck. Cunt. Love Is Revenge. As the signal went yellow on the other side of the intersection, a young black kid, maybe fourteen, detached himself from the kids by the BART station, walked toward the car and said quickly without looking directly at Frank, "Work work working, man, twenty does it."

"Better watch it, Homes, how you know I'm not the Man?" The light turned green. Frank drove on, here and there a band of gold light hitting a rooftop, a gable, a mural. The rest of the city could be wrapped in fog—Twin Peaks, the Avenues, North Beach—but the Mission was usually sunny. Sunny and third world, Frank thought. Go

downtown, come back and you noticed the people were
shoulder height—Mexicans, Chinese, Vietnamese, Fili-
pino. And up here, the streets smelled: stir-fry cooking,
perfume, fish markets, Mexican bakeries, coffee roasting,
people. Soon there'd be chickens and goats. Half San Francisco, half peasant village.

Frank glanced at the black kid in his rearview mirror
and then felt a little nervous. That was bullshit, his asking
Kramer to go to the project by himself; whenever there
was a case in the project, Frank almost always sent two.
Christ, what had he been thinking of? Still, Kramer was a
grownup, he would have said no if he didn't think he could
handle it. And Frank had told him to cut and run if things
were weird. Kramer did have good instincts. And he liked
taking chances, the jerk, out there surfing at sunrise . . .
Jesus. Frank wound up the narrow back streets toward
Holly Park, anxiously looking for Kramer's truck as he
drew within parking radius of their houses. Karen's car?
Cars were sandwiched into every available space and half
space up and down the narrow streets.

Still looking, he passed his intersection and noticed two
cop cars, blue lights flashing, parked in the middle of the
street. His stomach rolled over, and heart pounding, he
sped on, drove up several streets before finding a space.
By the time he had returned, the cops were gone, the street
was empty. Shifting his files and briefcase, jacket pockets
crammed with his Instamatic and film, he debated, then
walked around the corner and halfway down the next
block. He entered the driveway of the neighbor's house
which was behind his, confronted their backyard garden
and wooden fence. Debating, he found a broken board in
the fence, pushed his briefcase and files through, and then,
looking back at the neighbor's house, he carefully hitched
up his pants and climbed. Balanced on the top of the fence
in his suit, trying not to split the crotch of his pants, he
saw himself, stupid, ridiculous, paranoid? or just cautious?
He dropped into his yard, then climbed the back stairs and
let himself into the kitchen.

He stood in the dark. The silence told him there was no one there. He called. "Karen?" He opened his mouth to call again, sighed. She wasn't there. The cats came out of the shadows, purring, weaving in and out of his ankles. He dropped his stuff on the kitchen table. No one. He picked up the phone and listened. Dial tone, but nothing else—at least nothing he could detect. Tell-tale clicks, electronic noises. He didn't know if he'd be able to hear anything, anyway.

He replaced the receiver, then climbed up to the attic, moved to the front windows, and peered up and down the street. Except for cars and a couple of kids playing near the corner, there was no one. He slowly surveyed the front windows of the houses across the street. He peered into Kramer's, but couldn't tell who was home, what they were doing.

In the kitchen, the clock said five after eight. They were supposed to have met at eight. There were no signs of Karen or of her having stopped home. Frank switched on the TV, flicked the channels, ESPN, Yankees-Red Sox at Fenway. He watched, then turned away and spotted the light flashing on the answering machine, punched the *message* button. Attorneys. Appointments. Cancelled. Changed. Reminders. Melikian: "Frankie, Aram Melikian. Six p.m. I have word the grand jury is going to indict our client Ray Buchanan on charges of conspiracy to transport, sell, and distribute marijuana. Arraignment coming up in the next few days. I'll have Velma let you know. Let's get together tomorrow afternoon. We'll talk."

Ray to be indicted. Big surprise. Well, what had he expected? But there it was. And no word from Karen. Frank dropped into a kitchen chair. He spent several minutes returning calls and then gave it up. A cool breeze lifted the curtains above the sink. He watched them silently rise, fought off exhaustion and a feeling of desolation. He picked up his Polaroid, backed up to the door, and took a picture of the empty kitchen. Pulled the film out and watched the image silently emerge like falling smoke. The kitchen clock, the rising curtains. Clock at eight-twelve. He tossed the picture on the table, set water on to boil, ground coffee beans, sprinkled them into a fresh paper filter. So what did she want? She bitched about him—his drinking, his being erratic, his keeping things from her, his making and breaking dates, which was really his work—she knew that. Whatever he did, it wasn't right, and when he thought it was right, she changed the rules. So tonight it was eight and he was here at eight and now she wasn't here. No doubt she'd have a good reason.

Frank poured boiling water through the coffee filter and took the cup to the table. He watched Mattingly take a strike, sipped the coffee, walked to the window and looked out over the backyards and rooftops. The cool breeze passed over his face, the curtains rose, fell. High up, the soft blue of oncoming night filled him with longing. He went to the kitchen table, scrawled across the Polaroid: *I was here. Where were you?* He slipped a package of flower seeds into his pocket, walked across the street to Kramer's. Rang. June answered, smiled. "Steve just got back. He's sitting down to eat."

"Stevie's home and Snookie-Okums is waiting with dinner and warm arms."

Frank followed her in. Kramer was just taking a first bite of dinner. Kneeling on a chair at Kramer's elbow, Zack drew a picture with markers, crayons, pens, and pencils. Frank tousled Zack's hair.

"Hey, what's with pressure? Earlier, there were two cop cars on the street?"

June said, "A burglary. Mrs. Santos, five doors up."

"That's about the fourth in three weeks. Gotta be crack burglars, if they catch em it's going to turn out to be two or three of the same dudes coming up from the project, working the street. Remember Bobbie DuChan, crackhead blood, working that neighborhood till he killed the old man. Just like that."

Kramer put his fork down. Placed both his elbows on

the table and took a breath. Said quietly, "Frank, how about some dinner?"

"Or a glass of wine?" Kramer looked at June. Some kind of dirty look? Frank wasn't sure. The silent language of the married. He was half amused.

"Don't you know you're not supposed to offer Frankie booze? Specially after Frankie's fall last night. But hey, I could use a drop."

June poured him a glass of burgundy. "There's plenty of dinner." Frank went to the stove and fixed himself a plate.

"Where's Karen?"

"You tell me. You girls are in this thing together. Where is Karen? We were supposed to meet at eight. I'm here. She's not. Case rests." June was thoughtful. Frank said, "What?"

"Oh, sometimes I think the man-woman schism is no one's fault, just . . ." she shrugged. "You know, I think, men are in it for the highs."

Kramer said, "In what?"

"This. Life."

Frank and Kramer looked at each other. Kramer said, "And what are women in it for?"

June took a sip of her wine. "The long haul."

Frank said, "Now that that's been settled, all I have to say is that I was here at eight o'clock when we were supposed to meet." They ate in the silence of a charged, undefined mood. Finally, Frank said, "A moment of business, Steve?"

Kramer stopped chewing. "If it's business, ever so brief, please, señor."

"Right. People vs. Curtis Bledsoe. Any luck?"

"Kind of. But I've got to go back—a lot of the people I needed to talk to weren't around."

Frank ate quickly with no real appetite. He said quietly, "Hey, you know something. I'm jammed now, back to the wall, and you came through for me. I'll be there when you need me, Kramer. I won't forget it." Kramer shrugged. "No, I mean it, Steve."

Zack's magic marker screeched, and Frank remembered the flower seeds. He went to the refrigerator and rearranged the eggs until he had an empty carton, returned from the back porch with each cup filled with potting soil. Zack beside him, he pushed zinnia seeds into the soil, then watered them. "For you, my man, keep em watered when Mom tells you to. Pretty soon you'll have flowers."

Frank poured himself another glass of burgundy, walked into the front room, and looked across the street at his house. Still dark. The TV, flickering ghost, playing in the window, on the walls. He circled the dark front room, drank off the wine, began to feel it—big deal—and walked back into the kitchen, refilled his glass. He took a quick gulp, topped the glass off once more. Kramer sipped his coffee, put on a tape, an old Doors album, drifted into "Riders of the Storm." Frank watched his eyes. About now, when Kramer used to be Kramer, he'd smoke a joint, have another glass of wine. Frank saw hints of that distance coming into his eyes with the music. Most of the time, he thought he knew Kramer.

As a teaching assistant getting an M.A. in journalism, Kramer had been Frank's teacher one semester. His father dead almost four years, Frank was putting himself through school, painting houses and working as a chef. About halfway through the class, Kramer called Frank into his office and offered him a chair. "Your articles and essays are good and sometimes terrific—they're funny and inventive—and someone took time to teach you to write."

"Jesuits."

"Well, the Jesuits didn't teach you to fuck up. You've already missed too many classes. About half the times you are in class, you're stoned."

"Wait a second : .."

"I'm not finished. I know you're putting yourself through school. And I know you'll have a very good excuse for missing classes." Kramer held up his hand. "I'm in a rush right now. Here's the deal. If you don't miss any more classes, none, nada, and do quality work, you can probably still get an A. Otherwise, it's going to be a C or D." Frank started to speak, but Kramer stood. "I really am in a rush."

Kramer started down the hall. Frank was giving Kramer the finger when Kramer said over his shoulder, "Why do it if the guy can't see it? That's one thing I never understood." He turned around, and Frank started laughing. Kramer said, "Here, kill two birds with one stone. Write an essay on why I must say fuck you, Steve Kramer." He disappeared around the corner.

Uncertain whether or not Kramer was serious, Frank wrote the essay, relating his need to say fuck you and the pain he would suffer if he didn't to the fourteen stations of the cross. Kramer gave him an A for the essay. He came regularly to the classes, but missed two more, and Kramer wrote across his last article, "It could have been an A. I said come to *all* the classes." Kramer kept his word and gave him a C. One thing Frank knew, Kramer wouldn't take his crap. Frank watched Kramer come out of his distance.

Kramer said, "Earlier today you said you had something you wanted to talk about?"

Frank became aware of June who was sipping her coffee and browsing through the paper. "Hey, I'm in a red zone, you want to walk out with me?"

"Been out all day, but must be Frank's way of telling me something." He stood. "I'll be back in a little while." June said, "Kiss Zack. He's going to bed."

Kramer hugged Zack. Zack held out his arms for Frank. Frank kissed him goodnight, touched a fist to his chin. Kramer kissed June, she murmured something.

"Christ Almighty, Kramer, kiss her when you go in to take a pee, kiss her when you come out." Frank circled back into the kitchen, found his wine glass, and took one last gulp. Kramer threw on his jacket and they went out, walked up the street.

"Where's the car?"

Frank said, "The car's fine—maybe a little depressed, but basically fine. Let's take a walk."

They wound through the narrow back streets, then up toward Bernal Height, crossed the road leading to the grassy knoll at the top; they walked in silence, breathing hard against the incline. As they cleared the summit, the full force of the wind met them. Below, the city lights spread an incandescent glowing carpet of streets—Mission, Folsom, Valencia; single noises rose—a dog barking, a horn, a burst of music as a car turned a corner.

Frank pointed. "Hey, look at the Stick. Killer." The lights threw a soft glow up into the fog. "Who they playing?"

"Dodgers. Second night of three. Last night the fans rioted in the left field bleachers, tore the place apart."

"Yeah, the fans rioted. What a bunch of animals. I hate 'em all."

"What's the deal, you hate 'em all?"

"Hey, baruch atoy adonoi, don't start *Mother Jones* liberal with me. They throw rocks and bottles in left field, they throw em at me in the project when I come in trying to find a witness to save their asses. What's the deal? Maybe it was when they started killing each other for their hightops and jackets. Right down there in the park on Army Street, they murdered a sixteen-year-old kid for his hightops. Hope they got a good fit."

"If you didn't give a shit, you wouldn't be trying to figure things out for Curtis Bledsoe . . ."

"Let me tell you something. That figures itself out. I'm not talking justice here. I'm talking about playing the fucking game and winning. You think anyone really cares about bloods raping each other? Are you fucking serious? What's the matter, Steve? You mad? You think I'm an asshole?"

Kramer was silent. Finally he said, "I think you care and pretend not to."

Frank took a deep breath, let it out. "That's too touching.'' This wasn't what he wanted. "I care, you care, who cares. Hey, you know, what's real here is I'm not really an investigator. I'm a Juris Doctor hopefully somewhere between bar exams.''

Kramer laughed and took the out. "After all this, you'll make a good criminal lawyer. You know the drill.''

"If blood don't get me first in the projects.'' Kramer didn't bother with it. Frank drifted into an inconclusiveness. "You know, Steve, I've been thinking I don't know if I ever really loved Karen. Maybe it was more she was there at the right time and she was the solution to some of my problems.''

"Like what problems?''

"What problems?'' Frank felt something tighten in him. Strange. He'd known Kramer all this time, but he'd never been able to tell Kramer how or where Karen fit in his life. Perhaps he himself hadn't known. But right now, as he stood here looking down at the city, it suddenly seemed clear that marrying Karen had been intended as a way to change his life. Oh, Kramer knew that he'd married her in three weeks. Everyone knew that.

But Kramer didn't know—or anybody else—that when Frank married her, he'd been on the run two years. Tonight was the first time he'd ever seen it that way, even thought of it. Was it so? He looked over at Kramer outlined against the city lights. High above, the red lights of the transmission tower blinked, and behind them, the sprinkling of house and street lights ran down the back streets of Bernal Height as if it were a country village. Marrying Karen, a solution . . . He needed to go farther, tell Kramer something, hear something back. Now. Tonight. Before he went a day farther with Ray's case. He felt around for a first word. But when he thought back to that time, he had no idea where one thing stopped and the next began.

Should he start by telling him about the day he'd suddenly left Las Cruces? Kramer was the last person he'd seen. He'd thrown all of the stuff he could carry into the back of his pickup, left a note and some money on the

table for his two roommates—he was sharing a rundown
house near New Mexico State—and driven the few blocks
to Kramer's. Kramer was just kneeling down to put a hose
into a tree well when Frank pulled up to the curb. The palo
verde trees were in yellow bloom, the metallic yellow
prickly pear flowers translucent in the noon light.

Kramer said, "God, you look terrible, Frank. Is it just
the unsparing midday light or is this a preview of old
age?"

"Kramer, I need a favor. Can I store some stuff with
you."

"Where you going?"

Frank hesitated. "I've got to get out of here."

"Jesus, Frank, are you crazy? You've got five weeks
left to go until graduation, it's your last semester, and
you're done."

Frank shook his head. "Kramer, I don't have time for
this. I've got to go. Now. Can I leave some shit here. Yes
or no?"

Kramer stood up. "Yes. What's wrong?" Frank shook
his head, no, went to the truck, dropped the tailgate. Kramer shrugged, came up beside him. "What goes, what
stays?"

Frank studied the jumble. "The tools go. The TV. The
painting gear. The ladders. The stereo and speakers. The
books. I left a couple of chairs, a good kitchen table, and
a sofa back at the house. Take them, keep them, whatever."

Kramer helped him unload. Four or five trips and it was
all stacked in Kramer's front room. Sweating, dehydrated,
Frank gulped glasses of water over the kitchen sink. Between gulps, he said, "Steve, when you're ready to move,
if I still haven't come back for the stuff, keep what you
want, sell the rest. Don't ask me anything, Kramer. For
your benefit, I probably shouldn't even be seen here. It's
something I can't talk about, but I'll be okay."

Kramer started to ask, but changed his mind. "Okay,
Frank, I won't."

Frank said, "I haven't done anything to anyone. No one's been hurt, but just don't ask me about it. I can't talk." He had a last gulp of water and took off. Frank had never offered anything about that day, and Kramer had never again asked. It wandered off into an area of friendship where some things remain undefined.

He studied Kramer. So where should he begin now? Should he say: Remember that morning I came over and dropped my stuff off and left? It's twelve years ago already. Maybe say: Well, I was coming from the desert. I'd been out all night, driven halfway across the state, met a plane with three other drivers. Each of us took over half a ton of high quality marijuana in trucks. Ray drove one, I drove one, and the Morris brothers, Dickie and Charlie, each drove one. Their cousin, Jimmy Donovan, flew the plane.

Should he go on and tell it all: Remember seeing them around, Kramer? They managed and ran a mesquite steak grill . . . The Silver Stirrup? We used to drink in there. Jimmy Donovan was about five years older than me, had been shot down in Vietnam . . . He had that little hitch in his walk from where the doctors put his leg back together with screws and a metal rod. I had no idea Ray and Jimmy were tight until the morning Ray came by.

Ray. So that would mean telling Kramer about Ray, right? Was Ray the heart of the thing? Ray got him into it. Should he just come out and start telling Kramer about Ray? You know: Ray was there the same time you were. You might even have seen him play ball his first couple of years. Ray Buchanan. He was an All State baseball player from Ohio, a center fielder, first baseman, and a terrific hitter. Written up in the paper. Remember those great baseball teams when we were there? Sent a bunch of guys up to the Angels, Cardinals, Astros. Ray had it. He started his freshman year. He was hitting everything. Ripping the ball. Line drives. Home runs. That first year Ray said he could see the ball better than he'd ever seen it before. He could see the stitches, the rotation, see it big like it was in slow motion. Almost knew what they were going to throw. Hit .452. Can you dig that, .452? Sophomore year he was front-ended in the temple by a fastball in a game against UTEP and knocked cold. After that he struggled until he was benched, and then the coach took away his scholarship, and Ray—Ray didn't have any money—dropped out of school to figure things out.

Frank felt the long grass blowing at his feet. Did he just come out now and say these things? How Ray went off to the public library by himself and started studying all this weird shit—pre-Columbian art, Peruvian pottery, Navajo weaving, the weirdest shit. He took a course in Spanish. Always had his TV tuned to the Spanish station, blahacito, blahando. A few weeks after he started the Spanish class, we went into a bar in El Paso, he talks for an hour to the bartender in Spanish. I mean, he was really learning this stuff. Anyway, maybe a year later he came in one morning and asked me if I wanted to make two thousand dollars for a night's work, and I said, fuck yes, what night's work, I was working as a plumber's assistant, and Ray said, a night's driving, and I said, maybe you better explain.

Frank watched the red lights blinking on the Bernal tower. He recalled how they'd sat down in the kitchen, just Ray and himself, early morning sunlight flat and white-gold on the turquoise kitchen wall, and quiet and even, Ray said he was going to tell Frank something. If he wasn't interested, fine, nothing more to say, no questions asked, but Frank wasn't to breathe a word to anyone. Ray started with that. Ray ended with that. Not a word.

Here was the deal. There were over two tons of high quality marijuana coming across the border in thirty-pound bales. The plane would be landing out in the desert, there was an abandoned airfield in the middle of the state, no one within miles; Frank didn't have to know the whys and wherefores, but it was all signed, sealed, delivered. And actually, better for Frank if he didn't know. Mainly, there was nothing funky about what they were doing; it wasn't the movies, there were no guns, no car chases, whatever.

They were dealing with a high-level Mexican organization, everyone on both sides was in business and needed the other side, there was no room for any bullshit.

Hey, they'd done it before, they'd do it again, but there was always some risk. Ray pushed back in his chair and the flat rising sun came in the window and turned his precise blue eyes white. If anything happened, Ray would cover the lawyer, he'd be there, don't worry, but the main thing in that situation was not to panic, Ray would take care of him. If he couldn't beat it, there would be jail time. However it went, he was expected to keep his mouth shut. Nothing was going to happen, but he should know it from top to bottom.

When Ray finished, Frank felt a hard laugh rise abruptly, got hold of it. He realized the contempt was for himself. Everyone who lived in southern New Mexico knew the Mexican border was right out there—fifty miles—and that day and night stuff was coming across on foot, by plane, by truck, by car, in body cavities, any way in between. So he'd been killing himself working and sometimes feeling like a big wheeler-dealer selling a few ounces of dumb blond weed, and here was Ray not saying a word to anyone, just quietly reading his way through the public library, learning Spanish, playing tennis, and running tons across the border.

Then Frank said, "Why are you trusting me, Ray?"

And Ray just smiled, "Hey, I know what I know."

Frank would often wonder what Ray knew. He looked out at the white glow over Candlestick. Dodgers and Giants. All of the suckers out there freezing in the Stick, the owners and business people up in their warm boxes making the money. Maybe now it would be enough just to tell Kramer that someone asked him if he wanted to make some money driving one night. Or start by telling him about meeting the plane. But if he left out the players, there'd be no real way to make Kramer understand. Understand what? Frank looked out at the Bay Bridge hanging out over the dark water and puzzled it. He wasn't exactly sure.

In the end, of course, he had gone. There had never been any question in his mind that he wouldn't. Ray had been right, he knew what he knew, he could count on Frank. He and Ray had driven to a small town hours from Las Cruces in the middle of nowhere and gone to a safe house—just a suburban house in the dark—picked up a couple of four-wheel drive trucks, and then, night now, they had turned, followed a two-lane road, turned off onto another road, driven on, until Ray pulled off onto a narrow shoulder, removed the fuses on both of the vans to kill the brake and inside lights, and then, a little farther ahead, Ray swung onto a dirt road. Pitching and rolling as they drove through washes and arroyos, mesquite and palo verde branches whipping back out of the dark, they finally came up onto even ground. There they got out and stood in the silence. Miles from anywhere, Frank looked up into the spring sky blazing with stars, the Milky Way; he saw the stars as he hadn't remembered seeing them since he'd been a boy. The desert smelled of cooling heat, dust, creosote.

Ray walked off into the dark and in a few minutes, a single light, the brightness of a struck match, appeared. A short time later, another in the opposite direction. Then Ray was back beside him and said simply the Morris brothers are waiting over there—he pointed into the dark. And then, a little later, but moments before Frank heard anything, Ray said, here he is—stay close to me, stay away from the props, Frank.

Frank heard the engines, high, distant, and the blacked-out plane came low, ran down the valley, faded, came back, lower, louder, and then, dust swept up around them in a wave, the plane was down, turning, coming back, Ray yelled, let's go.

For years after, he would dream about it in crazy ways, the red light bulb burning in the cavernous interior, the bales, the thick resinous smell, dark shapes moving in and out, the Morris brothers, Jimmy Donovan, Ray, everyone moving, no one talking, the Morris brothers loaded and pulling away first, headed back toward the road, then Ray and himself still loading, pulling clear, Jimmy taking off into the dark, the sound of the plane fading, the silence and stars. In dreams, there was confusion. He couldn't see, he was loading bails, he was naked, he was being chased. Sometimes he'd come awake exhausted, an endless task he could never finish. Or startle awake terrified.

But awake, it always came back to him, that one moment after the plane had gone and Ray came walking back to him in the deep silence, and said, follow me. Ray turned and started toward his truck. Frank could sense his dark shape, hear his footsteps. Suddenly Ray stopped and was motionless. He seemed to be listening. Frank listened. It was a moment which had been with him ever since. Ray's footsteps stopping. His motionlessness. The certainty Frank had that Ray was listening into something, though there was nothing to hear. Then Ray said, "I know a back road out. We'll take that instead. It starts at the far end of the valley. Stay right behind me."

They'd spent hours following the back road in the dark, half arroyo, half wash, rocks suddenly spearing the heavily loaded trucks, four-wheel drives grinding and whining, the trucks lurching in and out of ditches, branches whipping back out of the dark, screeching along the body. The sky was washing out light, the stars fading by the time they reached a hardtop county road, and Frank could see the trucks rise out of the dark, dented, covered with dust, scratched.

They had made it back to the safe house, an empty house with a swimming pool, the bottom covered with a fine silt. With the trucks locked in the garage, Ray had gone to a pay phone, and Frank had plunged into the pool. He remembered the slow-motion rise of silt in a cloud off the bottom as he dove, his surfacing, and then looking up at Ray, who kneeled and said quietly, Frank, something's happened to the Morrises and Jimmy. None of them are where they're supposed to be. Get dry and get out of here.

I'm putting you on a bus back to Las Cruces. When you get there, leave town. I don't know what's happened yet, but you didn't stand to make enough to take any more risks.

Ray paid him off, two thousand dollars, and put him on the bus, and that was the last he'd seen him for several years. Later, in bits and pieces, he'd learned from Ray what happened. Their trouble had started over in a small field outside Albuquerque where Jimmy had been going to rent the plane. The manager of the field had gotten suspicious after a previous trip when he'd noticed the seats had been taken out and put back slightly askew and several prop blades were gouged, as though they'd been landed at an unimproved field. He'd notified U.S. Customs and the DEA who had placed a transponder in the plane. The best pilot in the world—and Jimmy was good—couldn't have gotten rid of them. They'd followed the signal to the New Mexico border, waited for the plane to return, and followed it to its landing in the desert. Afterward, they'd intercepted the Morris brothers with their two loaded trucks as they came out onto the road. They'd been waiting for Donovan back at the airfield.

The rest of it, too, had come out in a legal opinion. You could find it in the law library. In fact, Frank had. A dry piece of legalese which had found its way through the appellate courts and gone no farther. Not the opinion of the court that the defendants' fourth amendment rights had been violated by the placing of the transponder . . . one judge dissented. The court's opinion that the officer's statement that he would take into consideration the cooperation of Mr. James Donovan in his statements implicating Richard and Charles Morris did not in and of itself constitute a promise of leniency to Mr. Donovan.

What the legalese didn't say was that quite simply, once in custody, Jimmy had been tricked into giving the investigators his cousins, Dickie and Charlie, in return for what he thought would be leniency. He'd been conned and hadn't even made a deal that stood up. They'd all gone to prison.

There had also been mention of two trucks. Only two. Not four. Frank would remember that moment when Ray had suddenly stopped and he'd gone motionless. What had Ray sensed? Frank would never know. Just that Ray knew something. No matter how Frank thought about it, all he could finally say was that Ray got him into it. And Ray got him out. And in his silent way, Ray had been there for him ever since.

Frank muddled all of this. The dread. Three years. Moving. Changing jobs. Karen. The simplest things he'd never been able to explain to Kramer—why he hadn't finished that last semester. What could he say now? He puzzled it, looking for a first word, a connection. He decided he couldn't tell Kramer any of it.

He stared down at the city lights below. "Let me ask you something, Kramer. What would you do if you had a case come in, but you felt too close to it, some of the people, to see it clearly. Say you weren't sure what to think about the defendant—or your friendship with him. Call it a blind spot. Maybe you'd end up making some kind of big mistake. What would you do?"

"The question's the answer, right? Drop the case. What kind of mistake could you make?"

"I don't even know, exactly, just something. Let me finish. What if it involved a friend, a close friend, someone like yourself, Kramer, where you went back a long way, things weren't really all that clear, who owed who, where things started, where they stopped. If I were the defendant, you my investigator, you wouldn't walk out on me, would you, Steve?"

Kramer was silent for a time. "No, I wouldn't walk out on you. You can't walk out on your friends. But I guess if you thought you'd do the guy more harm than good by staying, than it might be better to tell him up front that you had to drop the case for his good. Get him another investigator."

Frank shook his head. "You're right, but you're wrong."

"What's the case?"

"I'll tell you sometime. I'm not clear. I've got to figure out a couple of things." Frank suddenly felt exhausted. "Maybe just get some sleep. I'm just not sure I can trust myself here."

"How do you mean?"

"I don't even know. I just have a funny feeling." He looked at Kramer. "Hey, Steve, let me ask you something. Did you think I'd been drinking when I came into the house tonight?"

"I hadn't really thought about it."

"No? That look you gave June when she offered me some wine?"

"What look?"

"The truth, Steve."

"What look?"

Frank felt a wave of uncertainty. Was he seeing things or were people lying to him? Kramer? Little things, big things, he wasn't sure.

Steve said, "Had you been?"

"I don't know, had I?"

"I told you I never really thought about it."

"Yeah, you didn't, huh? Okay, Slick."

"Got me coming and going here, Frankie. If I say yes, I'm conspiring against you with my wife in the kitchen. If I say no, that I hadn't thought about it—which is true—then I'm lying."

Frank saw it Kramer's way, lost interest in the whole thing. Kramer said, "Come on, Frank, what's happening here? You don't trust me? Don't trust me, don't talk to me."

The city threw its silvery white loom behind Kramer. Fog was starting to roll in over Twin Peaks, some of the lights were smudging out. Frank watched the lights on the Bay Bridge, beyond, the lights downtown.

"You know, Kramer, when we were first married,

Karen told me that all she ever wanted was for us to tell the truth. Okay, so you remember how I was working in Old Pueblo Lodge outside of Taos. The afternoon I met Karen I had some chick's bra in my jacket pocket from the night before, I'd been screwing my way through the waitresses, I looked at them and thought, 'Should I go around twice? Or marry Karen?' '' They laughed. ''Why Karen? Why then? Why not?'' Why bother telling Kramer if he wasn't telling him the whole thing? Tell him what he could, see where it led. ''She was from the East. It was time to go East, young man, change my life. Yeah, I knew it was romantic, but why not. Tell me why not, Kramer?''

''I'm not saying anything.''

''We were married by a justice of the peace in Los Alamos. Why Los Alamos? Why not? We went for a drive and that's where we ended up. Our wedding pictures were Karen and I driving down the road, I held up a snapshooter at arm's length, we put our faces together, shot three pictures, almost ran off the road. When her father heard that we were married, he didn't talk to me for two years. Her mother's never liked me. I wasn't good enough for Snookie-Okums. You know, Snooks is the real thing. Eastern girl's schools, RISD. Masters in Art History. What's she doing marrying some guy from New Mexico State?

''Anyway, it was a trip. Met and married in three weeks. And then Karen went back to Boston—she was just out for a jaunt, you know, clear the head, visit a girlfriend, check out the red rock and petroglyphs, and fuck a cowboy, or at least someone wearing turquoise, who turned out to be me. Had to get back to her job. She was working for a graphic designer back then. Tres now, tres gnarly, tres career girl. Same shit she's doing now. She's very good, really. Anyway, she was going to come back in a month for a five-day visit. I was going to take care of a few obligations, and then make a complete break and go live in the East—maybe three months. Tres gnarly, right?

''Fine? Fine.'' Frank applauded in the dark. ''Karen leaves and I take a trip back down to Albuquerque to get some of my things and ran into an old girlfriend. Rebecca Castillo—did I ever tell you about Becky?''

"Yeah, as a matter of fact, you have.''

"Hey, baruch atoy adonoi, Steve, can I tell the story? She was Castilian, strangely enough, like seeing how her name was Castillo. They look down their long white Spanish noses at all the other beaners. I ran into Becky and you know, we'd had a thing, once, she was really a nice woman, the long and short of it is, we ended up going to bed. Maybe it was hello, maybe goodbye to my old life, who knows, but there it was. Not what I intended, but no big deal. Anyway, Karen comes back for her five-day visit—did I ever tell you about this?''

"No.''

"I don't know how I could not have told you this. Maybe I told you and you forgot—ever think about that?'' Kramer laughed. "You know, she comes back, we're staying in my little cabin in the orchard behind the lodge. We're making love, it's all great, Karen is telling me how much she loves me, how happy she is that we're married, that she feels like we belong to each other, and then she makes this little speech about how anyone can have a big formal wedding, but we can have a real marriage of true hearts if we'll always tell the truth, never be afraid.

"She sits up and says, If there's anything either of us have any doubts about telling, anything at all that might stand between us, then let's share them now. Okay, did I have anything I wanted to share? I said no. She said, 'Anything at all.' The Becky business hadn't even occurred to me.

"Long and short here, Stevie, is that she keeps it up, I finally do think of Becky, and then I begin to ask myself, 'Is Karen for real? Does she really mean this?' I wondered if she was daring me. At the same time, I knew I shouldn't say anything. I mean, I just knew. But finally, I really had to see where she was. If she meant it. Or what. I guess I was calling her bluff.''

"Well, it was a mistake. I didn't even finish telling

Karen about Becky. She went crazy. She burst into tears, ran outside. You know, when you tell people the truth, they don't really want it. They can't deal with it. I don't think she meant to set me up. She just couldn't handle it, but didn't know herself. But I knew. I really knew before I told her.

"Sometimes I think our marriage was over that night. We've stayed together, but she's had lovers, I've had lovers, if that's what you want to call them. Lately, she's telling me I'm a typical adult child of an alcoholic: I keep things to myself, I'm secretive, I hide things; a lot of other stuff—I'm compulsive, a perfectionist, I structure things so that I can't possibly succeed, I have to fail—I did just fail the bar, didn't I? Though she doesn't know that yet. Prescient. Hey, everyone's life can be bent to someone else's theory.

"Karen's a reader—a self-actualizer—with an active imagination. You know, the whole nine yards, the dream journal, get in touch with your feelings. And I love that in her. But what the fuck, Steve. It's none of her theories about me. She just doesn't like to remember certain things she did. Once she asked me to tell her the truth. I took her at her word and told her the truth. I'd made a mistake about Becky. I told her. It was a truth she didn't want. She's as bad as my father. One minute charming, next furious, next demanding the impossible. She's always silently changing the rules."

Frank gazed over the city. "That night I told her about Becky, I finally gave up trying to talk to her. I bought a bottle of vodka and took a long drive off to Chama. Karen and I have, as they say, gone on from there."

In the distance, Candlestick threw up a gauzy white light into the fog. Beyond everything he'd just said about Karen, Frank knew he loved her, tenderly, perhaps even desperately, in a way which eluded his articulation. In what he'd told Kramer, somehow he hadn't come close to it. There was a long silence, which distilled into the certainty that there was nothing more to say, and Frank and Kramer turned and slowly started down from the Height.

Frank had turned on the TV and drifted into half-dreams when he startled awake to the clatter of a key in the lock. Karen came into the front hall with a soft intake of chill night air. Frank checked the clock. 10:20. She walked past him, dropped her bag on the kitchen table, shook her hair out over her collar, and unzipped her jacket. One of the cats leaped into her arms and she smoothed its head against her cheek and murmured to it. Frank watched her. Her face was young, open, beautiful—the face he sometimes caught glimpses of after they'd been making love. He suddenly felt suspicious, jealous. Where had she been? The cat purred loudly into the room. Frank stood, and squinting against the kitchen light, followed her into the kitchen just as Karen spotted the Polaroid on the table. She picked it up, read out loud, "I was here, where were you?"

She dropped the picture on the table, rubbed the cat against her cheek. "Oh, Frank . . ." She placed the cat on the table, took Frank's hand. "You've got a perfect right to be mad, specially after what I said this morning, but I've got the best news. . . ."

"Hit me. I could use a little."

"It's more than a little. Bradley Harwood's secretary called me at work today. . . ."

"The Bradley Harwood? Director, San Francisco Art Museum. . . . His very own self?"

"The Bradley Harwood. Only he's not at all like that: *The*. He turns out to be so nice, so unpretentious, so smart . . . Anyway. I'd sent him my portfolio months ago in response to an ad for an assistant to the director. No response." She shrugged. "There must have been three hundred applications for that position. I figured mine ended up lost behind a filing cabinet or whatever. Anyway. His secretary tells me Harwood's been extremely busy, but could I come in for an interview on such short notice? Just come as you are. It was already 3:30." Karen shrugged.

"I mean, look at me." Frank looked at her. Tight skirt. Jacket. Harwood must have looked at her, too. "No time to change. Take me as I am.

"I give Jeanette some excuse and I'm out of there. I'm downtown and in Harwood's office at five o'clock. His secretary shows me in and I can see my resume and slides are right there on his desk. For a few minutes I was nervous and then . . ." She opened her arms. "It was just like all pretenses or distances melted away. We were just talking about everything. The new installations over at Camera Work. Some of my teachers at RISD. And—he *loved* my work and resume. I mean, really. Then he said, 'This is such a pleasure, and I want to keep it up, but I'm starved. Join me for dinner.' I did call, Frank, but the line was busy and then there wasn't time to call back."

"Gee, Snooks, you sound as bad as me."

"Oh, Frank. We went to the Ritz Carlton and all the time we're just talking, I mean, it was a real rapport, and in the middle of dinner, right then and there, he offers me the job as his assistant!

"I know I probably should have played it a little cool and held out for something just because you should, but there was no point. My God. I accepted on the spot. I'll assist in writing grants, preparing shows—he says he's going to have me curate a show almost immediately . . . he has something very specific in mind he thinks I'd be perfect for . . ."

"I know something you'd be perfect for, Snooks. Hey, just as long as the job has a dental plan, babe. I've had a toothache lately."

She shoved him playfully. "Actually, I think it does. I'm just so happy."

Frank put his arms around her. "It's great. I'm happy for you."

She hugged him, pulled away. She hesitated. She seemed to have sniffed at him, reflexively, almost comically, like a dog. Shit, Frank remembered, he'd had a couple of glasses of wine at Kramer's, just nothing at all, but

what? she was going to think he'd been drinking in upper
case. DRINKING. She gave him an appraising glance, wavered, but then he saw she decided to let it go, at least for
the moment—she was wrong, anyway. "It *is* great. This
job takes me back to the art world, back to who I am, what
I'm about. It pays decently. I'm going to go in there tomorrow and tell Jeanette to stuff her job. I've taken so
much crap from that woman in the last couple of years,
been paid so little, done so much . . . I can't wait to see
the look on her face when I tell her." Karen laughed and
shrugged. "And now, just like that, I can walk away."
She laughed again. "It's unbelievable."

Frank deadpanned, "As long as there's a dental plan.
My molar hurts when I drink cold *and* hot."

Karen snapped her fingers. "Goodbye, Jeanette."

"What'd you have for dinner?"

"Alsatian Guinea Hen. And it was great. I enjoyed
every bite." She laughed again. "Brad Harwood was so
nice . . ."

"Oh, now it's gone from Bradley to Brad . . ."

"Frank, don't be jealous. And anyway, he's gay. And
sometimes people can have dinner together without trying
to get into each other's pants."

"I've heard of that. I think it happened once in 465
B.C. It's recorded in hieroglyphics on Amenhotep's pyr-
amid, south wall. 'Dinner. Kept pants on. Spent quiet time
in courtyard with my camel later.' Hey, Snooks. I'm happy
for you. Don't get too buttoned-down on me. I kinda like
you making video art I can't understand, being mad at me
when I can't, pretending you're not . . ."

"I'll *still* make videos, they're an important form,
Frank, they're . . ."

Frank laughed. "Whoa. Please. Make videos."

"This can be a new beginning for us. I feel so good
about it. We've had so much stress, our jobs, our sched-
ules—this will be time-consuming, too, but it's going to
be so great working for Harwood, but more than anything,
I just know we can pull together now . . . I mean,

there's no getting around it, we have some serious problems, and there are some things we're going to work on and change if . . ." She stopped abruptly. If what? "I mean, real changes, Frank. . . . Oh, shit, I was supposed to feed Myra's cat. That poor thing. I was supposed to feed him last night! Come with me, we'll keep talking."

She put her hand on Frank's arm, walked quickly down the hall. Frank followed her into the street, up three houses. Karen produced a key, let herself into a first floor duplex, groped, switched on the light. The cat meowed loudly, following Karen as she walked into the kitchen. "Oh, I know, you're starved, I'm sorry, yes, you're right, come on. . . ."

Frank wandered through the dark front room. "Where's Myra?"

"Vacation."

"Didn't know R.N.'s were entitled to vacations." Frank stopped by the front window, reached out, noticed several long peacock feathers drooping out of a large basket, smoothed one through his fingers. Extracted it. Touched it to his cheek. The secret life of an R.N. by Frank August. By day, Myra, in her white polyester uniform. . . . In the kitchen, the brittle clatter of dry cat food into an aluminum pan, all the time Karen talking to the cat, oh, yes, there's a good boy. . . . He heard water running, then the splash of houseplants being watered from room to room. Water pouring in the dark behind him. Frank smoothed the peacock feather to his cheek. Karen brushed past him, watered a dieffenbachia in the bay window. Broad dark leaves. Hair hanging over her face. Bent forward. Pouring. She deliberately placed the watering can on the floor beside the plant. Stood, but didn't turn.

Reaching for Frank, she backed up with a single step. He encircled her waist, smoothed the feather against her cheek, she fit her ass to his groin, the length of her body against him, legs, back, neck, perfumed hair to his chin, he slid his hands, her waist, breasts, face, the feather crushing between them, she turned her mouth to his hand, took a finger between her teeth, bit, a quickening of pain, suddenly he was tangled hard in his underwear, she reached back between his legs, shaped him with her hand, freed him from his pants, her skirt slid up to her waist, Frank bent his knees, lowered himself, she stretched her panties to one side at the crotch, fit him in her in one movement, stiffened and gasped, her wetness, she moved quickly, awkwardly, stumbling with each thrust, she rose on her toes, head back, at the same time she tried to push herself back against him and bend forward to receive him more deeply, with a sudden deep breath, she gave it up, pulled away, turned to face him, again gathering her skirt high around her waist, Frank's pants at midthigh, he crouched slightly, she climbed onto him, wrapped her legs around his waist, fit herself onto him, clung to his shoulders, they moved quickly, slow, quick, Frank staggered once, twice into the window, Karen's cheeks hollowed, lips pursed, eyes closed in concentration as she came, trembled, came again, Frank came, the room growing light, his legs heavy, he staggered. . . .

Moments later, Karen alighted softly, still holding onto him, her face pressed to his chest. She turned her mouth up to find his mouth. "Jesus, Frank, I love it when it just happens like that."

"Next time you do the standing and I get to be the one who does the acrobatic part. Equal treatment, right? Whose idea was this, anyway?"

"No one's, I think. That's why it was wonderful. It was kind of there and waiting."

Frank ran his fingertip along the glass. "Hey, Christ, we cracked Myra's window." Frank touched the long diagonal break. "Think she'll notice it?"

"No . . . because you'll have fixed it." She laughed, pulled down her skirt, hugged him again, picked up the watering can. She swept through the house, turned out the kitchen light, locked the front door, and they walked quietly, arm in arm back toward their house.

"So nice, Frank. . . ."

"Been a while, hasn't it?"

"A long while. I know you're there. I can feel you. But what happens to us? How does it get to be so long?"

"I don't know."

They stepped into the front hall. As Karen walked ahead, and Frank closed the door, he felt the darkness of the front room behind him, and again, as it had been this morning, he felt a terrible presence within the house. He took a deep breath and followed Karen into the kitchen and then up the stairs to the second attic space. She spread her arms. "So nice what you've done. When we moved in, it was a grimy attic. You opened it up, put in the sky-light, the bathroom. It will be great when you finish it." She disappeared into the bathroom. "Haven't heard any-thing on the bar today?"

"No." Just a few more days to pull things together and figure out how to tell her. A few days didn't matter. Now wasn't the time. He could hear her brushing her teeth, washing up. She came out. "I know you've passed. You'll make a terrific lawyer."

He placed his wallet and keys on his dresser, pulled out a drawer. He stared into the drawer, studying the contents; hey, hadn't his address book been under the calculator? She had been going through his things; she was looking for something. What? She could get so crazy at times, be so suspicious—in response to what she called his drinking, his being erratic, and then, once she was convinced, of what? of what she called his being secretive, his erratic behavior, she'd just kind of go tilt. He remembered her saying, "Frank, I'll do whatever I have to do. . . ." Even tonight she'd said, "There are some things we're going to have to change if . . ." If what? She was always laying down conditions, then silently changing the rules. He never said *if* to her. In a way, Karen was impossible to please, which might be, Frank sensed, part of why he loved her.

She slipped into bed. He took off his clothes, glanced up into the skylight, the gelatinous darkness massed be-yond, slipped in beside her. She lay quietly. Frank closed his eyes, felt the weight of the day, the jail, Ray walking toward him in the orange jumpsuit of a prisoner, the first weeks of his marriage to Karen. . . . Frank, did you pass the bar? No. But he'd tell her. He'd get to it. Hey, he told her certain things and then in other moods they came back at him upside down and backward. Karen's body gave a sudden jerk as she drifted into sleep. She turned away from him, curled up. Her breath deepened. She had a new job. She was going back into the art world. Things would get better between them *if* . . .

Frank felt for her, turned on his side. Tomorrow morning, he'd get up and . . . With sudden conviction, he knew Kramer was right, he'd have to drop the case, there was something in this which made it impossible for him to trust himself. One day of it had made him crazy. Faraway in the house, he heard the phone ringing, his message machine kick on, the garbled underwater voice. A beep. Last night. Kramer's machine. Anybody home? He drifted toward the darkness of the night before, but no matter how hard he tried, he couldn't find his way back in. Blackout. As he slid into a jagged sleep, he knew something was over, maybe for good, and just beginning.

II

SEMI-ERECT, BETWEEN DREAM and memory, Frank held onto sleep a little longer; he was back in the first weeks when he'd met Karen, the white sunlight of the high canyon reaching across the windowsill and sheet, the sweet smell of pine needles close, New Mexico, everything connected. . . .

Frank opened his eyes and looked up into the skylight. The hush and muted white of early morning and summer fog. Even before he felt for Karen, he knew the bed was empty. Suddenly recalling the failed bar exam, Frank took a deep breath against a stab of anxiety and sat up. He spotted a note on her pillow:

"Frank—I'm off for an early morning swim. I'm so excited about the new job. I just want things to be better for both of us. They can be! You mumbled and thrashed around in your sleep last night. I know you have things bothering you, real things. Why not talk about them—if not to me, then Kramer, or maybe a counselor. Would you consider AA? Whether you actually drink or not, alcohol is a problem for you. And even though I didn't want to say anything, I did smell alcohol on you last night. (The complexities of the ways I become complicit? Co-opted?) One way or the other, we are going to have to face some things. I want us to have the life I always knew we could when I met you and which I keep catching glimpses of. I love you, Karen."

Frank smoothed his hand across his chest. Talk to Kramer. AA. Actually, he'd done that number: six or seven months ago. A Sunday morning. Across the street, Kramer washing his truck. Under a crushing nausea and headache, Frank took the hose, then leaned forward and held the stream over his scalp.

"Hangover?"

Frank nodded. "Kramer, you have to tell me how you kicked it."

"Well, vato, it just started looking endless."

"You said you felt crazy for a while after you cold-turkeyed."

"Maybe the worst part was that I didn't know it at the time. I hated everything, the world looked ugly and boring. Here I was married to this wonderful woman and I felt dead inside for two years."

"So when'd you start feeling better again?"

Kramer made a hard jet with his thumb over the hose and rinsed the hubcap. "When Zack was born, I think. Come on." In the kitchen, Kramer dried his hands, and opening a phone book, he leafed the pages quickly. "Frank, you know, we've had this exact conversation about quitting a hundred times before. I can't explain something I don't understand myself." He wrote down a number and dialed. He asked questions quickly, jotted down information, hung up. "There's an AA meeting over on Folsom right near Precita Park—starts in about half an hour. I'll go with you."

Frank said, "Why should I go to AA when you didn't have to?"

Kramer, he realized, had somehow done it again. He'd been calling Frank's bluff since he'd warned him not to miss any more classes and given him a C when he had. He was calling his bluff now.

Back outside, Kramer sprawled across the front seat toweling the dash and instruments.

"It's beautiful, Kramer. I've got a favor to ask." Kramer went on wiping his speedometer. "Someone's after me about money. Can you handle lending me three hundred bucks?"

Kramer studied Frank. "Gotta be today?" He smiled. "Course it does." Kramer went in the house, dug out a checkbook, wrote Frank a check. "Not too long in getting back on this, okay, Frankie?"

Moved, Frank said, "I'll pay you back." He hesitated. "Steve, this isn't going for, you know, booze—grass, whatever."

Kramer said, "I didn't ask."

"You still have time for that AA meeting? Folsom, is it? You ever been to one?"

"Never. What's to lose?"

Frank dropped Karen's note back onto the bed. Imagined Karen gliding through clear, cold water. Laps. The echoes of the pool. Heart and lungs gearing up into a big cleansing overdrive. Later, a hot shower. In two weeks, she starts a new job. Assistant to the director, San Francisco Art Museum. He was happy for her. Maybe now things could be better. She'd walk out of the pool. Everything cool and clear and the whole day in front of her. Slim. He'd been slim a few months ago. Frank zapped on the TV against the silence of the house. The TV blared into the room.

Downstairs, he made coffee, turned on the small tv, and went through the *Chronicle*, looking for some news about the bust; strangely, there was nothing. Too soon. He found some Chinese food in cartons in the back of the refrigerator, dumped it into a Corning Ware dish, and microwaved it. Reading the paper, watching "Today," he ate, Joe sitting on the floor looking up at him, Sally standing beside the dish on the table. He flicked the channel to "Good Morning America," all the time feeding choice bits of shrimp and chicken to each cat with his fork as they purred loudly into the room. He considered the cats as they delicately licked the inside of the dish. "Karen gone swimming this morning, guys? Or what?"

He answered himself in a high-pitched cat voice. "We dunno, Frank. Dinner with Brad Harwood last night. Gay guy, though. Maybe. Never know with Karen. New job."

Frank poured himself another cup of coffee. Cracked Myra's window last night. Never enjoyed breaking a window more. He circled the first floor rooms looking for his briefcase, found it just inside the back door where he'd dropped it last night, remembered climbing the backyard fence to get to his house. Seemed like someone else. Stupid? Cautious? Paranoid?

Frank went through his files, quickly making notes of details he had to take care of to stave off the most pressing cases, but found himself thinking about Sarah Anne, the way they had come to rest tangled just inside the front door of that house over in the Haight. Ray's girl with the legs and bearing that could silence a restaurant.

He searched through his jail notes from yesterday morning—meeting with Melikian this afternoon; what did he tell Melikian, what leave out, and then he realized he had no idea how to talk about this to Aram, how to separate what he would not say from what he knew. This wasn't just another case. Part of this thing was his world. But which part? After the obvious, where did you draw the line?

Then he knew with certainty that he was going to make a mistake. He was going to miss something or give something away. He'd known it last night. And Kramer'd told him what to do: Take yourself off the case. And this morning, that looked right. He'd have to distance himself from Ray. There was no other way. His getting more tangled in this thing wasn't going to help Ray. And his giving something away, the wrong thing at the wrong time to the wrong person—a piece of information, something perhaps even more harmful—would hurt Ray, hurt himself.

He called his office and got his recorded message. Just as the tone sounded, Gloria picked up. "Gloria . . . just coming in or did I get you out of the girl's room?"

"Upstairs making coffee. Frank, we all use the same bathroom in the hall, remember?"

"Right. Just called to see who's come in, who's working what."

"Everyone got in very early this morning. John. Kramer just came by after surfing, said he was going to do more on Curtis Bledsoe."

Frank hesitated. "Hair all full of gnarly salt-water curls?"

"Yes, but he went out in the courtyard and shampooed his head in the garden with the hose."

"The six lawyers upstairs must have loved that."

"Soap in the geraniums. Left his board and wet suit behind your desk, but said don't freak, he'll be in later to pick it up, said something about looking for Ashanti Flowers' sisters."

Frank had meant for Kramer to pair up with John to go into the project, but too late now. But early was good, it was still quiet, though he'd have to watch out for those goddamned dogs. He didn't know which was worse, blood or his dogs—dobermans, shepherds. Frank took the rest of his messages and then suddenly remembered the money thing. He'd written $2500 to John in an uncovered check yesterday. He had maybe a couple of days to come up with the money. He felt a rise of panic.

"Gloria . . . listen, keep calling attorneys. Get checks mailed in to us. Today. Or, better yet, pick them up. I've got to cover over two thousand dollars I wrote to John. If I don't, it all comes tumbling down. What about that skip trace on Sarah Anne Gillette?"

"I've started making calls and checking. I've got a friend in Mill Valley who will check out the P.O. for me, I'll try DataSearch."

"You're the greatest. Mondo killer."

"Oh, Frank, one last thing. I misplaced a message here—I see I took it at nine o'clock yesterday morning. A Gina called. She didn't leave her last name. Said she was returning your call of last night, that you'd know who she was and what it was about. Nothing more."

They hung up at the same time. Gina. Jesus. Two nights ago. Again he heard his voice droning out of Kramer's message machine. Anybody home? Beyond his voice, darkness. Where was he? Some bar. He hadn't been in touch with Gina in weeks, months. She was better left alone. God knows what he'd gone on about. She said he'd know. That was one of the sadder ironies; he apparently would be the last to know. Had he asked her to go away with him?

Frank spent another twenty minutes sorting case files

out and straightening up. Upstairs, he spotted Karen's note. He reread it—mumbled in your sleep. Said what? Names? Gina's? Talk to Kramer. Would you consider AA?

He'd called Kramer's bluff—or Kramer'd called his. He'd gone—they'd gone—to the AA meeting together that Sunday morning. First, Frank had borrowed the three hundred, though he really hadn't needed it. Now Frank clearly understood it had been to test Kramer, see if . . . what? If he was willing, really there, before Frank took this weird step: AA? Anyway, it had been fairly painless. Somehow moving. Too many smokers and coffee drinkers, but no big deal. They'd started by reading the twelve steps, like school children droning the pledge of allegiance. Hi, I'm so and so, and I'm an alcoholic. A few skid-row types, but a lot of ordinary looking men and women. And Gina, who was a guest speaker. Hi, I'm Gina and I'm an alcoholic and drug addict. Sober six years and thankful. Wasn't always that way. Hell of a monologue about her drinking and drugging culminating in her boyfriend totalling the car. She came to with him gone through the windshield and lying out on the hood of the car—dead. She was drenched with gasoline. They'd used the Jaws of Life to pry her out. Gina. Auburn hair in tumbledown cascades, cigarette voice like Edith Piaf.

Afterward, Kramer took off, and they—Gina and he—had gone for a short walk in Precita Park, sat down on a bench. His first meeting? Yep, sure was. Last, too, though he didn't say so. They talked a little about drinking and then she'd smiled gently at him and said, "I'm attracted to you, but I'm not going to sleep with you."

"So who asked?"

She gave him a rueful, sweet glance. "I needed to say it."

Frank dead-panned, "Maybe I'll get lucky."

She laughed, covered her hand with his, withdrew it, but didn't say anything more. They'd talked a while more and then, just before leaving, they'd exchanged phone numbers.

Without saying more to Kramer, or anything to Karen, without going to any more meetings, he stopped drinking. He realized Kramer's cold-turkeying booze wasn't such a big deal after all. It was nothing. You just do it. Or, you don't do it. Except for several times each day when he'd have a steep lurch of craving, a hollow in the mouth, and wolf a candy bar, it seemed surprisingly easy. He felt a release of energy—a precipitous restlessness, almost as though he could work nonstop, fifteen hours at a stretch. He started jogging miles each day. He'd run from Holly Park to The Embarcadero. Or the other way, up Mission toward Daly City. He'd run around Delores Park. He ran everywhere. Miles. He didn't fight with Karen. But he also didn't really do much of anything with her. They walked by each other, but now without any kind of edge between them. They were almost like brother and sister, roommates. He had a vague edge of sexual desire for her, but something was missing, and he couldn't quite find his way to the center of it, initiate anything. And she seemed to mirror this. No booze, no edge.

As the days went by, his pants loosened; he noticed himself slimming, his skin tightening over his muscles and bones. He'd think about Gina. Part of him had the sensation that he was very high and also holding his breath and listening into himself for some indication of what, if anything, came next. Part had the feeling he was going very fast, maybe like someone who'd been shot into the air and as yet has no sensation of speed. He sensed he'd been avoiding getting in touch with her. He, of course, had been right in his instinct. Once he contacted her, in a hesitant, faltering way, they started sleeping with each other. What was there to say? It was there or it wasn't. You did or you didn't. Yet he didn't think it was particularly about sex.

After the first time, leaving her, he said, "I've got a funny request. Now that I'm not drinking, can I stay in touch by writing to you? I run numbers on people all day on the phone. I'd like to set this apart."

She nodded and that's the way they'd left it. He didn't

want to explain how he messed with people all day on the phone, you could be stoned, drunk, no one saw your face or knew what you really felt. He didn't want any of that with Gina.

He wrote her. What was this? He wrote that he was glad he knew her, glad she was there. Before long, he was writing her almost every day. They were tender, thoughtful letters. They were about everything. He wrote her how he didn't know why, but that he would always work for the defense. He loved that moment when the case was brought to trial: People of California vs. whoever. A whole lot of people against one. He loved being with that one.

He wrote her that day by day, you dealt with all kinds of people, but you had to make sure that you didn't adopt their methods and become one of them; at the same time, you couldn't let them con you, lie to you, bullshit you, get over; there was a fine line between you and them, and you had to make sure you didn't wake up one morning and find yourself on the wrong side of that line, or worse, not even know you were, find that you had turned into one of them. . . . And didn't know it had happened.

He xeroxed the letters and put them into a folder—his letters, her replies—in a chronological order. He kept them in his office and locked them in a file drawer, and sometimes he would take them out in a quiet moment and reread them and gazing at the soft shadow of the grating on the frosted glass, drift away from the sound of voices in the street, the ringing of the telephone. . . .

They'd gone on sleeping together: an hour here in late afternoon, a couple of hours in early evening when he was supposed to be serving a subpoena or interviewing a witness. She had gentle hands, but it had not been the kind of blind passion it had been with Karen. Afterward, he would sit naked in her easy chair by the window, sometimes talking, sometimes just looking out at the street and across the rooftops. He could say nothing or talk; either way, she seemed completely at ease. She was accepting.

After he'd leave Gina, he could still hear the flow of

her voice, slightly hoarse, thick, musical in her letters. He'd be driving or walking somewhere: . . . So long since I've let or wanted to let anyone get close to me . . . years. Maybe since the accident. I knew this might happen when we walked out together after that AA meeting on Sunday and I could feel something, that silence, between us. . . . She wrote: After you left, I kept seeing the struck look on your face as you came. . . . The tender way you looked at me. I think of your life with a longing. . . . I think you're exactly the way I'd be if I were a man. . . .

He'd find himself daydreaming that he could just go away with Gina, that he could fold up his business, write Karen a letter saying it was better he leave her, make a clean break of it, let her keep what little they had. He thought about starting over with Gina, maybe having a kid. Kramer said that after he'd quit drinking he'd felt dead for two years until Zack was born. He'd think about changing his name, going to New Zealand, maybe Hong Kong. . . . Part of him knew this was completely crazy, but another part of him kept thinking, I could do it, I could get my share of the money from Ray. . . . Karen: something now seemed too unresolvable with her, trusting her, her trusting him. He'd think about that money, just the fact that it was there, how it was his backup and his future, his main connection to something big, undefined, yet to come.

Several months after that Sunday morning AA meeting, he reached into his dresser for his turquoise cufflinks, stopped, and studied the drawer. Shirts. Snapshots. A pocketknife. Batteries. Film. But no cufflinks. He pulled out the second drawer—there they were. But what were they doing in that drawer? He studied the drawer again; his things had definitely been rearranged.

He sat down on the bed. Then he realized the obvious: Karen had been going through his things because she suspected there was someone else, and she'd been looking for some confirmation, a picture, letters, maybe a phone number written on a card or matchbook, some little memento.

How did she know? She knew the same way he knew when it had been her—something in the gaze not completely returned, an intangible self-consciousness in the speech, a slight watchfulness and absence. She knew, but didn't have proof.

For the next couple of weeks, Frank watched. Now he saw that Karen seemed to be methodically going through her closet, her drawers, her books, letters, and photographs, her cameras and prints, whatever, as though taking inventory. She was taking clothes to Good Will, sending things to the cleaners. But Karen had fits of compulsiveness where she periodically did things like this. A used suitcase appeared in the back of the closet, joined two of her others. Frank didn't know anything for sure.

But he remembered how it had once happened. He'd come home after a law class, and she'd been gone. Stayed away two months. It had been a series of letters, hysterical phone calls. I can't think with you around. I can't work. I'm always distracted. It's your energy. I haven't taken a picture I've liked in two years. Maybe I shouldn't be married to anyone. Eventually, she'd come back, apologized profusely, said she was wrong, but said she didn't want him asking questions—who, what, where, nothing had happened—or she'd leave again, no, she loved him more than ever. Somehow, they'd resumed.

One afternoon at Gina's, Frank knew Karen was gone again. He stood suddenly, separating himself from Gina, and lurched into the bathroom. His heart started racing erratically, filled up his chest, and burning, pressed against his ribs. He yanked the shower on and threw himself under the cold water.

Hair dripping, Frank stepped out of the bathroom, a towel around his waist. Gina, undressed, had draped his shirt loosely over her shoulders, tie still buttoned into the collar, and was sitting on the end of the bed. She smoked a cigarette and daydreamed through the smoke as it drew toward the open window. She turned and gave him a soft, expectant glance.

"Gina, forgive me. I've just remembered something. It's an emergency." He started pulling on his pants, shoes and socks. His legs were still wet.

She stood up, held the shirt at her shoulders. He looked at her naked and wished she were dressed. "Are you okay, Frank? Jesus, you're so pale. Why don't you just take a second and lie down. Can I help?"

He shook his head, reached for his shirt. "Gina, please. Excuse me, I've got to dress." She shrugged out of the shirt and stood in front of him naked. She folded her arms over her breasts, and then fully self-conscious, went for a robe. "Gina, I'll explain everything later. I've just got to run now." He pulled on the shirt, buttoned it quickly. Combing his hair with his fingers, he kissed her on the cheek. He was still gasping for breath as he drove, an emergency room? After driving several blocks, he pulled over and noticed he was in front of a neighborhood bar. Inside, the familiar half-light, the stale smell of beer and wood. TV. Basketball. He ordered a straight shot of vodka. "Stoli."

The bartender poured the shot. He raised it, touched his lips to the vodka. No booze for seventeen weeks. He drank off the shot, caught his breath, followed the burning down into his throat and stomach and felt a heat and ease spread through his chest. "Hit me, again." The bartender nodded and poured. Frank waited, trying to watch the game, but it was just noise and the stop and go of chaotic figures. He drank the shot and then felt something let go in him.

Gina. That awful moment when he reached for his shirt. He'd have to send her a shirt. A box of shirts. He'd do it later.

"Got a phone in here?"

The bartender pointed to the back of the bar. He called Karen at work. Would she even be there? He saw her emptied closet. When he heard her voice, he felt an enormous momentary relief—she wasn't gone. "How're you doing?"

"We're just going into an art director's meeting. What's up?"

"Just thought I'd say hello." Without forethought, he said, "We have some problems, but I want you to know that I love you."

She said quietly, "That's nice to hear, Frank. Nice to hear you say it. It's been a while. A long while."

Suddenly, again, he felt almost desperate, but he couldn't say any more—he was afraid if he went farther, she'd know something was weird. Hell, she already knew. She'd been going through his stuff. He couldn't lose her.

"Everything okay, Frank?"

"Fine. I just had a minute."

"What time are you getting through this afternoon?"

"I don't know, shouldn't be too late."

"I think I can put some things on hold and get out of here a little early. Why don't we meet home around six . . . I'll stop at the store. It's been a while since we've had time for dinner together. Let's cook and go to an early movie. How's that sound?"

"Sounds right to me."

Just before they hung up, Karen said, "Frank . . . it was sweet of you to call."

Frank drove, found himself on Van Ness and followed it past Fort Mason, down toward Ghirardelli Square, where he spotted a space, and on impulse, parked. He walked toward the concrete Municipal Pier curling out into the bay. Wind buffeting in his ears and whipping his pants legs, he leaned hard against the cold gusts, his face and scalp turning cold. A fine misting spray caught in the wind, darkened the concrete, rippled puddles, salted his lips and eyelashes, and he walked until he reached the end, looked down into the boiling chop. He was a good swimmer, but he wondered how long he'd have in this water if he fell in—currents, hypothermia, the seas. The buffeting gusts brought the churn of a heavily loaded container ship's engines across the water, and Frank watched its waterline and exploding bow wave as it worked its way past Alcatraz and headed out toward the Golden Gate.

He measured the distance across the freezing, greenish black water, white caps spilling in every direction. He'd had a drink. Two drinks. Two shots of vodka. What was it one way or the other? He didn't feel well—his heart, his blood pressure, something. He'd get a physical. Before that, he hadn't touched a drop in weeks, seventeen weeks this Sunday, and it hadn't been all that tough. There'd been this thing with Gina. It had just happened. Frank hadn't really gone looking for it. He saw her standing in front of him naked as he took his shirt. Across the bay, Sausalito, green, disappeared under low fog smoking in over the headlands. Turning, he started back toward the city.

They sat at the counter cutting vegetables for a salad. Karen had come in earlier, kissed him on the cheek and set down a grocery bag. She seemed calm, sure of herself, self-possessed. She changed into rubber sandals, jeans, and a burgundy silk tank top. She put on a CD, *belexa, tropical*, and now, as they cut and chopped, they moved easily in the kitchen, Karen setting on a pot to boil, now taking out pasta. From time to time, she would lean across him to take something from the spice rack, open a drawer. They listened to the music and cooked, the smell of garlic, basil, heat and steam, filling the kitchen, a cool breeze slipping through the open window above the sink.

Just before they sat down to dinner, Karen walked the length of the front hall; Frank looked after her, the tight rise of her ass in her jeans, liquid spill of the silk top, its folds and sheen, her white shoulders. She turned the dead bolt in the front door, the hard click bringing a stab of desire to Frank's chest; she closed the outer door to the hall as she came back, and then served the pasta, took out the warm French bread, and lowered the lights in the kitchen.

They ate quietly, the food warming, pleasing them, and then Karen said, "This is nice, Frank. I loved you calling me this afternoon. I can feel you're here with me now. You're not thinking about your work, you're not worried, crazy, angry. You're just here. It's so nice when you're here. Where do you go when you're away?''

Frank knew what she meant, but didn't want to get into anything with her now. It would only take a word, a glance to set her off. He never knew. ''Not sure. I wish I did. I'm here now.'' She had to be suspicious because of his afternoon call.

She said, ''I've seen some changes in you in the last weeks. You've gone back to running. I haven't seen you . . .'' She checked herself. He knew she'd been going to say drink. ''. . . as moody or losing your temper. When you're slim like this, you look so good. So handsome— really, you're such a turn-on. You were like this when we met.''

Strange, he thought, she likes what Gina brought out in me, what returned when I started seeing Gina. He looked at Karen's face, her small features, her smooth skin and lips. He saw again how beautiful she was, her expression open and curious, and now he could see her sexual face, which had the simple openness of a young girl's; this was how he imagined she'd looked when she'd been fourteen, fifteen, open, expectant. In the beginning, he'd been able to see this face for days, weeks at a time, and then it had disappeared for long periods, would sometimes reappear, though thickened with a sullenness or anger, and that, too, would excite him, and then again, that face would disappear and though he knew it was still there, it was beyond him, just beneath the surface of another face set over it. This other was a face locked tight with will, ambition, compulsion to succeed at her work, daily strain, with self-reproach, a woman he admired and understood, but didn't particularly care for; it was humorless and unforgiving; it was the face of a woman who thought she had to be set against him to keep the hardness of her will burning bright.

But now, here again, he could see her sexual face, beautiful, he reached over and took her hand, she squeezed his hand, and then very deliberately, she picked up her plate and set it aside. Shoving her chair back and standing, she pushed his chair away from the table, slid onto his lap, fit her shoulders against his chest, wrapped her arms around his neck and kissed him deeply, and they started to make love with a fierce, sexual edge, this extension of their battle of wills sharply reversed, and which had been entirely missing with Gina, popping of her Levi snap, the tangle of her pubic hair, her lifting her hips and shrugging down her jeans as she went on kissing him so he could reach her wetness, her standing, straddling his hand, undoing his belt as she went on kissing him, both of them trembling . . .

They were lying on the living room sofa, jeans still tangled around one of Karen's ankles, blouse still on. They were quiet some time before Karen said, ''One of us is always playing for the last word.'' She shaped his cheek, traced his jaw. ''I don't know why. That one part of me, I think it's there because of something in you. Another part of me wants to wipe the slate clean, start over, get it right this time. I know there's no one else I'll ever love.''

He nodded. He knew it was true. It had to be her. It was as if they were locked into a terrible game in which the winner would be the one who made the last move, but then, both would lose because to win definitively, the game would have to be over, each would lose the other. It was the one thing that terrified Frank.

In the morning she called in sick, and Frank turned the volume down on the message machine. They made love and slept the whole day and on into the night, and the next morning, they both went to work. For several nights it was like that—getting home from work early, making love— and as Frank went about his day, he could feel her skin on his, feel her face close to him, her breath on his neck as she dozed; then slowly, work piled up, Frank missed dinner one night trying to serve subpoenas, another night looking for a witness, afterward he had a couple of beers or shots to cool out, when he got home, he was moody and his breath smelled of alcohol and Karen withdrew, he started getting home so tired and late that he stopped jogging, and he could feel himself putting on weight, feel Karen turning off to the change; imperceptibly, Frank felt their closeness slipping away, and though he could still sense that sexual edge between them—it was always there—he couldn't reach it.

One morning, just after she'd left for work, he opened the door and looked into Karen's closet: her clothes all sorted and dry-cleaned and the suitcases neatly lined up against the back wall. Had she known about the affair with Gina, but couldn't figure it out or prove it? Had she done what she could to panic him, take him back and stem the threat? The closet was exactly the way it had been when he'd first thought she was leaving. Was that a message? A warning? Or was she still looking for the right moment to leave again? He closed the door.

And Gina? He'd meant to write her, but he didn't know what to say and couldn't get back to that part in himself. Before he could figure it out, she wrote him: Frank, it's alright. Somehow I understand. I'm here. Gina. He put the letter into the folder with all of her others, was amazed to see that there were dozens of letters, long and short, his and hers. There were also several playful nude pictures she'd once sent him—another of him naked taken when he'd been sitting in the green easy chair by the window: mirror on the wall behind, her face hidden by the camera, but her shoulders, breasts, pubic triangle also clearly reflected. He took out his lighter, stood over the wastebasket, but just as the flame singed the Polaroids, he pulled it back. He put the pictures and letters together in their envelope and locked them in the filing cabinet.

Finally, all of the lines were smudged, getting off booze, being in love with Gina, or had he in the end just been trying to get laid? And Gina, with her I'm-here-for-you—was that realistic? Was that any of the women he'd ever known? At times he thought she was just playing a waiting game. Her con was no-con, just another con. In the end, it was just out there, the sound of her voice, some-thing unbridgeable in himself.

And what, how had it all begun? Exactly as Karen had requested. He'd talked to Kramer and they'd gone to AA ... Frank walked quickly down the front hall. As for Karen, he knew that she was still going through his draw-ers, his wallet, his jacket pockets, even his car, looking for proof that he was either still having his affair or that he'd had an affair. Though there was nothing to find lying around the house, he was sure she'd never stop looking. It was too weird. She wouldn't let it go, he realized, be-cause she'd seen him change—he'd stopped drinking, slimmed down. She knew someone or something had re-ally affected him, and she'd have to find out who or what. Maybe now, though, with her new job, she'd be happier, stop looking for proof, move on. That's what he wanted.

Frank put his hand on the doorknob. Yesterday at this time, he'd been invisible. He'd had money, a connection with something, possibility. Then Melikian had called. Feeling naked, the protective cover of money gone, he opened the door and stepped into the street, took a deep breath against the fear clenching his stomach.

All the way down to the Hall, cutting in and out of traffic, Frank worded and reworded what he'd say to Ray; was he really afraid he'd make some kind of major mistake? Did he just want out? In the parking lot, he quickly went through his pockets, walked across the lot into the Hall. Stepping out of the elevator on the sixth floor, he showed his ID, and signing in, nodded to the deputy. "What, Timmy, we've done this five hundred times. You think one of these days I'll be packing heat or a grenade?"

"Never know, Frank. One day, a guy wakes up, he's got a wonderful idea. Come on, I've gotta job to do here."

Frank opened the briefcase. Tim looked inside, closed it.

He turned toward the cell block. "They're crazy today.'' Shouts, TV's, radios. A din. ''Who we looking for this morning?''

''Raymond Buchanan.''

A few minutes later, Ray walked in front of him, and again they went down the narrow hallway and into one of the small rooms. Frank closed the door and turned. Ray stood against the far wall on the other side of the table. There was something different about him. Circles under his eyes. Obviously, he still hadn't slept well, and his face was shadowed with a thick black beard. That was it. Ray was fastidious, and Frank had never seen him unshaven before. And there was something else, something in Ray's eyes, perhaps a realization settling; maybe panic, maybe just the jail. Neither sat. Frank said offhandedly, ''How're you doing this morning, Ray?''

''I'm okay. Actually, I'm bugged.'' He nodded his head back toward the cell block. ''Some guy started screaming about six o'clock this morning. They finally took him away. He went crazy. He was eating his own shit.''

''That's a new one,'' Frank said. ''Look, we'll have you out of here soon.''

Frank hesitated. Just jump in and say it? He phrased and rephrased a possible opening: Ray, I've been thinking about my working as your investigator . . . Ray, listen to me, I've got something important to tell you . . . Nothing was right. Or, those were the words, but he still couldn't hear himself saying them. Frank put his briefcase on the table. ''Not a word about it in the news this morning.'' Ray nodded. ''I'll tell you when it surfaces. Talked to anyone since yesterday?''

Ray fumbled a cigarette out of his chest pocket. Frank helped him light it.

''Ray . . .'' he glanced toward the window. ''You can tell me everything.'' The moment he said it he realized he couldn't have said anything more ironic to Ray.

Ray seemed distracted. ''I talked to Melikian for a few minutes yesterday afternoon. He was in a rush. Says there's not much happening until my arraignment.'' Ray brought both hands to his mouth, took the cigarette out.

"Well, the more time goes by, the better."

Ray puffed his cheeks. "Spoke to Marla later." Ray nodded. "The DEA and local sheriffs broke in the front door of the house about two in the morning—one minute she's sleeping, the next second there's this loud bang— she said they split the front door with a battering ram. Then there are guys running all over the house with handguns, assault rifles, she wakes up, there's two guys holding guns on her . . . You know, she's sleeping naked." Ray lowered his voice. "She never had a clue." Ray lowered his voice more. "She wasn't charged; they let her go. Not knowing protected her."

Hey, in a way it really did protect people, their not knowing. Maybe kept them from temptation, too. Karen. Said he'd been talking in his sleep. Saying what? And her going through his things . . . ? "Ray, they had to have had search warrants ready and when they busted you, they just turned their other teams lose. That's what that was. Looking for drugs, money, names, scales, whatever."

"Marla didn't have any idea what it was about. She thought they were going to rape her."

"Yeah, they love it."

"I told her I'd explain everything when I bailed, but she said the cops said it was dope, that I was a major dope dealer—talk like that on the phone—that they had just busted me over in San Francisco, that she wasn't going to be seeing much of me from now on. She said when they saw the look on her face, one of them just laughed and told her to get dressed. I mean, it's personal to these guys, Frank." Ray shook his head. "They just tore the house to pieces."

Ray's beautiful house. Frank had always loved that house, envied its location deep in the pines up on one side of Mill Valley. Two stories. Glass. Redwood. Beautiful decks. Hardwood floors. Ray had a 1929 green Rolls Royce Phantom I in the garage. A black Lancia with an aluminum body. A Harley Sportster. Walk out the back door, and there was a vegetable and flower garden. Look back inside. Paintings. Navajo rugs. He could imagine the house after the DEA had finished with it.

"Yeah, once they've got their chance, they like to piss out their territory. They never pull a drawer, look, and push it closed when they can yank it out, dump everything on the floor, and kick through the junk."

Ray conceded a nod. Frank realized Ray had changed the subject and still had omitted telling him, what? Had there been any other visitors beside Melikian?

Frank glanced back at the window. "Money alright?"

"What am I going to do, buy a color TV in here?" Ray shrugged. "I'll be alright." But he didn't sound convinced. Frank didn't like what was coming off Ray—he'd felt it coming off other defendants, the smell of the sixth floor, jail time, people who'd given them up or were going to give them away, whatever they had never liked in themselves and had hoped to beat. Desperation.

They seemed to be winding down. Frank thought, just do it, just say the words: Ray, I've been thinking, because we're so close—we go back a long way, we're friends; it's in your best interests, I don't think I should handle this investigation for you . . . If I make a mistake—because we're close, or some error in judgement, it could do a lot of damage.

Frank took a deep breath. Just do it. Get it over with. Say it. He felt a great numbness come over him: saw—or more, felt an emptiness, a room he'd been in or had to go into. Vacant. Desolate. An expanse of empty blue sky outside. Part of Frank knew he recognized it, almost like a word or name he was trying to remember. He took another deep breath, but couldn't say anything to Ray; he couldn't take himself off this case now, tomorrow, next week. Frank said, "Okay, Ray, nothing much happening yet, but let a few days go by, we'll get you bailed out of here, you'll get a night's sleep; Melikian's good, the best, he always finds a way; an illegal wiretap or search warrant, something, the case will fall apart, things will work out. Just hang tough.''

He put his hand on his briefcase. Ray said, ''Frank, don't forget what we talked about yesterday.''

Frank nodded. ''I'll take care of everything.''

A deputy looked in the window, moved on. Ray nodded, raised his two hands cuffed together, pointed at Frank. ''A name. You take care of me, I'll take care of you. I don't need to know how you get it. You're good. When you get it, I know it will be right. Just get it.''

Frank turned toward the door.

''Frank. Stop. Listen to me a minute. I know you think I'm tired and weirded-out. I am. But I'm picking up on things. I've seen Jack Adams in here. I've seen Sammy. But I haven't seen Dean Miller. Miller's the guy who was Jack's contact; he set up the deal.''

''I remember. Dean Miller.''

''He handled the sale. The details. Money. Time. Place.''

''Right.''

''I haven't seen him.''

''Last time you saw him, they had a gun pointed at him, they were shoving him in a car.''

''Right.''

''Ray, look, maybe he's on another part of the floor. It's big in there.''

''I haven't seen him, Frank. No one's seen him.''

Frank nodded. Sighed. ''Okay, Ray, I'll check it out. Relax, buddy, I'm on your side. I'll take care of things for you.''

Frank opened the door to the hall, and a deputy came for Ray and led him back into the cell block. Frank watched him disappear inside. As Tim came to let him out, Frank said, ''Little disturbance in here this morning, some guy went crazy?''

Tim nodded. ''Guy in there trying to beat a murder rap.'' He leaned closer to Frank. ''Playing crazy. By the time we took him away to the psych ward, he was eating his own shit.'' Tim smiled, said flatly, ''But he isn't crazy.''

''Sounds fucking crazy to me.''

Tim leaned back and shook his head. ''Hey, you're an investigator, you're supposed to know something, not like some of these lawyers.'' Frank felt the class thing. Us and them. You and I.

''So what, a guy eating his own shit is not crazy? If I let you bend me over and fuck me, I'm not queer, I'm just . . . what?''

Tim leaned toward him, and now Frank felt something—menace? cunning?—coming out from behind the uniform. ''The guy wasn't crazy. He was eating his *own* shit. If he was really crazy, he'd be eating *another guy's* shit. *Then* he'd be crazy.'' Tim unlocked the door. ''Outta here, August. One of these days, we'll be locking you up for something. You got that look to me.'' Tim opened the door, holding his keys. ''Go on, Frankie.''

In the elevator down, Frank shook his head. Jesus, was Ray going to hold up in there or not? Yesterday, last thing, Ray says, find whoever put me in here. And again, today. And now, what? Dean Miller, whoever he was, Jack's contact, wasn't in the jail. Or, Ray hadn't seen him. Was it going to be every little thing? This wasn't what he expected from Ray. And he wasn't telling Ray yet, but if they set the high bail he thought they were going to set, and Melikian managed to kick the case over, he could be in there for months. Some of his defendants spent a year or two on the sixth and seventh floors behind their high bails before their cases came to trial. After their lawyers stopped taking their calls, they called Frank daily, getting crazier and crazier; no matter how crazy they got, Frank could rarely bring himself to refuse their calls. Too much fucking empathy. Part of him felt that if it hadn't been for a few breaks—a decent education, being born white—hey, not an answer, but there was no getting around eighty per-

cent of his defendants being black—whatever, it could
have been him.

As the elevator doors opened, he thought sardonically,
and still might be me. He walked into the lobby. Drop the
case. On the other hand, if Ray was going to get weird,
maybe the best place for Frank to be was right in the middle of the case so he could stay on top of things, keep the
right information in the right places, protect himself. A
dangerous place to be. Hey, Ray was going to remain under constant pressure to give names and make the best deal
he could for himself.

He walked to a pay phone. Maybe this would be a good
moment to call and apologize to Gina, feel out what he'd
told her; he propped his briefcase between his calves and
ankles, and dug out change, held the receiver to his ear.
He dropped the coins. As he heard them falling, the electronic tone of their passage awakened something in him.
Three or four weeks ago. The kitchen counter. A phone
number and date scratched on a pad. Ray's writing. Ray
rarely wrote down anything of importance. But just for the
hell of it, Frank copied them. Later, he'd find some way
to rattle Ray's cage over this. He stuck the note in his
pocket.

At home, he'd dialed the number. It was the desk of
the Colonial Inn in San Francisco. What? Ray meeting a
married woman there? Intending to explore it further,
Frank had dropped the note into his top drawer; now, he
realized, this was the motel where Sammy had gone to
wait for Ray's phone call with $500,000. It was as Ray
had said of himself; he'd gotten sloppy-sloppy after Sarah
Anne left. Ray at his best would never have written down
an important date and phone number, much less left it
lying around. Frank listened to the dial tone.

And, Frank recalled, he hadn't seen his note again.
Karen had to have found that number, called it just as he
had, discovered it was a motel, and God knows what conclusions she'd drawn. Or what she'd done. She'd been
going through his drawers and clothes, looking for some-

thing. So here's a motel and a date. That's something. The worst possibility. Without being able to define it further, he had to ask himself what she might have been able to do. She assumed he was having an affair. He knew how vengeful she could be. Tyrone Mayfield knocked over that ice cream store, killed the woman, got away; his girlfriend, what was her name? Revoyda, dimed him: 88-CRIME. Someone had dimed Ray . . . Muddled, Frank gave up on the call to Gina without dialing her number, replaced the receiver. Karen. Finding the number to the motel. She'd done something with that number. If nothing more, she'd assumed the worst about him. . . . *If* things don't change, Frank. . . .

He unlocked his car and tossed the briefcase across the seat. Glanced into the Honda beside him. A MacIntosh computer on the floor. Pretty dumb way to leave a computer. Smash and grab. A couple of disks in direct sunlight. Disks. Richie Davis. His business on disk. Maybe. In code. The DEA sent the disks off to be decoded. It was Ray who had assumed it was Richie's business, his ledgers. The paper had never actually said that. Farrell's case.

Frank got out, relocked his car. He walked back into the Hall. He took the stairs to the fourth floor, Homicide, caught his breath as he went down the corridor. Farrell's office. He hesitated. He had a vague idea how this should go now, but if things didn't go right, he could be buying a lot of trouble. And if he couldn't make Farrell go for it, he had no idea where he'd get another opportunity. . . .

Nerve failing completely, Frank retreated down to the men's room, rinsed his face; he unbuttoned his pants, straightened and tucked in his shirt. He looked at himself in the mirror. Most of it seemed clear to him, but beyond, he'd just have to go in there and make it up as he went along. What'd he have to lose? Everything, he thought, everything.

The door was slightly ajar, and he could see Farrell's empty desk and a bulletin board behind it. The board was covered with dozens of color snapshots, a random sampling of people who drifted by you in the Safeway. Ordinary looking people, except none of these people were smiling. They were people Farrell had business with. Suspects. Witnesses. Frank thought of what a superior court judge had said of a defendant who had gone crazy and killed three people. "Frank, the law's not for people like him—makes no difference." He's going to do what he's going to do, regardless. The law's for people like you and me." Frank studied the rows of faces, knocked and pushed open the door.

Farrell looked up from a filing cabinet, closed the drawer with a heavy metallic thud. He looked at Frank with those blue-white eyes. Husky eyes, Frank realized, eyes that belonged on a perfectly white, frozen landscape. Looking for some cue, an opening, Frank hesitated. If things weren't working, he could cut and run. Maybe. "Got a moment, Lieutenant?"

"Mr. August. August like the month." Maybe they could play it out on that level: banter, their status quo. "What can I do for you today? Pull a classified police report on a homicide? Better see the D.A.'s office for that. No, wait . . ." Farrell looked at Frank. "Speeding. Drunk driving. D.U.I. They're sending you to traffic school." Farrell looked Frank over. "Still no piece, I see."

"The very next thing on my agenda. I'm going straight to the gun exchange from here and order something— what'd you say yesterday? Oversized handguns."

"Excellent, Mr. August. Glad you pay attention." Farrell leaned back in his chair. "How can I be of service today?" Farrell looked at Frank with those overexposed eyes. If he'd been able to take his bar exam four years ago, Frank would have a nice quiet law office now. Frank said to himself, straight ahead, Farrell doesn't know dick. Do it. This time his voice came and he was committed to playing it out.

"Dennis, let me be up front. I have a defendant who's looking at some drug charges. Conspiracy to buy, sell, distribute. You know how it goes."

"I might."

"He's a business man who says he has no involvement and was set up."

"That's not too original, but okay, we'll say so."

"Right. Maybe he's lying to me. But maybe he's telling the truth. He could be telling the truth."

"Once in a while someone tells the truth."

"I'm not judge and jury. I don't have to make the call. But it would help me figure out a few things if I could nail this down. I don't want to go out on a limb for this guy until I confirm a few things—if I can."

Farrell nodded. "What's my connection?"

Frank's heart started to pound. This was a mistake. He took the leap. "Sometime back, you were in charge of the Richie Davis murder investigation." Farrell became very still. His face was blank. "I remembered reading an article about it in the *Chronicle*." Farrell still didn't say anything. "The paper said Richie Davis was a drug dealer."

Farrell listened.

Frank went on. "There were supposed to have been computer disks found in the house. They were in some kind of code. I heard there was some speculation they had his business on them." That was stretching it dangerously. They hadn't quite said that.

Farrell said, "Where'd you say you got this?"

"The *Chronicle*. I read the paper. It's part of my job."

"Didn't realize you were so conscientious. Or had such a good memory, Frank. Sure you've got it right?"

Frank didn't touch it. Straight ahead or he'd never make it. "Dennis, my defendant says he has no history of drug dealing; he claims he was set up. And there are some things which point to that. But he also *might* have a history. I need to know what's what if I'm going to have the right take on defending him."

"How do you connect him with Richie Davis?"

It was too late to turn back now. And maybe it could work out. "It was the first thing I thought of after I talked to my defendant. He's an art dealer, an importer. Richie

Davis was an art dealer. I remembered his case.''

"Didn't realize you were so interested in art."

"I took a flyer. I just asked him if he knew Davis to watch his reaction."

"And?"

Frank shrugged. "He didn't think anything of it. Up front said he knew him, he'd brought Richie a few art items. I mean, my point here, is that he had nothing he was trying to hide or protect. So I can see it both ways. Either he's kind of dumb to connect himself to a major leaguer like Davis. Or he's really got nothing to hide and he's an art dealer who's been set up by somebody."

"Where's all this lead?"

"Okay, I figure if the Davis disks were successfully decoded, and if they had the names of people Davis did business with, I want to know if my defendant's name was on those disks. If it was, I know he's lying to me, that he's got a drug-dealing history, that he wasn't set up—that he's a player, Dennis. His attorney and I want to confirm all we can before we go any farther."

Farrell picked up his pen. "What'd you say his name was?"

"I didn't."

"Who is it?"

"Can you do anything?"

"I can do some checking. What list, who and where, we'll see. Not to be cynical, Frank, but do you mind my asking what's in it for me?"

"The article said there were no leads, that the Davis murder wasn't solved. Maybe my guy can help you make a few connections. I know my guy wasn't involved in anything like a murder, but maybe he knew some people Davis knew. I just don't know.

"I thought we could work it this way. You give me a few questions you have—names, dates, whatever—relating to the Davis murder. I'll ask my defendant if he knows anything—if he does, I'll give it to you in a report. If he doesn't . . ." Frank shrugged. "I won't bullshit you. I'm emphasizing, Dennis, he may know nothing at all. In exchange, whatever he comes up with—something, nothing—you let me know if my defendant's name was on the Davis disks. That's all. Yes, it was. No, it wasn't. If it was, I'll know he's lying to his attorney and me.''

Frank's heart was pounding. Ray, he knew, was in no way connected to the Davis murder; he was sure of that. Would Ray himself have brought up the computer disks if he'd had anything to do with Davis's death? No, let Farrell look in Ray's direction, it would be okay. But if he could just get Farrell to tell him who was on the disk, then Frank could stop going crazy and suspecting everyone. If Ray's name was on the disks, it would tell him Ray had been under surveillance and that's what had brought him down. Then Frank could stop thinking about Karen finding phone numbers on little pieces of paper in his drawers and making calls. . . . The thought lost its focus. *That* was unbearable. The information would get Ray off his back, too: find a snitch and the rest of it.

"Okay, Frank, give me the name."

"One other thing, Lieutenant. Can we do this without jumping up his bail down the road, issuing subpoenas, all the rest of the pressure to make him deal, talk, whatever."

Farrell looked at Frank. Skin like a raw potato. He didn't answer.

"Is that a yes?"

Farrell leaned back in his chair. "Okay, Frank. Yes."

Frank's mouth lost its juice. He swallowed. Could he trust Farrell not to take things into his own hands. He'd seen cops lie repeatedly under oath. But nothing left to do now. "Ray Buchanan."

"Spell it."

Frank spelled it. Farrell wrote the name on a piece of paper.

"Check back with me in a day or so. I'll give you my little shopping list. Hey, Frank, I'll keep my word, but how much do you want to bet your defendant says he knows nothing?"

"I never bet against myself, Dennis. Anyway, what's there to lose for either of us? We both take a flyer."

Frank   softly   back-pedaled   toward   the   door. "Frank . . ." Frank turned. Farrell looked at him. He seemed both amused and annoyed. Farrell picked up a file on his desk and waved Frank out.

In the hall, Frank became aware that his shirt was damp with sweat. He loosened his tie, undid his top button. He walked slowly. Great, he'd just pulled Ray into the Davis murder investigation, and whatever heat Farrell might want to apply. Someone nodded as he passed, and without paying attention or recognizing him, Frank waved. Would Farrell keep his word and stay away from Ray? He walked to the stairs, shifting his briefcase. Hey, it would be alright. He knew what he was doing. He didn't think Ray was a murderer. And even if he was on the DEA list, it wouldn't change his case. That's what the DEA had to have started with. And Ray'd already been busted. No, Frank hadn't really given Farrell anything. Maybe he'd get some confirmation back. It was under control.

He reached the lobby. But something was still bugging him, had been bugging him the whole time he'd been in there with Farrell. As he skirted the metal detector on the way out, it came to him: maybe *his* name was on the DEA list. Technically, Frank knew that was impossible. He'd never done anything with Richie Davis. But he *had* been to Davis's house; he'd come and gone from Ray's. The DEA had all kinds of lists and computers. He realized he wasn't thinking straight. He'd once taken a hard elbow in a basketball game. His eye had filled up with blood and for weeks it had been like looking through a veil. It was like that, now. He realized his involvement was the blind spot in the middle of everything.

He pushed open the door, stepped outside. He'd just have to tough it out. He didn't know about Ray, but it would go a long way toward easing *his* mind to know if there was a snitch—if so, who. Halfway to his car, he changed directions and started for the bar across the street. Beer, he said to himself. Just beer. Only one. Maybe two. He glanced at his watch. He'd be meeting Melikian later this afternoon. One beer. He had to watch himself. This time he was going to keep things completely under control. He was going to hang with Aram, get back in his good graces, take all of his cues from Aram, play his game: Aram gave him big cases when he played it Aram's way. As he crossed the street, he remembered Dean Miller. Ray hadn't seen him on the sixth floor. So why should he see him, there were how many guys on the sixth floor? Hey, okay, he'd check it out for Ray. Dean Miller . . . and then who or what next would it be for Ray?

Frank was just coming out of the dry cleaners at Folsom and 18th when someone walking just ahead turned suddenly to face him, at the same moment, Frank sensing movement at his back, ducked to one side—a moment's darkness—he dropped his shirts, light starch on the collars and cuffs, please, swung his elbow, and felt it connect, the guy in front of him hit him with his fist, Frank jabbed him quickly, snapped his head, hit him again hard in the middle of the chest, the guy backed up, Frank quickly turned to face the one behind him, who raised a tire iron for a second shot. There were several rebar stakes in the easement between the street and sidewalk where someone was trying to grow grass and had secured a rope to keep people off. Frank yanked one out of the ground with both hands, and enraged, wild-eyed, he swung it twice, threshing the air with a low moan. In a momentary stand-off, the three stood panting, juiced with adrenalin, wild-eyed. "Come on, ass-holes!"

One said hoarsely, "Tell Ray he better not roll on us in jail!"

"Get off my fucking shirts!"

"He lost us a lot of money!"

"I don't know any Ray! Fuck your money!" Frank

swung the iron stake quickly, once, twice, the air singing hoarsely.

"He promised a clean deal, a milk run! Tell him he doesn't roll over on us or he's dead."

Frank advanced swinging the iron stake, knocked the tire iron out of the one guy's hand, and the two broke for a car idling at the curb, slid in, took off. Frank landed several quick blows across the trunk and a taillight before the car was out of reach. It was only after the car was gone that he realized he'd lost his chance to get the license plate. Enraged, he flung the rebar onto the pavement, picked up his scattered and crushed shirts. He fingered the stinging in his scalp, felt the warm dampness. Blood on his fingertips. Somehow he'd sensed the tire iron coming just in time to duck. Basketball—the break. He saw the gash wasn't going to amount to much—really, he didn't want to look like a schmuck for Melikian—suddenly laughed, short, angry and said outloud, "Shit, my wife can hit harder than you assholes!" He tossed his shirts into his car, then grabbed them and walked back into the dry cleaners. "Mrs. Ramirez, can you please run these through again?"

Surprised, she looked from him to the shirts. "You alright, Mr. August?" She handed him a paper towel.

He followed her gaze to the blood on his fingertips. "I'm fine. Same as before. Light starch on the collar and cuffs. Thank you." Blotting at the ooze in his scalp, he walked out.

Frank's appointment with Melikian was at three o'clock, and by two-thirty he'd cleaned up and recovered from his go-around on the sidewalk and was in his car with not such a great feeling about the whole thing. Still, he forced his attention to Melikian. There was no way he was going to mess up this chance for a reconciliation. He hadn't said ten words to Melikian in the last four months—or rather, Melikian hadn't said ten words to him; Aram had just frozen him out. Not a word, not a single referral. Quick nods passing in the Hall. And whatever the offense, he hadn't been able to find out. If it had been over Aram shorting him the two grand in People vs. Delaney, hey, Frank had no choice; he'd had to call Aram. There was no chance he was going to let Melikian, or anyone else, get down with that. If you did, you might as well wear a big hat with SCHMUCK written on it. Still, they'd always had a good working relationship. Rule number one: always let the lawyer be right and win. Frank knew the game. Yeah, sometimes there'd been minor disagreements, but never a reason to stop speaking.

Frank slowed and started looking for a parking space. Anyway, whatever it was in Aram's mind, Frank had pulled himself together and decided he was going to make the most of this. Aram had a thing about shoes. His father had probably given him some manly bullshit advice, son, you can always tell something about a man by his shoes; Aram always had shined shoes. Fine, Frank had gotten a shine. Aram was a nut about baseball and day by day knew the batting averages, RBI's of half the National and American leagues and of course the Dodgers. Frank had spent time reading the Sporting Green and was ready for a little schmooze about last night's game, the third of the home stand with the Dodgers. Then, thinking it over a little more, he realized that Aram thought of him as something of a street guy, a hustler—the way he'd worked while putting himself through college and law school. And so Frank thought fine, I'll give him that. Passing Buffalo Exchange, he'd noticed a wide, silk tie, Hong Kong: flowering red hibiscus, clouds, and stylized flying cranes, five bucks, already dry cleaned; he'd put on a mauve and purple pinstripe shirt for a brilliant clash. Worn the tie and shirt with a gray, double-breasted jacket. He'd be whoever Aram wanted him to be. But with shined shoes. Hey, it was a killer tie. Frank spotted a place, pulled over, backed in. He dropped some change in the meter, and, straightening the tie, he started the five-block walk to Melikian's office. It was quarter of three and he was on top of it.

*   *   *

He stopped when he reached the small Victorian. Nice building. Frank glanced down the drive. There it was, the Porsche. Melikian always backed in from the street while people screamed at him and Aram just waved them off. Suddenly unsure of himself—first and last he was here today only because Ray had requested him, not because of anything Aram and he had worked out—Frank walked up the front stairs, through the double doors of the vestibule— polished oval windows as big as dresser mirrors. Once more, he lightly fingered the gash in his scalp, which had dried up.

Velma looked up at him from her word processor. Tall, slim, Oriental, long black hair, late twenties. Velma Wong. They'd checked each other out more than once, had flirted in a cool way, but Frank had wisely concluded, no matter what, not Melikian's secretary. Frank stepped into the front hall. "How've you been, Velma?"

She nodded, very well. She stared at his tie. Tore her eyes away to glance down at the appointment book. She seemed lost or confused, and Frank thought, great, the usual high-handed Melikian runaround, she's going to tell me that he's held up for an hour, or canceling; his time is important, my time is what? It was always this way with Aram. She found the place, picked up the phone, called him. "Be just a minute."

Frank paced away from the desk, looked at the double closed doors beyond her, immersed himself in slow empty thoughts as he watched his shined cowboy boots pace across the patterns of the Persian rug. The doors opened behind him, and Aram, in yellow tie, pale blue shirt sleeves and white suspenders, emerged from behind the doors, walked quickly toward Frank and extended his hand ceremoniously. Frank took his hand. Never taking his eyes from Frank, Aram smiled, put his hand on Frank's shoulder. "Francis Ignatius August . . . Jesus Christ, how've you been? Been a while."

Frank thought, who's doing was that? but just smiled and nodded as though he hadn't noticed.

Aram was still smiling, still had his hand on Frank's shoulder, was searching his eyes as if to say, you can tell me whatever it is, I know a lot of people, but I care about you. He was in his expansive mode.

"Good to see you, Frank." He released the handshake, pressed lightly on his shoulder. "Come on in. Velma, no calls please. Go ahead, Frank."

Frank led the way into Aram's office, Aram closing the door behind him. The massive mahogany desk, a couple of plush chairs and a sofa in front. One wall, built-in bookcases, law books, wherein also resided William Saroyan's *The Daring Young Man on the Flying Trapeze*. Filing cabinets. Thick files stacked on the desk and on the floor alongside the wall. A chest-high safe. On his desk, a large color picture of Janice, Melikian's nice wife. There was a baseball signed by the starting line-up of the 1988 Dodgers; Frank could make out Tommy LaSorda. There was also a signed picture of Diane Feinstein: Thanks, Aram. In more confident days, Frank always said "For what?" And Melikian would just smile. And Frank would say, "I doubt if it was for that, dude-san." And Melikian would say, "You're an investigator, you're supposed to figure things out. If you want to know, go dig." And Frank would say laconically, "Someday I will."

Now Frank let his eyes slide over the picture and blanked his face. Take your cues from Aram.

Aram drifted back behind his desk, looked Frank up and down, shook his head and smiled appreciatively. "I've missed you, Frankie. Look at you . . . what? still wearing cowboy boots . . . Oh, Jesus and pointed toes. And look at this tie." He held out both hands. "Get this unbelievable tie!"

Frank looked down. "What? You don't like my tie?"

"I love your tie! Only you, Frank, only you. Where'd you get a tie like this—you don't have this kind of good taste—Karen picked this out for you . . . How is Karen?"

"Karen's great. Got a new job coming up at the San

Francisco Art Museum. Assistant to the director. She's ec-static. We're gnarly. Totally awesome.''

"Gnarly. Totally awesome," he repeated automatically, laughing as he was reminded of Frank's dialects and voices. He smiled, shook his head. "The tie, the shirt—purple . . .''

"Mauve is what the boys in the fashion industry call it, part of the total concept, I'm suure." Frank lisped out the sure, Valley Girl.

"Purple. Mauve. Suuure. I love it, Frank."

Frank shrugged, "Mondo killer? Thanks."

Aram. Six-four, barrel chest. Frank had seen him pony-tailed, but in the last few years, he'd been playing it straight. He had weird, blue-green eyes, a regular nose, but perhaps just a little wider, fatter than a nose should be, maybe a little surge of upward motion at the bridge, the nose of a goat or dolphin, an animal whose best expression would be a firm nudge. Stories still circulated about Aram as a wild-eyed public defender who'd been warned not to wear green hightops to try cases and who'd been held in contempt when he'd continued to do so. He, too, lived for that moment when the charges were read: People of California vs. whoever. All against one; in that, Frank and he were exactly the same. They loved being with that one. Hey, Frank could dig it. Part of Frank loved Aram. Aram deflated slightly, turned back to look around his desk, swept his fingers through his hair, a caress: I'm so busy, I'm so whatever. He picked up a yellow pad, put it down in the same place.

As though calling a meeting to order, Aram held out a hand, lowered his voice, thickening the air with confidences to come, conspiracy. "Sit down, Frankie, sit down."

They sat. Aram looked at Frank. Quick smile, shake of the head. "Well, I stopped in for a minute yesterday to see Ray, but had no real time to talk. This trial's taking up every minute. Tell me what you've got. Just run it down, what Ray told you."

Though he didn't need them, Frank pulled out his notes and looked them over, trying to compose himself. Okay, watch what you say to Aram. No opinions. Don't volunteer anything. Just keep it neutral: He said. He saw. He did. Let Aram ask the questions. From then on, Frank could reply he'd see, he didn't know, he'd find out. That was the best way to make sure he didn't let something slip with Aram. Melikian was clever. Frank started in. He represented Ray the way Ray represented himself to the world. Importer-exporter. Art dealer. He'd been having some financial problems. An opportunity came through his friend, Jack Adams, who'd dealt successfully several times with an organization. Ray knew nothing about these people, but he was in a money bind and the deal looked good. Grass. High quality. He was to bring a million in cash. Jack was to bring a million. Ray sent another friend to wait in a motel room with $500,000 in cash until Ray saw the bales and made sure everything looked right. Then he called him. Sam Coleman. The guy they were meeting was someone called Dean Miller. . . . Frank hesitated here: no, nothing more now. Don't say anything about Ray's insisting he hadn't seen Miller on the sixth floor. Keep it very simple. Frank finished the story with Ray's description of the bust. He didn't say anything to Melikian about Richie Davis, murdered; about his deal with Farrell to find out if Ray had gone under DEA surveillance through Davis's computer disks—he had no idea what Melikian would have said to that, but would probably scream. Melikian was an obsessive control freak. No, Frank would keep those things to himself.

As he finished, he was surprised by how simple the narrative details were. Three guys raised a couple of million in cash to buy a few tons of high quality Thai weed in bales. Somehow, all of them were busted. That was it. Nothing. He had cases where he ended up with fifty or sixty witnesses, six trial notebooks full of interviews, police reports, coroner's reports, etc; it took an hour to get all of the cards on the table; an hour to figure out the

players; an hour to narrate. It surprised him in the telling;
this simple story seemed to be completely different from
the one which had engulfed him. Only his stomach lurching with adrenalin could tell that story. And it bled away
at the edges in all directions: the heat and blue dome of
the New Mexico desert sky and some indefinable sense of
despair which always seemed to be with him; Ray standing
beside him in the dark thirteen years ago; Ray saying he'd
lost money in the pipeline, but not letting on anymore;
Frank, in going through the newspapers, recalling Richie
Davis, and then seeing in another article, that months later,
a trawler had been taken at sea with twenty tons of high
quality Thai weed; this, just a few weeks after Sarah Anne
had left Ray. There were a lot of other little details that
Frank wasn't sure what to do with yet: a phone number
written on a pad in Ray's kitchen, The Colonial Inn;
Karen's finding that number—she had, hadn't she? She'd
been going through his stuff; she had to have made some
assumptions when she saw it was a motel . . .

". . . Frank?"

"What?"

"Where'd you go? I just asked you where you knew
Ray Buchanan from." He reached up to finger the gash
on his head. And just a couple of hours ago there were the
two creeps who'd threatened Ray. He pulled his hand
back. All he had to do was break the scab and start bleed-
ing all over his collar in here. In a way, it was easier when
they were on the sidewalk in front of you swinging a tire
iron. You just hammered back.

"Oh, a few parties. He went out with a girl who Karen
knew from graduate school . . ." Frank shrugged to show
it was inconsequential. Even that little fantasy was imply-
ing too much of a connection. And Melikian was a guy
who was inclined to fill in gaps with his own ideas.

Melikian looked at him now. "Right, well, he made a
point of asking for you."

"You mentioned that yesterday."

Melikian looked down at his notes, swiveled in his

chair. "Okay, Frank, I have a good picture—clear enough,
for the time being. Write me an investigation report. Keep
it minimal. Address it to me. You interviewed the defendant. He said what you told me. Nothing else." Melikian
lowered his voice, a Melikian habit, a deft piece of theater—Melikian, king of schmooze—which said to the listener, you and me, baby. "There's no point in our helping
the prosecution with shared discovery full of ideas. Any
opinions or ideas, keep them with me right here in this
room.

"Frankie, I like it that Ray is a buyer, not a seller.
Down the road, maybe we can do something with that.
And specially with Ray having no priors. You said he had
no priors, right? No weapons at the bust." Frank nodded.
"Look, this is not a twenty dollar crack bust. This is something else. A couple of buddies get together and raise two
million bucks in cash. You don't just find two million
bucks on a street corner; it takes resources, planning, other
players. They then go to a seller, who's also got to have
people behind him. He's got two tons of high quality
weed—wish I had a little right now . . ."

Frank gave him what he wanted, "Yeeah. I heard that,
Slick." Jailhouse, broken diction, black.

Melikian smiled, sat up. Smoothed a suspender. "What
I'm saying, Frank, is that we have some charges—U.S. vs.
Buchanan—buy, sell, transport, distribute. We have a lot
of cash and a lot of good dope. We have an arrest. Someone calls it spaghetti. Maybe it is, maybe it isn't. But two
strands don't make spaghetti." He leaned back.

"Find out about the four defendants. Pull court files.
Miller. Buchanan. Adams. Coleman. Check out the affidavits for the search warrants—actually, I've got something I'm doing over at the U.S. District Court in the next
few days so I'll save you the trip. See what came back on
the warrants—check the evidence and make sure it's what
they say it is and the way they say it is: scales, dope,
whatever. Photograph it. Videotape the warehouse. Have
an electronics guy do a sweep of Ray's house for bugs.

Double check Ray's record to make sure he really doesn't have priors—maybe something slipped his mind. He won't be doing himself any favors by lying to us. I've gotta know how it really is before we go to bat. If there's something to find in here, find it for me, Frankie. You've got the gift.'' He smiled. ''You're obsessive. You're suspicious.'' He glanced at Frank and smiled more broadly. ''Those are compliments.'' Frank finished scrawling notes on a pad.

''How about the grand jury transcript?''

''Federal, remember. It's sealed. Grand juries are witch hunts and bullshit anyway . . .''

''Right. But without the transcript we don't know what they're trying to do with their case.''

''That's how it is dealing with the Feds. You never know what's going on and it's on a fast track. If I have to, I can make a Brady motion for disclosure, but see what you can do now. I mean, it's early. We don't know what's what. Today, it looks like one thing. In two weeks, we look a little more, it's a circus. Down the road, who knows, but if we can get something, Ray's a guy you can go to trial with . . . tall, handsome, gentle manner; you pack the jury with women, you sell them Ray. If you don't think good looks make a difference to a jury, then you shouldn't be a lawyer.'' He waved his hand, never mind, we'll deal with that when the time comes. ''How's Ray holding up in there?''

Frank shrugged. ''He's not having fun, but he's okay. Some guy was hauled off to the psych ward this morning after eating his own shit. Ray saw the whole thing.''

''Not what he's used to.''

''You know that big deputy in there, Tim Longenbach?'' Melikian nodded. ''It's his opinion that the guy wasn't really crazy—that he's playing crazy to beat his charges. According to Deputy Longenbach, if he's really crazy, he wouldn't be eating his own shit, he'd be eating someone else's.''

Frank and Melikian exchanged three different gradations of shrugs—so who's crazy—and let it go. Melikian glanced at his watch. "Check in with me every few days on this case." Aram scrawled a couple of notes on a yellow pad, placed them in a folder. He eased back in his chair. "Catch the Dodgers last night?"

Frank knew what Aram was looking for. "Two-run double in the seventh, three-one pitch, Kirk Gibson drills the slider . . ."

Aram nodded and extended his arms. "I had a clear view of it, second row, halfway down the third base line. Gibson just reached out and you could see him watch the ball onto his bat and slap that pitch, scored two runs . . . So pretty," Melikian shook his head, "so pretty."

Frank nodded. "He's got the stroke." Frank felt into the room; at this moment there seemed to be absolutely nothing wrong between them.

Aram looked at a calendar on his desk. "Jesus, I'm late, I've got to run. Walk out with me, Frank."

Frank stood and dropped his pad in his briefcase. When he glanced up, Aram was smiling at him. "I do like that tie." Frank undid the tie. "Frank! No way!"

Frank slid the tie from beneath his collar. "Aram, take the tie."

"Frank . . ."

"Please." Frank nodded. "Take it, Aram." He came around and gently draped it over Aram's head and shoulders, lightly let it go, held up his palms not to say any more.

Aram raised the tie and looked at it, nodded and said quietly, "Alright, Frank. I'll take it in this spirit. Thank you."

Frank closed his briefcase. "You know something, Frankie . . ." Aram went to a closet. "Maybe I've got something for you, too." He opened the door. A satin-finish Dodgers jacket hung on a wooden hanger and hook. He turned back. "What size are you. Forty-four long? Forty-six?"

"Sometimes one, sometimes the other."

Aram pulled out a tweed shooting jacket with a shoulder patch. Country squire style. "Try this. It's forty-six long. It's too small for me."

He helped Frank out of his jacket and into the shooting jacket.

Aram turned him and straightened the shoulders and lapels. "English." It didn't fit. Too loose. And Frank hated it. "What do you think?"

"Nice."

"Yeah, beautiful. Have it taken in a little. Perfect."

"It's new."

"Janice talked me into it. I wore it once." He shrugged. "Beautiful, but just not for me." Aram put up his two hands, done deal. He dropped several folders into his briefcase, conferred quickly with Velma, then angled Frank toward the back door, and in a moment, they were standing beside the Porsche. "Where's your car? You need a ride?"

"I'm fine."

Aram slid into his Porsche. "Touch base every forty-eight, seventy-two hours on Ray Buchanan—if you find anything, call me right away." He started the car, waved and took off.

Frank started toward his car. Melikian. Frank unbuttoned his top button, looked down. The tie? The jacket? Frank shook his head, what vaudeville, what a farce. But then, Melikian had seemed genuinely happy to see him. Maybe. Melikian was slick and knew how to play along when it suited him, too. So maybe there'd be cases in the future, maybe not. Referrals would tell him what was what. In the meantime, he'd play everything exactly Melikian's way. As he reached his car, he dumped the jacket in the back seat. Hey, he'd kind of liked that tie; it *had* been a real find: red hibiscus, clouds, white cranes with outstretched wings.

In his office, Frank quickly sorted through a pile of messages, then turned to Gloria. "Can we let the answering machine cover for a minute? Grab a pad. Ready? Here are four names." He dictated them: Dean Miller; Sam or Samuel Coleman; Jack Adams; and Ray Buchanan. "Okay, what I want you to do is check each of them out through the Muni and Superior Court Clerks of San Francisco County—it's a trip to the Hall. Go back, let's say, ten years. See if there are any cases; if there are, get the files and the sentencing abstract.

"Then, let's widen the field. Call DataSearch. The same four. I'll call the jail and get their D.O.B.'s. If any of them have addresses for driver's licenses outside S.F. County, check the Muni and Superior Court records of those counties." Frank spun the Rolodex. "Here, use Anita Chavez for that. I don't want you wasting time driving all over the place." He gave her Chavez's name and number. "There are fifty-eight counties in California and you can't cover them all, but let's start this way. Wait." Gloria continued writing quickly. He remembered that Ray had said in passing that Jack Adams had an ex-wife down around Leucadia. Southern Cal. "Check to see what county Leucadia is in and try that one for Jack Adams. And what the hell, you might as well try Orange County for Adams since you're looking down there."

"What case did you say this was, Frank?"

"Gloria, I'm rushed, I'll explain everything when I have a minute."

"I just wanted to know for time sheets, filing, and billing." She parted her hair back off her forehead.

He swung his swivel chair side to side, softened his voice. "I'm sorry, didn't mean to be short." He pulled out a blank folder, wrote Melikian across the front, and said, "Let's call it this for now. All expenses, correspondence, receipts, time sheets go in this." He placed it on her desk. "I'll take care of the rest later. How're you doing covering our check to John?"

"So far we're not getting much more than promises and unreturned phone calls."

"Keep after them. Make it your number one priority." She swung back to her desk. "And Gloria. I have a sexist task for you, if, that is, you won't feel too sullied."

"Try me, Frank. This might be time and a half."

"When you're over at the Hall checking the records, flirt with that assistant D.A., the one who flushes when you come in . . . what's his name?"

"Harrison . . . Ron Harrison."

"Dude's gonna have to hide his feelings better than that if he's gonna win cases. Pink equals a case of the hots for the defense's investigator. . . . Anyway, maybe you can get Harrison worked up enough to check the computer, see if any of these four have criminal cases pending. Nothing like a little tumescence to get information."

She swiveled back. "We'll see what we can do, Frank."

"I'll bet we'll see what we can do." She didn't say anything more, but he could see she was looking down and smiling. "Anyway, here we go. Adams. Jack Adams." She nodded. "It's a smooth name, you know." He glided the flat of his hand in mid air. "So try John. Jonathan. J. And the last name, beside Adams, try variations: Adamski, Adamson, whatever you can find. Look in the phone book for any other variations on Adams and run those. I don't care what it costs."

Frank picked up the phone and called the county jail, but of course it was busy. Goddamnit, he'd been right there this morning . . . too many things on his mind. And maybe he hadn't really taken Ray seriously. Now he was taking everything seriously. He banged down the phone, then dialed San Bruno, which rang and answered. He asked for Lazebiety Singletary, who'd been a witness in one of his cases and, as a prisoner clerk, had access to the computers. He came on and Frank identified himself.

"Whas happenin, Frank?"

"Actually, what it is, Zeb, I'm looking for a dude, supposed to be on the sixth floor, got a minute to check it out, or you jammed?"

"I'm cool, Frank. Who is it?"

"Dean Miller." Frank spelled the name. "Race: white. I don't have a D.O.B. or a SF number."

Frank heard keys punching. He swiveled back and forth, glanced up at Kramer's surfboard overhead on the ducts.

"Computer's got Donald Miller, Ralph Miller."

"No Dean Miller? White?"

"Donald Miller is black; Ralph Miller is white. But there is no Dean Miller, white."

"Middle initial for Ralph Miller?"

"No."

"D.O.B.?"

"12-7-35."

"Too old. So there's no Dean Miller now. Was there ever a Dean Miller booked in?"

"Not that I can see."

Frank waited for the burn of adrenalin to subside. "No Dean Miller ever booked in."

"No."

"Okay, Zeb. While we're at it, can I get D.O.B.'s for three others. Buchanan, Ray. Adams, Jack. Coleman, Samuel. Just booked in." Zeb pulled them up. "What do you need these days?"

"I'm tripping on Shakespeare—specially the tragedies."

"Seriously?"

"Straight-up."

Though Frank was surprised daily by what people did, he felt a kind of amazement enter some unfrequented part of him. "Well, I'm down with Shakespeare. I'll have the complete Shakespeare in your hands in a week. Comedies, tragedies, sonnets, the whole nine yards. Later."

Frank scribbled a note: Shakespeare/Zeb. Sat back. Then, from beneath his momentary surprise, he felt something else emerge; Ray had been right. Maybe for the wrong reasons, but he was right. Dean Miller was not on the sixth floor. He was not in any of the county jails. Frank shook his head. Ray was canny. He'd just made one big mistake in thirteen years, but he always knew something. Whatever or whoever had taken him down had to have

come at Ray from a completely unforeseeable direction.
He handed the D.O.B.'s to Gloria for DataSearch.

"And Gloria."

"One more thing, Frank?"

"Dean Miller. He's not in any of the three county jails.
If he's an undercover cop who makes a sting, then they
don't book him. Pay special attention to Dean Miller. It's
a million to one now that's his real name—I mean, this is
probably pointless—but some of these guys get cute and
love to play little games. I remember one guy, real name
was Wayne Clancy, or maybe it was Clancy Wayne, anyway, he just reversed it on undercover. Part of his psych,
his way of saying fuck you. I mean, anything's possible.
Maybe there's a variation on Dean Miller. So let's try a
longshot here. Call SFPD non-emergency number, identify
yourself, say you're having trouble reading a police report;
the name is obscured; the reporting officer looks to spell
his name something like Dean Miller. Get the clerk to try
the M's. Dean Miller. Don Muller. Play with it. See if she
can kick something back out that sounds close. Use the
first name as a last name. When she loses patience, call
back and start with another one." Frank stood. "With the
way things are going here, there's not much left to lose."
He stood and dusted off his knees. "Coffee?"

"Tea. Chamomile."

"Sleepy Time, isn't it? Hey, I don't want my employees too relaxed."

When he came back, Gloria was hanging up the phone.
He set the mug on her desk. She shook her head, no Dean
Miller or variations from SFPD. Frank sat at his desk, spun
the Rolodex. "Longshot time, Gloria." He found the
prison locater number, dialed. To get a prisoner's
whereabouts, you had to have either the CDC number or
his D.O.B. Ray had described Miller as white, in his mid-
thirties. Frank quickly made up a scattershot of four
D.O.B.'s as the phone rang, one of which would have put
Miller in his mid-thirties.

CDC answered. "California Department of Corrections."

Frank introduced himself as an investigator, and in his most appealing voice, said, "I'm wondering if you could help me. I'm looking for a witness in a death penalty case." He gave her the name and docket number of one of his death penalty cases. "His name is Dean Miller. I've reduced my search to four Dean Millers and I have four D.O.B.'s." Before she could say anything more, he gave her the four D.O.B.'s, knowing she wouldn't catch them or even try.

She said, "I can't do that."

"I know, but I'm running out of time and he's an important witness. I really need someone to step forward and help. It's a death penalty case."

The woman hesitated. "Go ahead."

He gave her the four bogus D.O.B.'s to make her think he legitimately had something. He'd done this before when he hadn't had the CDC number or D.O.B. If she had anyone by that name, she'd kick him back the right D.O.B., which now opened the door to more information.

She said, "I have no Dean Millers at all." She read him several Millers.

"White?"

"The only one who's white is Paul Miller. Born 4-2-72. What's he in for?"

"242. Assault. The last one is too young. Maybe I've got my information wrong. Maybe he's been released. Have you ever had a Dean Miller. On probation or parole?"

After a long pause, she said, "The computer shows no one by that name."

"Thank you for your help."

Frank hung up. "Well, gnarly. Portrait of a man spinning his wheels here. Dean Miller's not booked into any of the county jails now as a prisoner. He hasn't been in the CDC. He's not in SFPD, at least by that name. And that's not all so hard to understand, is it, Gloria? That's because Dean Miller's not really Dean Miller. So who's Dean Miller, Gloria?''

"I wish I knew, Frank, if for no other reason than to put a happier expression on your face.''

"*That* impulse," he said in a fey voice, "makes you my enabler. Co-dependent. Everyone's twelve step now.''

Frank watched Gloria think that over, take a sip of her tea, and decide not to take it up. Instead, she ventured gently, "If Dean Miller is not Dean Miller, I guess there's nothing for me to check out on him . . . for the time being.''

Distracted, Frank didn't answer. He fought back a feeling that the case against Ray was going to be tighter and more involved than he knew. He turned to her, "Go ahead with the other three names. I'll think of something to do about Dean Miller. And keep calling people who owe money. Please. Thank you. In advance." He paused, then added, "Without more, we can't do much on this now. It's too early, too something." His voice trailed off. "Dean Miller will surface soon enough; it's just going to be in a way we don't like." He corrected himself. "Going to be in a way *I* don't like.''

If asked at precisely what moment things started to slide, Frank would have been hard pressed to answer. Perhaps it was when Dean Miller didn't come up on anyone's computer. Perhaps earlier when Frank had hesitated dry-mouthed outside Farrell's office. Or, maybe it had been when he'd failed his bar exam a week ago. However he would have described it, in the next week, things silently started to slide like objects across a table slowly being tipped from beneath. The signs were everywhere as when a couple of days later he waited for the elevator down in the Hall.

"Frank.''

He started, recovered. "Lieutenant Farrell." Christ, why the fuck did Farrell keep playing this little game of coming right up behind him before he spoke? Frank fought to hide his flash of anger.

"Always so preoccupied lately."

Frank shrugged. "I take my work seriously."

"I'm sure. That's how we got acquainted, remember?" Frank gave him a vague non-committal reaction. If Farrell wanted to bring up Tyrone Mayfield, that was up to him. In trial, he'd won Farrell's grudging respect. Perhaps Frank had been foolish not to see that he might also have won Farrell's resentment.

"Hey, well, however it happened, you're just the guy I've been looking for. You still interested in our trade? A few questions on Davis, something on Buchanan?"

"Absolutely."

"So where you been? I thought you'd gotten cold feet."

"Not at all. I just didn't want to jam you, Dennis. Figured you'd say something when you were ready."

Farrell took an envelope out of his jacket pocket and handed it to Frank. "My questions for Buchanan. I've been ready. Somehow expected to see you the next day bright and early. You had that eager look on your face."

Frank took the envelope, but rather than let Farrell see his reaction, he decided to open it later. He slid it into his pocket. "When in doubt, just pick up the phone. I'm in the book."

Farrell put his hand on Frank's arm. "No, I knew I'd see you soon enough. And here we are."

Farrell's smile was ironic. Frank nodded, still didn't bite. "I'll take care of it and get right back to you." He patted his jacket pocket.

"And I'll have something for you soon from the Richie Davis case, I'm sure. Stay in touch."

Still off balance from Farrell's manner, Frank reached his office. Giordano turned from Gloria's desk. Long salt-and-pepper black hair hanging over his ears and collar—not a style, he just needed a haircut—he stopped when he saw

Frank. He held up Frank's check. It was stamped in block capitals: INSUFFICIENT FUNDS.

"Congratulations, Frank."

"Hey, whoa, Homes, I'll call the bank, there's a mix-up. Sit down, Slick."

"You and I know it's no mix-up. You did a number. It flew for a few days. It's over." John tore the check into small pieces over Frank's desk.

Frank said, "Well, that's one way."

"I'm gone."

Frank dropped his briefcase into his swivel chair. "Gnarly, dude-san, hey, I asked you to hold off a few days, I told you everyone's squeezing me, you ignore it, you come in and squeeze me, too, I fucking *told* you, why'd it have to be right then? Jesus, you'd walk out on me over a few bucks after I gave you a job here, trained you, nursed you through law school . . ."

"All of that's true, Frank, and like I said, I've always appreciated it, but you owe me money and I owe people money. Pay me now and we're home free."

Frank swept pieces of the torn check off his desk. "Yes-but me, go on, John, I don't need you now with an attitude like this; you forget I'm the rainmaker here!" He pointed at his framed license. "I'll get you your scratch. Be a couple of days." He glanced around. "These your case files?" John nodded. "Got anything else that's mine? No? Good, later, Slick. I'll mail you your check."

As John went up the stairs, Frank turned to Gloria, softened his voice. "Sorry for the scene."

"I'm sorry, too, Frank. I really thought I could cover the checks. No one came through."

"I'm the guy who wrote the bad check. Hey, I was forced. I understand Giordano, I might do what he's doing in his position, but somehow, I don't think so. It's no way to treat someone who took care of things for you." Frank shrugged. "I know, he's gotta draw his line somewhere." Frank looked at Giordano's files stacked on his desk, shook his head. "Too many cases. Gotta hand it to him;

he couldn't have picked a worse moment." He went to the ficus and started picking up leaves off the floor. "Did you water this thing?"

"No, I'm letting it dry out."

"Two weeks ago you were watering it, right?" She nodded. He swept up several handfuls of leaves, dumped them in the basket, switched on the stereo. "Okay. So it's you, me and Kramer for everything until I can make a few adjustments." Frank looked up at Kramer's wax and sand encrusted surfboard resting on the ducts overhead. "They're taking Bledsoe to trial in three weeks. I hope Kramer's getting close to something there. Bledsoe could do a lot of time over that rape."

Frank swept the remaining pieces of torn check off his blotter and into his cupped palm with the meticulous care of a headwaiter crumbing a table and neatly dumped them in the basket. Remembering Farrell's list, he sat down, opened the envelope, and reread the questions. Did Ray know two Colombians who went by the names of Hector Schmidt and Armando Martinez? Had he seen them in the Northern California area between March and July of . . . Had he ever seen Richie Davis with them? Had he ever heard Davis mention them? Did he know a Thai business- man named Nakorn . . . Did he know a woman, maybe thirty, with a flower tattooed on her left ankle who lived in North Beach . . . Frank had never heard of these people, never heard Ray mention them, which didn't necessarily mean anything. He glanced at his watch. He didn't have a good feeling about what he'd set in motion with Farrell, but he saw no other way. He had to find out something definite.

As he waited for Ray to come out of the mainline, Frank knew he was going to be very upset about his trade-out with Farrell. Still, he had no choice now. He'd have to tough it out and make this thing fly. He decided to float it almost as an afterthought. They went into the interview room, made small talk for a couple of minutes, and then

Frank mentioned his recent sidewalk tango. Ray listened tight-lipped to the end, shook his head. "They're in front of some people I really didn't want to involve myself with, but they had money." He shrugged. "Hey, they knew there was risk. That's what the big money's about. Risk. I don't need to tell you, just keep your eyes open."

"Nothing but good news." Frank stood in the interview room, crossed the floor in two steps. "Ray, I have something we need to talk about. . . ." He eased into it as off-handedly as possible; he'd been checking on some information which might start to answer some of Ray's questions on who set him up; some of it had led back toward Richie Davis; he'd been lucky enough to have a good connection with the homicide cop in charge of that investigation, and hey, in exchange for Ray's answering a few questions, the cop might be able to give them some answers and . . .

Ray's eyes went flat, as though he'd been slapped. He cut in. "You're going to ask me about Davis's murder for a cop, Frank?"

Frank lowered his voice. "Ray. Jesus, relax, he's just trying to get some background information. This goes on all the time."

Ray turned sideways in his chair. He glanced back at Frank.

"Christ, Frank! Connecting me to a murder!"

"You're not connected. It's under control. Just play along and it might lead us to some places we want to go. This guy's got access to information which might help us. You know, you've got to dance with these people a little."

"You've got this cop looking at me for a murder. . . ."

Ray stood suddenly. He was right. This had to have been a mistake. Keeping his tone even, Frank said, "He's not looking at you, Ray. Will you just go along with this and shine it on. If I can find out a few things, maybe we can get out of the woods. Jesus, did you think it would be easy? You took chances to do what you did. I'm taking a few chances here."

Ray glanced at Frank as though he couldn't get over his amazement. "Fuck, Frank, the harm's already been done." He shook his head.

Frank read the questions slowly. Did Ray know the names of two Colombians, Hector Schmidt and . . . To each question, Ray listened, shook his head no with an increasing contempt and impatience. When he'd finished, Frank shrugged. "Nothing, Ray?"

"Never head of any of those people. It's like TV. Two Colombians! A girl with a tattoo on her ankle. Come on. I can't believe you'd put me in this position for whatever the reason."

Frank said, "Hey, Ray. This guy asked me to do something for him; I'm doing it so he'll do something for me." Frank hesitated, became aware of the sharp smell of nervous sweat. "And it would be good if I could give Farrell a little something. Yeah, you heard Davis mention the Colombians, something. I mean, there's nothing that can be proven, Davis is dead, and if you say you knew a little of this and that, it looks like you cooperated, but it leads nowhere for him."

Ray said, "I don't know these people and I don't want any part of it. I didn't know Richie Davis very well. With Richie, it was all business. Then we went our separate ways."

Frank hesitated. Best to stop. He held up his hands. He doubted anyone would ever go to trial over Davis, anyway.

As they went out, Ray calmed down some. "Find out anything about Dean Miller? Because I still haven't seen him in here."

Now was definitely not the time. Moving toward a deputy to kill the conversation, Frank said, "I'm still checking out a couple of things. He may be in San Bruno. We'll talk."

They turned from each other without another word.

Trying to cover John's cases, Frank kicked it into overdrive and started to push. Going on too little sleep, cranking it up on espresso, letting down with a few shots—hey, he wasn't drinking, he didn't get drunk—falling asleep on the sofa in his office, things started to jumble and run together.

Things were still sliding a few days later when Frank came in and saw the message machine blinking. He pressed the button. "Francis Ignatius? Aram Melikian. I'm just leaving the office. Please call me at home."

He circled the kitchen once, dialed Melikian. The thought occurred to Frank that he should have gone to a pay phone. Aram came on. "Frankie ... How's the jacket?"

"The jacket. Oh ... Great. Yeah, great. Wore it the other night."

"Good." Melikian lowered his voice. "Frank, I just got hold of an affidavit for the search warrant used to get into Ray's house. It describes the investigation in some detail, though there are black holes, too. You know, ' ... we developed information through a confidential source.' Anyway, it's twenty single-spaced pages, all the i's dotted and t's crossed, written by a DEA case agent, Enrique Hernandez."

"That's the name of the guy who took Ray in the warehouse."

"According to the affidavit, they'd been trying to get Ray to sell to them for a year. They approached him several times, but he wouldn't. So finally, realizing Ray was feeling backed into a corner, they thought *they* could sell to him and what turned out to be his partners. They posed a DEA agent as a representative of an organization, had him go by the name ..."

Frank's stomach rolled over. "... of Dean Miller."

"How'd you know?" Frank didn't answer. Melikian laughed. "How'd you know, Frankie?"

Frank couldn't pull a wisecrack. "I figured a couple of things out."

"You're good, Frank. You fucking amaze me. But you see what we've got here now, don't you?" Frank waited.

"If Ray really has no priors—you're checking that out, right?"

"Double and triple checking, Aram. It's in the works."

"If he has no priors and the DEA induced Ray to buy from then, we've got a real case for entrapment. Entrapment: induced the defendant to do something he ordinarily wouldn't do: no priors. It could fly. They did it with DeLorean."

"It could fly."

"It's the DEA, Frankie. Keep checking things out. The DEA makes up its own rules; up is down, down is up. It's Wonderland. Anything goes. So pay attention to everything." Melikian quickly went on to the bond hearing tomorrow afternoon, again ran through the possibilities of taking Buchanan to trial behind an entrapment defense. "Frank, the guy who sold to Ray, how'd you know it was Dean Miller? Had you seen the affidavit?"

"No."

"So?"

Frank still couldn't muster the right touch of bravado to play the thing out. "My job to know."

Melikian laughed. Lowered his voice. "Okay, someday you'll tell me. Bond hearing tomorrow at two."

"Wouldn't miss it for the world," Frank said dryly.

Melikian laughed and hung up. Frank glanced toward the stairs. Climb. In a minute. The familiarity of this moment. Over and over. First, an arrest. Chaos. Names. Police reports. Witnesses. Affidavits. Police tapes. New witnesses. New names. Rumors. Someone mentioned some-one else. A first name. Then a last name. Or just a street or an address. Someone talked to someone. Another name. It peeled back, was peeling back now. Just that he was in it. He stared up into the dark at the top of the stairs.

Frank took a seat in the back of a courtroom in the Hall. Several days earlier, Coleman, Buchanan, and Adams had been arraigned and pleaded not guilty. Bond had been set at $500,000 for Ray Buchanan and Jack Adams, $300,000 for Sam Coleman, who had been portrayed as a lesser player, a follower. Now the three were appearing before a magistrate for a bond hearing. They had just been led in, each in a prisoner's orange jumpsuit, each accompanied by a sheriff's deputy. Each had his own attorney. After the preliminaries, the proceedings got down to business. The assistant U.S. Attorney, Bennett Winters, got up and started a statement characterizing the defendants as major drug dealers who were well organized and financed. He portrayed them as leaders in a major West Coast drug ring.

As Winters spoke, Frank watched the three. Jack Adams, with his country club good looks, tennis player's tan contrasting with his curly blond hair, his shoulders and size dwarfing his attorney. Frank could see damp crescents of sweat under his arms. In a detached way, Frank thought, poor schmuck, he took the wrong moment to get involved with Ray. And Sammy, nervous, heavy beard dark against his pale skin, tortoiseshell glasses, looked like an adolescent, a manager for a high-school football team, who'd wandered into the wrong room. Ray remained motionless, face unreadable; he seemed to have a silent space around him and looked at a point beyond the magistrate as if thinking about something else. Frank thought that if Jack and Sammy had to go to prison, Jack, with his looks, and Sammy, a pushover, were dead. However it came down, he thought Ray would be okay. Ray was a survivor.

Winters maintained that each of the defendants, given the penalties they were faced with and their abilities to come up with large amounts of cash, were considered flight risks and believed their present bonds to be appropriate. Jack Adams looked quickly at his attorney. Sammy seemed to gasp for air. Ray drew quietly on a yellow pad and never looked up.

When the U.S. attorney finished, Melikian got up and did a convincing job of depicting Ray as a hard-working businessman and member of the community who had never been convicted of anything, had not even an outstanding parking ticket—and who could be released on his own recognizance. His client, Mr. Buchanan, was looking forward to all legal proceedings and a speedy vindication of his reputation as an honest and well-known importer-exporter of Indian and Oriental artifacts.

. The attorneys for Jack Adams and Sammy did more or less the same things, though neither of them had Aram's flow of words, his mesmerizing way of speaking. No matter what Frank knew to be true, when he heard Aram speak, he could feel himself fall under the sway of Aram's words. *This* was the truth.

Several rows up from Frank, a man sat alone. He had thick, curly black hair and mustache, wide shoulders, was maybe in his mid to late thirties. When Frank had first come in, he turned and looked back at Frank, a single, hard glance which measured and recorded Frank. With that look, Frank had the feeling the man knew or recognized him, and even before Frank had spotted his nine millimeter pistol, he realized that this had to be the case agent, the guy who'd led the bust on Jack and Ray and Sammy and called himself Hernandez. Frank had intuitively blanked his face and looked away as he'd sat down. Heart pounding, he'd thought, he doesn't know or recognize me. How would he know me? Surveillance photographs? Someone's verbal description? Frank busied himself with a yellow pad. He doesn't know me. Frank had not looked his way again during the entire proceedings, though throughout, he had been aware of Hernandez sitting several rows up.

As the last attorney finished speaking, the magistrate said that he would take the arguments of the U.S. Attorney's office and defendants' attorneys under advisement and notify the defendants of his decision in several days. Each defendant was led out a side door to be returned to the sixth floor, and after a moment, Frank stood and exited quickly. •

Frank had just finished going through the whole thing with Ray—Dean Miller's being DEA, bad break, yeah, but wait, Ray, cool out, Melikian is good and is going to make this thing work to our advantage, hey, I know how it sounds . . . Frank had gone on to explain Melikian's defense strategies on entrapment. They'd fallen silent and the silence stretched out, thickened, and something else entered the small room—calculation, mistrust, Ray trying to make up his mind. A heavily tattooed trustee in a lime-colored uniform pushed a laundry cart down the corridor on noisy, clanking casters. Ray followed it with his eyes, glanced back at Frank. He stood up. In a lowered voice, he said, "Frank, every day this thing changes a little—now there's this new thing with Dean Miller . . ." He trailed off.

"That's the way it always is, Ray. Just when you think you've got a handle on it, it changes. Almost always that way."

"A DEA agent. I was buying from a DEA agent. Unbelievable. And I thought I'd make bail a few days ago, but I see the bond thing is going to drag, too. And if it's too high, I might not be getting out at all." Ray weighed that, came to a decision. "Frank, I need you to do something for me. We go back. We've had our disagreements," he shrugged, "but we go back. This is important and I know I can count on you to work it out." Ray's eyes went to the window and he stopped speaking. Outside, a deputy had chained several prisoners in a row to take them down to their hearings. Ray paused. "Frank, I want you to move some money for me."

"When?"

"As soon as possible. Tonight, if you can."

"Your money?"

Ray nodded. "My money."

Frank realized they were almost whispering. "Where is it?"

Ray said, "You know behind my house? You walk off the back deck, walk straight, just go back, there's some land." Frank nodded. Ray placed his two index fingers side by side on the table. "Here's my flower garden . . . those big sunflowers?"

"I know."

"This side's my vegetable garden."

"Right."

"Toward the back of the property, and right in between them, there's a compost pit."

Frank laughed, short and abrupt. "You're kidding, Ray."

"Hey, where else could you dig without people thinking about it or noticing any fresh holes in the soil?"

Frank laughed again. "You actually have money buried in your garden. Jesus, even Nancy Drew hid and found things in more original places than in a fucking garden." Frank shook his head. "It's either very smart or very dumb."

Ray said, "If it's still there, it's smart enough."

Frank nodded. That was true. But a compost pile. Well, maybe not so bad. Out in the hall, the deputy moved the chained prisoners toward the elevators. Frank heard the cell-block door slam.

"Hey, if I'd left it where it had been a few months ago, we wouldn't be having any conversation at all now."

"Where was it before?"

"Safe deposit boxes."

"Why'd you move it?"

"I woke up in the middle of the night about four months ago—I thought I heard someone breaking into my house and going through my things—I couldn't get back to sleep. I started thinking about the Feds. First thing in the morning, I got in the car, spent the day going to my safe deposit boxes, getting everything out. So where else was I going to put it? Tell me, Frank, where do you hide money? In the end, one way or the other, you have to bury it." Frank laughed. "Yeah, laugh, but if I hadn't, the Feds would be sitting on it right now."

Christ, Ray, one of the most willful and pragmatic people he knows, does this on the strength of a hunch. He moves his money. Buries it. Maybe he just felt something in motion. Or, that he was making it happen, but couldn't figure out how. Or how to stop it.

Frank shifted in his chair. Go up to Ray's house, which has just been the center of a lot of late-night, unwelcome attention. Now probably has neighbors worrying and wondering. And watching. Dig. How? In the dark? With a light? Get a bunch of cash out of there without anyone knowing what was going on. "Ray . . . listen to me. Now is really not the time to be going near your house."

Ray said, "It has to be done now. It's risky, but you can do it. I'll take care of some things for you, Frank, when you need them."

Frank closed his eyes. Later when things cooled down would be better. Couldn't Ray see that? Frank stared at the concrete between his boots. It was just one thing, then the next. He glanced quickly at Ray who watched him. Four months ago, Ray'd had a hunch; he'd moved his money. Ray did these things. He'd been right about Dean Miller. Almost right. But he'd been wrong about something very big because he was in here in the orange prison garb of the San Francisco County Jail.

"Really, Ray?"

"What?"

"A hunch?"

Ray nodded. "Why else would I have moved it?"

Frank laughed. It was all too weird, too big. This whole thing had an inner life of its own. "Where do you want it to go?"

"Back into safe deposit boxes." Ray spelled it out, the new false names, the five new banks.

"This is going to be great, me driving around with a bunch of money. Specially after your investors' recent chat with me. What is it, cash?"

"Cash and gold coins, a few stones."

Frank realized they were still whispering. "How'd you keep the cash from rotting?"

"Tupperware. It's fine."

"Tupperware, Ray?"

Ray shrugged. "Big tupperware containers." Frank could only shake his head. "It's fine, Frank. Can you do it tonight?"

"Boom. Just like that?"

"You don't have to park or go too near the house. As you're taking the road up the hill, there's a pullout. You'll see a mailbox, says Paulson. John Paulson. Park. There's a little trail, it'll take you up the hill under some trees, and you come up onto the back of my property. You'll recognize those big sunflowers—you'll get your bearings. As you're going up the trail—maybe halfway up—you'll hear a dog behind a fence, he'll bark for a minute, but no one ever comes out and he'll stop after you go by."

"Okay, great, Ray. A barking dog. And do I bring my own shovel? Do I rent one when I get there? Do I . . . ?"

"Should be one in the compost pile."

"Totally gnarly. Should be. I'll bring a shovel. Jesus. How many containers are there?"

"Five."

"How deep are they buried?"

Ray held his hands up to his forehead. "About like that."

"How big?"

Ray held up his hands to measure. "Each is maybe the size of a small suitcase."

"What do you think they'll give me if they bust me with a mountain of cash?"

Ray shrugged. "They bust you, I'll get you a lawyer."

"Just don't get me Melikian. Hey, I couldn't afford him, anyway."

Frank stood and stepped toward the door. "How much is there, Ray?" Ray's face blanked over. Frank laughed, once, short, abrupt. "What, Ray, you're sending me out to do this, you don't trust me enough to tell me how much it is?"

Ray smiled ruefully. "Ten thousand short of five million—that's the cash. Then the stones and gold coins, they're something else."

"Does anyone else know, have suspicions, whatever?"

Ray hesitated. "There are the two you met on the sidewalk. I did worry about bringing those people in. They may try to even things by getting my money."

"This just gets better and better."

"There's a neighborhood watch association, too."

"This is great, Ray. Can we let it cool off?"

"Frank, it has to be done now. If you're careful, it'll be fine. Just move quietly."

"What, were you a member of the neighborhood watch association?"

"Yeah, matter of fact I was." Frank laughed. "I thought it looked good. And hey, you know, people keep an eye on my house, I keep an eye on their place, fine with me. You know, they were my neighbors. I liked some of those people, they liked me."

"Any Rambo types up there?"

"John Paulson's a hunter and a little right wing, but ... I don't know. I mean, he gets a few ideas when he drinks, but just pay attention tonight, go the way I told you, things should be fine."

This time, as Ray was led back into the cell block, he did something he hadn't done before. He turned and looked back at Frank. Was there a last question on his face? They were friends, but hey, it was five million dollars, and each new conversation was full of undercurrents. Standing behind the white line on the floor, Frank nodded once and then turned for the elevator.

As he rode down, Frank realized that right from the beginning, willingly or unwillingly, Ray had revealed more of himself in the last two weeks than he had in over ten years of friendship; was this, entrusting five million dollars today, getting to the heart of Ray? The doors opened and Frank stepped into the flux of the lobby. No, he suddenly knew, he'd be at the heart of Ray if and when he could come up with a snitch. If there was a snitch. When he had that name and knew how this thing went together, then he'd get his read on something. And know

what came next. Then, maybe, he and Ray would be somewhere together.

The rest of the day was shot for Frank. He kept his appointments, but couldn't keep his mind on what he was
doing and by three, he phoned Gloria and told her to cancel
out the rest of his afternoon and went for a walk through
Chinatown; he looked in the shops, jostled with summer
tourists on the crowded sidewalks, drifted over into North
Beach, and slid into a sunny table at a backstreet cafe
where he had a couple of beers and read the paper. Fighting off the urge for a shot of vodka, he headed for home.
   On the top floor, he leaned on the windowsill, stared
out across the rooftops at the light standards at Candlestick, the cranes on Hunters Point touched golden by slanting sunlight. He went to his closet and dug around, settled
on a pair of blue denim overalls, a blue T-shirt, a pair of
hiking boots which were worn thin-soled and coming un-
ravelled, and put them on. He tucked a complete change
of clothes—jeans, a dark shirt, underwear and socks, hightops—in the gym bag. He dug out a couple of fraying
beach towels, rolled and jammed them into the bag. He
pulled an aluminum pack frame out of the closet. He tested
a flashlight's brightness against his palm, pushed the light
into the bag. As he straightened, he noticed the room and
stopped. Half the space had finished oak flooring; the other
half remained, plywood subflooring exposed. The bathroom was roughed in, but needed to be sheetrocked. It had
all been happening and then somehow he had lost the
thread and it had stopped. And now, why bother? He
would never own this house. A long shot at best.
   Frank picked up the remote, turned on the TV, greased
through the channels, settled on St. Louis-Pittsburgh on
ESPN, and returned to the windowsill. Now everything
was slowly sinking into flat light under a deepening blue
sky. Frank pushed into the closet, felt around on the shelf,
and pulled out a Glock 17 in a holster and a .44 revolver.
He held one in each hand and put the .44 back. He listened

into the house, and then slid the nine millimeter out of its holster, released the clip, rolled the ball of his thumb over the top three bullets, snapped the clip back into place. Heard Farrell saying, "What, Frank, no piece?"

In the last five years, he'd carried a gun maybe three times. For Frank, guns went with movies, TV, "The Rockford Files," "Miami Vice," cartoons. And trouble. As he'd explained to John when he'd first interviewed and trained him, "No matter what you've seen on the tube, we write reports about people. We need to know where to find records. We do good preparation for interviews. The job is reading people—knowing when to talk, when to shut up. We write reports about people, we don't shoot them."

He felt the weight of the gun in his hand. He needed this now because, what? He was going to dig up some money. Drug money. Two of Ray's angry and enraged investors were on the loose. He remembered hearing a D.A. in a prelim saying about a defendant charged with possession and a concealed weapon, "Guns and drugs go together like love and marriage." At the time, he'd laughed at the D.A.'s felicitous use of hyperbole. So here he was.

The last time he'd carried the .44, he'd been going into the project alone and too late in the day. Common sense said come back tomorrow, but he was pushing to finish up. He'd been in a dark stairwell, when a voice said, "Stop right there and put your hands on the wall, white motherfucker."

Frank knew that he would never put his hands on the wall and walk out alive, and without making any decision, he'd fumbled out the gun, almost dropping it, and hands shaking with the adrenalin rush, letting himself fall to his knees, he put a couple of shots up the stairs. With the deafening concussion filling his ears, he'd taken off. In a clearer moment, he knew the incident had come out of his poor decision to go into the project at that time.

Guns blurred things. Day in, day out, he saw the results of that blurring. Poor choices, no choices, uncertain intentions. By the time anyone got around to actually using the piece, Frank got the feeling the trigger had been pulled years before. Tyrone Mayfield in that ice cream store. The D.A. said, "He *chose* to use heroin, he *chose* to go into a store, he *chose* to take a gun..." Aggravation. Frank thought: he *chose* to be poor, he *chose* to be black, he *chose* to live in the project, he *chose* to have his father absent, he *chose* to have his mother use crack.... Frank's doll house had saved Tyrone's life. Frank weighed the Glock. On and off for days after the stairwell, the tactile penetrating smell of gunpowder released itself in his nostrils.

Frank put the gun back on the shelf, walked around the attic space. He watched Vince Coleman take ball four on a three-two pitch and trot down to first; in another moment, Barry Bonds caught a fly ball and ended the inning. Frank got up and took down the Glock. What was he actually going to do with a handgun? Shoot Ray's irate investor goons? Who knew. If a cop came by checking out Ray's house, was he supposed to shoot him? Murder with a special circumstance. Killing a cop. Or, let a cop take him with five million dollars? How many times had defendants told him how much money they'd had seized and how much of it actually turned up in evidence? Okay, and if a neighbor came by from the fucking neighborhood watch association, what then? Was he supposed to grease one of Ray's neighbors? Just show the gun? A deterrent in the dark? And who am I? Well, I'm Ray's pal.... So who was he in this thing? Uncertain, Frank placed the Glock in the gym bag, thought of Farrell with a grim satisfaction. Happy, Farrell? I'm carrying it. I'm supposed to have passed the bar and be a lawyer by now and heisting all of this legally.

He sat on the edge of the bed with the TV on at his back, the evening darkness seeping into the room; overhead, the skylight, too, was filling up with night. "Shit," he said softly. "Shit."

It was still maybe a little early, even with the drive

ahead, but he had to get out of here before Karen got back. The bag would be unexplainable. Hi, where you going at this hour? He couldn't remember, had she mentioned a meeting after work? Wherever she was, he'd better get out of here before she got home. As with much of his life, the bag had become inexplicable.

He walked to the pair of front windows under the roof-peak, looked carefully up and down the street. Downstairs, he debated leaving Karen a note, gone to a movie, and then, thinking better of it, he studied the street. He returned once more, took a package of heavy duty garbage bags from under the sink, stuffed half a dozen into the gym bag, grabbed the pack frame, and then he stepped out onto the porch, and walked quickly up to his car. He could see Venus, the thin, watery gold paring of the waxing moon.

The light was still fading as he felt the enormous space open up on the Golden Gate Bridge, and he divided his attention between traffic and looking out at the darkening, windswept water—below, a container ship emerging from just beneath the bridge—the last dilutions of the afterglow below the horizon, and the dark mass of the headland of Marin. Beyond, the flash of the lighthouse on Bonilla Point. On the other side, the big tower pulsed above Alcatraz, the old monster sinking into windswept darkness. Once you were in custody, you were theirs and little could protect you from either the guards or prisoners. One of his defendants had been a jailhouse rapist, Darrell Smith. Six-five, two-fifty. Very white skin. A single tattoo of a hummingbird, red, blue and gold, hovering at a flower, like a flush on his forearm. One of the young prisoners had sued the prison system for failing to protect him. After resisting Darrell's advances, he'd been taken into an empty cell by prearrangement and beaten unconscious by another prisoner. Darrell had come in. "I could have saved you if you'd been one of my kids." Then he'd raped him. In the interview room, Frank, couldn't keep his eyes from drifting back to the hummingbird on his forearm, its flush of

colors, and once when he looked up, Darrell caught his
eye with a faint smile, and Frank knew that little could
have saved him from Darrell Smith. Coming to the end of
the bridge, he decided to get off 101 and drive through
Sausalito just to give himself a little more time to pull
himself together. Thinking of Darrell Smith, Frank knew
that if things went wrong tonight, or down the road, he'd
make bail, do whatever he had to do, but that he'd never
go to prison. He'd become a fugitive, flee the country. He
took the Alexander Street exit and wound down into the
privileged Victorian pastoral of Sausalito.

In Mill Valley, The Depot and its surrounding shops. Right
on Throckmorton, left onto Blithedale, he followed it up
into the valley, took a right, the winding roads taking him
in as he wound farther up into the valley, the sweet smells
of dry grass, eucalyptus, the cooling of a warm summer
day drifting through the car. He drove slower and started
watching the mailboxes, and when he saw the name John
Paulson, he spotted the pullout, stopped, glanced past the
mailbox for the trail, thought he spotted a break in the
foliage, and then turned off the lights. He slumped down
in his seat and listened. Crickets. Quiet. Houselights back
through trees on both sides of the road.

By now, Ray's neighbors had to have noticed DEA or
IRS agents, Sheriff's deputies coming and going, and no
Ray or Marla around; though it wasn't yet in the paper,
people always knew when something had happened. Frank
listened to the car hood creaking as the engine cooled and
made himself push open the door and get out. He collected
the shovel from the trunk, closed the lid quietly, and
reached into the back seat for the gym bag. He felt for the
flashlight, dropped it in one oversize pocket; he pulled out
the gun, hesitated, and feeling both foolish and unhappy,
dropped it into the other.

Frank crossed the road, found the mailbox, and walked
past it. He again looked up and down the road for the loom
of car headlights, took out the flashlight, and held it ankle

high. He flicked it on quickly right above the ground, found the flow of the trail, switched if off. Walking slowly and flatfooted against the unevenness and incline of the trail, he started up, occasionally stopping to listen.

He'd been walking for a few minutes and sensed the trail rising into a darker thick area—trees, vines—when suddenly there was an explosive jangling and barking and Frank froze and ducked. Stumbling, walking quickly, he moved ahead, one hand feeling beside him, the barking and racket following him as the dog threw himself against the length of a fence hidden somewhere behind the trees and undergrowth. The dog kept it up, frantic, snarling, and then, reaching the end of his run, growling, whimpering, he broke it off. Frank felt around for a minute, realized the trail was taking a switchback, and then, simultaneously, he felt the space open out around him. He made out the dark shape of the hillside. Below, he could see several houses through the trees, the houses some distance apart: back decks, people, tiny inside, TVs glowing, faraway music, a laugh suddenly rising.

After a few more minutes he saw the dark roofline of Ray's house. It was completely black, a dark shape. Frank remembered the house lit up, the sound of music and laughing, an intense glow to the lights, the presence of the women—their hair, their eyes, their smell—moving over his skin as if in a fever, Ray, standing off to one side, a glass of wine in his hand. Frank felt his way around. Trying several times with his hand cupped around the flashlight, he found the compost pit. Maybe ten feet in diameter and neatly covered with straw. Wishing he'd asked for more precise directions—the middle, the side?—Frank crouched in the approximate middle of the pit and carefully raked the straw back with his fingers. Then he took up the shovel, switched off the flashlight, listened, and feeling his back exposed, he began to dig.

The compost smelled of rich soil, the sickly sweetness of decomposing garbage, manure, and straw, and gave off a slight warmth, as though it were the low grade meta-

bolism of an animal curled up and sleeping. The digging
was easy going, and as Frank worked, he thought of Karen
and how he had taught her to garden in the first years of
their marriage and how, laughing, she used to walk into
the shoulder-high corn or pick up a squash, "What a trip,
Frank, who would have believed it, I'm so glad I married
you."

Periodically, Frank shifted his feet to the other side of
the hole and dug down farther. Or, suddenly, he'd freeze,
hold his breath, listen, look around in the dark, then go
on. When he was shoulder deep and drenched with sweat,
Frank felt the shovel hit something and skid. He stopped.
He pulled out the flashlight, and shoved the beam into the
bottom of the hole and there was the opaque plastic of a
container, comforting in its ordinariness. Cut by the shovel,
a huge nightcrawler writhed around on itself, disgorging
its black juices; some kind of white, many-legged worms
or grubs seethed into the dark compost.

Frank began to widen the bottom of the hole, checking
with his hand every few strokes to feel for the container.
After a few more minutes, he switched on the light,
reached down, and wedging his fingers around the sides,
he pried out the first container, and set it beside the hole,
just about eye level. He listened. He wiped his hands,
sweaty and caked with dirt, on his pants, shined the light
into the hole, and sweeping away another layer of dirt, saw
the second container. He widened the bottom of the hole,
removed the container, and placed it beside the first. He
dug sidewise and found the third container. In a short time,
he had removed all five containers. He hoisted himself up
out of the hole.

Crouching, he looked around and listened. He emptied
his pockets, stripped off his clothes, rolled them into a ball,
and tossed them into the bottom of the hole. Then, he
carefully filled the pit in, smoothed out the compost, and
replaced the straw. He felt into the gym bag, pulled out a
couple of garbage bags, and split the containers into them.
Carrying everything, he quietly approached the house and

then felt along until he found a spigot and hose.

He placed the gun on the gym bag, crouched naked, turned on the hose, rinsed off, and suddenly chilled and covered with goosepimples, he dried himself with one of the towels and put on clean clothes, slipped on his high-tops, tossed the towel into a garbage bag. Had he forgotten anything? He thought not. He also knew that anyone who had been paying attention to Ray's place—DEA, IRS, neighbors, or any of Ray's interested money people— would, if they were keeping an eye on things, know there had been a visitor.

He arranged the containers on the pack frame, lashed them on with duct tape, and carrying everything, he started down, periodically stopping to rest, or switch things around in his hands. It seemed to take a long time. Down off the open space of the hillside. Into the undergrowth and deeper blackness of the trees. The fence-rattling bark-ing dog, which again started Frank's heart exploding in his chest. After what felt like a very long time, he sensed the road, then saw the mailbox.

He carefully put everything down, and composing him-self, he stepped out into road. In the driveway light on the other side of the road—it hadn't been on before—he spot-ted a boy and girl walking behind a collie. The girl was maybe twenty, the boy a little older. Her face and lips had a soft, open vulnerability; the boy was quiet. He walked with his arm around her shoulders, she, her hand in his back pocket, cupping the shape of his ass. In that moment, before the girl called the dog quickly—Toto, Toto—and the dog stayed, Frank felt overwhelmed by a recognition and nostalgia for their closeness, simple lust and sexual belief, love? the summer night, silent and endless.

Keeping his face down, he said, "How ya doin?" in a soft voice. The boy said, "Okay." Frank saw the girl tighten her arm and turn her friend, and they started back down the road in the other direction. Toto. Toto, come on. Frank walked to his car. When he didn't see them in the mirror, he recrossed the road, felt for everything up on the trail, and quickly, in two trips, dumped it all in the trunk. He surveyed it—pack frame, shovel, gym bag, took a quick inventory of the garbage bags, five containers—and slammed the trunk.

Though it was just as Ray had said it would be, he was still incredulous. Five million dollars buried in his garden. A compost pile. And just left there, overlooked by the DEA. Unbelievable.

He pushed the Glock back under the front seat, started the car, Y-turned and slowly, started rolling down the hill. Pulled on his lights. Ahead, he spotted the girl and boy and her collie and as he came up on them, he hesitated, and then, on the off chance either of them, feeling diligent or nervous, was noting license plates, he killed his headlights. Running with only his parking lights, he passed slowly and rolled around a curve before he reached for the switch. Just as the lights came on, something rose out of the dark, the back end of a pickup, parked and angled too far out, he swerved, and just sideswiped the pickup with a loud grinding crunch. In the next moment, house lights came on back in the trees, and Frank floored it, taking the curves with his tires screeching. He was almost into the outskirts of town, driving a little too fast and trying to slow himself down, when he came up on a stop sign and a right turn. By the time he braked, he had rolled most of the way through the stop sign. Throckmorton and Blithedale.

In another moment, there was a blue strobe and siren, and Frank went blank and thought, floor it, go, GO, but another part of him said, it's just the stop sign, he doesn't know anything, the pickup, the money, nothing, pull over. Run and you're dead. Pull over, Frank. Bluff. Play the game. He placed his hands high on the steering wheel where the cop could see them. A spotlight came on, found its way through his back window, and squinting in the white light, blue strobe rippling, Frank waited for the cop and tried to figure out where he was sideswiped. The passenger side. The side away from the approaching cop.

The cop came alongside and shined his light in the window and Frank waited. Just let him lead. The cop shined the light on his face, asked for his license. Frank pulled out his wallet and opened it wide to show his investigator's ID. The cop glanced at it, then looked at Frank's face. Frank pulled out his license and gave it to the cop.

"Registration." Frank pulled his registration from the glove box and noticed his hands were shaking. The cop had his flashlight on his hands, and Frank thought he noticed, too. "Alright, Mr. August, step out of the car please." Frank stepped out into the spotlight. The cop looked him up and down. Frank noticed he was maybe late twenties. "Walk toward me." Frank walked toward him. "Walk away." Frank walked away. "Keep walking." Frank kept walking. "Stop there. Come back. Okay. Touch your hand to your chin." Frank touched his hand to his chin. The cop said, "I've been following you for the last half mile. Your driving's erratic. Speeding up. Slowing down. You just ran a stop sign. Where've you been?"

Frank knew it was going to be a breathalyzer, that it was going to get more complicated, that if he was going to go for it, he'd better go for it now. He knew the cop had seen his investigator's ID and taken time to read it. That might have made just enough of an impression: us and them. "I've been up visiting a friend, John Paulson." Frank gave the road. The cop's face showed nothing, "Officer, I understand, you're doing your job, I work with a lot of you guys—you know Dennis Farrell, Lieutenant over in San Francisco? Homicide." He shook his head, no. Frank ran through some names quickly. The cop didn't say anything.

Then Frank realized that he still had the faint odor of the compost pile on him and that the cop literally smelled him and knew something wasn't right, but couldn't quite define it; he could see the cop was nervous and was leaning toward Frank with all of his senses aware like an animal's trying to pick up something which he knew was there—some combination of Frank's nervous sweat, a ripe odor, something else which Frank was giving off.

He said to Frank, "Turn around and put your hands on the hood of the car." Frank did. The cop patted him down, found nothing. "Stand up and step back into the spotlight." Frank followed his directions. The cop took a flashlight and shined it into the front and back seats. Once again to the front seat where he held it on the floor and darkspace under the seat. Frank had slipped the Glock in there. Where it had skidded and ended up after winding down the curving valley roads, Frank had no idea. For police to pursue a search, the gun had to be in view. Which never stopped anyone. Whenever police reports mentioned guns seized in searches, they were always "in plain view." The flashlight beam moved around the car. Back to Frank's face. "Follow my finger." The cop moved his finger toward the bridge of Frank's nose until he was cross-eyed. He stepped away, walked toward the back of the car, hesitated at the trunk, and then something caught his attention. He shined his flashlight the length of the car. He ran his hand along the passenger side. "This is fresh. What happened here?"

"My wife did that yesterday. San Francisco parking." He shrugged, trying to suggest wives, parking, us guys, you know how it goes. The cop was having none of it. He stepped back out and shined the light into Frank's eyes, studied him.

"Stand here. Don't move."

Keeping his eyes on him, the cop walked slowly back toward his car and got in. Frank stood motionless in the spotlight, trying to look unconcerned, which was hard when you were both blinded and scared. He saw the cop start punching his license and registration into the computer. There were five million unexplainable dollars in the trunk which the cop had been thinking about opening when he'd spotted the sideswiped fenders and doors. That card had yet to be played. Frank squinted into the white spotlight. His heart was pounding.

After a long time, the cop opened his door and walked

toward Frank. He handed him back his license·and registration. "Get in your car and go."

Frank nodded. "I really appreciate . . ."

The cop leveled his index finger at Frank and said in a barely restrained voice, "If you say one more word, I'm taking you in. Get going now before I change my mind."

Frank turned, got in his car, and drove.

Back through Marin. Back across the Golden Gate Bridge. Lombard. Van Ness. Mission. Relieved and exhausted, he wound up to Holly Park, and turned into his street, which was completely parked up. He cruised slowly by his house, dark. He looked up at the second-floor attic windows. Blinds closed, the room appeared dark, but Karen could be reading with the halogen light.

Pulling over, he double-parked and quietly let himself in. He walked through the darkened first floor room, into the kitchen, and stood by the staircase. The door was slightly ajar. He peered up. Dark. And quiet. He listened, walked back through the house, opened the trunk, and grabbing the tupperware containers, he walked quickly through the front door, down the hall, and opening a closet door, he felt around in the dark, pushing things back; he dumped them in the back of the closet and pulled the door closed. He reopened it and smelled. Compost. Pushed the door closed.

A few minutes later, he returned from parking the car, locked and bolted the front door, and placed the gun out of sight on the topmost shelf of the floor to ceiling bookshelf. In the bathroom, he started a shower; he opened the window, extricated a pint bottle from behind the tub, took a few hits. He leaned on the windowsill and peered out into the dark, the steam rising at his back and drawing out over his shoulders into the night. He watched it dissipate into the air. Then he stepped into the hot shower and groaned as the last hours and days uncoiled in him. He felt his legs give way to exhaustion, then his whole body, and he sat down under the stream and closed his eyes.

In a thick terry cloth robe, he turned on the small tube, settled on a movie. He felt for a chair and sat in the dark. Karen's steps creaked as she descended the stairs. She came toward him, put her hand on his cheek. "Where've you been so late?"

"Looking for a witness."

"Couldn't call?"

"Once and for all, gotta get a car phone."

"Find her?"

"Him, Karen. A two hundred and fifty pound Samoan. Once I got him going, he talked for two hours. You interrupt people with phone calls, they start having second thoughts about what they're saying, clam up."

She smoothed his cheek, kissed him, hesitated. He suddenly knew she must smell the vodka on him. She didn't say anything. Christ, once again, he hadn't really drunk. Okay, he'd had the equivalent of a shot—two shots; he'd had a drink, but he wasn't a drunk. Yes, once in a while he did get drunk. But that wasn't the problem. It was her constant thinking the worst which was bugging him. He didn't have the energy for it now.

"Got a statement and got him to sign it before he changed his mind."

"Good, Frank. We seem to be missing each other again."

"Once this big case clears out, we'll have time."

"Jeanette flipped when I told her I was quitting. Did I tell you that?"

"No, wish I could have seen her."

"More like hear her." They laughed softly. "She went world-class ballistic." Karen put her arms around him. "Frank," she said quietly. "Please . . ." She didn't say anymore. Frank put his arms around her. He felt awful.

"I'll be up in a few minutes, babe. I just need a second to sit here and unwind."

"I wish I could sit with you, but I'm exhausted. I'm going up."

"I might just watch a few minutes of this movie."

She kissed him lightly on the lips. He would have given anything not to have the sting of vodka on them. He wanted to say, it's not what you think. No point. He listened to her steps creaking up into the dark on the stairs, heard her walking overhead. Somehow their timing was completely off.

He retrieved the gun from the shelf and lay down on the sofa in the middle room. Hiding the gun in the cushions by his hand and covering himself with a blanket, he dozed. He started awake, felt for the gun, dozed. Several times he went to the front and back windows to look out and finally he fell into an exhausted sleep which was thick with broken, low-ceilinged rooms and anger. He had the money.

Dressed, Karen said, "What, how'd you end up here?" Chill morning light in the window behind her.

The TV was still on. "Just couldn't sleep." He pushed himself up on one elbow, felt the gun slide against his back. "Didn't want to wake you." He smelled coffee.

"I've got to be at work. Jeanette's taking every opportunity to make me miserable in these last days. I'm trying not to leave her openings. Why couldn't you sleep?" He shrugged. "Frank, you're taking on too much, you're killing yourself. And the last couple of weeks, even when you do sleep, you thrash around, you groan, you sweat; a couple of nights ago you called out, 'Dad!' You should get a physical. You're exhausted." She looked at him, her eyes moving back and forth over his face. "I've got to go." He sensed everything she was holding back. She leaned forward and kissed him, stood quickly. She started down the hall, then stopped. "I don't want to wear these shoes." She kicked them off, went to the closet. "Seen my gray flats?"

Frank blurted, "They're upstairs!"

Karen hesitated. "No, I looked. I think they're in here." Karen pulled open the closet door. There were the five tupperware containers piled in the back. Frank suddenly groaned and grabbed his stomach. "OH! Christ, Karen, help me!"

She turned. "Frankie!"

"Oh, shit, babe. . . ."

"What?" She kneeled beside him, panicked.

"Please. . . ." he groaned. "Upstairs . . . in the medicine chest. . . . There's some Alka-Seltzer and a codeine."

"Frank, we don't just mask pain. . . ."

"I know. Please. . . ." He lay back on the sofa, holding his stomach. Karen ran through the kitchen and up the stairs. Frank leapt to the closet, pushed the containers as far back as they could go, and looking wildly around, grabbed a sleeping bag, unzipped it, and flung it over the containers. Tossed a jacket and a poncho over protruding corners. He fell back on the sofa just before she returned with the Alka-Seltzer, codeine, and a glass of water. He groaned. She raised his head, dropped the Alka-Seltzer in the water, helped him swallow the codeine. "Promise me you'll take the morning off and see a doctor."

"I will, babe, I absolutely will."

"What do you think it is?"

"Maybe some tacos I ate yesterday, funny little tacorea over on Valencia. Not too clean. Must have been."

Karen smoothed his hair. Kissed him. "If I go, will you be alright? Call me in a couple of hours?"

He nodded. Distracted, Karen stood, once again approached the closet, and confronted the jumbled contents. "Sleeping bags, a poncho . . . just a mess." She picked up a shirt and hung it on a hanger. Frank groaned suddenly. "Oh, God, Karen. . . ."

She turned. "Frank. . . ." She toed aside a fallen jacket. Her gray shoes. "I knew they were here." She slipped them on. She crossed her arms, shook her head. "Frank, this closet is such a tangle. We have to make more time for ourselves to take care of the small things like this—to make room for us. Well, can't now. Always not now, not now." She closed the closet door.

She kneeled beside him. "I know you're overworked,

but let's take an afternoon off, drive up to Tennessee Valley, take a picnic. In another few days I'm through working for Jeanette, then I start my new job. It's a new life. Let's enjoy our lives together.''

Holding his stomach, Frank lay back on the sofa and nodded. He could feel the gun pressing against his back. She kissed him again, went down the hall, and then she was gone. He stood, placed the gun on the kitchen table and spat out the codeine. He poured himself a cup of coffee, reconsidered, and then took the sodden codeine tablet. Why not? He didn't feel all that great. Upstairs, he pulled down several cardboard file boxes. Then he went to the front door and picked up the *Chronicle*. A four-column headline: *Major West Coast Drug Ring Smashed*. Below, there was a picture of a smiling U.S. Attorney, James Rhodes, a microphone in front of him. Press conference. Late yesterday afternoon. He sat at a table surrounded by local politicians and law enforcement officials. The table was piled high with stacks of money. Bales of marijuana. Scales.

Frank skimmed the story. High quality . . . sophisticated methods . . . large   volume . . . ingenious. . . . There   was nothing he didn't already know, except that Ray was being portrayed as the ring leader, which was going to make things tougher. Believed to have handled over 100 million dollars in the last ten years. Yesterday's bond hearing. . . .

Frank walked slowly back toward the kitchen table. Maybe he had gotten the money just in time. Ray right again. Frank closed the doors to the middle room, locked them, and hung a sheet over each window. He wiped the five plastic containers clean with a damp towel and pushed back the sofa and coffee table. He vacuumed up the crumbling dried compost.

He put together the cardboard files and a stack of the 9"×12" boxes, and then opening the first container, and cutting through the layers of plastic, he checked the money. Everything was in good condition. He laid out the packages of bills—stacks of hundreds—fit as many as he could into the 9"×12" boxes. Then he started on the next container. One container had a small pouch with unset diamonds. Another, a box of gold Krugerrands. One held a simple envelope with pictures of a couple making love in a number of positions. Their faces weren't shown. Frank was sure the woman was Sarah. Overwhelmed with a steep and unanticipated arousal, Frank flipped through the prints, maybe thirty-six color shots, probably taken with a camera mounted on a tripod with a time release; he put the pictures back in the envelope and placed them in his pocket, and then he took out a stack of hundreds. He counted out fifteen thousand dollars, hesitated, and stopped. Fifteen.

He looked at it. What the fuck. This would do it. Pay John, kick in a little extra to smooth things out. Apologize. It wasn't too late. John was a good guy. Money would grease it now. Then he could pay Kramer whatever he owed him for his work, plus the three hundred bucks he'd borrowed, four months on that, and then bring Gloria up to date. Pay a bunch of back bills. Hold onto some so he'd have enough to put the business on hold, let his money come through the pipeline from lawyers and the courts. Shut down in a couple of months, take time off, and do a full-time study for the bar exam, this time blanket the thing and pass and stop fooling with it. Once he was a lawyer, his schlepping street days would be over. He'd sit in his office and send someone else out. He'd be home free.

He saw himself standing in that cop's white spotlight. Walk toward me. Touch your chin. The cop leaning toward him, picking up on whatever he was giving off. Good cop. But he'd let himself get distracted for a second. Like Ray. If the cop had been just a little better than good, Frank would be in jail right now. Hey, the fact was, Frank knew he was pretty good, himself; he had pulled it off for Ray. He'd toughed it out with the cop. Ray owed him. Frank glanced at the boxes of cash. A little gold. Some diamonds. He saw himself and Gina. Boston? Would that be far enough? London? Or go with Karen? Someplace English speaking. Maybe Australia or New Zealand. A law office, a new name.

Fifteen K. Ray owed him that much. And Ray would never miss it. He stood, shoved the fifteen thousand into his pocket. Where now? Everyone was out there: the Feds, the DEA, the IRS ... there was no way he was going to deposit this money. Anyway, anything over ten grand had to be reported to the Feds by the banks under RICO. If they were watching, they'd see new accounts. Upstairs, he opened and closed drawers, spun around here and there; he couldn't leave the money around with Karen, either, not with her going through his things. No way. Confused, he divided the money into roughly two stacks and shoved it into the toes of his cowboy boots. He'd think of a better place later.

Downstairs, he placed the balance of the cash in five ordinary, cardboard file boxes. He uncovered the windows and changed into a blue suit. He hesitated, then put on a shoulder holster, and fit the Glock into it, which showed like a tumor. Ridiculous. He changed into a pair of slacks and Melikian's oversized English shooting jacket, which finally served some purpose by enveloping him and the gun. If Aram could seen him now....

Frank looked down at the boxes and then impulsively, he opened one and refilled a tupperware container with cash. He cursed, took off the jacket and gun, and went down the back stairs to look for his shovel before he remembered it was still in the car trunk. He looked around his yard, studied the place where other years there had been the large vegetable and flower garden. Dried and overgrown. He walked to the back fence, looked over into the neighbor's backyard. Their shovel leaned up against the back door. He hoisted himself up on the fence. When he reached the top, he had one of those clarifying wideangle lens views of himself and his life which froze him: good slacks about to catch on a nail; five million bucks on the floor in the house; the Glock he didn't want to use anyway out of reach on the kitchen table; the neighbor's shovel thirty yards away; and a carved up Richie Davis hanging upside down in a tilting house with fifty-six thousand dollars in cash surrounding a pool of his blood. Frank lowered himself carefully back into his yard.

He spent the rest of the morning taking all of Ray's money to five different safe deposit boxes and putting it under false names as instructed. As he drove toward his office, he could feel the pressure of the keys in his pockets. There no longer seemed to be much of a question of his taking the money. He just didn't want to be stupid about things. It was more a question of when. With the money, he could start over.

Frank buttoned and smoothed his jacket as he stepped into the small courtyard behind his office, deadbolted the door to the street. In the hall, Gloria was just backing out of the office. "Don't bother locking up, Gloria."

She turned. "Ah, Frank, I'm just breaking for lunch. I've left all of your messages on your desk. And I have an address you were looking for—the skip trace—Sarah Anne Gillette."

"Nice going. How'd you do it? Wasn't through postal forwarding, that's for sure."

She shook her head no. "You thought she might have a sister in Sacramento and that turned out to be true. Tracy Gillette. I told the sister I was her Allstate Insurance agent and that Sarah Anne had cancelled her policy; we wanted to mail her a refund."

Frank laughed. "That's good, Gloria. You're catching on."

"You taught me that one. Sarah Anne has no phone— or at least none that's being given out. But Tracy gave an address. It's all there on the desk. What case is this?"

"Oh, it's nothing—witness in a small criminal case, but she had to be found. You're the one person I can always count on." Frank reached into his wallet, pulled out a twenty. "Have a nice lunch."

"Frank . . ."

He pushed it into her hand. "Go somewhere nice with a view, take a couple of hours. Eat an avocado salad and an enchilada for me. Well, actually, if it's for me, better make it three enchiladas."

She hesitated, then leaned over and kissed him on the check. "Thank you, Frank. That's lovely of you."

"I have my moments."

She went down the hall. As she reached the door, Frank said, "Those names I gave you the other day. Adams. Buchanan. Coleman? Criminal charges or previous convictions?"

"I'm still checking. So far I've turned up nothing in San Francisco County. Nothing on Adams in Southern California. They look clear."

He nodded and waved her out, went in and shuffled through his messages, found Sarah Anne's address. Pacific Grove. Maybe three hours south. Would kill the better part of a day on a round trip. What was she doing in Pacific Grove? He folded the note into his wallet. He looked at John's empty desk. He picked up the phone, dialed John's number, hung up before it rang. He'd pay John, the turkey, but now, Frank decided, he'd let John sweat a little for squeezing him like that. He knew John desperately wanted his job back. Yeah, it would make life a little tougher for Frank not to have him, but he couldn't just let John get away with that.

He flicked on the stereo, studied the ficus. Still losing leaves. "Goddamnit." He felt the soil. Dry. He shook his head and scooped up a handful of the dried leaves. Last year about this time Ray thinks Sarah Anne's on to him. He takes a calculated risk: damage control. He tells her everything. She hears him out and goes crazy. This she extends to include Frank whom she fucks on a floor in a hallway to add the right element of squalor, and thus to prove a point to herself; that he would screw his buddy's girl and that she would screw her boyfriend's buddy, or however she saw it: people really *aren't* nice. A few days later, she's gone. A month, six weeks later, one of Ray's

big cargos is taken by the Coast Guard. Coincidence?
Frank sat back in his chair, watching shapes moving past
his windows, and absentmindedly fingering the safe deposit keys in his pocket. It was time to see Sarah Anne. It
was also time to go reassure Ray that his money was safe.

Frank handed Ray the envelope and watched his face. Ray
slid out the first pictures, glanced up at Frank, looked embarrassed, smiled uncomfortably, pushed the prints back
in. Frank shrugged. "Somehow says it all."

Ray said, "I'd forgotten about these." He closed the
envelope, slid the pictures back to Frank.

Frank dropped them in his pocket. "They'll be safe
with me."

Ray smiled at him. It was the first time Frank had seen
Ray really smile in here. "How was it?"

"A little spooky. Actually, I almost ended up in here
with you, courtesy of some nervous driving and an almost
smart cop. Everything's safe."

"Okay, Frankie." Ray stood. "Okay. You did it for
me."

"I can't stay. I've gotta take care of a few things. Just
wanted you to know. You saw the article in the *Chronicle*
portraying you as the Great Ringleader." Ray nodded.
"It'll make the going tougher, but we'll still find a way.
I'm working on a few things."

Ray nodded. They started for the door. Before they
reached it, Ray put his handcuffed hands in front of Frank.
"Frankie . . . I know you clipped a little. How much?"

"Five, Ray."

"Okay, Frank, you got ten. Fine. There's more for you
when you get me the snitch. Twenty more. But Frank . . ."

Ray looked at him: precise blue eyes. For an instant
Frank saw something he'd never seen in them before, felt
something he'd never felt from Ray. It jolted from his
stomach and chest, a sudden feeling he wasn't quite catching his breath when he said a little more quickly and
hoarsely than he wanted, "Hey, buddy, what do you think

I am. I'm taking risks for you. I'm trying to save your ass in here.''

"I know. But five million cash is tough for anyone. Just be careful, Frank.'' He stepped back. "After you. I've got no place I have to be just now.''

Frank went out the door first. Whatever he did about the money, he knew he'd have to think it through. He'd just seen someone he'd never seen before in Ray.

The first diffuse gray light was seeping in the windows as Frank started awake. Reluctant to separate from Karen's warm body, he slid out from under the covers, and naked in the chill room, walked to the front window; if he saw a light in Kramer's house, maybe he'd go over. He had to talk to someone. He looked up and down the street and saw someone moving near the corner—Kramer, wet suit over one shoulder, surfboard under his arm. Thirty-nine years old. He loved Kramer for this. Kramer slid the board into the back of the pickup, dropped his wet suit in the cab, and was gone. Frank turned from the window, dressed quietly, and as the white light rose to the windows, he stood motionless over Karen.

Lips slightly parted, she breathed softly. He watched the taut surface of her eyelids ripple like a startled school of fish. Her small features were so simple, open, and pretty as she slept. She hadn't, he realized, asked him again about the bar exam; she seemed absent, resigned. Wasn't this how she'd been just before she'd moved out four years ago?

He straightened and walked quietly across the room. God-damnit, he should at least get some carpet remnants and cover this half-floored room. As he reached the stairs, he hesitated, shifted his weight to the firm section closest to the outside wall, and stepped down. Something he was forgetting? The Glock was back on the shelf. The five safe deposit keys were under a loose floorboard in the closet, his shoes on top. He looked over toward her closet, where her two bags had remained packed. Since February. He

hadn't ever said anything to her about them, but he was
always aware of those packed bags. Things were going to
be better with her new job, but . . . he realized as he stood
on the first step that he was half hoping for her to stir and
call him: Frank. Step by step, Frank went quietly down
the stairs.

He pulled into the McDonald's drive-thru, ordered breakfast, the food tasting of styrofoam, and then, the lidded
coffee hot between his legs and warming his crotch, he
pulled out and picked up 101 South. Driving fast, running
up behind cars and forcing them to give way or changing
lanes himself, Frank slid through traffic. San Mateo. San
Jose. Then the Santa Clara Valley opening up, he headed
toward Gilroy, swung west, and wound through the low
coast range. As he slipped down into a thick, early morning fog, the temperature dropped, and the windshield
beaded and streamed with condensing moisture. He pulled
on his headlights and heater, and slowing, felt his way
along. Monterey. The fog thickened, thinned out in
places—a disembodied field, a house, a tree appeared—
closed in to where he could barely see beyond his hood.
Then patches of the main street of Pacific Grove—early
morning, deserted, Victorian. A pair of diffuse headlights
floated toward him, the outline of a car appeared, drifted
away. Frank pulled over, studied a map across his steering
wheel, and then rolled forward. Beyond, he could see the
fog swirling, and sensing an enormous space, he realized
that beyond the road, there was nothing—the vastness of
Monterey Bay, the Pacific. From somewhere, the sound of
a fog horn. He drove carefully, getting out several times
to locate house numbers before he found the right address.

He checked his watch—almost eight. From what he
could make out, the house appeared to be a large, well-
kept Victorian on a rising lawn close to the street. Did she
have a room or apartment here? And what did you do in
a town like this? From across the road, he could hear the
sound of waves, hypnotic, slow, so close he expected he

could look down and see them lapping at his feet. And from somewhere, he heard a voice, Charlie or Carlie, and then a laugh. The fog distorted the sound and he had no idea which direction the voice had come from. Wiping the moisture from his chin, he started up the walk.

On the porch, he leaned toward the double doors, peered in the window. Someone had just come down the stairs, and opening a newspaper, was walking down a hall. Frank looked up: a thickly carpeted staircase, steep; a varnished oak bannister. Frank watched the unknown person disappear into an interior room, the far wall rippling with light.

He stepped inside. Soft voices at the top of the stairs, footsteps. He moved quietly down the hall to a front room with several long tables, a log fire throwing heat and light into the room. Several people talked quietly and helped themselves to coffee. Frank said to the nearest woman, "Excuse me, I need to make a delivery—Sarah Anne Gillette—is she here?"

The woman, straight silver hair, makeup, eyeliner, too purple eyeshadow—what was it like to do all that before eight a.m.?—looked Frank up and down, and then pointed toward a door close to the fireplace—leather, heavy brass tacks top and bottom, a polished plate; Frank pushed the swinging door and stepped into a kitchen—gas stove, mixing bowls on a counter, bacon and eggs frying, muffins rising in an oven, and a woman with long hair, her back to him at the stove. She wore tight jeans, an apron around her waist, a pullover. She glanced up. Black hair with a purplish sheen. Something incongruous. It was her, but her hair had grown down below her shoulders and . . . she'd dyed it black. Jesus. Beautiful and weird against her pale skin and blue eyes. He wouldn't have recognized her. She stood motionless at the stove, and then, the bacon spattering, she jumped slightly.

"How ya doin, Sarah Anne?"

"Actually, Frank, dispensing with all of the niceties—" he'd forgotten how her hoarse voice turned him on—"like hello, how are you, what are you doing here, how did you find me, I'm not great at this very moment."

"Not anything to do with my walking through the door, I hope."

"No, but about twenty-five people are on their way down to breakfast, they're heading up to Monterey Acquarium, and neither of my two highschool girls has shown up this morning."

"Not running a house of ill repute?"

"A bed and breakfast."

Frank took off his leather jacket, pulled on an apron, and looked around the kitchen. "I cooked breakfast, lunch and dinner for two years at a resort." He went to the sink, washed and dried his hands, and studied a menu. "There's no handling money. It's all paid up, right?" She nodded. "Okay. I'll be right back with the rest of the orders. You okay with this?"

"Frank, can you really cook?"

"I can cook." Frank smoothed his apron and walked out into the dining room, put another log on the fire, and he moved from table to table taking orders. In the kitchen, he started cooking blueberry and buckwheat pancakes, laying out plates on the counters, filling coffee carafes, ducking out to serve, until things were going along at a high speed. As things progressed, they started clearing tables. Occasionally, they'd brush by each other at the stove or counter in the quiet, easy rhythm of flirtation.

As the dining room cleared out, Sarah Anne came in, gave him a couple of last orders, and then, putting her hand on his shoulder, she kissed him on the cheek. "You were great. Make yourself something."

"What's yours?"

She put down several plates. "I'm not too hungry."

Frank made them breakfast, and they poured coffee, checked the dining room once more, and pulled up stools at adjacent sides of the island. She put her hand on his.

"Thanks again, Frank. You're good." He shrugged. "What are you doing here?"

"Came down here to help you cook breakfast." She smiled and shrugged. "Actually, I'm at a death penalty seminar over at Asilomar. Lawyers, investigators."

"And you were just driving by?" Frank nodded. She shook her head no. "Frank, I'm not in the phone book or under information."

"Sarah Anne, I had some work to do up toward Sacramento the other day and remembered you once said you had a sister up there. She gave me the address, I realized I had this seminar down here . . ." he shrugged.

Sarah Anne got up, pushed open the dining room door, returned. "There's a straggler out there." She went back to the stove and put on a couple of eggs and pancakes. She still had that tight dancer's walk. She made a plate. Refilled the coffee carafe, their coffees, again went back out and returned, brushed her hair off her cheek. "My sister gave you my address?"

"She shouldn't have?"

Sarah Anne tipped her head. "She never gives my address out."

Frank nodded. "I feel the same way, myself." He waited, but she didn't say anymore. "You let your hair grow out. And dyed it."

"I felt like a change."

"It's a change. If I hadn't been expecting to find you here, I wouldn't have recognized you." Frank took a swallow of his coffee. "Make you feel different?"

"From what?"

"Well, good question. From before?"

"Before what?"

Frank shrugged, let it go. "I could use a change. Maybe I should grow a beard." He sniffed. "What's that bad smell in here. I get whiffs of it. Acrid."

She pointed at a wall gas heater. "That's Charlie. He's supposed to be neutered, but he sprayed on the heater, which is great every time I turn it on. Nothing gets the smell out."

Frank realized he was getting nowhere. He liked her.

He pushed ahead. "Heard from Ray lately?"

"No." She flushed and her face closed. She shook her head slowly. "You know, I had such a good feeling about you a minute ago even though your story doesn't make sense—the way you just came in here and helped me— but now, it's a bad feeling knowing it was this."

"One thing doesn't have to exclude the other. I was glad to help you."

She shrugged.

"Sarah, you could help me. Have you heard from anyone else?"

"You mean connected to Ray?"

Frank shrugged. "Whoever."

She didn't answer. Frank went over to his jacket and took out the front page article. Watching her face, he placed it in front of her—the front page picture of the U.S. attorney. She picked up the clipping, studied the picture, and then started to read. After she reached Ray's name, she glanced at Frank with a panicky look. Still sitting, she hunched over the article, both elbows on the table, palms cradling her cheeks, her hair falling forward. Frank realized that she had hidden her face completely and he could no longer see her expression. When she finished, she asked, "Is he okay?"

Frank said, "Is being in jail okay?"

She pushed the article toward him. "Is this why you're here?"

"I've been over at Asilomar."

She said, "The death penalty seminar at Asilomar is in a week."

"I like to settle in early."

"I get a schedule of events and read it closely. It's my business to know what groups are in the area."

Frank said, "Good. Then let's stop dancing and talk. You're with Ray a few years and everything goes along fine with his business. Then Ray tells you about his real line of work last September. Apparently, it didn't meet your expectations or approval. You leave. Six weeks after he tells you the truth about himself, the Coast Guard takes a ship. Ray's cargo from Thailand. They don't get Ray. They haven't figured out how to pull that off yet. But they put a big hole in his economics. Major. And that's step one. Step two is he doesn't dare make a move. And when he does, finally, gee whiz, there they are, just waiting. I find you here, almost a year later, you've dyed your hair, you've crawled into the bucolic woodwork . . ."

"Just go."

"You know, Sarah Anne, anybody can do anything. I see it all the time. You made a a very definitive point of showing me that. You're Ray's girl, but you and I end up on the floor together . . ." He stopped. This wasn't what he'd meant to say.

"Out, Frank." She pointed at the door.

"If you'd do me, why wouldn't you dime Ray?"

"Catholic guilt poisons your world," she said with hatred and conviction. "You've got it written all over you. As one who spent twelve years in parochial school, I know when I'm in the presence of it. And if *you'd* do me, why wouldn't *you* dime Ray?"

Reeling in confusion from her outburst, he recovered enough to say, "Listen, I knew you were upset that day we ran into each other in North Beach, but I didn't understand what it was all about; now I know. I even sympathize. Someone you love turns out to be not quite the person you'd thought or hoped they were. You wouldn't be the first person who dialed 88-CRIME on her boyfriend."

She turned her back on him and walked in the other direction, reached the stove, stood with her arms crossed. "Just leave, Frank," she said in a low, flat voice.

He reached for his jacket. Dropped his card on the counter. "I'm sorry to upset you, Sarah Anne. I always liked you. If you want to talk to me, there's my number." She picked up the card and flung it after him. Halfway through the dining room, he realized he was still wearing the apron; he slipped out of it, folded it over once neatly, and laid it across the back of a chair.

Outside, Frank squinted. The fog was burning off with a blinding, silver-white glare, and he could see down the bluff and just make out a stretch of cove beach and the water, gray and gelatinous with the thin beginnings of blue. It was hot and cold, clammy and humid, all at once. He sat in his car, shaking his head, wondering if the way it had gotten out of hand had been completely his fault or if she hadn't been primed for something emotional—he *had* walked in on her; she had buried herself down here and she *had* changed the way she looked; people did that all the time. But the moment he'd shown her the article, he could feel the chemistry change: high pitched. Her. Him. You'd do me. A real mistake on his part. He felt engulfed by her voice, ". . . Catholic guilt . . . you dime Ray . . ." He started the long drive back.

Pacific Grove seemed another country, another life. A couple of hours ago, he'd arrived home to the close, mid-afternoon silence of the house, the phone ringing, Gloria, reminding him that tonight was the Golden Dragon at six.

He glanced at his watch. Now ten after six, and Kramer, June, Zack and Karen were all late. From here, they were supposed to leave for Chinatown and be in the Dragon by six-fifteen. These scams were starting to wear him down. Still, he had to get this right or he'd look like an idiot. The Golden Dragon: two partners, and Duane Chin, the silent partner, suspected the other, who was also the manager—Delores Woo—of pocketing cash and skimming a lot of the profits. Chin's lawyer had hired Frank a while ago: get me some proof, do it any way you want. Frank had decided to kill two birds with one stone. He'd put together this dinner, inviting maybe twenty-five people, and on the way, he'd make this a celebration of Karen's last day of work for Jeanette; he'd pay back invitations; schmooze a few attorneys; court a couple of others; and overall look like a good guy. He would feed six hundred dollars of Chin's money into his own restaurant, pay the check in cash—he'd xeroxed the money to make a record of the serial numbers—and then see if or how much or where the money showed up in the books, or if, as he'd suspected, the money mostly disappeared into Delores Woo's pocket. He'd get the dinner receipts for proof, write his investigation report, and that would make Chin's case.

On the porch, he glanced over at Kramer's. No one. He looked for Karen's car. What a moment they'd all picked to be late. He'd give it another five minutes and then leave without them. In the bathroom, he reached behind the tub, found the bottle of vodka, unscrewed the lid. Felt the pressure of the mouth against his lips, but didn't drink. He replaced the bottle, put on water for coffee. He called the Golden Dragon, asked for Delores Woo, and when she came on, he identified himself and told her to go ahead and seat and serve people as they came in—appetizers, drinks, put it all on his bill.

Then everyone was in the kitchen at once. Frank and Karen, Kramer and June and Zack. Frank extended his hand. "Low five, dude-san." Zack slapped his hand. Frank hugged the boy.

Karen said, "Frank, I'm really sorry I'm late, but there was an accident on Hospital Curve, tied up everything." She sang and did a little dance. "But this was my last day with Jeanette." Frank hugged her. June and Kramer clapped. "Do I have a minute to change?"

"Go for it, Snookie-Okums."

Frank turned off the boiling water, poured it into the filter. "Coffee? Kramer? June?" They shook their heads no. Frank took a scalding swallow, another. "Ready for a free meal, Kramer?"

"Always."

"Listen to him, always. How're you doing on People vs. Bledsoe?"

"Moving along. Ashanti's got a sister named Marvella. Spoke to her this afternoon."

"And?" Kramer and Frank had drifted toward the

kitchen window. "Ashanti's got two other sisters, both whores, as it's turning out."

Frank wiped the sweat from his forehead. "Ashanti's a ho, bubba."

"Yeah, you were right."

"Proving it, that's the game."

"Here it is from her own sisters."

"None of em would make the greatest witnesses, but it'll never go to trial now. Plain English is Bledsoe's gonna beat it. So Curtis, he luck out, dude-san. And he didn't cop a plea. Deadly stupid, but I kind of like him for it, actually. Did you get statements—get em signed? You know, close on it?"

"Well, that was the catch. Marvella's trip was, yeah, we'll tell you anything here. Let me write it up as a statement, but wouldn't sign it. They laughed at me."

"We'll have the last laugh. And I'll give it to you. We'll go back and you can serve them subpoenas, we'll threaten to put them on the stand, say they're whores, their sister's a whore . . . We've got you to testify what they told you and you won't discredit too easy. Bledsoe's attorney will run the scenario back to the prosecutor: bitch be a ho, we got half the neighborhood'll testify, her own sisters. People vs. Bledsoe is history. Hey, great going, Kramer. If someone walked in the door now and offered me a thousand up front, we'd turn Ashanti into a white virgin from Kansas."

Frank checked his wallet for the sting money. His heart and words were speeding half a step ahead from two cups of coffee; he was rolling; as they stepped out on the porch, Frank reached down and took Zack's hand, "Me and you, dude-san, we're in the street now, pay attention. I got your back, you got my back?" Zack nodded. Zack's small hand in his, Frank suddenly wanted a son.

They walked in a straggling group up the street toward the car. With the slanting sun catching the roof peaks, the soft blue sky overhead, a dinnertime silence, Frank knew things were going to work. He was going to bag Delores Woo; Duane Chin's attorney would be happy, kick him back some Chinatown cases; the thing with Curtis Bledsoe was just about a done deal; he'd stop fooling around and pay John, get him to come back to work; there'd be some breakthrough in this thing with Ray and who knew? maybe Melikian and he would walk Ray, too. Somewhere out there was the five million, and he'd know when and what to do about that when the time came.

He held Zack's hand and watched Karen just ahead. Her face was flushed, her eyes bright, and he knew she was lit up over the sting. The fact was, bitch at him as she did, his hustles, which were really necessitated by his business, she fed off and loved his schemes, always had, always would. Just wouldn't cop to it. Frank looked down at Zack and squeezed his hand gently.

At the car, Frank pulled out a bottle of Windex, washed the windows with comic ceremony, piled everyone in, and they wound down toward Folsom. Karen held Zack on her lap, smoothed his hair, kissed and joked with him, her high mood spilling out into playfulness and affection. Frank and Kramer kibitzed front to back seat, the Giants, Dodgers, Cincinnati, cases, and at the same time Frank thought ahead. He'd have to remember to pick up the dinner check receipts. They'd be his evidence. With twenty-five people, there would be three or four checks, maybe more. Duane Chin characterized Delores Woo as being shrewd and suspicious. A big party like this, she'd be watching him. Under the pretense of seeing if there was a separate room which could handle his group, he'd stopped in sometime back. Made-up, manicured, coiffed, in perfectly tailored clothes, he knew that nothing got by her; she had given him a close look. She might know something was up tonight, play it straight and run all the money into the books where it belonged; if she did that, he'd look like an idiot: nothing missing. If he fucked up, then what? He'd never get to do this again without making her impossibly suspicious. It would be better to let Karen pick up the receipts, maybe pretend he was a little drunk and didn't know or care what was happening.

The light changed. "Karen, listen to me," he said in a low voice, "I want you to do something ... you listening?" Tickling Zack, she nodded, and Zack squirmed and laughed. "When we leave the restaurant, pick up all the dinner receipts." Karen and Zack giggled. "The receipts. And the itemized strip from the cash register. Everything they have in writing, get it. If she asks, just say it's a business expense."

Karen nodded and smoothed Zack's hair back, sniffed his scalp. "Oh, this kid smell's so good. What a sweetheart." She wrapped her arms around his chest and held him tight, and Zack sat back against her, the wind riffling his hair. Karen, Frank knew, wanted a child—both of them did—but there was always some intangible obstacle. Ahead, Frank saw a parking garage and pulled in not far from where Green and Columbus came together.

Inside, a waiter led them up an ornate staircase with a wide red railing and stylized, elongated golden dragons as balusters and directed them to a smaller dining room. Half of it was sectioned off with Chinese screens and behind them, four large tables were already filled. Frank could see a round of appetizers and drinks had been served. As he came into view, there were calls and a smattering of applause and whistles. Hey, Frankie. Frank let himself be taken into the ebullient mood of the room, making the rounds, shaking hands, smiling as he was introduced to wives, kids, joking with everyone.

Delores Woo, lacquered and sprayed, every hair in place, appeared with her head waiter, and Frank coordinated the ordering, and then continued to move from person to person and table to table. He sat in his place as a beer came, raised it, put it down. He never drank in front of Karen. Not anymore. He stood and continued to circulate. Delores Woo sat at a table off to one side, and oversaw the party, the waiters, the delivery of food. In a short time, a parade of waiters arrived with trays full of steaming platters. Plates and bottles and more dishes came and were cleared away. Occasionally, Frank glanced over at Karen and could see that laughing, eyes bright, she was giddy, and from time to time, he'd catch her watching Delores Woo's face, fascinated by the thin line of deception.

Eventually, the party wound down, and people started thanking Frank and straggling away to get kids home to bed. Frank circled behind Karen's chair and whispered, "Okay, I'll be sending Delores over to you—pick up the change. Keep it separate from other money. Take care of things like I told you." Karen nodded.

When the dinner checks came, feigning drunken indifference, Frank dealt out a pile of cash, and then, suddenly excusing himself, said, "Bathroom? My wife will pick up the change." He waved vaguely toward Karen, and smiling indulgently at Frank's drunken carefree attitude, Delores Woo nodded. Good, Frank thought, pocket the whole thing tonight. Make me a winner.

Pleased, happy, Frank drove out of the parking garage. He knew he'd pulled it off. After Chin's accountant had gone through the books, Frank would be kind of curious to know just how much she was screwing her partner. But write the report, bill it out, hey, he was done with Duane Chin/Delores Woo—unless, he had to testify down the road. Unlikely.

Beside him, Zack was nodding off to sleep on Kramer's lap. From the back seat, Karen squeezed his shoulder and he touched her hand. They drove up Stockton. Once, bright headlights pulled up right behind them, and Frank knew it was Ray's investors back, but in another few blocks, whoever they were turned off, and Frank calmed down, and finding a place to park, Frank and Karen said their goodnights.

In the kitchen, Frank sank into a chair. "Whew, I'm whipped, but we did it. Better give me the paperwork now while I think of it."

"What?" She was in the other room.

"The receipts. The strip from the cash register. And the rest of the change." She came in and counted the change onto the table. "That's what Delores Woo gave you back for change?"

"Exactly." She leaned over and gave him a deep kiss, moved against him.

He laughed, kissed her back, fought off a sudden rise of desire. "Uno momento, por favor. Where're the receipts? The total from the register."

"What receipts?"

He looked at her. "You were supposed to pick up the receipts for the dinner. The strip from the register. I told you on the way down. 'Pick up the receipts. The strip from the register.' "

Karen took a deep breath, blinked and kept her eyes closed. "Frank, I really don't think you told me to pick up the receipts."

"Karen, please. You were tickling Zack. You nodded. And then again, on the way out, I said take care of things like I told you. You nodded again."

"I know, Frank. Take care of things—I wasn't sure what you were talking about. Then Delores Woo gave me the change and I thought that was it."

"I told you in the car on the way down. Pick. Up. The. Receipts. You nodded! What were you nodding at?"

"I don't remember. There was so much noise and confusion in the car, everyone laughing, the radio on, you and Kramer talking, June telling me something. . . . Frank, God, I'm sorry. Can I go back down and get them?"

Frank shook his head. "It would tip her off, tip her off in red neon letters. She's canny. She'd put every cent of that money into her books."

"Okay, Frank, please don't get so upset, what if you don't have the receipts?"

"My client doesn't have a case—they're the evidence; I've just wasted six hundred bucks of Dennis Chin's money, blown my fee, made myself look like a half-wit, dumped future referrals in the crapper, and there's really no other way now to catch Delores Woo red-handed since I can't put on that little circus twice.''

"I really don't think you told me. You know, Frank, when you pass the bar exam you won't have to be fighting these battles all the time, you can come up out of this. Did you hear on it yet?''

"Look, Karen, now's as good a time as any. I didn't pass. Okay?''

"You just found out?''

"I found out a few weeks ago.''

Karen sat down. "Oh, Christ, Frank, I knew something was bothering you. I should have known it was this.''

"Yeah, the bar. I was looking for a good time to let you know. There's never a time just to sit down and talk.''

"You're smart enough. What is it, you don't want to put on a suit every day? You don't deserve to be a lawyer and do better?''

"The fact is, Karen, you didn't pick up the receipts tonight when I asked you to and you said you would. And I failed the bar—and not by much—because I work full time. Big mystery here.''

"Day by day, I feel like I'm losing you to something—alcohol, secretiveness, scams. You bring it into the house with you every time you come in; you're followed by another presence. It clings to you like the smell of smoke.'' She turned from the window. She took his hand. "Frank, you're looking for boundaries, the impossible; you're trying to make booze your limit, your father and your mother. You can't beat them. No one can. They've got you whipped.''

He took back his hand. No matter what he said, he couldn't convince her he wasn't really drinking. He drank a little, but he wasn't really drinking. This was *her* fear. And somehow, he always played into her hands.

"One of these days you're going to have to stop playing the control game . . . let go. Trust. It will be an enormous weight off your shoulders. But you've got to take that first step.''

Absentmindedly, Frank pocketed the change from the Dragon. He did have the xerox of the money he'd passed Delores; maybe he could bluff Chin's lawyer with just that.

''I watch you, Frank, and you're amazing. You keep all these balls in the air at once. People, business, cases. And you keep everyone out where you want them. Me included. You let me know just what you want me to know.'' She drifted into another focus, almost talking to herself. ''You're so good at giving everyone a different story and making them believe you. So good. I sometimes wonder what would happen to you if we could get all the people with all your different stories in the same room at the same time.'' She fell silent and contemplated that thought. ''With so many stories, do you know what to believe about yourself anymore?'' She picked up one of the cats, turned. ''You stay with me, Frank, because I'm the only person you can't con and you don't know what to do with that. The day you could con me, you'd leave me.''

Frank said, ''Karen, tonight earlier, we're going down the street on the way to the restaurant, and I see your face—you're happy, you're excited, it's the sting—and I know you wouldn't have it any different from me. It turns you on.''

She sighed. ''I want things to be the way they used to be with us. I want us to have time together. I want us to have a flower and vegetable garden. We've always had a big garden. I loved doing that with you. What's happened?''

Frank shrugged. ''We both work full time.''

''We worked full time when we planted the garden.'' She started for the stairs. ''This was supposed to be a celebration of my last day working for Jeanette. Coming up?''

''In a minute.''

She went up a couple of steps and then stopped. She half turned back. Without looking at him, she said, ''And

I think there's something—something big—you're still not telling me."

He had to love Karen. She knew she hadn't gotten it all, the thing she'd been looking for in his dresser drawers, wherever else. Gina. And something more. Ray. And he knew she wouldn't quit until she found it. Was tonight's mix-up her fault? Or his? Hey, he'd asked her to pick up the receipts. But maybe he never should have. It was all so tangled.

Head down, Frank was on his way up the stairs in the Hall. "Jesus, Frank . . ."

Frank jerked to a stop. Dennis Farrell. Their heads were a foot apart.

"Sorry, Dennis."

"You almost ran me over. Always take the stairs at a half-gallop with your head down?"

"Only on Tuesdays." Shifting a couple of files, Farrell looked him over. They eased toward the back of the landing as people moved up and down at the blind turn.

"You look terrible. Color. Circles under your eyes. Maybe it's the hours or the company you're keeping." Farrell said, "Allow me. . . ." He reached out and straightened Frank's tie, then half turning Frank around, untangled the back which looped out from under the collar. "You talk to your defendant, Ray Buchanan?"

"As a matter of fact, I have."

"And? He have any answers to my questions?"

Frank hesitated. He wasn't ready for this. When Ray wouldn't admit to knowing anything, Frank had tentatively made up a few answers to Farrell's questions just to give him something. But then, who knew, maybe Farrell had tossed in one or two ludicrously false questions to catch Ray out. Frank wasn't ready to pull it off. "Dennis, the truth is, my guy says he knows nothing."

"Surprise."

"Yeah, I know how it sounds, but I read him as telling the truth. He really doesn't know." Frank shrugged.

"What can I say? I didn't guarantee anything. I said I'd try. I could have lied. You'd never have been the wiser."

"Maybe, maybe not."

"I'm leveling with you."

"Okay, relax, Frank. Maybe I shouldn't do this, since you've got nothing, but down the road you'll do something for me—won't you?" Frank nodded. "Ray Buchanan was on Davis's disks—there were ledgers. So when the code got broken, the DEA started to watch him. Your client, Ray Buchanan is a major dealer. Millions, Frank. If he's telling you he wasn't involved with Davis or dealing, he's lying. That's what you said you wanted to know, isn't it? If he was on Davis's disks."

"It helps me straighten out my case, deal with his attorney, you know?"

"All too well." Farrell gave Frank a peculiar smile. Was Frank in the DEA computer? If so, had Farrell picked up on it? "Anything else I can help you with, Frank?"

Frank shook his head, no. "Thanks. That's a big help."

"I'll bet. Hey, I'll see you around, Frank."

"What do you drink, Dennis?"

"I don't. Why?"

"Thought I'd give you a bottle of something. Christmas."

"It's July. We've got a long way to go to Christmas." Farrell started down the stairs.

"Dennis."

"Sir?"

"What *did* happen to Richie Davis?" Frank wanted to hear Farrell's version of it. "I read in the paper he was pretty beat up."

"Davis wasn't just beat up. When we found Davis, he was hanging upside down from a rope over a beam in his living room. Someone spent a long time carving him up with a very sharp knife. Maybe Colombians. That's their kind of business. Or maybe it was someone who wanted it to look like Colombians. A long time carving, a long time dying. He was bled like a sheep. We needed boots to walk in the living room. There was money lying all around him. Wasn't robbery. Not with that kind of money left.''

''Not robbery. So?''

Farrell shrugged. ''Davis seems to have been a quick study who got bored easily and started dealing. It got bigger and bigger. By the time we found him hanging in his living room, he was dealing everything big time.''

Farrell shifted his files to his other hand, hitched up his pants. ''You know, some of these guys, they get so much money, it's like they float out into space, they lose all connection to reality.''

Frank shrugged. ''And?''

Farrell said, ''Colombians front their coke and float their dealers large loans. You sell off some coke, you pay off your loan. I think Davis stopped paying off his loans. Without knowing it, he thought he'd got so big he could say fuck you to anyone. So they came for him. Whoever did it took their time. And left the money lying around Davis's body when they finished. They wanted their message to be clear: *You* don't say fuck you to *us*. *We* say fuck you to *you*. You've been around awhile, Frank. I'm sure you know what we're talking about here. Anyone else out there who's getting ideas thinks twice.''

Farrell turned, then said, ''Frank, I think you're a bright guy.'' He became thoughtful. ''Sometimes we get tired, overworked, make some bad decisions when we're tired. Listening?''

''I'm listening.''

''Maybe get some sleep, relax a little. Take a few minutes, get your tie on straight in the morning. You know what I mean.''

Dennis turned and started down. Against his better judgement, Frank said, ''If you thought it was Colombians, why did you have me talk to Buchanan?''

''Why not? It was a freebie. And who knows, maybe I'm wrong. Maybe it wasn't Colombians. Anybody can get a rope and a sharp knife. The case is still open.''

Farrell turned and went down the stairs. Frank looked

after him. Bad decisions. Get some sleep. Was he on those
DEA files or not? Farrell seemed to be warning him he
was. But then again, maybe it was just Farrell playing his
avuncular games.

At home, Frank replayed his answering machine. A
long, early-morning message from Melikian. In a hearing
late yesterday afternoon, Ray's bond had been reduced to
three hundred fifty thousand dollars—the magistrate had
originally wanted five hundred thousand. Jack Adams and
Sam Coleman were each set at one hundred thousand; the
prosecution was still portraying Ray as the ringleader. Melikian would take care of the bond details.

Frank and Ray rode the elevator down from the sixth floor,
Ray now dressed in slacks, a shirt, and sports jacket. The
doors opened, Frank touched Ray's arm and pointed, and
they went through the lobby. Outside, Ray stopped; he
squinted, shaded his eyes with his hand, and turned his
face up to the sky. "Whatever happens, I'm not going back
in there." Frank nodded. Ray took a deep breath.

"What do you want to do first?"

"This may sound weird, but all the time I've been in
there, I kept thinking I wanted to see the horizon."

"Poetic. We take a drive out to Ocean Beach?"

Ray nodded. "That's good. That's really good."

"Over here." Frank steered him, and they started an-
gling across the parking lot. "On the way, maybe we
swing by the Marina, check out that sublet I told you
about—I was supposed to let the guy know. He's a friend
of mine. If you want it, you got it. That's one less thing
you'll have to worry about. It's furnished. All you've got
to do is pay the rent and take the key."

As they drove across town, Ray, elbow out the window,
looked at the women, shaking his head, his long black hair,
which had grown over his ears, blowing back from his
head. Ray said, "Hey, I gotta get a coffee. You?" Frank
nodded, handed him a twenty, and Ray bolted from the
car into an espresso shop. By the time Frank circled the

block, Ray was back with a bag of Italian pastry and two coffees to go. Frank laughed at Ray wolfing the pastry, licking the filling from his fingers, crumbs falling in his lap.

"Frank, you know, I'd like to stop and get some shampoo and if this place is decent, just get it right now, take a shower and scrub the fucking sixth floor off me."

Frank swung by Safeway, waited while Ray went in, came out a few minutes later with a bottle of red wine, shampoo, blades, Dove, and a large bottle of Scope. They parked over at the Marina, and Ray stood looking at the lush green in front, the boats, their hulls incandescent with waterlight. A hard afternoon bay breeze was blowing in and kites plummeted and fluttered, and beyond, sailboats clearing the calm inside the breakwater, raised their sails and heeled into the afternoon chop. They walked across the Green and Frank found the condo. Inside, the manager took them up. The apartment was sunny and open, well furnished, and had a view of the Bay.

The owner being a friend of Frank's, they dispensed with the credit report and deposit, went through some paperwork, and the manager gave them a key. After he'd left, Ray opened a door, and looked in at a row of suits, jackets, and slacks. "Melikian tells me the Feds will let me go up to my house one of these days and take my clothes and a few personal things out of the house." He went into the kitchen and opened a couple of cabinets until he found glasses. He poured Frank a large glass of wine, took the bottle, and went in to take a hot shower. Frank put the wine on the counter, looked out from the balcony at the Green, and then returned and took a big swallow.

They went down into the sand, and chill wind blowing back their jackets and shirts, winding their pants around their legs, they made their way across Ocean Beach and stopped where the recent high tide mark had darkened the sand. A fine mist silvered the air, and the wind-driven waves exploded, blinding in the sunlight. They walked down the hard-packed sand, avoiding the occasional long reach of a wave. Neither talked. A park ranger came silently cantering down the beach and Frank and Ray stopped to watch, the horse's hooves throwing sand.

Ray said, "That wouldn't be too bad a life, would it?"

Frank shook his head, no. He wasn't sure either of them believed it. They walked on, Ray stopping to pick up a lightbulb, a snarl of monofilament and a lure, a wooden spoon—and reluctantly discarding each. Then they turned around and went back to the car.

Ray glanced at his watch. "I said I'd meet Marla in front of the apartment at four-thirty. I don't want to be late."

"What're you going to tell her?"

He shrugged, "I have no idea. I kissed her goodnight two weeks ago. I was supposed to be gone a few hours. A while later a bunch of guys kicked in my door with drawn guns." He shook his head. "What do I tell her? It won't happen again, honey?" They started back through Golden Gate Park. "What do you think my chances of beating it are?"

Frank shrugged. "I'm still checking things out. If I can give Melikian some ammunition, maybe he can get a plea. You've got no priors. You had no guns with you. If he can plead you, and with parole, who knows. You go in, you come out. Maybe you do, what, for a first offense, three, four years, maybe less with parole when everyone stops the bullshit. Maybe Melikian gets you a medium security federal prison; it will be different than the sixth floor county jail, you get to lift weights with a nicer class of guy, a mayor, a city manager taking kickbacks. . . . Don't make me speculate now, the cards aren't all dealt."

Ray said, "I can't go back to prison."

"Slow down, Ray, this afternoon you're out. It's great. You're out for a while."

"You've got everything in the safe deposits . . . The keys are put away safe somewhere?" Frank nodded. "Hold the keys for now. Until I see what's what, they're probably safer with you than me. Maybe they're safer with you anyway. Those guys who said hello to you represent some people who make me very nervous. I know they'll be watching to see where I go, what I do.''

"They like me, too.''

"If I can't beat it, I'm going to eat the bond, take everything in the safe deposits, disappear.''

Ray wasn't usually impulsive, but it sounded like he'd go on short notice. Maybe Frank would have to make up his mind within an hour or two of Ray's call. Take the money. Where would Frank go? He had to start figuring it out. Frank said, "The Feds thought you were a flight risk.''

"I hate to make the Feds right about me twice, but I can't go back in.'' They passed the Arboretum, the beautiful lawn, the flowers, the white glassed structure. "Been in there, Frank?''

"Oh, yeah, nice, isn't it?''

"Green and mysterious. Just beautiful. I'd build myself one and live in it if I could.''

"Look, for the time being, you don't have to make any decisions. Let Melikian work the case. That's what you're paying him for. Maybe we'll come up with something. I found an illegal wire tap in a smaller case of this kind a couple of years ago. That threw the thing out. Fruits of the poisonous tree. Nothing here yet, but you never know what you'll find and we're just starting. If Melikian can't pull anything off for you and you still wanna run,'' Frank shrugged, "cross that bridge then. It means being a fugitive for the rest of your life.''

Frank wanted to go when *he* was ready, not when Ray panicked. Again Ray became silent. They were approaching the Marina. Frank saw Marla's car pulling up.

"Frank, whatever happens, I want the name of the snitch. You've got to do that for me. Don't humor me.'' Ray put his hand on the door handle as Frank parked.

"Ray, don't get out. Sit back a second. Let me tell you something. Once and for all. The DEA got your name through Davis's disk. I've had someone who headed the Davis case look at the DEA file.''

"Who?"

Frank said, "Just trust me on this. I got it. It's reliable.''

"But who told you?"

"Someone you can't approach, Ray. Trust me." Ray was getting impossible. He couldn't give Ray Dennis Farrell's name. What was the point, anyway? "Ray, man, I can't tell you, or I'd never get anything out of this guy again. You don't need to know who on this. Please.''

Ray sank back in the car seat and stared ahead. At the other end of the block they could see Marla. Ray pulled Frank's rearview mirror to his side, "Look like shit," he said. Ray pushed the mirror back. "Was it Sarah Anne? Level with me, Frank?"

"What do I have to say to make you believe me? The DEA. Dean Miller was DEA. It all fits.''

"Are you trying to protect her?"

"Oh, look, Ray." Frank shook his head. "Get together with Marla now, relax, we'll talk later." Ray looked at Frank, his small blue eyes blank with disbelief. He turned away and smoothed his hands through his hair. They remained silent. They watched Marla coming down the sidewalk. Frank didn't know her well enough to read her expression. Ray pulled open the door. Frank opened his fist and held three thick, tightly rolled joints in his palm. Ray looked at Frank. Smiled an ironic smile. Took the three joints and dropped them in his jacket pocket.

"Thanks." Ray glanced down the sidewalk. "Frank, it may have been the DEA that did me . . .''

"It *was* DEA. Please believe me on this.''

Ray nodded. "I believe you." There was a hard gaze of obstinancy on his face. "But there was also someone else in it. Find her. Or him. Or them. I know this, Frank, or else I'm wrong and crazy about everything. Remember, I can't recover what I lost of yours, but there'll be more money in it for you." He swung his legs out of the car. "And hey, I'm not kidding, watch yourself.''

Marla reached the car. Ray reintroduced them, and she leaned down into the car to nod hello. She was better looking than Sarah Anne, but she didn't interest him. As far as he could see, she was just a pretty girl. There was too much strain in her to do more than force a smile, and it suddenly dawned on Frank that he, they, were all getting older. Frank checked his rearview mirror as a car came up too quickly. Passed. A day hadn't gone by that he hadn't regretted taking this fucking case.

Frank fit the second key into the deadbolt, pushed open the door and stepped into the dark front hall, and then, hearing something—a door opening, a footstep?—he stiffened. Karen? He opened his mouth, but didn't call her name. Nettled, one of the cats came quickly down the hall, crooked its tail, set its ears back.

He took a step, another. The small TV lay on its side near the back door. He looked up, listened. His Glock and .44 were upstairs on the closet shelf. He hoped. Christ, he'd hate to get blown away with his own guns, although, perhaps as slight compensation, he probably would never know they were his. On his immediate left, the door to the back stairs was closed. Had he left it like that? Impossible to know. If someone was hiding in there, better to leave it closed and let him hide. Most likely he—or they—just wanted to get away. Although, if they were coked or dusted, there was no telling what they'd do next. Bobby DuChan. Tyrone Mayfield. Kill you.

The back door was wide open. He quietly crossed the kitchen and looked into the yard, across the back fence, and into the surrounding back yards. No one. He glanced up into the scraggly hackberry tree branches. He recrossed the kitchen, opened the closet in the front room, and reached in for an aluminum softball bat. He walked to the stairs.

Feeling terrified, gripping the bat with both hands and holding it raised, he started up the dark stairs. As his head came level with the floor, he stopped, raised the bat higher.

He looked into the darkening room. The big TV was right in front of him. There were drawers dumped out. Clothes and junk scattered everywhere, the mattress thrown off the box spring. Either he went up or down. He stepped up in a quick crouch, crossed the space to the closet, and jammed the bat into his clothes, pushed into the bathroom, and in another moment, was in Karen's closet. No one. Becoming aware of glass crunching underfoot, his hoarse breathing subsiding, he went to the sink and gulped cold water from the tap, splashed water in his face, and walked into the closet. He groped on the shelf. One gun. Both guns. He picked up the Glock and walked to the front window, checked the street; at the back window, he surveyed the patchwork of backyards and decks. He walked into the bathroom and took a piss, not quite as satisfying as he'd first anticipated.

The room was torn up. He put down the gun and waded into the stuff, trying to figure out what was missing: Karen's Nikon, which had been on her dresser. Also, her camcorder. They'd snatched her cameras, but missed his guns. Glass in their picture frames was smashed. He could feel the fury which had been brought into the room. Someone very high, very crazy, very angry, very frustrated, and then some. Then he remembered the fifteen grand and froze. He'd stuck the money in his cowboy boots. Sick, he walked into the closet. The boots were gone. He sank to his knees, groped under his clothes, searching wildly and haphazardly through the room and house until, in the middle of the kitchen, he suddenly let go and lay on his back on the floor and groaned.

After some time, broken images, in what passed for thinking, started coming to him. Cop cars in the street a couple of weeks ago. Mrs. Santos. Crack burglars. Blood coming up the hill from the project. He returned to his closet. Heart pounding, he kneeled in the back and pried up the loose plank. The five keys to the safe deposit boxes. He put them in his pocket. Crack burglars. Or someone, those two creeps, looking for something—the keys to the safe deposits? Did they even know anything about safe deposits? If they'd been watching him, they'd seen him make his run to five banks that morning. So was this for real? Or staged, someone trying to make it look like crack burglars?

Frank placed the .44 under the plank in the closet, and pushing the Glock into the back of his pants, turning on lights as he went through the rest of the house, he walked up the street and crossed over to Mrs. Santos', rang the bell. One of her teenage sons answered and Frank asked for his mother. She nodded, a vague, neighbor's greeting as she came to the door. Frank said, "I heard you were burglarized a few weeks ago. How was your house? I mean, was it very messed up?"

"Not too bad. A few things dropped or knocked over. The back door was forced with a crowbar. I had to have a carpenter and locksmith. It's still not right."

"But the house wasn't too bad?"

"No. Someone come in your house?"

Frank nodded, yes. Mrs. Santos was, of course, very sympathetic. They talked a moment, Frank thanked her and started back up the street, went into his house. Fifteen thousand gone. Five million left. Then, remembering Otis, a former defendant, he made a phone call.

Frank couldn't have said he was crazy about the guy, who called himself Doc; he was a small, Camel smoking cracker, maybe forty, with a seamed smoker's face, a Southern drawl, and long brown hair combed, pompadour and ducktail, into a glossy perfection which had stopped square in the middle of 1956's Heartbreak Hotel Memphis. When he'd walked in, Doc had smiled, squeezed off a shot at him with a pointed index finger. "Frank something. Dude who bought the .44 last year." Now Doc stood with his back to Frank and studied a rack of shotguns. Several lay across the counter.

Frank said, "Maybe Remington. Semiautomatic. Something with a choke." Frank waited as morning sun caught

Doc's Camel going up in smoke. All in all, last night had not been fun. The upstairs had been pretty well pulled together by the time Karen had come in, glass swept up, big TV reconnected to the cable and tuned to a ball game. He'd told Karen a while after she'd come home happy from work. Her first day on the new job and she went out the door singing. He didn't describe the mess, the sense of unleashed fury. He had followed her up the stairs. "Let's call the police."

"What're they going to do? There are dozens of police reports filed like this every day and tossed in a bin. There's absolutely no point, specially because we don't have insurance."

They'd gone around on that and then it had just drifted off unresolved. Exhausted, they had more or less given up on the day, and had slept badly, tossing, turning, Frank with the Glock hidden under the mattress on his side. He had no sensation of sleeping, and the night had seemed endless, every house and street sound resonating as an image, a confusion, the two creeps with their tire iron over him turning into Bobbie DuChan. . . . Several times Frank had found himself standing at the front or back window looking up and down the street or into darkened backyards lit only by a neighhor's outside light; and Karen had said, "What's happening, Frank, what *is* happening? Why do you keep getting up?" And he'd mumble, "It's okay," return to bed, and slide into that same twilight.

Just before he'd left the house, Karen said, "Frank what *is* happening?"

"Remember those crack burglars who did Mrs. Santos' house a few weeks ago? It's them. Gotta be. Hey, I'm glad we weren't here." He took her hand. "Just as long as we're together and stay together, I know everything can be alright."

Halfway down the street, he realized he'd forgotten his briefcase, and as he pushed open the front door, she hung up the phone suddenly—he thought he saw her jump— and ducked into the bathroom. She closed the door. A moment later, he heard the lock snap and the shower start. Sometimes Karen was so weird.

Now Doc walked toward him with the shotgun, lifted it to his shoulder, and then eased it across the counter to Frank. "Remington 1100. Semi. Choke. Twenty gauge. Four in the magazine, one in the chamber. Sweet gun. When the chips are down, you don't need to aim. You just put up a wall of lead." He mimed quick pumping action from the waist.

Frank turned away from Doc and raised it to his shoulder. Felt right. Good balance. He checked it over. Pumped it once. Pulled the trigger. Laid it on the counter. This was the one.

Doc said, "Going bird hunting?"

"Eventually."

"Make sure you don't get caught out of season. Fine's stiff. Mind, I ain't saying don't hunt out of season. Just don't get caught." He laughed, his hoarse squeezed laugh.

"Let me have a box of shells, too. Double O buckshot."

"That's not bird shot."

Frank said, "These are big birds."

Just as Frank was getting ready to go, Doc said, "You know something?"

"Probably not."

"I think you're gonna shoot some cans."

"Yeah? Cans?"

"Afri-cans. Puerto Ri-cans. Morro-cans," Doc started laughing, "Domin-i-cans . . ."

"How about just plain Ameri-cans?" Frank started backing up toward the door.

"Yeah, good for that, too."

"See ya round, Doc."

Frank walked toward his car. One thing he knew for sure. There was no way he was again walking into his house empty-handed under yesterday's circumstances. Or anywhere else. And he wasn't going to be relying on the hit or miss of a handgun.

He glanced at his watch and drove fast. He was pretty sure Otis would wait, but then, why push it. He was relieved when he saw him at Dolores and 19th. Frank barely slowed enough to give him time to get in, and then Frank was driving fast.

"S'happenin', Homes?"

They slapped hands. Otis. Six-two. Lean. Face like a ten year old. He'd been up for a manslaughter rap Frank had defended through the P.D.'s office a couple of years ago down in the project; they'd walked him and justifiably so when Frank had come up with a couple of reliable witnesses who had born out Otis's self-defense story. Frank turned up Clipper Street. Keep away from the project where Otis wouldn't be seen talking with him, that was the thing.

"How're ya doin?"

"I'm good. I'm takin my GED next month."

"That's great." They talked back and forth and then Frank came to the point. "I got ripped off pretty good last night, Otis. I think it was guys in the project. Crackheads. Can you keep an ear to the ground for me?" Frank pushed a handful of twenties into his hand. "I want to get it back. A lot of money. Cameras."

Otis pushed the money back, nodded, "I'll listen. I'll look."

"How's your mom?"

"Better. She's got new medication for her blood pressure."

"Give her my best and take this fucking money." Frank pushed the twenties back into his hand. "If not for yourself, then for her."

Otis took the money. Frank drove on. "You be safe getting out here, Otis?" Otis nodded at the next corner. "Thanks. Call me at my office if you get anything. Be careful."

"You, too. If it's there, I'll hear it or see it."

They slapped hands, Otis got out, and Frank drove

away quickly, watching Otis recede in the rearview mirror. Maybe. Maybe not.

Frank was in a clean white shirt and blue suit.

It had been the usual with Aram. The big handshake and arm around the shoulder; the guided walk into the inner sanctum of the office. There'd been the usual schmooze, and then they had cut the bullshit and come to the point, which was U.S. vs. Ray Buchanan. Now Frank was expanding on his last investigation report; while it checked out so far that Ray had no priors, Frank had confirmed from someone high up in the Richie Davis murder investigation that Ray's name had been on the Davis disks, which were ledgers recording detailed transactions: weights, dollar amounts, dates. And therefore, Aram should be advised: that if they continued with the entrapment defense, this evidence pertaining to the defendant's predisposition would be, as Aram knew, admissible by the prosecution. "I mean, Aram, Ray left a trail."

Melikian swiveled behind his desk as he considered this. Frank felt as if he were skidding, and, at the same time, he was trying to remember something. What? Before Melikian could come to any conclusion, Frank said, "Jack . . . Jack Adams. Sam Coleman."

"You've run them. No priors. Nothing pending."

Frank nodded. No illegal wiretaps. The sweep of Ray's house had revealed no bugs. But he had the feeling he'd missed something.

Melikian turned a pencil over and over. "Actually, I was coming to Jack Adams." He stood. He swung open the door on a waist-high safe. There were several bundles of cash lying in the bottom. Melikian pointed and said, "Jack Adams came by today. You know, they made bail yesterday. Adams's bond was one hundred grand. He comes by," he glanced at his watch, "maybe three hours ago. He opens a briefcase, and puts this money on my desk."

They looked down at the cash.

"How much?"

"Twenty-five thousand. All he says is, 'Make sure Ray gets this money.' I said, 'Why?' He said, 'I've got to help Ray. I feel responsible.' "

"I'm not sure I get it."

Aram swung the safe door shut. "I do. Things went wrong. Jack thinks he brought Ray into this trouble. I suggested it was the other way around, that Ray had the DEA all over him for months, but Jack just shook his head. He didn't spell it out any more than that, but he didn't really have to. A guy doesn't give another guy twenty-five thousand dollars in cash if he doesn't have strong feelings." Aram shrugged. "Didn't you tell me they were tennis partners?"

Frank nodded. "Tennis partners, played all the time. Why didn't Jack just give Ray the money himself?"

Aram picked up the baseball signed by the Dodgers and turned it over slowly, looking at the signatures. He fitted two fingers across the stitched seams as though he were going to throw a curve. "When he put the money on my desk, he said, 'This'll be safe with you, won't it?' Maybe that says it all. SAFE. These guys are out on bail after a couple of weeks on the sixth floor. There's the huge shock of having M-16's stuck in their faces, their houses torn apart—you know, their lives are chaos. Where'd Dean Miller come from? Who else is out there? Who do you believe? Who's turned state's evidence, who's watching? What, I have to explain paranoia to you?"

Frank shrugged.

"In that frame of mind, you've got cash, you don't give it to the guy directly. Give it to his lawyer, put it in a safe, let things get sorted out. I told him, 'Go back to your bail bondsman, have him make out a certified check in Ray's name.' You know, these days cash is dirty. Someone gives you cash, maybe they're trying to set you up."

"Paranoia, Aram?"

"When *you* feel it, it's paranoia. When *I* feel it, that's the way it really is."

Frank laughed. "So what'd he say when you told him to get a check?"

"Said he didn't have time. Somehow I got the idea that this was Jack's swan song—goodbye, so long, sayonara."

"He's jumping?"

"He's gone."

"Did he say so?"

"Of course not, but there was just something coming off him, final gestures. Very good looking guy. I can't see him making it in prison. He'd be dead in the joint." Melikian caressed his head. They looked down at the bundle of cash, and then Aram closed the safe.

"So where are we?"

Velma beeped him. "Frank, I've got a meeting. We'll pick this up. Let me think the whole thing over. Maybe we're plea-bargaining if I can get some kind of ammunition. Maybe we can go to trial behind entrapment. Whatever we're doing, I need something more." Velma beeped again.

Frank walked to the door. Melikian picked up the receiver. Frank said, "Could you do something, Aram?"

"What, Frank?"

"Could you ask the Prosecutor—what's his name, Winters?—what he knows about Jack Adams? Sam Coleman?" Frank had sworn he wouldn't do this with Melikian. Melikian often took these unsolicited suggestions as challenges, or who knew how? Things just had a way of coming back funny.

A look of annoyance crossed Aram's face. He nodded tolerantly. "Alright, Frank, I'll ask him. Adams. Coleman. What's he going to tell me?"

"I'm not sure. What's to lose? You were the one who said that when it was the DEA, anything goes. Up is down." He could see from the look on Melikian's face he'd already said too much.

*   *   *

In the morning, Frank left for the office, but instead of taking his turn, he crossed Market and continued on Van Ness; the car was travelling by itself and he let it go. Left on Lombard and then he found himself funnelling into traffic onto the Golden Gate Bridge, the spans and cables unspooling themselves overhead. He continued on 101 into Marin, got off at Mill Valley. After a few minutes, the Marin Racquet and Tennis Club came into view and Frank pulled into the parking lot. He turned off the engine. Birds. The soft whump of tennis balls, a teaching pro giving instruction and encouragement. The rattle of a diving board, and a lifeguard's warning to a couple of children: Don't run!

Frank slid back in his seat and lit a cigarette, quietly watched the smoke dissipating in the sunlight. Then he got out of the car. Jack's white Mercedes hadn't been far from here. Beside it, Ray's Porsche. A summer day maybe a year ago. Frank cut across the lawn, followed the courts until he came to the one where Ray and Jack had been playing. It was empty. He walked beside the court until he'd stood where he'd been the first time he met Jack. There was a white metal lawn chair a few steps away, and Frank pulled it to him and sat down. He took a drag on the cigarette, gazed through the smoke at the sunlit court. Afternoon. They were in a sweat. They'd come off the court, side by side. Tired. Pleased. Ray had introduced Jack. They'd shaken hands. Something in Jack's glance? Or was Frank reaching for it now? Maybe Karen was right about him: he was just paranoid—or *too* paranoid, whatever that might be.

Frank looked out at the court. Something, a certainty or gravity went out of him. Service court. Alleys. Backcourt. Baseline. Serve. Volley. He slapped the net; the cable sang softly, and as it died, he turned and walked back to the car. He drove out of the lot, and then circling once, he returned to his space, went into the clubhouse.

He hesitated, his eyes adjusting to the shadowy corridor, and then he followed an arrow and sign. Sudden close slam and crack, Frank flinched; two men, almost in a violent embrace, shirts plastered to their backs with sweat, faces flushed red, caromed off the back glass of a racquetball court a foot away, and one spun to face the shot coming off the front wall.

Frank went to a pay phone and picked up the book. When in doubt, always try the obvious. Jack Adams. Not listed. He called information, and when he reached Jack's number, a recording said, "I'm sorry, that number is no longer in service, if you think you've . . ." Maybe Melikian was right. Jack had jumped.

Collecting himself outside the club office, Frank stepped in. There was a good-looking woman in command, sweater over her shoulders against the air conditioning, chain sweaterguard across her throat, a few smile lines and maybe a bit too much early tanning past her prime. Her blond, frosted hair was gelled up off her forehead. Gray eyes, but no flirtation in them. Slightly rounded, one hundred and forty-five pound women like this quietly ran everything.

"Good morning. I was supposed to meet Jack Adams here at 10:15—do you know Jack?" She nodded. "Looks like one of us got it wrong. I'm wondering if you can give me his home address; my address book is locked in the trunk of my other car. I'd like to drop by his house and see what's what—wrong day, wrong time, something. He's not listed."

"I'm sorry, we don't give out any information on our members."

"I understand, but Jack and I were roommates at Stanford; I'm just up for a few days and we were counting on getting together."

"This is a private club. The members pay for their privacy." She wavered, then shook her head. "I'm sorry."

Frank thought, good for you, stand your ground. "I'll

just leave him a note.'' The secretary pushed over a memo pad. Stalling, he sat in a chair inside the door and glanced around the office. Filing cabinets. Computer. Small bathroom. A fluorescent light flickering on and off overhead. She watched him closely. He wrote a note, handed it to her.

''Which way's the bar and restaurant? I'll wait for him there.''

''Out and to your left. Come to stairs. Straight up.''

''Straight, straight and straight. Kind of directions I like.''

He smiled at her and went up to the bar, sat down, signaled the bartender: a beer. A newspaper. After a while, the secretary came in and sat at a table with another woman and they ordered lunch. Frank nodded at her, folded the paper and went out. Downstairs, he noticed an electrical box as he made his way along the corridor. He opened the metal cover and studied the labels on the circuits, then continued on to the office.

A girl, maybe high school, maybe college, reading Stephen King's *Pet Sematary*. He smiled. ''Hi. Electrician. Gonna finally get that light taken care of so you don't go blind reading. Could you do me a favor, make sure I don't get electrocuted?''

''Okay.''

''I just need to double-check the labels on the circuits. There's a box,'' he walked her out into the corridor and pointed. ''Open the door, you'll see bottom left, a switch like a big light switch, number 14. I think it's for this office, but I just want to be sure. When I wave, will you throw it for a second, then throw it back again.''

She put down the book and went to the box. Frank walked back to the filing cabinet. Pulled out a drawer. Another. *Members*. In a few moments, he found the membership file: Jack Adams. He reached in, took everything out, and crammed the papers inside his shirt. He walked to the door and waved at the girl.

"Now." The lights in the office went dark. "Okay. That's the one. Turn it back." She flicked the switch, the lights came on. "Back a little later with parts." He smiled as he passed her. "How's the book?"

"Not bad. Good. A little dopey, but interesting."

"That Stephen King, whatta guy. Musta had a bad childhood."

She smiled at him and shrugged.

Half a mile up the road, Frank pulled out his Thomas Guide, and studied the streets until he found Ridgewood. Jack walking toward him. His shaking hands with Jack. Something? He saw it in Jack. Or, knew that Jack saw it in him. Something? Was it there? Frank drove on through Mill Valley, checking streets against the map, and then turned onto a winding country road, and started noting the mailboxes and numbers as he went. The trailing branches of eucalyptus dappled the road with shade and the air smelled of sunlight, flowers. He spotted a number on a mailbox, matched it with Jack's address, and turned into a gravel drive which rose slightly as it went up toward a glass and redwood house with a deck along one side. Frank stopped beside a silver Plymouth Voyager. He followed the flagstone walk to the front door, rang. A woman answered. "Hi. Is this the home of Jack Adams?"

"Just a minute." She seemed completely distracted. She called into the house. A man came to the door. Wire-rim glasses, wild, graying hair. A kid, maybe five, fit between their legs.

"I'm looking for a friend of mine. Jack Adams." He repeated the address.

"Just a second." The man came back. "That's this address. Right." He smiled. "It's not that I don't know my own address, but we just moved in."

"When?"

"Yesterday."

Frank could see boxes stacked in the living room. "Did you rent the house from Jack Adams?"

"I don't know anything about a Jack Adams. We rented the house from a realtor. Leased it."

"Not from Jack Adams."

"I think the woman in the real estate office said the house had just come open—that's all I know. She didn't say who owned it. They handled the lease."

"Real estate office in town?"

He ducked into the living room, returned with a card, handed it to Frank. "Century 21 office right in the middle of town."

Frank thanked him. In the car, he studied the house. He'd had the idea from what Ray had said that Jack owned the place, in which case, it would have been seized by the IRS as Ray's house had been. Frank double-checked the Marin Racquet and Tennis Club membership file against the address on the house. They matched. It was the right house.

In a convenience store in Mill Valley, Frank dialed the number off the Century 21 card, Donna Green, and after being placed on hold, he was put through. "Donna Green?"

"This is she."

"Bill August of August Realty. I'm calling about your listing up on Ridgewood." He gave her the address and described the Jack Adams house, said he'd had a chance to drive by yesterday and look it over. "I've got a client who saw the house during a party earlier this year and loved it. Totally loved it. She's interested in exploring the possibility of buying. I'm on my way through town in a while, and I'm wondering if you could pull the listing for me."

Ms. Green explained that the house had just been leased, but she'd be in until four if he wanted to drop by. Frank thanked her and again called his office. Gloria answered. "Gloria, Frank here. Listen, something important. Can you call Sacramento and see if there's a developer who has a company or business registered to Jack Adams. If nothing under Adams, try variations. What we did when we looked for his priors in the alpha indexes. He has an office in Mill Valley. I'll call back in half an hour. Gloria, if you don't get anything on that, call DataSearch and check the U.C.C.''

Frank walked back to his car, dug a tie out of his trunk, straightened himself in a store window's reflection as he passed, and took a slow walk over to Century 21. He spent several minutes looking at the listings and couldn't help but feel a growing resentment at the frequent recurrence of the figures 750, 800, and 900 before the three zeros.

Inside, he was directed to Donna Green, who came out from behind her desk with a hard click of heels. Padded shoulders in her jacket added to a sense of her forthrightness. Well-coiffed and groomed, though three earrings in one lobe told Frank she also might be about something else. Frank straightened his tie as he walked toward her, shook hands—pleasant scent of hand lotion—and sorting through his cards of fictitious businesses, gave her one: August and Associates, Realty.

"Donna Green. That was fast. Seemed like you just hung up.''

Frank smiled indulgently. "Car phone. Thanks for making time to see me. As I mentioned when I called, I've got a client who's crazy about the house on Ridgewood, one of those love affairs, everything's right, the view, the location, you know how irrational that can be—sometimes I think in those cases some unconscious chord has been struck, maybe a house someone grew up in . . .'' Donna nodded. "So anyway, I thought I'd touch base here and see where the owner might be on selling. You mentioned the house was currently under lease.''

"That's right.''

"Wait a minute. My client described the owner as, what'd she say his name was? Jack Adams, tall, blond, good looking.''

She shook her head. "He's not the owner. Jack Adams was the previous leasee, but he just terminated his agreement in the last couple of weeks. Broke it actually. Forfeited his deposit and last month's rent.''

Frank said, ''My client said he was the owner.''

''No, he leased. But he wasn't tall and blond.''

''No? My client described him as tall and blond. Maybe she had a crush on Jack Adams and not the house. Confused the two. Tall, blond, and redwood.''

Donna smiled. ''Maybe she did, but the man who signed the lease agreement was stocky, strong looking, and had thick, curly black hair and a mustache.''

''That was Jack Adams?''

''That was Jack Adams.''

''Black hair?'' She nodded. ''And that lease agreement was just terminated?''

''Within the last couple of weeks. Days, actually.''

''So who *does* own the house?''

She handed him a xerox of the listings and pointed at the name. ''Robert Gardener.''

''Who's he? Not tall and blond by any chance?''

Donna smiled. ''Robert Gardener is a seventy-five year old lawyer and businessman with thick silver hair who's been quietly buying up property since the Fifties around Marin. We take care of some of his rental and leasing arrangements.''

Frank nodded. ''And right now, he's just leasing and letting everything appreciate. Doesn't sound like someone who'd ever feel pressure to sell.''

Donna Green nodded. ''That's exactly right.''

''Well. Okay. Let me get back to my client and see if she wants to pursue this. Or, maybe it's just Jack Adams she's really pursuing.''

Donna loosened up and smiled widely, ''Maybe. But which Jack Adams? Tall and blond or stocky and dark?''

Frank shrugged. ''I don't know. I'm a realtor, not a dating service. Anyway, it's starting to sound like the tall blond guy is a figment of her imagination—too much of a good party.''

"If it were my choice, I wouldn't be interested in the man who signed the lease agreement."

"The dark one. Why not?"

"There was something explosive about him. All business, but with a real edge. Not my kind of guy."

Frank thought that over. "Thanks for your time. I'll give a report to my client. Maybe you can sound out Mr. Gardener, though it doesn't sound hopeful. I'll call you in a week."

"A week is fine. Thanks."

They shook hands. "Thank *you*, Donna Green."

Outside, Frank walked over to the Depot, ordered an espresso, and sat down outside in the shade. Jack Adams. Stocky. Dark-haired. Explosive. Frank had no idea who that might be. Maybe an office manager of Jack's, someone who'd done the paperwork for him on the lease, maybe represented himself as Jack to make things simpler and get it done. Had he actually called himself Jack Adams or had Donna Green just assumed he was? Frank finished his coffee, called Gloria from a pay phone. "Frank here, checking back. What'd Sacramento have on Jack Adams?"

"Nothing."

"No business, nothing incorporated, nothing in Mill Valley?"

"Nada."

"Okay, you checked variations? Adamski? Whatever?"

"Yes."

"Okay, go ahead and follow up with DataSearch. Gotta run. Any money come in today?"

"Three hundred and fifty dollars. Also, a slew of bills."

"Gloria, are we still afloat?"

"Barely."

"John Giordano. I'll tell you. He make a pass at coming back to work."

"Not a word."

"I saw Giordano through law school. Three years. Took

care of the guy. Never mind. I owe you and Kramer my
life these last few weeks. You've both been there. See
you."

Frank walked over to a bench, watched the slow swirl
of cars, the movement of people in and out of the overpriced shops. Frank was happiest in a good home supply
depot. Nails, lumber, power tools. He felt himself taken in
by sunlight translucent in a flower garden across the street:
agapanthus, nasturtium, gloxinia. He resisted the urge to
go over and rub his cheek against their petals. He drifted
back to the beautiful view from Jack's yard. Half of Mill
Valley. Frank was sure Ray had said Jack owned that
house. And that he had an office in Mill Valley. But maybe
not. Maybe Frank had gotten it wrong. He fought the rise
of dread in his stomach. Hey, the confusion over the house
and office didn't necessarily mean anything. Ray said Jack
had an office. Had Ray actually ever seen his office? He'd
confirm a few details.

Frank returned to the pay phone, called Pacific Bell in
San Francisco, got put through to records, and asked for
Mr. Blake.

In a minute, Blake picked up. "Whitey, Frank August
here. How are you?"

"Frankie, I'm good. Very settled now."

Frank had handled a landlord/tenant case on Whitey's
behalf several years ago. The landlord had evicted Whitey
to move into the unit himself—legal—but then raised the
rent and moved in a new tenant: illegal. Frank had sent
Gloria to inquire about the apartment out on the Avenues;
the landlord had stepped all over his dick looking at her
tight skirt, asked her out for dinner, given her his phone
number and address, told him who'd lived in Whitey's
unit, how long, all of it. This information had won a set-
tlement for Blake.

"Listen, Whitey, can I ask you for something?"

"Anything. Name it."

"I'm trying to figure out a few things for a couple of
clients. Can you get me copies of their telephone records

for the last year and a half. Two, make it two years.''

"Ask me something hard, Frank.''

"That's all.'' Frank gave him Ray Buchanan's number and address. Jack Adams. "Both Mill Valley residents. Jack Adams should have a second number beside the residence. A business, don't know it offhand.''

"If it's there, I'll find it. When do you need them?''

"Now. Today, Whitey.'' Frank thought, three weeks ago was when I needed them. Six months ago.

"Soon as we hang up, I'm on it. I'll have someone run them by your office. Same place?''

"Same place.''

"Give it to me again.'' Frank gave him the address. "Before five okay?''

"Perfect. Give them to Gloria of tight skirt fame. Thanks, Whitey.''

"Hey, I take care of guys who take care of me.''

Frank crossed to the overpriced liquor store, spent a little too long looking at a bottle of Stolichnaya, finally not buying, and feeling vindicated, he drove back to San Francisco.

When Frank reached his office after five, the building had a somnolent and unanimously deserted feeling, the upstairs windows slanting with late afternoon sunlight. Frank peered in at the law library, the mahogany desk, and then suddenly recalled that today was their—the building's—day to play the Public Defender's office in softball. He was going to miss the game, but too late now. He went down the long narrow staircase to his office.

Inside, there were two brown manilla envelopes on his desk and a note from Gloria: "Hand-delivered at 4:45 via messenger from Mr. Blake. DataSearch turned up no businesses for Jack Adams/variations.''

Frank locked the door, tuned in the jazz station, and dropped on the sofa, jumped as someone whacked the window grating outside. He opened one of the brown manilla envelopes. There was a note from Whitey. "Frank, there was no second business phone listed under Jack Adams. These are his residential phone records. They go back thirteen months at the number and address you gave me in Mill Valley and terminate at the customer's request five days ago.''

As the light gradually faded outside—still a patch of blue in the clear top windows—Frank went through Jack Adams's phone records. There was nothing extraordinary, really, except that for a developer who had no business phone, there were not many long distance calls. Frank had expected calls all over the state, calls to banks, who knew what else. But what Frank did quickly notice was that there were long distance calls to the same number in Santa Monica repeated three, four, five times a week, fairly long calls, half an hour, forty, fifty minutes, week after week, month after month.

Frank copied the number and, switching on his desk light in the darkening office, turned to Ray's phone records. They were slim and after going through several months, Frank laughed softly, and knew he would not find anything. There were no long distance calls. It was one of the first things Ray had impressed upon Frank years ago. Don't talk to people. Don't talk on the phone. There'd been no wiretap on Ray's phone, no bugs in his house, but even if there had been, there would have been nothing to hear. Ray, he knew, used pay phones and almost always only made quick calls. You wanted to talk to Ray, you met him somewhere of his chosing. Frank returned the phone records to their envelopes and locked them in a file drawer. He glanced at his watch. Too late for the library. Spinning the Rolodex to Axelrod, he dialed. Before the phone could ring, he hung up.

It was almost dark as Frank parked his car on Twenty-second and Mission and started walking. The air was heavy with the sweet smell of a Mexican bakery, fry cooking, the cloy of perfume, noise, movement, low riders turning a corner with the bass thud of Bazooka speakers. Frank had walked this street morning, noon and night, and at odd hours in between for the nine months he'd apprenticed with Axelrod when he'd realized he didn't have time or money to take the bar. Frank couldn't think of anyone he'd ever hated working for more.

They'd fought their way through the whole nine months until Frank had finally just walked out. Murray. Here was this guy, who had not a single social grace. He stood too close when he talked, and on top of that, he misted his listener with saliva. Over the last four years, they had come to an uneasy truce.

Now Frank stopped at the darkened storefront, made out a number of deserted desks in the shadows, and rang the bell. Stepping back to the curb, he looked up at the second floor windows. A night light? Frank rang the bell again, longer, louder, heard it jangle somewhere deep in the building. Records were Murray's big trip. And, in the last couple of years, records on line. Computer records. He liked to boast he paid thirty thousand a year for data bank services—property titles, bank accounts, credit reports, whatever—and that he could do almost everything he had to do without leaving his office, his phone, his computers—i.e. did not fucking have to talk to people. Talking to people was messy. Murray said, hey, give me a guy's social security number or license plate and in twelve hours I'll tell you everything about him. Politicians, lawyers, all kinds of players paid him a lot of money to do just that. He'd say to Frank, watch the papers—next two weeks. What, Murray? Just watch. And there it would be. Whoever. Money laundering, kickbacks, racketeering. Names named. Many of these things started with Murray, his computer, a few intuitions. Like a kid connecting numbered dots, Murray could look at bank records, credit cards, mortgages, the flow of money, and draw unique conclusions. Frank knew that Murray would be the last person he would want after him. He leaned on the bell, and then Frank thought he saw someone moving in the shadows. Murray peered through the glass at Frank, made an exas-

perated gesture, and started fooling with the deadbolts. He
yanked open the door in anger.

"Fuck, Murray, answer your door much?"

"Well, Jesus Christ, Frank, I thought you were one of
the fucking neighborhood asshole kids." Murray misted
him with saliva. Four years might never have passed.
"Shit, it's eight, fuck you want?"

Frank saw the gun tucked into Murray's belt. "Blow
your lizard off with that thing jammed in your pants. What
is this, the movies?"

Murray's glasses glinted in the light. "Fucking baseheads. Some fucking spic blew away a kid right there last
week." Murray sighted his finger at the opposite corner.

"Yeah, I read about it."

"So fuck you asking me why I come to the door with
a piece. Lucky I came at all."

"Well, what are you doing here at eight o'clock?"

"Working on something."

Frank knew there would be no point in asking him, but
couldn't resist. "What?"

Murray went flat dead on him. "Something."

Frank laughed. Aside from Ray, Murray was the most
suspicious person he'd ever known. Actually, Murray was
in a class by himself. It would have been interesting to see
Ray and Murray locked together in a white tile bathroom
for forty-eight hours. Hi, who are you? Someone. Yourself? Someone else.

"Well, fuck, Frank, now that you've interrupted me,
fuck you want?" He misted Frank again.

"Murray, I just wanted to look at your crisscross directories. Very simple."

Murray said, "Why don't you fucking spend a fucking
buck and get your own."

"So charge me for the look-see."

Murray desisted, let him in. Frank followed him up the
darkened stairs, increasingly thankful with every step he
was no longer subject to Axelrod's moods, whims, com-
pulsions and explosive temper. He came up onto the sec-

ond floor, a long room lined with windows facing west. Heat from the summer day still lingered and a small fan turned in the corner. Beyond the row of windows, a line of rooftops submerged into a single black mass.

Frank reflexively walked toward where his old desk had been. There was now a table covered with a printer, two computer screens side by side glowing soft green, a keyboard, folders, papers; the floor beneath was a tangle of wires and telephone lines leading to modems. Within reach, a microfiche viewer, a Canon copy machine, and a fax machine. Sensing Murray's proprietary nervousness, he glanced at the screen—rows of names, number and letter codes, all illegible hieroglyphics to Frank—and turned toward Murray's desk, the only other source of light in the darkening office.

"I won't take up much of your time. Directories, Murray?"

"They're on CD-ROM now, but my fucking drive just went down. Check the books." Murray nodded toward the shelves. "Same place. Where you looking?"

"L.A. Santa Monica. I've got the number; I want the name and address."

"Lower left-hand shelf. Try third or fourth from the bottom."

Frank crouched. The titles were impossible to make out in the dark. Sensing both Murray's impatience and his resistance to anything being disturbed, Frank struck a match. "I've got it."

Murray didn't turn on the light. Now in unreadable Murray Axelrod–land and not wanting to disturb Murray more by switching on an overhead light, Frank walked toward his desk; he placed the directory in the circle of light, sat in Murray's chair and opened the book, could see Murray silhouetted against the faded window light, the green glow from the computer screens throwing a soft pattern on his hand. The warm room was permeated with Murray's inept desire to do something social confounded with his obsessive drive to return to his computerized da-

tabanks, these impulses in turn warring with an urgent and
overwhelming desire to get Frank out of his chair—it was
his! Frank laughed quietly and made an exaggerated show
of settling himself into the swivel chair.

Murray paced once, twice, stopped and blurted, "What
are you working on, Frank?"

"Oh, nothing much."

"Smegma. You come shaking my door after eight,
you're working on something."

"Just passing up your street."

Murray made a sound, a cross between assent and contempt. It wasn't the answer Murray wanted, but it was the
only one he would have respected. Frank flipped through
the pages, matched the first three numbers of the Adams
Santa Monica number with the three at the top, ran his
finger down the column, stopped, checked and double-
checked each successive number, matched all the numbers,
followed the numbers out to a name: Howard Rosenthal.
He copied it down along with the address and slipped the
paper back in his wallet. He also noted from the symbol
that it was a moderately affluent area. He blanked to nothing more than the declarative sentence: Jack Adams called
Howard Rosenthal in Santa Monica for weeks and months.
What? Was Ray's tall, blond, good-looking tennis partner
queer on some guy named Howard Rosenthal? Beyond
that, Frank had no other thoughts, but to tip back and remain in Murray's swivel chair and see what Murray did
next. He left the directory open. Murray paced, blurted,
"Find it, Frank?"

"Found something." Frank stood and replaced the directory. "How's biz?"

"Killer. I'm making twice as much as I ever was and
I don't have to go out and talk to all the scumbag assholes
anymore, don't have to go into the jails, the prisons, the
fucking streets and hallways and kitchens and bed-
rooms. . . ." They started tromping down the dark stairs.
"I just punch in commands. You're alive and breathing,
even if you're nobody, you leave a paper trail behind you

ten miles long, ten miles wide. Even the smart ones. I pull it up and sooner or later, I read it like the fucking paper.'' On the first floor, the silver streetlight caught the glint of Murray's glasses, the piece jammed into his pants as he checked the sidewalk and then undid the deadbolts.

"Thanks, Murray. Let's get together soon and I'll buy you a drink."

Frank stepped out. "Watch your back, Frank; there's a bunch of douche-bag baseheads running around out there blow you away for the fuck of it and a bunch of asshole lawyers and investigators who'd walk them for fifty cents," Murray said, working himself into a vehement rage.

"Yeah, I'm one of them." The door slammed, the deadbolts snapped into place, one two three, and Murray sank back out of sight. Frank took a deep breath in relief, started walking. Jack Adams called Howard Rosenthal in Santa Monica. Four, five times a week. For months. What was that? There was probably nothing to do until morning. He could call the number tonight and, what? ask for Howard Rosenthal, but a phone call now to the wrong person could bitch things. He walked toward the Mexican bakery—had he eaten? The same Mexican woman who'd been there four years ago, a little wider, sold him two pumpkin empanadas and, holding them in their wax paper, he bolted one, then the other.

He drove slowly back toward Mission, hesitated just before turning toward home and then rocketed across Mission and Valencia, started for the park. Within a few blocks, he drove into the fog and driving on, he reached the field and recognized several of the cars parked down the block. Opening his trunk, he changed into a pair of hightops and a sweat shirt. Behind the screen, floods poured down a silver light onto the infield and Frank could just make out the pitcher, batter and the outline of the guy playing second.

"Hey, Frankie, always on time. Where've you been?"

"Some guys work for a living."

"What inning is it?"

"Seventh."

Someone called, take my place, I gotta go, and walking in from center field, handed Frank a glove. "Bring it in to the office tomorrow." Someone else put a beer in Frank's hand, and he drifted out toward center, took a swallow, and placed the can at his feet. Frank could just make out the pitcher in motion. A moment later, the whump of the bat, someone called, center field, right field. Frank looked up but couldn't see the ball—just a fine, silvery curtain of mist burning and falling in front of the white lights.

Afterward, a trip to the nearest bar. Two blocks. A beer. Two. In the bathroom, someone produced a line. Shouldn't. Just this one. A shot of vodka waiting on the table. Who bought the round? Hey, thanks. Enough. Jesus, Frank, going home? Come on. . . .

Dry-mouthed, Frank opened his eyes. Across the room, Karen had set up a table, and there were transparencies of pictures, slides, notes, folders, and a vase filled with flowers. He heard her coming up the stairs and rolled away, closed his eyes. She walked to the bed, stood over him. She said, "Don't, Frank. I know you're awake. Here."

He rolled over, half-heartedly faked waking. She handed him a glass of juice, placed a cup of coffee on the floor. He sat up, thankfully drank the juice. She walked over to the table, picked up a transparency, held it to the light. She said calmly, "I can see that nothing I say or do will make a difference in the overall picture."

"It was softball . . . the whole office was there. We went out afterward. I don't know . . ."

She said softly, almost tenderly, "Don't, Frank. Somehow it's beneath us both. I hate to hear you in that posture." He took his cue from her tone and shut up, sipped the coffee. "You know, everything's working for me now. I have the urge to take pictures again, I love my new job, and I feel good about myself. I don't want to lead my life dreading the call from SFPD that you're in a morgue on a tray, a drunk driving stat. Are you trying to kill your-self?"

"No, babe."

"Am I taking you up with me—are we going up to-gether—or are you going down alone?"

"Babe . . ."

"I love to make love with you, but I don't like it when you come in from some place high and smelling of breath mints and cigarette smoke and try to fuck me in the middle of the night."

"Oh, Karen, babe . . . listen to me . . ."

"Please. A couple of days ago you said you'd stop in to see my new office. It's got a beautiful view. I want you to meet Brad Harwood. You'd like him. Most of me wants you to meet him. A little part of me is nervous; you can be very funny at other people's expense. . . ." She held another transparency to the window light.

"Oh, come on, Karen. . . . Don't make me out to be so bad. And about seeing your new office, I told you, I'd love to. Things will ease off. I'll stop by. We'll go to lunch. Things will settle down."

"Do you believe it when you say it?"

Could she really have so little faith in him? "I believe and mean it."

She carefully replaced the transparency in its sleeve. "Okay, Frank, all I can say is one of these days, I'm going to get all the stories in the same room with you and we'll see what's what."

"You keep saying that. What does *that* mean?"

"I think it means I love you and want to find you again. And if I have to take drastic steps, I will."

"Whew, babe, that's cryptic and heavy."

"Isn't it, though. I'll see you later. Sometimes I think you'd like me to give up on us to give you an out into . . . into what, Frank? Oblivion? Is that where you think you belong? Anyway, I'm not going to. See ya later, Slick." She kissed him lightly on the cheek.

He smiled at her passing parody of the street, lisped back to her in black diction, "Awright, Mama." When she was gone, Frank got up. It could have been worse with Karen. The thing that scared him was that last night's stumble in the bar had taken him completely by surprise. Frank walked to the window and looked down into the backyard at the unplanted garden, a scrabble of weeds, a faded shadow. He'd loved walking out into that garden in August, corn up to his shoulders; he'd loved sitting down between the rows, stretching out, staring up at the blue sky, the heat of the ground, the smell of the soil around him. He'd loved being enveloped in that greenness.

Last night suddenly rose clearly in focus: the computer screen glowing in Murray's dark office. The crisscross directory. Jack Adams had called a number in Santa Monica several times a week for months: a Howard Rosenthal. Jack Adams and Rosenthal were lovers? Frank saw Jack Adams walking toward him on the tennis court. It hardly fit; but who knew. . . .

He leaned on the windowsill, wondering about Howard Rosenthal when the phone rang. Gloria. She had a message from an Otis Wilson. She read: "Frank, I think the guy you want is Khalid Lewis. Five-ten. Twenty. Thin. He started driving a white 80 Camaro. New purchase. Last three, four days. California license: 986 MKL. Parks it around the project. Basehead. Carries a Davis .380. Be real careful."

Frank thanked Gloria. It was the only time in his life he wished he could have dialed 911. A basehead with a handgun truly terrified him and Frank had no idea where things might end up with his carrying the Glock, but he couldn't go empty-handed. With no plan other than to see if he could find the car, wincing from a splitting headache, he ran down to Van Ness and Army and slowly cruised the streets around the project—Folsom, Lucky, 25th, Lilac. . . . It was early morning, gray and quiet. Turning from 25th into Horace, he saw the Camaro and drove past, parked half a block down. He walked to the car and tried the door. It was unlocked, which was all he wanted to know. There was a club on the steering wheel. Love that car, Khalid.

He walked back to his car, waited awhile, and then had to give it up to keep an appointment. Toward evening, he returned, this time with a roll of duct tape, found the car gone, once more cruised the streets, and saw the Camaro over on Lilac. Again he tried the front door which was unlocked. Again, the club was on the wheel. This time Frank decided he would wait it out. He slumped in the front seat of his car, Giants and Reds, the shrill cries of kids playing on the sidewalk, hits of adrenalin coming and going. It was almost dark, but even before the man approached the car, Frank knew by the emaciated cheeks and herky-jerky movements of a basehead that this was Khalid Lewis. Frank slid out of his car just as Lewis got into the Camaro.

He was hamstrung with unlocking the club when Frank opened the passenger side door, slid in, and jammed the Glock hard into Lewis's ribs. "Freeze, blood!" For a second he was afraid he'd pulled the trigger. Lewis didn't move. Frank trembled with rage, trying not to shoot him. "Give me the gun!" Lewis didn't move. "Give me the fucking gun!" Lewis started to reach down and Frank went crazy and hit him across the mouth with the Glock, reached over Lewis, and grabbed the gun out of his waist. Exactly as Otis had said, a Davis .380. Khalid reached up to wipe the blood from his mouth. Frank snatched the club off the wheel. "Drive!" Lewis started the car, and terrified, he could barely work out of his space. Frank saw his cowboy boots on Lewis and hit him again. He was afraid he was going to kill him. "Where you want me to go?"

"Shut up! Take a left here."

They turned onto Army. "You gonna kill me?"

Frank jammed the Glock hard into Lewis's ribs. "Shut up!" Frank shouted. "Drive!" Lewis drove. "Turn right at Evans!" Lewis turned. They drove a while. "Right here!" They turned onto Toland. "Pull over!" Lewis pulled over. They were in the empty lots of the Farmer's Market, which was deserted. "Open the fucking door!"

Holding onto his collar, gun pressed to his head, Frank slid across the seat and pushed him out. "Sit!" Lewis sat, Frank kneeling behind him, Glock to his head. He could feel Lewis trembling. "Take off the fucking boots!" Lewis struggled with the boots. One. The other. "Where's my money?"

"I don't have no . . ."

Frank walloped him across the head with the gun. "You're dead, blood!"

"In the trunk!"

"Open it."

Holding on to him, Frank walked him back to the trunk. Lewis opened it. The light came on. Karen's Nikon. The camcorder. A brown paper bag. Frank held it open in the light. "How fucking much is left?"

"Eleven thousand. . . ."

Frank hit him again with the gun. He stuffed the money into his pants. He grabbed the duct tape out of his jacket, taped Lewis's hands behind his back, taped his mouth. "Get in."

Lewis got into the trunk. Frank grabbed the cameras. He held the gun to Lewis's head. "You piece of shit! Come up my street again, you better be strapped. I'll kill you!" He slammed the trunk, picked up his boots and the cameras, drove back, parked. He wiped down the car, not that Lewis would ever go to the cops, and took off. He went to a pay phone, called the SFPD, and told them there was a guy in the trunk on . . . He gave them the location. "Hey, he's fine, take your time. And make sure you ask him how he ended up in there." Frank hung up. There were almost eleven thousand dollars left. Five hundred to be mailed certified check to Otis and his mother. For their safety, he didn't dare go near them.

He couldn't remember when he'd felt better. In the morning, when Karen saw the cameras on the kitchen counter, she burst out laughing, but Frank wouldn't tell her how he'd done it. Frank. Please. It wasn't a story he could tell or she'd understand. She laughed. "I love you. You're impossible and you amaze me."

Good, that was enough. Let her be amazed. Let her start believing in him a little.

He had Khalid Lewis, he had the cameras, he had most of the money, which was now under the floorboard in his closet; he also had a phone number in Santa Monica listed under the name of Howard Rosenthal. So? Then it was simple. The obvious. When you want basic information, go back to basics. Everyone drives; everyone has a driver's license. He called the DMV and requested Joan Santiago, a woman he'd talked with often enough to have a playful flirtation going; he asked for something on Howard Rosenthal.

"Okay, Frank, give me a name and location." He did. "Hold for a second." He heard her start to punch computer keys before the line went silent. When she came back on, she intoned, Howard Rosenthal. Santa Monica. Date of birth: July 10, 1954. Height: six-three. Weight: 205. Restrictions: none. Car: 1988, BMW. No liens on the car. No moving violations. No accidents. She gave him Rosenthal's social security number.

"You have his place of employment?"

"Nothing in the computer."

Frank thanked Joan, asked her to do him a favor sometime—she laughed once, I will—and hung up.

He gave the cats a half can of tuna each and stroked their upright tails as they purred. He reread the DMV information on Rosenthal. BMW. No liens. So the guy had bought a BMW, paid thirty thousand cash up front? He was either making a good salary somewhere, had a nice Daddy or a rich girlfriend or boyfriend who liked sweetie-pie a lot.

Donna Green had said Jack Adams was a stocky, curly haired guy, dark. Could the dark, curly haired guy actually have been Howard Rosenthal? Donna Green had been shorter than he, maybe five-seven. He glanced at his DMV notes. Six-three. Even though Donna was shorter, she couldn't have mistaken five-eleven, six feet, stocky for six-three, 205, could she? The guy who'd been Jack's contact for the buy, the one who'd called himself Dean Miller, and who'd been busted with them, but never booked into the jail . . . Could this be him? Jack calls him, Jack's in touch with him right up until the night of the bust. Frank was completely confused.

He called Ray's number in the Marina apartment and a woman answered. Marla. "Hi, this is Frank August, I'm working on something for Ray, is he in?" He heard a hand go over the phone, muffled talk.

Ray answered in a reticent voice. Frank knew he hated phones. Whenever he talked, he shifted slowly from side to side as if he were on a teeter-totter.

"Ray . . . Frank, relax, I'm not going to say anything. There were three of you together on the night you went to do business. You understand me?"

"Uh huh."

"There was a fourth guy who was Jack's contact—you went to meet him. He was taken but was never booked, remember?"

"Right."

"Was he maybe my height and build, stocky, dark?"

"No. Five-nine, slim," he heard Ray draw a deep, nervous breath. "Reddish hair. Completely average looking. Like a kid, twenty-eight, thirty. Even baby-faced."

"Not stocky."

"No."

"Okay, Ray, how are you?"

"Not bad."

"Ray, your tennis partner own his house?"

"Right."

"Didn't rent or lease?"

"Owned."

"Had an office?"

"Right."

"Okay, I'll be back in touch."

Ray made a vague sound which was his telephone goodbye. Frank paced the kitchen. Jack Adams told Ray he owned his house. And had an office in Mill Valley. Frank had gotten them right. They just happened not to be true.

He thought about himself talking to Donna Green. Maybe Howard Rosenthal wasn't a stocky guy. He didn't have to be the stocky guy Donna Green met. Maybe he was the slim guy who called himself Dean Miller. But glancing at the DMV notes, Frank shook his head. There was just no way five-nine could be mistaken for six-three, no way.

Frank slapped his briefcase shut and had reached the front door when he returned to the table and called Melikian's office. Velma answered; then Melikian came on. "Francis Ignatius August, what's happening?"

"I'm working on some things, but you remember our last conversation."

"Which part?"

"The end, where I asked you to talk to the Prosecutor about Jack Adams, Sam Coleman."

"I do. And I talked to him."

Frank tried to sound relaxed. "He give you anything at all?"

Melikian paused. "I asked him if he knew anything about those guys he wanted to tell me; he was noncommittal, and so I told him I was getting ready to file a Brady motion for disclosure of their informant. I thought I'd test those waters."

"What did he do with that?"

"He didn't look happy. Then he said, 'You don't have such a great case. Start filing motions now and that will take away the possibility of there being any deals down the road. We'll go all the way on you.' "

"What'd you say?"

"Nothing. I got up to leave."

"And?"

"When I reached the door, Winters called me back and softened a little. 'Aram, I'll tell you what. Just hold on a few days. Don't file the Brady. Don't do anything until I get back to you.' "

"That's where you left it?"

"That's it. If I file the Brady and force him to disclose his informant's ID as a potential witness, word gets out he doesn't protect his snitches, and he's in trouble. I'm not sure what's up, but Winters got very uncomfortable when I suggested a Brady motion."

"So he's got you on hold while he does some figuring."

"I'm assuming. Looking that way more and more."

"Maybe offer you a plea."

"I'm hoping. We'll see. Could be a break. Hey, I'm already twenty minutes late for a meeting. If you've got something more for me, call."

Frank knew his pushing Melikian to go back to the Prosecutor would be completely overlooked by Melikian. That Melikian would never thank him. That Melikian would remember it only as his having made a right move at the right time—if it worked out to a counter offer or a plea that Melikian wanted. Otherwise, it would probably just register as more of Frank's paranoia, you know how he is, difficult, etc.

He picked up his briefcase. So, what was happening? Maybe things were working the way Melikian thought, maybe not. Jack Adams didn't own a house he said he owned. Didn't have a business he claimed he had. At least not registered to his name. He had a bunch of phone calls to some guy named Howard Rosenthal in Santa Monica. And that Rosenthal had a new BMW and didn't make car payments.

On his way to the office, Frank remembered that Giordano had a buddy who was in the D.A.'s office in L.A. Working class and activist, Giordano was still, underneath the street-smarts, idealistic at forty; like Frank, he could only work for the defense, though Frank, minimizing his own sympathies, loved to bait John and was constantly amazed at how often Giordano would rise to the baiting, "What, John, he's poor, he's black, his father used to beat him, his mother was alcoholic, he's got a license to kill?"

"That's not what I'm saying at all, Frank, but . . ." And off they'd go. Anyway, Giordano had mixed feelings about his buddy's being with the D.A.'s office. On the one hand, he'd landed a good job, it was a good career opportunity, and when he'd learned the ins and outs of prosecution, he'd probably turn it around and go into a private criminal practice. But for now, he was on the wrong side. Frank tried to recall his name. Funny name. Glover. First or last? Glover Dupray. Dupray Glover? Preppy looking guy with wire-rim glasses. Funny how those preppy guys always had two names which both sounded like last names.

The red light turned and someone honked behind Frank. He could take the flyer with Dupray himself but he'd probably not get too far. Giordano was the way to Dupray. They were buddies. So could he ask Giordano? This was giving John the chance he had to have been looking for to kick him in the balls. Serve them up on a silver platter. First thing, of course, was to let John know he had his money. No telling with John, he still might not come back to work now. And Frank wasn't sure he was going to ask him.

In the office, Gloria gave Frank his messages. "Kramer wants to talk to you. He's going to have be be out of town for a week or ten days."

"Starting when?"

"I'm not sure. He said he'll be home this afternoon between three and four."

"It won't help if Kramer goes now." Frank gazed back and forth along the time line on the murder case, switched on the radio. "Coffee yet?" Gloria shook her head no. "Would you mind fixing us each one. And I need just a moment here of privacy. If you don't mind. Please. Thank you in advance."

She went up the stairs. Frank spun the Rolodex. He knew a couple of investigators in L.A. . . . No, he'd have to take a stab with Giordano. John answered on about the tenth ring. Sleeping late, I see. Going to hell not working. Frank checked himself. "John, Frank August. How's it going?"

There was a long silence. "How ya doin', Frank?"

"Fine. Hope I'm not disturbing you."

"Just getting out of the shower."

"I can call back."

"You got me now. What's up?"

"I've got your money?"

"Yeah? Really?"

"Surprised?"

"No. Yeah."

Frank desperately needed John to come back to work. There was a long silence. Frank listened to see if he would ask for his job back. If Frank would offer. The silence extended. Frank didn't hear either of them talking. "Yeah, so come on in, Gloria will have it for you in cash in an envelope."

"Okay, Frank. I will."

Frank decided the best way was direct appeal. "John, I know we've had our disagreements, but I'm hoping we can put them aside for a minute." John didn't say anything. "I have a case that's taking me through the L.A.D.A.'s office. I need someone who's there, who can go in today, and see if there are files on a couple of guys; if so, what's in them."

"And?"

"Your friend, Glover Dupray, is with that office." Again there was a long silence from John. "Hey, I know you're mad at me." John still didn't say anything. Frank reached for the idealist, the working class Sixties activist. "Look, John, this request isn't about you and me. It's about a defendant. I think the guy's been set up. The case is too long to explain now, but if I can't clarify a couple of things, my guy's going to go in the dumper for something I know he didn't do. He's innocent. But I've got to be able to prove some things about a couple of other guys." John remained silent. Frank made a last appeal. "Why make an innocent defendant suffer because I had a cash flow problem?"

"What do you want, Frank?"

"Could you just talk to Glover Dupray, tell him what I've told you, ask him to help us?"

"Help *you*, Frank."

"Okay, help *me*, John. Help my defendant. I need him to call me. That's all. Just have him call me."

There was another long silence. "You be there awhile?"

"An hour or two."

Short and curt, which was all John could manage, he said, "I'll see what I can do."

"Thanks. I appreciate it."

"Don't think you're doing a number on me, Frank. I know ninety-five percent of what you're telling me is bullshit." Frank smiled and thought affectionately, good for you, Slick. "But if it would help walk a guy who's being set up, I'll try it anyway."

Gloria set hot coffee in front of Frank, and he playfully kissed her hand and took a deep swallow. He looked at his watch. "Gloria, let's leave the lines open for the next hour or so. We'll let the machine take messages. Got some billings and reports to catch up on?"

She nodded. Frank handed her a sealed envelope with Giordano's name. "John's money. Just put it in a safe place. He'll be in." He handed her another envelope with her name on it.

She smiled. "I knew you'd figure it out somehow."

"Yeah, it's the somehow that's making me nervous."

They busied themselves at their respective desks. Each time the machine answered, Frank jumped and listened. Over an hour had gone by when Glover Dupray called.

Frank picked up, they said hello, Frank reminded him they'd met a couple of years ago, and then Glover said, "John told me you needed help with a couple of case files. You wouldn't have the case numbers?"

Frank decided not to bother with the story he'd given John. "I'm not even sure if these guys have done anything or if it's landed in your office. So it's just a shot in the dark."

"Okay, well, give me their names and I'll see what I can find."

Frank gave him two names. Jack Adams. Howard Rosenthal.

"You be at this number awhile?"

"I'll be here." Frank went on trying to keep his mind on paperwork.

After a while, Dupray called back. "There's nothing whatsoever on a Jack Adams. I went back ten years."

"Nothing?"

"Nothing. Jack. John. Variations. But there was a file on Howard Rosenthal. Problem is: the file's been pulled. There's nothing—no preliminary hearing transcripts, nada."

"What is there?"

"Just a record of his initial appearance for selling four kilos of coke on March 27, 1989 to an undercover cop and that he entered a plea of not guilty."

"There's the BMW without a lien. Cash."

"What's that?"

"I just realized how he paid cash for his car. So they've pulled his file."

"Looks that way."

"Is there a picture of him? Booking sheet?"

"There's no picture, either."

"Okay, Glover. Rosenthal. Busted March 27, 1989." Frank wrote down the date. "Many thanks to you and John Giordano. I hope I can return the favor some day."

Frank hung up. "Gloria, keep things going as best you can—the illusion that there is still an August and Associates will do. I'm a one-time college student, former house painter, sometime tiler and framer and chef, presently a law student between bar exams on the verge of reentering one of my former occupations.''

"Where'll you be?"

"The main library." He glanced at his watch. "Believe it just opened."

In the periodical room, Frank inserted the microfilm for the L.A. *Times*, month of March, 1989. He brought the image into focus and slowly began to scroll forward to March 27, 1989. Nothing. In the Metro section of May 5th, he noticed a short article near the bottom of the page. *Santa Monica Man Pleads Not Guilty.* Frank began to read. Howard Rosenthal, arrested and charged with dealing four kilos of cocaine to an undercover DEA agent, today entered a plea of not guilty. . . . Rosenthal, who was a tennis star at the University of Florida, and who was once ranked thirty-ninth in the world, was a teaching tennis pro at the Beverly Hills Country Club.

Frank fiddled with the focus on the machine. Rosenthal, a tennis player. Jack Adams, a tennis player. So these guys were teammates at the University of Florida? Or were teaching pros together? Or roommates? And what, a year of phone calls from Mill Valley to Santa Monica, they were lovers? Frank came to the end of the column and worked his way through the blur of images to where the column continued onto the last page of Metro.

Even when he saw the picture of Howard Rosenthal and brought it into focus, there was one long last pause in Frank—a chaos beyond the constraints of grammar and declarative sentences—before Frank could conclude: Jack Adams is Howard Rosenthal. Then, he fumbled the sentence into reverse; Howard Rosenthal is Jack Adams. He felt something go through his chest, a pain, what his deepest self always knew was there in people. A false bottom. Lies. Hadn't he seen or sensed it? Or had it been deflected by his sharing Ray's blindspot? Ray had never doubted that Jack Adams was his buddy and tennis partner. That much in this tangled nightmare was a given. If Frank had removed himself from the case, would another investigator have been able to spot this? Dean Miller hadn't been booked into the jail, but Jack was. Absolutely nothing led in his direction. And the other day, after Melikian had shown him the twenty-five thousand Jack had left Ray, if there had ever been any doubts, that had removed them. DEA: up was down. As Melikian had said, "Assume nothing. It's the DEA. Up is down."

Now things seemed so simple. The DEA had gotten hold of Rosenthal: a tennis star. And Ray had surfaced on the Richie Davis disks at about the same time. The DEA knew Ray was a tennis player. And they couldn't get Ray to sell to them. Not after Davis's murder. But they had Rosenthal and they gave him a plea—maybe a long probation, no jail time—if he'd turn for them, take an identity and cover story, drive someone's confiscated Mercedes. He was perfect. He looked the part. They'd set him up in a house with a phony business, walked him onto a tennis court with Ray: get Ray to talk, do a deal with him, set him up. And it hadn't been easy. It had taken almost a year. But Rosenthal had done what no one else had been able to do with Ray. Hey, you had to hand it to Rosenthal. He'd done what he'd had to do. He'd pulled it off. It was just the coincidence of Rosenthal's being a tennis player, no more, no less, Ray's being a tennis player, and a DEA agent's spotting it, which had brought them together.

Frank stared at the picture. A smiling Rosenthal, curly blond hair, no doubt before the bust. Frank couldn't move. A guy who looked like this named Howard Rosenthal? Frank put his head in his hands, closed his eyes, the machine humming. And the stocky, explosive guy who Donna Green said had signed the lease as Jack Adams? Now Frank saw him. At the bond hearing, he'd turned and looked at Frank. A hard stare. Stocky, curly dark hair. Frank had seen his nine millimeter and knew that this had to be the case agent, the one who'd called himself Hernandez, who'd led the bust and taunted Ray all the way back to the jail. Whatever Donna Green had felt—explosive, an edge—Frank, too, had felt that day at the hearing. So he was the one who had to have come in and signed the lease, paid on the house with DEA money, set Rosenthal up in his place in Mill Valley.

Frank forced himself to stand. He stared at the image of Rosenthal, rerolled the film, switched off the machine and returned the spool.

Outside, he looked across at City Hall. Jack Adams/Howard Rosenthal called his home phone back in Santa Monica for a year, three, four, five times a week. Who'd he been calling? A girlfriend, no doubt. Maybe a boyfriend. Didn't make any difference now, and Frank wasn't going to try the number. No sense risking a warning to anyone.

Frank went to a pay phone and called Ray's number. The girl, Marla? answered. Again the hand over the receiver.

"Ray, Frank. Can you meet me?"

"When?"

"Now. Just walk out of your apartment, across the Marina Green and meet me right in front of the main gate to the yacht club. Take a short walk with me."

"I'll be there."

Frank cut across the Green. Several people were flying kites in the stiff wind. They swooped toward the ground, tails snapping. Frank spotted Ray. As they shook hands, Frank noticed the calluses from his tennis hand were gone; he had color back in his face, had gotten a haircut, and looked somewhat revived. They fell in side by side and walked silently for a minute before Frank said into the wind, "The night you went to do business . . ." Ray nodded. "I know this is a long shot, but you didn't, by any chance, happen to record the serial numbers of the bills you used when you went to the buy?"

Ray glanced at him, his eyes blue-white, small and precise in the sunlight.

"As a matter of fact, I recorded some."

"Can we get them?"

"What for?"

"Follow up a couple of ideas I have."

"Got something to write with?" Frank patted his jacket pocket. They were coming to a bench along the walk toward Crissy Field, and they sat. "Take out your pad."

"You've got them with you?" Ray nodded. "How did you know I was going to ask?"

"I didn't. Ready?"

Confused, Frank placed the pad on his knee. "Yeah, sure."

Ray closed his eyes and was still. He seemed to recede beneath his skin. The wind gusted cold off the bay, riffled his shiny black hair. In a quiet, precise voice, as though he were reading an eye chart, he began to dictate. Frank stared at him, then wrote quickly. Ray went on reciting in a flat, expressionless voice for several minutes and then stopped and opened his eyes. "Enough."

Frank looked down at the rows of serial numbers: a letter, eight numbers, a letter. "Jesus Christ, what is this, Ray? You're not joking?"

"It's a memory system I taught myself. A big house, furniture in the rooms, drawers in the furniture, each one contains something; I'll explain it sometime."

Frank was always amazed by Ray. Always. And how could a guy with this much canniness and discipline have left a motel phone number and date on a pad in his kitchen? Because he'd stopped caring after Sarah Anne left. Had to be.

Frank was still shaking his head when Ray gave him a sidelong glance. "About five years ago, I thought I wanted to go to medical school—don't laugh—and be a surgeon. I like precision. Ophthalmology. Eye surgery. They're doing things now with cataracts, radial keratotomy, lasers. I

knew I could just soak up that anatomy and chemistry."
Ray shrugged.

Stupified, Frank stared at the columns of serial numbers. Ray stood and they continued on down the walk, Ray a few steps ahead of him. Frank looked at his back. The closer he got to Ray, the less he knew him.

It was just after one when Melikian buzzed Velma, and she nodded, "Go ahead, Frank . . . He's got just a couple of minutes, then he's on his way to a meeting in San Mateo."

Frank nodded. "I'll be a minute."

As Frank stepped into the office, Melikian was standing behind his desk. "Frankie . . ."

"Aram, I know you're jammed. Please don't let me interrupt you. I just wanted to check something out—is your safe open?"

Aram nodded, "Safe's open. What'd you want to check?"

Frank mumbled, "The Jack Adams money."

Distracted, Melikian nodded and went on skimming through files. Frank pushed open the safe door, kneeled. The twenty-five thousand cash which Jack Adams—Rosenthal—had dropped off was still neatly stacked in the bottom of the safe. Frank pulled out the list of serial numbers Ray had given him, unbundled the cash, and quickly started sorting through the hundreds. After matching six or seven numbers, he quickly broke it off and shoved the list back into his shirt pocket. Behind him, Melikian was still scratching notes on a yellow pad. Frank replaced the bundles. They were the same bills Ray had used to make his buy. It was Ray's money. The DEA had given it to Rosenthal to funnel back to Ray. A last diversion. What perverse fuckers. They hadn't missed a trick.

Frank stood and straightened his pants. Now he saw the whole of it from beginning to end. After setting Ray up, Rosenthal had taken the bust with him, gone through the charade of pretending his case was active, the bond hear-

ing, staying in jail, all of it. The D.A.'s deal with Rosenthal
down in L.A. had to have been to cover him—that's why
Winters had balked when Aram had threatened with the
Brady motion. And why he would probably rather plea-
bargain than give up Rosenthal's identity. The last of it
was making this show of helping Ray with this pile of
cash—Ray's cash—and pretending to jump a bail he'd
never had to make. Now he could disappear and that was
it, Jack jumped. Hey, these guys were good. It was also
probably seventeen shades of prosecution misconduct.

In a distracted voice, Melikian said, "What are you doing, Frank?"

"Just trying to figure out something about this money."

"And?"

Frank hesitated. Now wasn't the time to tell Melikian.
Or anyone. No way. He had to take all of this in, figure it
out. "I don't know."

"What were you thinking?"

"I thought this money might have come from another
bust—another defendant of mine in a different case—that
there might be some connection between these guys."

"And?"

"Didn't pan out. I know you're jammed so I'm not
going to bug you now." Melikian was still sorting files
into his briefcase. "You said Winters asked you not to file
the Brady motion until he contacted you again."

"Right."

"And he hasn't gotten back to you yet?"

"No."

"Let me know when he does." Melikian nodded,
closed his briefcase and groped for the jacket hanging over
the back of his chair. He didn't meet Frank's eyes. Frank
stood. "I'll be back in touch."

"Sorry it didn't pan for you."

"What it is, my man."

S TOPPED AT A light on Mission, Frank watched the swirl of people moving in and out of the produce, poultry and fish markets. Ahead, a lowrider's bass thudded something. Frank drank his third espresso from a to-go cup. If he could maintain speed, nothing would fall or hit the ground; he felt the silent momentum, the icy clarity of sunlight on the chrome bumper in front of him, fought the rising undercurrent of dread. He glanced at his watch. Ten after three. Gloria had said Kramer would be home between three and four.

Again he saw the image of Jack Adams blurring to a stop, then coming into focus in the library projector; there was the name beneath: Howard Rosenthal. Closing his eyes, Ray began to recite serial numbers in a monotone. And one by one, there were the numbers matching the bills in Melikian's safe. There could be no doubt how this had been put together.

Hey, if he handed it over that Jack Adams was Howard Rosenthal to Melikian, then Aram wouldn't have to file any Brady motions with the court or play any more games. He'd know where he stood. And if Melikian went to trial behind that, he would try to discredit Rosenthal. Maybe he could make the entrapment defense fly. He says to the jury, look at Rosenthal, a coke dealer, a felon, a guy who spent a year getting close to Ray—it took him a whole year! That's how eager Ray was to be involved. Eventually, yes, he drew Ray in. How? He tempted him with a pile of cash—and, yes, Ray turned out to be human; he saw the money and he was seduced, as anyone of us with the best intentions and strongest will might be. Ray has no record. He has no prior convictions; he doesn't even have any prior arrests. Frank could just hear Melikian going on to the jury: But Rosenthal? What did Rosenthal have to gain? Everything! He was told by the DEA that if he could get Ray, he'd get his freedom.

Frank licked his dry lips. He could see things going a lot of different ways. There were the Davis ledgers of Ray's previous transactions with him—four, five years old.

How long would they be admissible as evidence? There were a lot of things to consider. . . .

One thing Frank knew for sure. Once he gave Rosenthal to Melikian, whatever was going to happen would from then on be completely out of his hands, and Melikian, in his autocratic way, would call the shots. Screw Melikian. If anyone was going to be in control, it was Frank.

A couple of cholos on the corner, shirts blowing open, pants high, yelled, "How much for the Caddy, vato?" He shook his head no. The light changed. Then again, Frank could see it another way. He gives the name to Melikian; Melikian decides, yeah, definitely, he'll go to trial, he'll walk Ray, and so this now puts Rosenthal on the stand as the Government's star witness. Rosenthal is no dummy. He'd sold himself to Ray, a very tough sell. And once he's up there, and Rosenthal talks, who knew who else he'd give them; Rosenthal knew that Ray and Frank were buddies. Hey, Frank was in the middle of this. Given the opportunity, Rosenthal would never be able to make himself look better than by giving the prosecution the defense's investigator.

Frank drank off the espresso. But if Rosenthal's name never went through Melikian, Frank wouldn't be taking any chances on what might or might not come up from Rosenthal; he wouldn't be hurting Ray much by withholding the name, since Melikian and the prosecution would just continue on course to a plea bargain. Things might work out.

A couple of blocks from his house, Frank saw Kramer's truck parked; he slowed, pulled into a space behind it. As he started down the street, it came to him, obliquely, in the rhythm of his stride, that hey, if he'd gone to all this trouble to find out about Jack Adams, and he wasn't going to give the name to Melikian—he wasn't, was he?—then he might as well give the name to Ray and collect twenty thousand dollars. Ray had always said there was someone. Ray wanted the name. Frank had the name. Hey, on one level alone, that's what he did, found things out and sold the information. He didn't know what Ray would do with the name, but that wasn't his problem. He found out a lot of things for a lot of people, got paid, and then they did what they did . . . the next thing they had in them. He'd found out a long time ago that he couldn't be judge and jury to everything that went across his desk. That wasn't his job.

He stepped up onto Kramer's porch and rang the bell. It became clear; Ray deserved the name. The bottom line was friendship. Kramer opened the door.

"What's shakin, Slick?"

"Just got in a few minutes ago." In the kitchen, Frank noticed several containers on the windowsill in the sun. Zinnias. "Those were the flower seeds you gave Zack back when. Remember?"

"Oh, yeah, Jesus, here they are. I'd completely forgotten. Killer." Frank turned to Kramer. "Hey, Gloria tells me you're on your way to L.A. in a few days."

"I've got to interview some Salvadoran refugees who were tortured by the right wing repression."

Frank paced. "There's no way you can put off going?"

"I really can't, Frank, I've had my work on a back burner for the last three weeks. The *Mother Jones* article is already late."

"You couldn't possibly put it off a few more days?"

Something evasive in Kramer's glance? "Frankie, listen, if I could, I would. I really would."

"No, I understand, it was wrong of me to ask. That's okay, Steve, you've been there for me, man. I won't ever forget it. I'll get something figured out. Save me an hour before you go so we can update on what you've been working on—the details."

"We can do that now."

Frank shook his head, "Tomorrow, maybe. Not now." Frank fought off his uneasiness, and then, giving in to it, he walked to the door of the living room and switched on the stereo. He found a rock station and turned it up loud. Frank returned to the kitchen. He lowered his voice.

"Steve, I want to talk to you about a couple of things." Frank said, "What if you had the name of someone who screwed your friend, and your amigo wanted that name?"

"Who?"

"Who's not important, Steve."

"Well, what would he do if he had the name? The friend?"

"I don't know."

"No idea? You just said he was your friend."

"I still don't know what he'd do. He's not like you and me. I just think maybe he needs to know how some things went together."

"Do you know him or not?"

"I think I do and then he keeps surprising me. I can't be judge and jury to everything. When I started this business, I tried that, I was a smart ass, I thought I'd know everything for everyone. It drove me crazy. Now I handle my part and pass it on and it works better. This guy's a friend of mine. He wants a piece of information. I've got it." Frank didn't say anything about the twenty thousand.

Kramer gazed at the zinnias on the windowsill, touched the soil. "Okay, so? What do you want to do about your friend? Give him the name?"

Frank shrugged. "We go back a long time. He did something once which got me out of trouble. He's taken some risks, looked out for some of my interests, never asked a lot of questions. He's always been there for me. That's a friend, isn't it?"

"Could be."

"That's a friend, Kramer. Hey, we go back a long time. If you had information about someone who was doing me, wouldn't you give it to me?"

"Probably. But if I thought you were going to get into something stupid, I really don't know."

"So who are you to decide what's stupid for me?"

"Sometimes that's part of friendship."

"I think it's part of friendship not to second-guess your friends. If you had some information about someone who

had hurt me, you'd give it to me. I know you would."
Kramer stared at the floor and didn't answer. "What,
you'd just leave me out there?"

Kramer glanced up too suddenly. "I'd give it to you.
If I thought it would hurt you not to know."

Frank nodded. "That's all I'm talking about. Buying
and selling information, you do it, I do it all the time. Look
at the Curtis Bledsoe-Ashanti Flowers thing. Bledsoe's up
for rape, assault, heavy jail time. He raped her, beat the
shit out of her. Doesn't matter. We turn Ashanti into a ho,
dude. Sold that information back to the attorneys—kinda
cheap, considering it's saving Bledsoe from ten years in
the slammer—and behind that information, Bledsoe's lawyers get him a deal, probation, instead of Soledad. Is it
fair? Is it justice? No. What is it? It's a game."

"Yeah, but . . ."

"Hold on, Steve, before you go getting up on my leg,
is that so or not so, what I just said."

"It's so."

"Right, and you played your part, dude-san. It's called
the criminal justice system. It's a factory that processes
crime."

Frank saw a bottle of opened red wine on the counter,
uncorked it, threw open a cabinet, and filled a glass almost
to the top. "Okay?" He held up the bottle. Kramer
shrugged. "How about you, Steve?" He held up the glass.

Kramer went in and turned down the stereo. Frank took
a swallow of the red wine, followed its warmth. Another.
"But hey, Steve, what am I talking about? You do it every
day. Journalism. I know you suck your people on to get
em where you want; you were telling me about that Latino
general, what was his name?"

"Which one?"

They looked at each other and laughed.

"Which general? The one who was telling you his little
horror stories about the people he'd tortured and exe-
cuted—first I had their women raped in front of them, then
I made them beg, then I cut off a finger, then I shot them—

and then he made some weird little joke and waited for you to laugh and you hated this fucker but you laughed because you both knew if you didn't laugh, he wasn't going to keep talking and the bottom line here for you—cause you were looking for information, Slick—was to keep him talking. Am I right or am I wrong?" Kramer nodded. "Is that the story you told me or not?"

"Yeah, that was Enrique Baldenegro and you're right."

"And when that fucker said laugh, Jewboy, or I pull the plug on this interview, you laughed with señor torturer and murderer, didn't you?" Frank took a deep swallow of his wine. "Baldenegro had that laugh on you. He said, let me see you dance a little, fucker. You're a player, Stevie, like everyone else, so don't go getting up on my leg here."

"I'm not. You asked me what I thought."

"Right, and I'm telling you a few things, too. Your shit stinks like everyone else's." Kramer's eyes flashed, his posture stiffened. "Don't like hearing that, Kramer?"

Kramer went to the cabinet, took out a jelly jar with Fred Flintstone chasing a green dinosaur on it. He filled the glass with wine and drank half.

Frank smiled. "Good for you." Kramer finished it, banged the glass on the counter. "Good for fucking you, Slick. First one in six, seven years?"

"Six." Kramer wiped his mouth. He held up the glass. "It's nothing to me, Frank. Just nothing. June matters. Zack matters. My friends matter. My work matters." He held the glass up. "The rest, none of it matters." He shrugged, turned the glass over. "That's what I think of the whole thing." Kramer looked at Frank sharply. "What, it's a big deal, you want to see me do it again? Fine." Kramer filled the glass again, drank half.

"Whoa, Homes, you're not used to it." Frank could feel the crazy edge in Kramer surfacing.

Kramer said, "Now you're trying to stop me." Kramer took another big swallow.

"Tell me something, Kramer. It's always there, isn't it?

You're exactly the same person and it's always there and it never goes away.''

Kramer nodded. ''All the parts are always there. Maybe the proportions change a little.''

''So how do you do it?''

''You're going to have to figure it out for yourself.''

Frank picked up the bottle and filled his glass. ''You laugh when the Latino general says laugh so you can get your story. Hey, it's a buy-and-sell world, Stevie.'' Frank took another swallow of wine. ''So someone does you. Whatd'ya think, shouldn't I give you the name?''

Kramer said, ''What if you turned out to be wrong? You had the wrong person.''

''I'm not wrong.''

Frank placed his empty glass in the sink. Kramer didn't meet his eyes. Melikian, too, had looked away into his briefcase the whole time he'd been in his office. What, were these guys up to something?

Kramer followed him to the front door and let him out. In the middle of the street, Frank looked at his house; a small, old Victorian on a narrow, sunny street; overhead, the sky was high, faraway, blue. Rosenthal had conned Ray for a whole fucking year, pretended to be his friend. With an uncertain feeling of belligerent regret—should he have talked to Kramer?—Frank headed for his car.

Frank looked up from his office desk, took a swallow of vodka. Through the clear top panes, he could see the blue sky slowly darkening into night. The stereo uncoiled soft loops of jazz into the stillness. He had turned off his message machine and wasn't answering the phone's occasional ringing, including one long series that might be Karen. He tipped back in his chair. A couple of hours earlier he had called Gina—could he stop in later, there was something he wanted to talk to her about? She hesitated, ''Yes, come over, Frank, we have a lot to talk about.'' Later would be about now. What *did* they have to talk about?

He took another swallow of vodka, winced at its heat

and hardness. Since he talked to Gina, he hadn't stopped thinking about the five safe deposit keys, which were now locked in the filing cabinet, along with her letters. There was something good about himself in those letters. He was going to reread them. Twenty pounds lighter, too. And didn't drink. And Karen, Frank knew, had felt her between them and had packed to leave; then they'd spent three days making love and he could see Karen's face again, open, tender, and it was like when they'd met, and then slowly it had slipped through their fingers; it was always just out of reach. With Karen, he wanted to drink. With Gina, he'd been okay. Maybe.

He realized he was starved, but food seemed impossible; he called, ordered a medium pepperoni and sausage, gave the office address: have the delivery boy ring the bell. He pushed back in his chair, spun the Rolodex, refilled his glass, and decided that he wanted to talk to George Buckner. High school. Basketball team. Now a bond salesman in Manhattan. He got an answering machine, hung up, dialed Kramer, got his answering machine, Frank drew on a yellow pad as he left his message: "Hey, Kramer . . . listen, I . . ." He understood Kramer's drinking this afternoon was to show that drinking no longer had a hold on him, and that's why we'll always be friends, though I don't approve of your choice of glassware—Fred Flintstone chasing a green dinosaur.

He sighed and took another swallow of vodka, noticed most of the bottle was gone. When? He shook it. Frank dug out his wallet, fumbled up another number, dialed, somewhere faraway in the building, the doorbell rang a long time, Frank didn't hear, he heard himself talking, he scrawled on the pad, the building was silent, the room got close and airless, and Frank hanging up the receiver, stood, banging the swivel chair against the wall. Focussing on the window across the room, he took a step, the room lurched, spun, he grabbed for his desk, took another couple of steps and made it to the sofa.

*   *   *

Through a close, enshrouding nausea, Frank heard the phone ringing. It rang a long time, then stopped. Soft jazz. He opened his eyes. Green light of the stereo receiver above him on the shelf. And high above that, balanced on the ducts, Kramer's board, bright red, skeg like a razor. He swallowed, closed his eyes, felt a place he'd been close back over him. An island. Heavily wooded, trees growing right up to the runway. Puget Sound. George Buckner, his father's Cessna, everyone tripping on acid, four of them. George revving the engines for takeoff, he released the brake, they were just rolling forward when Frank sensed a blur of movement, then a thud and wrenching vibration, the canopy splashed red. When they climbed out, a doe was lying on the runway; it had bolted from the trees and been cut in half by the prop, and a perfectly formed fawn, beautiful, delicate, untouched, was still enfolded within her. Frank opened his eyes and forced himself to sit up. The room was slowly whirling. He stood unsteadily, and stepping over his fallen files, he walked to the door. He froze. Listened. Someone out there?

He listened hard. He swallowed, trying to get some saliva. He walked back to his desk, sat down. In a light sweat, he glanced down at the yellow pad. His writing was jagged, bent forward like someone leaning into a hurricane. He remembered coming to the office. Calling Gina. Jesus, he was supposed to meet Gina sometime. He looked at his watch. It was 3:30 in the morning. Who had he called? He turned the pad around looking for clues. Flintstone. Why had he written that? Through the tangle of weaving lines and doodles, Frank made out a phrase: *jackadams*= and scrawled over that, *howrosenthal* and over that he had written a phone number. He pulled out his wallet, matched the number with one on a card. It was Ray's apartment number at the Marina. He had called Ray.

He stood queasily and suddenly knew that he might make it out of the building, but also knew that there was someone waiting for him between the building and his car. Those two creeps. More. Or others. They were through fooling with him. They were out there. His car was parked two blocks down toward Mission to the east. The loaded shotgun in the trunk. The thing now was not to panic. Okay, he'd go out on the second-floor sundeck beside the kitchen. Drop to the ground. Ten feet. Stay behind the building. Go through the neighbor's lot. Cross the alley. And he wouldn't go to his car. He'd do the unexpected. He'd leave it. He fought off the terrible pain in his head, looked down at the letters on the pad. *jackadams=*. He had no memory, but here it was; he'd called Ray. It was a hole in him.

He felt another surge of panic, closed his eyes into that terrible acid trip, the canopy streaming red with prop-blown blood, the perfectly formed fetus of the fawn still undisturbed and enfolded within the doe's uterus, and kneeling, looking close, he'd seen the tiny eyelids and nostrils and hooves. . . .

He dialed his home phone, and Karen answered, voice hoarse with sleep, but nervous. "Karen . . ."

"Christ, where are you? I've been calling all over. You know I sleep badly when you're out. My God, Frank." Her voice was choked.

"Can you come pick me up at the office?" There was a pause. He was about to say he'd fallen asleep, but even though this was true, he'd used it too many times. "There's something going on. I need your help."

"What's going on, Frank?"

It was too big to say. Ray. Jack Adams. The black and white picture skidding to a stop in the L.A. *Times*. Rosenthal. Other things, too, all too much to go into with her. Frank could only think of the loaded Remington in the trunk of his car, how far it was. "I can't explain, but can you help me?"

"Frank . . ."

"Please."

"What can I do, Frank?" Resigned, but more awake. "I'd do anything to help you."

"Just drive to the office and pick me up. But listen,

don't come up to the building itself. Drive to the corner of Smith and Ivy. That's two blocks to the west.''

"I know where it is.''

"Wait, listen to me. Drive to the intersection, slow but don't stop, and I'll be there. Leave the passenger side door unlocked . . . I'll get in.''

"What is it, Frank?''

"I told you, I can't explain, and I can't talk on this phone, but it's something to do with a case. Just come now.''

"I'll be there in twenty minutes." She hung up.

He stood and scooping files up off the floor, he placed them on the desk. He dropped the empty bottle of vodka into the basket, covered it with some paper, unlocked the filing cabinet and took out a brown manila envelope, felt the five safe deposit keys within. Turning off the light, he stepped carefully onto his desk, reached up and placed the envelope out of sight on top of Kramer's surfboard. In the dark, he relocked the cabinet, and then, ripping the top sheets off the yellow pad, he tore the pages into tiny pieces. Flintstone. *jackadams=*. Christ, he'd called Ray. He'd given him Rosenthal. He went to the door.

Holding his breath, he listened; slowly working the bolt back, he eased open the door and stepped out into the darkened hall. In the bathroom, he gulped water from the tap, retched once, splashed his face, and then quietly climbed the long, narrow stairway to the second floor. He listened into the enormous dark building, and eased down the hall toward the kitchen. He opened the door to the sundeck and crouching, made his way to the back of the deck, climbed over, let himself down arm's length, hung and dropped several feet into the alley. Dizzy, he cut through a lot, an alley, and down the street to the intersection of Smith and Ivy.

After a few minutes, Karen came slowly rolling through the intersection, and he jogged out to meet the moving car, yanked open the passenger-side door, and jumped in. "Go. Jesus, GO!''

She stepped on it as he looked back. "What's going on, Frank?"

"I can't explain. I really can't."

She drove on in silence, and then said, "My god, you're living your life like it's some kind of weird movie." She reached over and touched his forehead and face. "You're sweating. You look just awful. You reek of alcohol." She shifted, drove on, Frank looking ahead. "Frank, I can help you. Let me help you. Let me back in."

Frank closed his eyes. He glanced back as lights came up quickly, passed them. He could see Karen was freaked. What was the best approach to her now? "I'll do whatever you think is best."

As she wound through second, she took her hand off the gear shift and squeezed his hand. "Okay, Frank, okay." They drove up Valencia, Karen alternately fitting her hand to his between shifting gears, neither saying anything more.

Slumped in an easy chair by the window, Frank tried to sip warm tea mixed with milk and honey which Karen had brought him. Sally, the Siamese, curled in his lap; Joe stood on his knee. Hands shaking, Frank extended a table-spoonful of tea, and Joe spattered his knees as he drank. Still brushing her hair, Karen burst from the bathroom and shook her head at the scene. "Frank . . ."

He'd slept briefly, sleep like something high-pitched and electronic. Now, exhausted, sick, he watched Karen moving around the bedroom as she finished dressing. She was making an elaborate show of nursing him, which he, not wishing to play the penitent, ignored.

". . . you're not going to drink that now after the spoon's been in the cat's mouth."

He took a sip of the tea. "The worse that happens is six months from now, I fall off the sofa licking my parts, break my neck and then you don't have to worry any-more."

Karen stopped a few steps away. "Is there anything you

want before I go. More tea?'' He shook his head. ''You need fluids, Frank. Can you try toast?''

''Not yet. Thanks again for coming last night. I keep telling you how sorry I am, but I don't know if you believe me. It's a case I'm doing, Karen, it's wrapped me up. It's just too involved and I can't talk about it now. . . .''

She nodded, but he could see she didn't believe him. She kissed him on top of his head. ''No more now. We're talking tonight, Frank. No matter what, be here. That's all I have to say. Be here.''

''I'll be here.''

He heard the front door slam, waited, went downstairs and made some toast, gingerly took a bite. Then he went in, felt behind the bathtub, and found the vodka. One swallow to ease the hangover. He took a sip, winced, another hard swallow. He took another sip, felt worse, felt better. With one more gulp, he finished the bottle and realized he had to talk to Kramer, get a hold on something.

Across the street, he rang Kramer's bell, but there was no answer. Fuck it, he didn't need to talk to Kramer or anyone else. He looked for his car before he remembered he'd left it by the office last night; he walked out to Van Ness to catch a bus, stopped off for a quick vodka. . . . Sometime later, he was driving, the afternoon blurred. Then he was down at Union Square with the street people drinking from a bottle as night came on. Later, he was with Gina and for an hour she was the most beautiful woman he'd ever seen—ever. Leave with me, Gina, we'll go somewhere, leave now, don't think about it, let's do it. All your life you've wanted to go away. Admit it. I have. I've got five million dollars, we go away, we make it work. . . . A while later he was enraged at Gina and driving somewhere alone, she had held his hand, she had talked softly, she had tried to take him to see her sponsor from AA. . . .

Then again, it was another day. The next day? And Frank remembered that Karen had wanted him to see her new office and hey, he hadn't made time, and that was really wrong, but he'd stop in now. He was getting out of the car when the sun caught him and he saw himself in a shop window, hair wild, shirttail out, and realized no way, and you know, he didn't want to see her office or anyone else's office, it was all self-important lies, offices, phones, everyone keeping up the bullshit and pretending what? And later still he exploded into a shoving match with some yup in a suit who'd looked down his nose at Frank, sucker punched him, Frank had recovered, knocked him to the sidewalk, had to be restrained, broke free, took off.

Much later—when?—he was home, sprawled in his bed, sweating, sick, dry-heaving, no idea what day it was, and Karen and Kramer were standing over him, both of them talking in low voices. Then they were gone and it was another day, he was feeling a little better, sitting in a chair, hands shaking. Karen was saying, ". . . and Frank this Saturday we are meeting. We'll make it a lunch. We're talking. And this time you will keep your word and be there. I know the thought of food doesn't seem very appetizing right now, but you'll feel better by then."

"Okay."

"No matter what you have to do, this comes first."

"Okay. I will be there."

"Here at noon; we'll go together for a one o'clock lunch."

"Okay. Let's see your new office afterward. I want to see it. I'm sorry, Karen."

"I know you are. Okay. Good. My office afterward."

"I'll be here. Noon. One o'clock lunch. We'll go together." He held up Joe. "Can I bring the guys."

"Frank," she said in a level voice. "Don't be here or make a joke of it and see what happens." She surveyed the room once more, looking for anything she might have forgotten. "I'm tied up in a meeting this morning, but if you need me, call. There's broth for you in the refrigerator. Have something. Drink before Saturday, Frank, or don't keep our date and I'm gone."

"Karen, whatever it was, it's over. I know it. I have

the feeling I'll never drink again, as a matter of fact."

She didn't answer and went out.

Frank switched on "Today" and taking comfort in the background ordinariness of TV, he stood unsteadily, groped into the kitchen, microwaved the broth and sipped a few spoonfuls. Upstairs, he dozed into the background of TV voices. Blurred. Gina. God, something bad happened with her. Then he saw some guy hitting the sidewalk in front of him. Hit him, hadn't he? He felt a bruise on the back of his head. Then a terrible clarity: Frank jerked upright, wide awake: somewhere back four or five days ago, he'd given Rosenthal to Ray. He sipped the broth. . . . But no one knew Frank had found out Jack Adams was Howard Rosenthal. If the Feds had a tap on his office line, then maybe they'd heard him talk to Ray. Rule number one: never talk on the phone. He'd talked. Ray always had one more surprise in him for Frank: the other day, the sound of Ray reciting those serial numbers in a flat monotone. *That* was weird. Hey, whatever Ray did now, Rosenthal had it coming. There was little enough justice in the courts. So if he'd given Ray Rosenthal, then that was between those two. Friendship was the bottom line here. But if the Government's snitch ended up dead, it would go right back to Ray. And from Ray, back to Frank. Accessory to a murder. Frank eased back on the bed. The cats curled up on him as he slipped into a light doze inhabited by answering machine voices—Gloria, a succession of attorneys, Kramer, Gloria again. Between him and that phone call nights ago, a canyon of confusion, a blur. . . .

He was just out of the shower, still nauseated, early afternoon, the ball game on, when he recognized Melikian's voice recording on the answering machine. He picked up. "Frank . . . Frank? That you? Aram here. Jesus, where are you today? I've been calling for days, no one could find you, your own secretary doesn't know where you are."

"I've been working a case in the field. Hold on." Frank

fumbled with the message machine. "Okay, go ahead."

"Winters got back to me first thing this morning on Ray Buchanan. You remember where we left it. My part: There's an informant in here. We're not guilty: entrapment. What and who do you really want? Tell me something or I'm filing my Brady motion for disclosure. Remember?"

"I remember."

"And he said, hold on, don't do anything until I get back to you: don't file any motions. You remember the sequence, right?"

"I remember. Absolutely."

"Okay, so here's what Winters comes back with yesterday. He says, 'If you make a Brady motion for us to disclose our informants, and your motion is granted, I'm going to dump my case, and your guy will walk. You'll win.'

" 'But,' he says to me, 'if you file your motion, and the court rules against you, I'll put Ray away for a hundred fucking years. You'll never make your case for Ray. You'll have a bitch of a time making an entrapment case. I'll bury him. So there it is.'

"You know, Frank, this reminds me of that prosecutor down in San Diego. What was his name? He fucked up, gave away the identity of one of his snitches by mistake, she was killed a week later. Someone emptied an AK-47 into her as she got into her car. You remember that?"

"Michael Ott was the prosecutor. He killed himself two years later. People said he couldn't get over it."

"That's the one. Well, that wouldn't be the problem with Winters; he'd get over it. But he doesn't like it when he can't protect his snitches. Maybe he wants to use this guy again."

"So you lay off the motion to disclose and what will he give you in return?"

"He says, 'Melikian, I'll do you a real favor. The case agent Hernandez got a couple of throw-ins on this bust. He got Sammy. He got Jack Adams.' " Frank shook his head at the smoothness of the pretext which Winters was keeping up on Jack Adams. " 'So I'll give Ray forty-eight months if you don't file your motion for disclosure.' "

"That's the offer."

"Carrot and stick. File your motion, you sink or swim. That's it."

"What'd you tell him?"

"I told him I had a case, I'd file my motion, I could win, but would reconsider taking an offer for twenty-four months."

"And?"

"Winters screamed."

"Loud?"

"Loud. But when he got done screaming, he came back with thirty-six months. I tried for thirty, but thirty-six was his number and I took it. Thirty-six months is good, damned good. We get Ray a medium security prison, Ray's out on probation in eighteen months, what? it's nothing. He's moved millions of tax free dollars."

"Jesus, Aram, we're on a phone."

"I'm just talking to you. Allegedly."

"And if you took it to trial?"

"You know, given the evidence, Ray has a winnable case, but I don't have the informant's name and if the court ruled against me on the motion to disclose, then where am I? Winters said, start filing motions and have the court rule against you, and we'll bury you. Hey, I've got to take Winters at his word and think of Ray and what I'd be exposing him to here."

Frank straightened the towel around his waist. Maybe he could meet Melikian somewhere, give him the name; if Winters didn't want Rosenthal's identity exposed, maybe that could get the case thrown out right there: we know who he is; stop right here. But Frank was uncertain he'd given the name to Ray; or, he couldn't risk telling Melikian and then have it turn out he had given the name. No way. Not now. Today, he gives Melikian Rosenthal, Rosenthal turns up dead down the road, the Feds come straight back to Ray, Melikian, and Frank, who is now an accessory to a murder, with a respected attorney to be subpoenaed to testify that his former investigator uncovered the Government informer's identity. And did what with it? Gave it to his client, Ray Buchanan, who turned around and had the guy killed.

"You there? Frank?"

"I'm here."

"So I'll be in touch with Buchanan on this latest development. I think he'll be happy. There will be some details to clean up, but this will cover it for now."

Frank wondered how killing a Government informant would look on a presentence report.

"Okay, Frank, we'll be in touch. I'll see you Saturday . . ." He stopped abruptly.

"What're we doing Saturday?"

"Nothing. I said I'll see you later."

"Saturday?"

"Did I say Saturday?"

"Yeah, just now."

"It couldn't have been Saturday. I've got tickets to the Giants game. I must have been thinking of Tom Gutweiler. We're sitting together, and I was just going to give him a call. You want to come, I'll make a call and get you a ticket. We're right behind third base, six rows up. Great seats."

"Saturday? Who they playing?"

"Cincinnati. Giants are a game behind them. Should be a dogfight."

"I'd like to see that, but I've got something I'm doing with Karen. If I miss it, she'll kill me. Afternooner?"

"Two o'clock."

"Yeah, can't make it."

"Okay, we'll be in touch."

"Nice going on the plea bargain."

"My job."

"You think Buchanan will take it?"

"He'd be crazy not to. When I get through talking to

Ray, he'll take it. Given what he's looking at, it's a good deal. I'm gone." Melikian hung up.

Saturday? Frank held the receiver. Then, realizing he was standing naked in a puddle of water and holding a phone in his hand, he hung up, and went upstairs to dress.

Frank watched Cal Ripken Jr. fight off a series of three-two pitches before getting a soft single just over the short-stop's outstretched glove. Becoming aware of an insistent rapping, someone calling? he inched up the front blind, looked down on Kramer, who was on the front walk shading his eyes and surveying the house. Frank went down to let him in. He quickly rebolted the door. "Let's go up-stairs, Slick." Temples pounding, Frank followed Kramer. Kramer circled the room, watched the ball game, circled. "What's the score?"

"Six-three Baltimore, bottom of the fifth. Kramer, for Christ's sake, please sit down, you're wearing out my eye-balls already. Oh, stop, Kramer! What! Just say it!"

"I'm not saying anything."

"You're saying it with your expression. Okay, hey, I fucked up big time. I have no explanation. None. I saw you do it more than once, Slick, back before you got your halo."

"Course I did it. Everyone was worried, was all."

"It's over. Please. Talk to me without this or leave."

"Okay, Frank. I took you to AA once. That's it for me. I'm not a believer in enforcement. You'll do it when you're ready. I'm leaving for L.A. in a few hours. I wanted to catch up with you before I go."

"A few hours? I thought you were leaving, when?"

"You lost a few days, remember? This was the day. Evening flight."

"Interviews? Salvadorans?" Kramer nodded. "Hey, ask em if they heard the one, what did Christ tell the Mexicans before he died?" Kramer waited. "He said, 'Y'all play dumb until I get back.' "

"These people will be rolling in the aisles over that one."

"You'll be back, when'd you say?"

"Ten days."

"So who's with June and Zack?"

"Her sister Mona is coming to stay for a week."

"That'll be nice; when blood comes in the window, there'll be two styrene instead of one. I guess he'll have em on the half shell." Frank went to his closet and came out with the Glock. "It's loaded. All she has to do is pull back the slide, hold it with two hands, and keep squeezing the trigger."

"I can't have that around the house with Zack into everything."

"He'd never be able to pull back the slide. Take it, Homes."

Kramer didn't take the gun. "June wouldn't use it even if she knew how."

Frank dropped it on the bed. "Okay, alright, I'll keep an eye on em. Your kid is my kid."

Kramer pulled a wrinkled spiral notebook from his back pocket. "I've got some notes here, I thought I'd update you on the cases I've been working."

Frank turned on the stereo until the ball game was submerged, pulled a wicker chair over close to Kramer's easy chair. They were maybe an arm's length apart. Frank said into the music, "Did I call you a few nights ago?"

"Maybe. Yeah. You're always calling."

"Did I talk to you?"

"No, you talked to the machine."

"Did I say anything about a guy named Jack?"

"No."

"Howard?"

"Nothing about a Howard."

"What did I talk about?"

"You talked about, well, you said you understood my drinking. Or not drinking."

"I didn't tell you anything about a Jack or a Howard?"

"No."

"You're sure?"

"No, Frank. Hey, man, you disappeared on us."

"Do me a favor? Can you erase all messages before you leave?"

Kramer nodded, sure. Frank slid toward inconclusiveness. He said, "Remember a morning, this was, God, literally years ago now, 1978, spring, I was a junior? New Mexico State? I'd been up all night, I brought over a lot of my stuff and left it at your place?" Kramer nodded. "There were only a few weeks left in the semester. I couldn't explain any of it and I couldn't stick around."

"You disappeared completely. Three years later I get a card out of the blue telling me you'd married Karen."

Frank glanced into the upper part of the window. The empty blue sky. In a drifting, halting beginning—a phrase, several sentences, Frank backed into a meandering monologue, turning the music up as he did so. Years ago. Ray. The desert. Jimmy Donovan. The Morris brothers. He didn't mention Ray by name: He said, "A friend." A friend took us out a back way. If it hadn't been for him, Kramer, I would have gone to prison, too. Almost three years of running. Taking jobs, leaving jobs, wondering if anyone had given me up. When I met Karen, she was an out, Kramer. After a few years this friend got back into the business, I had money with him, not much, but I left it there and it would double. Hey, I'm not Aram Melikian, I didn't have a father who owned half of Fresno. . . . The money was my future. "Do you believe me, Kramer?"

"I believe you, Frankie. What would it mean if I didn't believe you?"

Frank shrugged. "I don't know." Frank meandered on about the last few weeks starting with Ray's bust, Richie Davis's murder a year ago. His disks with names, names leading to DEA surveillance on his friend. Ray and Jack buddies, tennis partners. Frank's finding out Adams was Rosenthal and putting it all together; that's how the DEA had finally gotten to his friend. Tennis. They were tennis players. That's what it was, Kramer. That's what the Feds were betting on. Friendship. Tennis.

Kramer said, "So these are the guys you were talking about the other day—your friend wanted the name of the informant. The snitch was his buddy, his tennis partner set him up."

"Right. And my friend was so convinced it couldn't be him no one looked that way; hey, like I told you, his partner took the bust with them, went to the slam with them, bailed out with them, you know it was just a perfect con, and maybe that's why I didn't start looking until late in the game. Same blind spot as my friend. I had a feeling I shouldn't take this case. You told me not to first night I asked. Always follow your intuitions."

The baseball and heavy metal were a tiderip of noise around them, and Kramer stood and turned down the baseball game. "Did you give your buddy the snitch, Frank?"

"I know I called him."

"How do you know?"

"I found his number and some names written on my pad. I called him, Kramer."

"But you don't know for sure if you gave him the name."

"Right. Not for sure."

"Why don't you just ask him?"

Frank shook his head. "It wouldn't work, Steve. He'd know I was second-guessing myself for some reason and just say no to whatever I asked. Or even that I'd called at all. That's just so much the better for him if he plans to go ahead on something."

"You're saying you wouldn't believe him, Frank, no matter what he said."

"Not in this. Hey, he's got his interests to protect, too. If I fuck up and he wanted to keep it to himself, he'd do it. I can respect that. If I lose control, you know," Frank shrugged, "you make mistakes, you gotta pay."

"So you're telling me there's no real way for you to know for sure now?"

"I'll know for sure when sometime down the road the Feds come knocking on my door."

Kramer stood. "Little late, then. Would your friend kill someone?"

"Anyone can be anything. I see it every day. Jimmy Donovan twelve years ago turned state's evidence on his cousins. This friend of mine from the first has always surprised me, at times, amazed me. I'd say anything is possible here. I can't imagine him doing it himself. He'd probably have it done. He's got the money to cover that."

"Frank, did you give this guy the name or not? Just dig down into yourself."

"I'm telling you I don't know what to believe. Part of me says I didn't. It's not in his best interests to grease the DEA's snitch. It's going to point back one way. Part of me says, hey, I didn't give anybody anything. But then, I think about it more. My friend took this other guy to be his friend. They ate together, drank together. They played tennis every day. Finally, he trusted this guy enough to put up a million in cash on a deal. You know, the guy did him.

"If I did something to you, Kramer—you're one of my best friends—and you lost your business, your wife, what could you do to me? Anything, right?"

Kramer, uncomfortable, looked away. Frank said, "You know, one of the weirder little spin-offs of these last few weeks is that Karen thinks I'm a complete nut case. She doesn't know about any of this, what I'm saying to you, I can't tell her anything because who knows with Karen? I think she's come to believe I'm delusional. Course I've more than played into her hands by having a few cocktails, but I'm okay now." Frank shrugged, veered again. "Bottom line. I don't know what my friend would do with the name, Kramer. I just don't know."

Kramer checked his watch, put his spiral notebook away.

"You know, Homes, I leave out the names of the players here because it's safer for you. Who knows where this might end up. If you were ever subpoenaed, this way you don't have to lie on the stand. You don't know anything." Frank added, "I'd deny we ever had this conversation, anyway. Hey, it's all lies between people."

"Then don't talk to me, Frankie."

"Spare me the bullshit. You know what I'm saying." Frank went into his closet, under the floorboard, returned, counted five hundred dollars into Kramer's hand, squeezed his hand into a fist around the bills. "What I borrowed. Thanks, Slick. Sorry I took so long."

Kramer looked at the money. "It was only three."

"The rest is interest. I've been an asshole. Always take money. Don't say any more. I want you to have it. Here's the rest for your case work." Frank counted out another fifteen hundred.

"It's too much."

"I want you to have it." Frank wandered back into the closet and came out with pants and shirts on hangers. A couple of sports coats. He laid them on the bed, held a pair of almost new jeans up to Kramer. "Try these on. What're you?"

"Thirty-four."

"I was, but I've put on too much weight. Nothing fits."

"You'll lose the weight. These are almost new."

Frank held clothes up in front of Steve, separated them into piles. There were several large stacks by the time he'd finished. "Take them, Steve." Again, Kramer shook his head, no. Frank bundled them into a pile and placed them by the stairs. "You don't want em, then they're going to Goodwill. Suit yourself." Frank picked up the Glock. "Take the piece, Homes, and leave the ACLU mentality for the Jewish lawyers. A guy gets into your house, black, white or green, he's not there to talk about the fucking weather. Someday I'll tell you about my little friend Khalid and his Davis .380 and a little ride we took together." Frank shrugged, "Okay, if that's the way you want it. I'll watch your family for you. Hey, if anything ever happened to you, Steve, I'd want you to know I'd look after your kid.'' Kramer looked at Frank questioningly. "What? I hope you'd do the same for me. You're looking at me like I'm going to die soon. I've got a hangover is what it is. I fell off, but I'm okay now. It's over.''

Kramer surveyed the room, the piles of clothes, the gun, the TV, and stereo, both blasting. He was trying to make up his mind about something.

"What, Kramer?"

"I'll see you when I get back."

"Just slam the door when you go out and then try it and make sure it's locked."

When Frank thought he was gone, Kramer came back up. "Frank."

"You want the clothes. Take the clothes."

Whatever it was, it went out of Kramer. "I'll see you soon."

This time Frank heard the front door slam and then turned back to the ball game. Pacing aimlessly around the room, he found himself standing in the back of Karen's closet looking down at the two suitcases which she had silently packed in February when he'd still been having his affair with Gina. He had stopped drinking and slimmed down and Karen had *liked* that. She just hadn't known that it was coming out of his being with another woman. She'd never let on that she'd known or not known for sure about Gina. He knew she'd tried to find out. He looked down at the two suitcases, and then, gathering a handful of her dress, he inhaled her scent.

Freshly showered, Karen came up, hair in a towel turban. Saturday, a little after noon, and he was in the easy chair, watching a ball game, where he'd been Friday and through Saturday morning, engulfed by a lapping tide of TV. Last night, after a short sleep, he'd awakened beside her, sweating, there it was again, a room he had to go into, a terrible presence within, the atmosphere thick and palpable on his skin like a fog. Now she ran the blowdrier, shrill, finished and called from the bathroom. "Just about ready, Frank?"

"Oh, sure, absolutely. Ready."

Fitting a blouse into her skirt, buttoning the waist, she came out looking him over. "Like that?"

"Like what?"

"You haven't changed, showered."

"I'm okay." She returned with a laundered shirt. "What's wrong with the one I've got on?"

"Frank, the shirt is rumpled and there's a spot on it. You've been wearing it for two days."

"You want me to change my shirt, I'll change my shirt."

Frank changed. He looked her over. Tight skirt, blouse, open toe shoes. "You, Snookie-Okums, look fit to kill."

Outside, June and Zack were just getting into Kramer's Toyota pickup. Frank kneeled and hugged Zack. "The bash, dude-san. McGwire." Zack smiled and they touched forearms. "Awright. Totally awesome." Frank straightened, holding Zack's hand. "How you doing, June?"

"Good, we're just on the way to the bus station to pick up Mona; she'll be with us while Steve's gone."

"Keep your doors locked and bolted."

Karen checked her watch. "We're off for lunch."

"June, you need me for anything, I'm here for you. Anything. You name it. I'll check in on you later."

June nodded, thanks, looked quickly at Karen, and helping Zack with his seatbelt, got in and drove off.

Silent, Karen drove. Strangely, there seemed to be hardly anything to say about his fuckup—he'd apologized too many times already—and she wasn't asking for anything more, threatening, nada. She had a portfolio she wanted to drop off in the Upper Haight on the way to lunch, take a second, and he'd shrugged, fine, okay. They drove on, Karen checking her watch, a nervous fluttering glance; she found a place and parked. She picked up the portfolio. "This'll only take a second. Come meet this woman, I work with her, she's kind of neat."

Frank shrugged. "That's okay, I'll wait here. Another time."

"Come on, Frank, are we together this afternoon or not?"

Frank sighed. Just roll with it. They got out, and Frank followed her toward a well-kept, two story Victorian in the middle of the block. She pressed the bell, the latch release sounded, and Karen let them into the vestibule, and then was buzzed through a door to a carpeted staircase. "Jesus, your friend, she just lets people in without asking who they are . . . she'll wind up dead."

Karen climbed a step ahead of him. "She was expecting me, that's all." She reached a second floor, opened the door, and disappeared. Reaching the landing and catching his breath, Frank followed her in. Hands in pockets, a couple of men, their postures familiar: Aram Melikian, sports jacket, tie, slacks; John Giordano, black and red aloha shirt, beside him.

Confused, Frank glanced at his watch. Almost 1:30. "Thought you were going to Giants-Reds at two with Gutweiler, Aram?"

Not quite meeting Frank's look, Melikian said, "Changed my plans. How're ya doing, Frankie?"

Frank looked at Karen. "What is this? Where are we?" A door was ajar and inside, he could see chairs, a sofa. Again someone familiar. "Jesus Christ. Is that you, Buckner?"

"How're ya doing, Frank?"

"Thought you were in Manhattan." At the sight of George Buckner, he felt the airless nausea of the other night, office spinning, the island runway, the deer cut in half. A woman he didn't know walked toward him. Midthirties. Authority in her walk and posture. "This your friend, Karen?"

"This is Germaine Blumenthal. Come in, sit down, and she'll explain."

"Georgie, remember St. John's-Albuquerque High, we're all tied up in the playoffs; this is senior year, George

and I are the guards, thirteen seconds left, we're bringing
the ball up-court and Georgie feels the pressure and throws
the ball into the stands, I mean, no one is there to take
Georgie's pass. Albuquerque inbounds, scores with three
seconds left and wins. Remember that, George?''

George didn't answer. Frank said, ''Ms. Blumenthal,
you've got something to explain, let's hear it out here. I'll
listen.''

''I'll be glad to. Karen—and this hasn't been easy for
her—has called together a group of people whom she feels
are important to you.''

''What's your role in this?''

''I'm a psychotherapist specializing in these meetings.
We call them interventions.''

''Thank you.'' He turned to Karen. ''Does she always
stay in this persona? I mean, is it her?''

Karen said, ''I'm sorry it's this way, Frank.''

''Thought you and I were having lunch and a quiet
afternoon together.'' She shrugged. ''Snooks tell a little
fibby?''

''And I'm sorry for that, too, but it was the only way
I could get you here.''

''What's an intervention, Ms. Blumenthal? M.D. or
Ph.D. this afternoon?''

''Ph.D. with a specialty in alcohol and drug related
problems.''

''Was it the Mom, the difficult Dad, both, or the impossible boyfriend we had in our early twenties?''

''We're here to talk about you today. An intervention
is when a group of people meet with an individual and tell
how they see that person. It's done in the spirit of love,
giving and trust.''

''Hey, last few days, I fucked up. I admit it, though I
don't see how it's anyone else's business. I've apologized.
It's over now.''

Karen shook her head. ''It's not about that. If you'd
just come in and listen. No one's here to put you down.
We're trying to help you.''

"You said you'd take drastic steps. Gotta hand it to you."

"I want to save our marriage."

"And drag the whole world into it. Everyone cares about me. Unbelievable. Kind of "This Is Your Life." I didn't know I had so many friends. Any other surprises? Anyone else back there? Gloria?"

"Gloria couldn't make it."

"But you tried to get her."

"Yes, I did. I asked her. I know you think highly of her."

"Thanks, honey. Yeah, I do. Gloria's okay. Maybe that's why she's not here. Kramer? Wouldn't make it."

"Kramer went to L.A."

"But did Kramer really go to L.A., Karen? Or is that another sham, like our lunch date?" She nodded. "You asked him?"

"Of course I asked him. I know you're close."

"And he wouldn't come. Couldn't get him to buy it." All of Kramer's evasive glances, pauses, the way he'd kept looking at Frank, his final coming back before he left now made sense; Kramer had been trying to make up his mind whether or not to tell Frank. His compromise had been not to come, but not to tell Frank, either. Christ, Kramer! "Couldn't con Kramer. Or half-conned him. Something like that. Looks like you at least got him to cooperate enough to shut up."

"Frank, I don't want to get a phone call in the middle of the night that you're dead—though it's not from a lack of your trying."

Frank turned to Aram, "Cops take a dude off the street, they gotta Mirandize him, someone's gotta charge him, then there's a prelim. You don't like me, don't talk to me. Aram, wouldn't you rather be at the Giants game? Hey, you almost let the cat out of the bag the other day when we talked. 'See you Saturday.' That's not like you. But nice recovery, I gotta hand that to you. Giants-Reds."

Aram said quietly, "Frank, I wouldn't do anything to hurt you. Hey, I've been there before."

"I heard that. You took a thirty-day detour two years ago. Snowblind. I pretended not to know where you went. I never told anyone."

"You'll be okay. Just hear people out. We all care about you."

"The way you did when you knocked two thousand bucks off my bill to protect your client—legitimate hours, Aram. I made your case."

"Frank . . ."

"Where was your loyalty in that, Aram? To me or your felon client? It's okay, Aram. I understand. You play hard-ball.

"What about you, Homes?" He looked at Giordano. "What're you here for? I got in money trouble, you fucked me around, I still made every penny up to you. What's in it for you today? Or you just love me like Aram?"

"When you're on top of it, Frank, you're the best."

"Well, thanks for coming everyone, but I'm not into this circus." He backed out to the landing. Karen and Germaine exchanged looks. "Does she still get her fee if I don't stick around? Maybe a kill rate? I'll leave you to negotiate."

Karen followed him out and closed the door behind her. It was just the two of them. They were standing at the top of the stairs.

"Karen, I've got to hand it to you."

"You've just disappeared on me behind a wall of secrecy and booze. I want you back. I want to save our marriage."

"And drag the whole world into it. This is really something. And the way you put it together. Seamless. I never saw it coming."

"The other night when I came down to your office and picked you up, Frank—if you could have seen yourself. When you got in the car, you said you'd do whatever I thought was best. Next day you said we'd talk. Then I came home to find you've gone off on a four-day drunk. Oh, Frank, it's been a long time coming. You're begging for help.''

He took a step down.

''Frank, either go in and hear what everyone has to say or I'm leaving you. Hear us out, and I'll stick with you and we'll see it through.''

Part of him, detached, watched Karen with fascination; she was good, a real player. Was she bluffing? He took another step down the stairs.

''Frank. I love you, but it has to change. For you, it's a tough choice. Love. Or booze and hustles. You don't trust.'' It was like the first time when she'd said tell the truth, we'll always tell the truth, and he'd wanted to believe her—or try her. She'd burned him on that. She liked to say she was the only one he couldn't con; that's why he stayed with her. ''Go back in, Frank, we'll have a life. Go down those stairs, go into the street, and it's over, you can have the street for a wife. I'm gone.''

He saw her bags packed in the closet. She held out her hand. Then, with one arm extended, she stepped toward him the way you'd approach an animal, a bird, one step, two, until she was beside him. Then she put her arm around him. He said quietly, ''There's nothing wrong with me. I'm just overworked and exhausted. I have money problems. There's never been time to study for the bar. A few other things. That's what it's all about. I did go on a couple of drunks, but . . .'' He shrugged. ''I've had times when I haven't had a drink for months.''

''I know, babe. Hear what your close friends and colleagues have to say, that's all.''

''And get up tomorrow and work with them after this humiliation?''

''It's not humiliation. It's help. I don't want to leave you, but I will.''

Frank looked down the stairs to the bottom. He looked at Karen. He knew he should call her bluff, but he didn't dare. He couldn't bear the thought of her leaving him.

*   *   *

As Germaine Blumenthal closed the doors, Frank caught her exchange of looks with Karen; they'd won? Fine, he'd coast through this now, and later he and Karen would settle it. Part of him, fascinated, was still watching her. Whatever she was doing, it was a seamless performance. He had to love her for this alone.

Frank picked out a chair, and then John sat. Karen took the place next to him. Then he realized he couldn't see her face or keep her in view without twisting around. Aram circled the room, took a place out of Frank's direct line of sight, and George eased himself down across from Frank. An uncertain quiet descended, so pious, so somber, like the beginning of a trial or funeral, but just as Frank was about to make a crack, the mood of it eluded him; he couldn't find his voice. He recalled Karen's saying: if I could get all the stories in the same room with you at the same time. . . . She hadn't gotten all of them, but she'd gotten a lot of them. He'd played into her hands and she was taking her shot.

Germaine Blumenthal joined the circle and thanked everyone for coming. She went on to lay out the ground rules. Everything was to be said in a caring way—indeed, that was the spirit of the day and this meeting: love and caring. There was to be no vindictiveness. This was to be constructive. She said, "I'd like to start by getting people's impressions of what they see happening to you."

She paused. No one said anything. Karen said, "I'll start." She launched a determined statement about why she'd called the intervention. It was her perception that Frank was on a downward slide and while it was said you couldn't help people until they hit bottom, often that was too late. By calling people together to tell a person what they saw, you could put a dent in his denial and raise the bottom. That's what she hoped to do here today. In the last year Frank had become incredibly cynical. And in the last six weeks, he'd just been over the line. She started detailing Frank's erratic and unpredictable behavior: his long hours; his repeatedly failing to keep his dates with her; his wild mood swings; and his letting himself go physically. She went on. There was his suspiciousness, his cynicism, his paranoia. As Karen spoke, Frank looked at George; he had sat close to him at his father's funeral—the shadowy cathedral, its vast nave overhead; his father's flag-draped coffin dwarfed by the high altar; the mass; and afterward, the blinding glare in the cemetery; the long coffin hovering on its shadow over the open grave. Frank felt a queasy lurch and softening in his stomach, took a deep breath and let it out slowly.

Aram was speaking. It wasn't his usual mesmerizing wave of language. He spoke a phrase or two, halted. He said that he thought of Frank as a special friend. Difficult, yes, but rewarding. Someone he could count on in the larger sense. As an investigator, he could do amazing things with people and situations. He was often brilliant and intuitive. He'd say now in front of everyone, Frank had made many of his cases. But though Aram recognized there was a lot of stress in what Frank did—the difficult people, the impossible hours, the deadlines, the dangers—he still thought Frank went too far—his contesting of money and fees, his aggressiveness; specific incidents were brought up.

Now John was speaking. God, he loved Frank. He really did. Frank had taken him on and patiently taught him how things worked. He knew he'd be a much better lawyer for his having worked with Frank. Hey, he loved Frank's spirit, his ingenuity, his talents; he was a guy he always wanted on his side—he never could have put himself through law school if Frank hadn't cut him slack. But the money games, the outbursts of temper, this last and latest standoff over the money Frank had owed him . . .

George Buckner shifted in his chair and started to speak, but his voice broke. He cleared his throat, started again. George spoke about how close they'd been—altar boys together, the Jesuits, the time Frank had smashed that boat senior year when Brother Malcolm accused him of not having built it himself. Everyone loved him for finally standing up to Malcolm; he'd bullied them for years. They'd been starting guards Junior and Senior years. Hesitating, George went on to say he loved Frank, but hey, the phone calls, three, four in the morning when Frank was drunk, waking his wife, his quarrelsome behavior, his irrationality, his taking offense at a remark and hanging up the phone . . .

Frank could feel Karen beside him, but couldn't bring himself to turn and look at her. Again, Frank thought, did I give Rosenthal up to Ray? Kramer said, dig down into yourself, did you or didn't you? He surveyed the circle of shoes, Melikian's Gucci loafers; Giordano's cowboy boots—Christ, cowboy boots and a black aloha shirt, red roses, no less. . . . If Frank could just know for sure what he'd done about Rosenthal, he'd be closer to knowing what to believe about himself: did he belong in this room now? He raised his eyes, but didn't meet Melikian's gaze. Fuck the Brady motion, Winters' power play and plea bargain; he had the snitch. If he gave Melikian the name, Winters would have to move to dismiss rather than let it come to light, and Ray would walk. Or, Melikian could go to trial and win on entrapment; he'd make mincemeat of Rosenthal. It *was* entrapment. The right defense for the wrong reason. Not to mention the prosecution's misconduct. Fuck, tell Melikian now, they could walk out of here together, make it to the Giants game by the fourth inning. There was so much none of them knew here today. And so much Frank didn't dare say. Not now. Maybe never.

Now Germaine Blumenthal, Ph.D., was speaking again. Each of today's participants had written Frank a letter telling him what they were prepared to do if he didn't stop his drinking. They were going to read them out loud. Frank looked her over. Well-coiffed, rings, mid-thirties careerist. He could stand up and put her through the window. Still, Frank remained seated as Karen unfolded a piece of paper. He didn't look at her. She quietly started reading something. When she finished, she said, "Remember that,

Frank?'' He shook his head. She said those were their wedding vows which they'd written the night before driving off to get married. "I meant them then, I mean them now. I'm here, Frank. But if you don't stop, I'm going. I'll serve you with divorce papers and we're through.''

He didn't say anything. Aram Melikian read his letter. Clean up and we'll do cases together; we'll be friends. Keep drinking, I won't take your calls, I'll walk by you and look the other way in the Hall; we'll be finished.

Then John. As each of them went on in that vein, Frank wondered what Kramer might have said if he'd chosen to be here. But then, maybe the fact that Kramer hadn't come today said everything—that he was basically okay and Kramer knew it. If he was really over the line, wouldn't Kramer have shown up here? Kramer had always called his bluff. But why hadn't Kramer tipped him off this was coming instead of ducking out and splitting for L.A.? Everyone always had a cover story: Kramer's was interviewing Salvadorans.

George finished reading his letter and there was an awkward pause. Raising her eyebrows in inquiry, Blumenthal was looking at Karen. Karen said quietly, "Okay, I'll bring it up." She turned to Frank. "Where all of this leads in practical terms is this." He didn't look at her. "There's a thirty-day inpatient detox and rehab center in Dallas. One of the best. Counselors, a structured program. I've made a reservation. There's a late afternoon flight and their people will be waiting for you on the other end at the airport. I want you to go, Frank." Frank didn't say anything. "Frank?"

Frank shook his head. "I mean, come on, Karen."

"Have you been listening to everyone?"

"Those places cost a fortune."

"Money's not a question. We'll cover it."

"Look, Karen. Ms. Blumenthal. Everyone. Thank you for coming today. I heard it all. Thanks for your concern. I won't drink anymore. I can't take a hike for thirty days."

"It's either that or I'm leaving, Frank."

"Karen, I've got over forty cases open, I've got nine death penalty cases. I can't just walk out on my obligations."

Karen said, "I'm not unreasonable. I know what you're doing. But it's all been thought out. We'll contact your lawyers, refer your cases . . ."

"Some of them have been going on for over two years; I can't just refer this stuff; I've got people I've built relationships with; Christ, it would take someone a week just to read the discovery in People vs. Perez, alone."

"John and Gloria have offered to keep things going until you get back. I'll go in, pay your bills, take care of the paperwork, do whatever needs doing."

Frank shook his head no. "It just won't work, Karen; it won't work practically."

"It will work. It can work. It has to work." She stood, picked up her purse. "We make it work or I'm gone."

"It's either do this or I'm gone. Let's have this out in front of a few people."

"It's not people. Everyone here knows you, Frank. And there's nothing to have out. Detox, get counseling, come back, stay straight, or I'm gone now. That's all that's left." Karen remained standing.

Frank said quietly, "Could you please sit down?"

"I'll sit, but . . ."

"I heard the terms. Could you still sit. Please." Karen sat. "Thank you. You're saying I leave town this afternoon. Do thirty days in some gulag. No one knows where I've gone or what I'm doing."

"Right."

"You're saying give you the keys to my office."

"Yes, I'll take care of things."

Frank remained silent. "Fine, I speak my mind, that's trust and honesty? Let's share?"

"Yes."

"Then I'll say it here that I don't trust Karen to have the keys to my business."

"Of course you don't trust, Frank. God, read Germaine's book on that issue alone. You let me—everyone—see just a little bit of what you want. That's precisely why we're all here today in one room. You've frozen me out. Look, it's all such a vicious circle. But at some point, you have to break out.

"Frank, if I didn't have your interests at heart, would I have gone to all this trouble? Would people have come if they didn't care about you?"

He didn't answer. She said, "I'll pay your bills. I won't go into your files. John and Gloria will collect your messages; John can refer your cases, serve as a liaison—and that's it. I know how hard it is for you to trust. I understand. We understand. But it's okay. It's time for us to move on."

"And if I don't play it your way, you'll leave."

"That's right, Frank."

"Trust, but a power play, too, right?"

Karen didn't answer. Frank looked past George into the upper part of the window. Blue sky. Branches. Something queasy, a terrible feeling, his father's hospital room. Do it my way or I'll leave. "Never mind the timing or what I have to do. I have to take your trip."

"Frank, if people don't go under these circumstances, they don't ever go."

Germaine Blumenthal nodded.

"And you get the keys to my business?"

"I'll take care of it for you, Frank."

Frank remained silent. He knew she had him off balance. That he should just get up and walk. But he was sure she'd leave. He heard a voice saying, watch out. Another part of him was indifferent, almost hypnotized. Then, too, it might be good to get out of town for a while, let things chill. His having given Ray the Feds' snitch terrified Frank. He was fascinated watching Karen. She was such a player. Here she was challenging him. He had to call her bluff. And who knew, maybe something could change. He reached into his pocket, took out a ring of keys. "Okay, Karen, I'll give you the keys. And I'll go. I'm not in the throes of alcoholism or drug abuse or whatever else—five, seven months ago I quit cold turkey. . . . I mean, I can control it.'' Germaine and Karen exchanged looks again. ''Hey, I know, it's all my denial. That's the new buzz word. You all want to pay for my rest, fine. I'll stop home, pack a bag.''

Karen said, ''I have your bag packed in the trunk.''

He smiled at her. ''Snookie-Okums has thought of everything. In the trunk. Drastic. You figured I'd try to make some kind of getaway?'' He sorted three keys off his ring. She held out her hand. Frank held the keys. ''You know, first I have to stop by my office and take care of a few things.''

''John and George will go with you. I'll be at the Delta counter at five. If you're not there, I'm moving out and serving you with divorce papers and a restraining order this week.''

''You already said that. Must like the way it sounds. Gotta hand it to you, Karen.''

''If this is what it takes, then this is what it takes.''

''You said you'd do something drastic. Least you keep your word.''

''See you at Delta at five.'' She took out a checkbook and walked over to Germaine's desk. She hugged Germaine.

Frank said, ''Sisterhood.'' Karen leaned over the corner of her desk and wrote out a check for four hundred dollars. Frank rolled his eyes at Germaine. ''Not a bad hustle for two hours work, doctor.''

He went out through the waiting room. As he reached the landing, he became aware of George and John keeping up with him. He turned to them. ''Relax, I'm not going to lead you on a chase. First, I need a ride to my office. I don't have a car. Second,'' he started down the stairs, ''I want to say I'm not crazy. Karen, whew, she did a real number, whatd'ya think, maybe the best thing for me is not to show up at Delta and let her leave, that was textbook Karen at the top of her game, you guys saw it with your own eyes. Whatd'ya say we go out catch the second half of the Giants game, my treat. . . .''

They reached the sidewalk. George indicated a new white Buick Regal. "Come on, Frankie. No trouble. Please."

"Hey, Georgie, you did throw the fucking ball away in the last thirteen seconds. The pressure got to you." George unlocked the Buick and slid in. Frank was aware of John right behind him. He turned and smiled. "You're standing there so I won't make a break, right, John Giordano?"

Frank pretended to dribble a basketball and feinted to his right, and John spread both his arms. Frank laughed, turned and got in the front seat. "I'll just sit in da front between youse twos. Or, Johnnie G. sit in da back like ina thriller when deys takin da guy for a ride and deys gonna shootem or if deys not gonna mess up da car deys gonna use da piano wire. . . ."

John laughed and got in back. Just before they pulled away, Frank made another feint for the door handle. John grabbed at him, and this time after an awkward moment, they started laughing. Frank turned. "Karen conned you guys. Totally." He laughed and noticed them exchange quiet glances of doubt. Again it came to him that George had been at his father's funeral sixteen years ago, an isolated event which seemed to exist only for Frank; his eyes filling with tears, he pretended to scratch his temple and looked out the driver's side window.

Frank unlocked his office door. "I've got a couple of things to take care of in here by myself. Want to wait outside?" Buckner and Giordano exchanged looks. "Hey, relax, I said I'd meet Karen at Delta, I'll meet her. There's no way out of here, anyway. John, you know there are gratings on the window. What'm I gonna do, crawl through the ducts?"

John said, "We'll wait out here." George sank onto a broken-down sofa by the stairs and picked up an old copy of *Sports Illustrated*.

As Frank closed and locked the door, he felt the nightmarish airlessness of the other evening close over him. The room spinning, the darkened windows. He stepped up onto his desk, groped around the top of Kramer's surfboard, found the envelope. He checked. All five keys, still there. He placed them in his pocket. It was now or never.

Frank went to the window and quietly slid it up. He studied the wire mesh grating, went to a closet, took a set of Phillips screwdrivers out of a tool box. There was a pint of vodka. He took that, too, and went to work on the grating.

Giordano called. "How're you doing in there, Frank?"

"Fine. A couple of more calls and I'm ready. Be there in a minute."

He finished with the last screw and lowered the grating to the sidewalk. Beyond, the sidewalk, parked cars, the street. Frank returned to his desk, opened the top drawer to get his checkbook. He looked down at the picture of his father. He sank down and stared out the window. Shit. Today was Saturday, the banks were closed. Still, he could take off now, hide out for a day, wait until the banks opened Monday morning. But what was he going to do? Drive—and fly—everywhere with three suitcases full of cash. And where?

Once he left, that would be it with Karen. Everyone. Kramer. John. Melikian. His business. The bar. And Ray would always be back there somewhere. If Ray wanted to kill Rosenthal because he'd befriended him to betray him, what would he do to Frank, old friend, who took five million bucks while supposedly trying to defend him? Frank had felt what he'd do that day in the jail when Ray had basically warned him. Frank didn't doubt Ray. Never had. Goddamnit, he just wasn't ready to run. His timing was off.

He closed the top drawer. He had to marvel at Karen. His whole trip was reading people and catching them off balance and now here was this little masterpiece from Karen; he hadn't had a clue what was coming.

Giordano knocked again. "You still there, Frank?"

"Goddamnit, I'm still here! Be out in a minute."

Still, he sat without moving. Then Frank realized he was within moments of becoming Rosenthal. Worse. Because he *was* Ray's friend. How could he have gone so far? Maybe it was a weakness not to be able to go farther. Weakness or strength? Frank walked to the window, unscrewed the vodka bottle and took a drink.

John came up the sidewalk and looked at Frank sitting on the windowsill, drinking, grate on the walk. He started laughing. "What the fuck are you doing, Frank?"

"I'm supposed to be a drunk. I'm drinking. Drink?"

"Not right now." John changed his mind. "Yeah, sure, why not?"

Frank handed down the bottle and John took a belt. "Think you could stop me if I climbed out now?" John passed the bottle.

"Be a good fight, Frank."

"Pretty good, but you'd lose." Frank took another swallow of the vodka. "Look, Johnie G., Karen's conning us, somehow."

"You see cons everywhere. How?"

"I don't know, Slick, but she is." Frank handed down the bottle. John drank.

"I'm charged with getting you to the airport, dude-san. I will. After that, it's your call. I think she'll leave you if you don't show. What do you think?"

"I think she says I'm a drunk, gimme a drink." John passed the bottle back. "Pass me the grating and hold it." John held the grating and Frank started replacing the screws.

"What was this about, Frank?"

"Coming within a moment of something bad. I think. Or maybe I'm not strong enough. Or maybe it's just because it's Saturday and the banks are closed. Who really fucking knows? Hold this thing still, will you?"

"I am."

"Buckner doesn't need to know about this, does he?"

John laughed. "No."

They finished the grating, Frank closed the window. He saw John's shape poised outside the window and laughed. When he dialed Ray's, Marla answered. After the usual hem and haw and the hand over the mouthpiece, Ray came on, voice tense. "Ray, you know who this is, right?"

"Right."

"Okay, meet me by the Marina where we met last time. Twenty minutes. Okay?" Frank hung up.

In the hall, he said to John, "Hey, we gotta make one more stop."

"We don't have time."

"Ten minutes. I can't leave until you take me there. Don't waste time arguing, let's just go. Karen probably figured extra time in and the flight doesn't leave until six-thirty or seven. I *know* Karen. You guys only know what she told you." John opened his mouth. "Don't talk, John. Let's just go. You owe me that much. I promise it'll be fine."

At the Yacht Harbor, Frank saw Ray standing alone. "Stop here. I'll be right back." John looked at him. "John, if I was gonna go, I woulda done it by now. Please. Thank you. I'll be right back." Frank got out of the car and walked quickly toward Ray. He had the envelope folded up in his hand and as he approached Ray, Frank shook his hand with a two-handed clasp. Ray felt the envelope and took it into his hand.

"I can't hold these for you anymore. Safe deposit keys. I'll be away for a while. I don't need to tell you to be careful. Hey, Melikian told me the details about the plea bargain. I think he's done okay for you."

"He has, but I can't go to prison."

Frank shrugged. "I don't have time to talk, Ray. Given all the ins and outs and what it could be if you got the max, I'd listen to Melikian. But in the end, it's got to be your decision. Including jumping. Means being a fugitive." Ray, his precise, brilliant blue eyes, his groomed look. It was a surface, Frank realized, he'd never been able to read. There was always one more surprise with Ray. He ventured, "It's all up to you. Everything." But Ray didn't acknowledge Frank's phone call of the other night or Rosenthal or indicate what he might do with the name. Frank hesitated. Did I call you the other night? Tell you about Rosenthal? What would be the point? One way or the other, Frank wouldn't believe him anyway.

Ray said, "Where you going, Frank?"

"You'd laugh if I told you. I'll be back soon." Ray looked at him quizzically and then let it go. "Hey, I'm outta time, I've gotta book. Go back to Melikian and listen to him; he's got your case covered." Frank started walking. "Put those keys somewhere safe."

"Frank." Frank turned again. "You took care of things for me." Ray nodded, squeezed his fist with the five keys. "Everything. I knew you'd come through for me. I won't forget."

Feeling a catch of fear, Frank nodded. He'd taken care of everything for Ray. He walked quickly back toward the waiting car.

Karen stopped her pacing in front of the Delta counter. It was a quarter after five. She shook her head at his lateness, his smell of breath mints, but didn't say anything and handed him his ticket. "It's Gate 12. I already checked your bag." Buckner and Giordano followed a few steps behind. Karen took his arm. As they walked, she fit herself to his side and step and spoke softly, "Frank, I know this is hard. It's unbelievably hard for me. I admit it, I've contributed, it's not just you, it's us, but you're the only man I've ever been able to love. If I were stronger, maybe I could leave you, that would probably be better for both of us, but I still believe we can make it together; do the program, come back, I'll be waiting here; stay straight, we'll have a life together, we'll go on, someday we'll look back on this and laugh about it. . . ." They reached the gate. The passenger area was already deserted.

Face suddenly flushed with emotion, George Buckner hugged Frank hard. Frank let him, but didn't respond. John shook his hand. "Okay, Frank, okay now. We'll take care of things here. Don't worry."

Karen walked him aside. "I love you, Frank." She hugged and kissed him. "I'll be here when you get back."

He handed the stewardess his ticket. "Karen, which bag am I looking for when I get there?"

"The gray one with the zipper compartment. I packed your clothes, razor, a couple of thrillers. Two counselors from Saint Teresa's will meet you. They know the flight number and have a description of you. Frank?" She squeezed his hand. "You'll be able to love me after this, won't you?"

He was surprised to find his voice gone, then hoarsely, "Wouldn't be a whole lot of reason for going if I couldn't, would there?"

She shook her head no. "Yes, if you couldn't love me, then going just for you alone would be a good reason."

The flight attendant said, "You'll have to board now."

Karen hugged him. "It was the only way, Frank." He stepped into the tunnel and started down. "Frank." He turned. "The keys. To the office."

He handed her the three keys and walked down the sloping passage to the plane. Just before the tunnel elbowed, he looked back. Small against the airport doorway, Karen remained motionless. She looked like she was miles away.

As Karen had arranged, two counselors met Frank at the airport and drove him to a clean and modern facility in a suburban section of Dallas. The sun had already set here. The counselors brought Frank to a 24-hour nursing unit where he was given a physical, blood and urine specimens were taken, and a medical evaluation was made. After filling out admissions paperwork, Frank was led to his unit and brought to a room, a simple, institutional room, dresser, closet, toilet, and two beds—he'd be getting a roommate tomorrow. The counselor finished up and left him alone, and he stepped out, walked the length of the corridor. He tried the door at the end, which was locked, walked back toward the TV lounge, the reception area, noted two pay phones, again tried another outer door, also locked. Through a window, he could see a simple white cross spotlit on the lawn. Moths swarmed in and out of the light. He took a deep breath and smelled the air; it was reminiscent of a hundred places he'd been. It was an institution, clean, modern, efficiently run, expensive, with a gleam of linoleum at the end of the hall, a subdued, background smell of disinfectant and floor wax, red EXIT signs. Except for its being well-kept, it could have been any of a number of prison wings. Hospitals. Schools. A place one finished up with, a place always there, a place one always came back to. He wandered down the hall to his room, and sat on the bed. Leaving his bag unpacked, he stretched out.

He could be anyone anywhere. He stared up at the ceiling. The meeting in Germaine Blumenthal's office already seemed faraway, an old memory that had happened to someone else. He'd felt like this at times when he'd been on the run those three years after Ray and he had almost been caught. He'd be somewhere one morning, have a job, friends, then suddenly have the feeling he'd better leave. Next day, all of the people he'd been day-to-day with would be memories. Yeah, his business might already be ruined, but then again maybe John and Gloria and Karen could keep it afloat until he came back. Maybe clients would find out where he'd been, maybe not. He really had no idea how the expense of this place was going to be met—what? six, eight thousand dollars, something like that. If he'd been able to set this kind of money aside so he could take the bar exam, he'd have passed. Karen's way of looking at it was that she was saving his life. He still didn't think he'd had any choice. She'd said, go down the stairs now, you can have the street for a wife. He knew she'd meant it. Karen had forced this on him because she loved him. Or said she did. This was her way of loving him. He closed his eyes and tried to ignore the hollow feeling in his mouth.

On and off during the night, he kept seeing the circle of faces in Blumenthal's office, which also felt like a court-room—Giordano, Buckner, Melikian, Karen, Blumenthal; he heard them speaking, heard himself replying endlessly, as he had not done during the intervention; felt the pres-ence of other people, Kramer, Ray, Gloria, his father some-where near, and beyond, crowding at the periphery, others, some of the nuns who'd taught him in grade school, his high-school basketball coach . . . faces and voices pressing in, everyone talking: all the stories in the same room.

After breakfast, he was met by a counselor and taken to his office, and they continued the lengthy intake proce-dures. There were more questions about his recent alcohol and drug use. Then he was given a detailed form to fill out, a psychosocial history. Family. Childhood. Schooling. Important events. Family drug and alcohol use. The effects of his use of chemicals on himself. Others. When begun. How much. Effect on work. On marriage. Incidents. Cost in terms of work. Money. Injuries. To himself. To others.

The counselor went on to describe the program's having strong roots in twelve-step recovery. There would be meet-ings with groups which worked on the steps. There were anger groups. Addiction groups. Confrontation groups. Peer groups. One-to-one counseling. A daily journal. And written assignments on each of the twelve steps. Frank was given reading material on all of them. It was also explained that if people didn't participate as best they could, they were out of the program; there were too many people who were waiting to get in.

Afterward, Frank went to his first meeting, a step-one group. Step one was written on a blackboard and read out loud in unison: We admitted that we were powerless over alcohol . . . that our lives had become unmanageable.

And the group began.

Frank had been in two days when Karen called to ask how the program was going. No, she hadn't had a chance to get to the office yet, but it looked like John and Gloria were covering pretty well. Relax, Frank, it'll work out. Knowing she wanted to hear something encouraging, Frank gave her an idea of the routine—group therapy, keeping a daily journal and discussing it one to one in meetings with counselors . . . How was the food? It was served in a cafeteria, and, hey, it wasn't bad. She ended with, "I love you, Frank." He forced himself to say quickly, "I love you, too.

After he hung up, he paced and noticed the beginnings of a wild mood swing. He was furious at George Buckner— Christ, how could George have done this to him!—and couldn't keep himself from calling him at home in New York. When he got his answering machine, he slammed down the phone. A while later he was completely indifferent and couldn't understand why he'd been so angry. The third night he was there, he had the terrible dream, a room he had to go into, and he awakened sweating. Where was he? There was the shape of his newly arrived roommate sleeping in the other bed. Frank walked into the corridor. The red EXIT sign. Somehow, he felt faintly surprised, yet that it was right, too, that he be in this place, no place, limbo. He'd always known he'd deserved this. Unable to face his bed, the dark room, he dozed on the sofa in the empty TV lounge.

That night—was it the third, or the fourth?—Frank called June, got Kramer's number in L.A., and connected with him in the evening. "Steven Kramer?"

Frank heard him hesitate. "That's me."

"This is Officer Innocente Trujillo of the San Francisco Police Department . . ."

"Frank?"

"None other. What's happening, Slick?"

"Don't do Officer Trujillo again. Christ, I thought something had happened to Zack or June. Where are you?"

"I'm in the gulag. Dallas, Texas. No place. A building with a bunch of guys. Women's section, too. We don't fraternize. Hey, you knew what was happening. Snookie-Okums sent me to the gulag. Don't pretend you didn't know."

"I'm not pretending anything. I didn't know that you went. Or that you stayed."

"No one ever knows anything. I went. I've stayed. They've got locks on the doors. We're paying guests."

There was a pause. "So how is it?"

"Boring. Half interesting. Inmates eat, talk, obsess, whine, cry, regress, manipulate, regret, cry again, bullshit. Variations on: nobody cares; I don't care; fuck you. It's giving me a chance to rest and eat good food for a change. Hey, you knew Karen was going to do this to me, Steve."

"I wouldn't put it that way."

"Yeah, the way it worked, she did it to me. But you didn't warn me. You shoulda told me, Steve."

"Why? What did I know? I'd never heard of an intervention before. It wasn't anything I personally wanted to get involved in."

"You could have said something."

"Karen said, 'I want to talk to you, it's important, but first I need you to promise you won't talk to Frank about what I'm going to tell you out of a fucked-up sense of loyalty. If you really care about him, you won't tell.' Once she told me, it was like, you're going to do this with Frank? But what am I going to do now? I promised her I wouldn't say anything."

"She set you up, extracted a promise before you knew what it was about—she conned you. Did you think I needed to get sat down by my friends and colleagues? To get an either go or I'm leaving you?"

"I didn't come to it, did I?"

There was some static. "She said she was putting a dent

in my denial. Good one, huh? If it had been you in my place, I would have warned you, dude-san."

"I couldn't figure it out."

"That's Karen. She's good at that shit. Okay, Steve, I didn't call to get in your face. And actually, depending on what hour of the day you ask me, I've come to think it was a very loving thing she did. I don't think she was right. I don't think I needed it. My denial of course. She cuts out your tongue and makes you doubt yourself. But you gotta hand it to her, she's got huevos, dude-san." Kramer didn't answer. "Hey, you tell your Salvadorans my beaner joke?"

"Not yet, Frank. I'm working on finding just the perfect opening. Families murdered, tortured, kids disappeared. There's gotta be a place for a joke like that."

"Hey, y'all play dumb until I get back. I'll call you. I gotta get off now. This is a pay phone and someone's giving me the evil eye. A fellow substance abuser. You know how manipulative they can be, right? Lemme give you the number here."

In the morning, Frank watched the counselors admitting a new patient: rumpled, gray-faced, with a disoriented gaze and circles under his eyes. . . . When Frank turned, a guy he'd noticed in several group sessions was watching him. Clean-shaven, short-haired, maybe a few years older than Frank, with an attentive gaze and an ironic smile. It was the smile, sardonic, sympathetic, which Frank had noticed.

"Funky, isn't it?" He nodded after the new patient and extended his hand. "Stan Buddenhagen. *Doctor* Stan Buddenhagen," he said with an edge. "*Patient* Stan Buddenhagen here."

"Frank August." They shook hands.

"You looked like that your first morning. Toxic. *I* looked like that when I came in three weeks ago, though I couldn't see it in a mirror. Gray. Bled." Buddenhagen checked his watch. "You going to the group meeting now?" Frank nodded and they fell in step. Buddenhagen said, "What I hear people saying in the group over and over is, 'I don't love myself, I don't accept myself, I don't forgive myself. I want to be king, I don't trust anybody, I'm angry, I'm hurt, fuck you.'"

"Yeah, it's something like that."

They went in to the gathering group. The counselor arrived, and they started, different people speaking, some crying, some angry, some irritated, and it was as Buddenhagen had just said: I don't love myself, I don't accept myself . . . Right on until lunch. As they were walking to the cafeteria, someone said, "There's a call for Frank August," and Frank went to the pay phone.

"Frank!"

"Johnnie G., that you, Slick?"

"Yeah, Frank, I just got in. There are files dumped on the floor, stuff has been burned in the wastebasket, the office is trashed!"

"What's happened?"

"I just spoke to Tom Gutweiler out in the hall. He came in first thing this morning, smelled smoke and ran down with a fire extinguisher to find Karen dumping files on the floor. The wastebasket was full of smoking stuff. I wanted to warn you, Frank."

"Warn me? Thanks. What can I do now?"

"I don't know, but she's gonna do something."

"She's already done it."

"Do something more."

"Hey, I told you guys last Saturday she was running a number."

"If I'd known she was going to do this . . ."

"Yeah, if you'd known. She wanted the keys to my office, there's the bottom line. She got em, too. Love. Trust. That's great."

"What's she looking for?"

"I don't know, but I'd appreciate your doing a couple of things now. Please."

"Okay, Frank. Jesus. I'm sorry."

"Clean up as much as you can. And even though it's

too late, call a locksmith, have him change all the locks to the office. You keep a set of keys and give Gloria a set. And call me back as soon as you know anything else.''

Frank hung up and went to the dining room, but could only pick at his food. Someone came to the door and announced, ''Phone call for Frank August.''

He walked to the phone. Karen. Her voice high, crazy. ''You fucker, I'm going to kill you.'' He didn't try to answer. ''It wasn't just letters, but there were even a few nice cozy pictures of the two of you naked in a mirror.'' That's what he'd forgotten! And the letters! His. Hers. Gina. Frank remembered holding his lighter to a picture, pulling it back. ''At least it was her place. Did she have nice tits, Frank? A nice juicy little pussy? Let me read a letter to you? Gosh, there are so many I can hardly make up my mind. And what do you think, Frank, should I read one of yours or one of hers? Here's a part I really like. 'I love that tender struck look on your face, the way you looked at me when you came.' How's that, Frank? She's kind of a poet, isn't she? 'That tender struck look.' I mean, I never saw it quite that way. And you write back to her, 'If things don't get better, I'll have to leave Karen.' Frank, I'm going to have one of those slimy creeps you're always defending beat your brains out. You wrote her about us, about me, you wrote about our marriage, you just tell her everything. Here I was starved for tenderness and openness and these fucking letters are full of it. And all the time I was trying everything with you, everything. Here, fucker, let me read more . . .''

''Karen, congratulations. I really mean that. You looked until you finally found something. First you went through the house. Nothing there. But you couldn't leave it alone. So you pressed on. Maybe the office. But how were you going to get the keys to the office. Maybe you can sell Frank's friends on his being a drunk, pack Frank off, get the keys. I played right into your hands. Well, you sold it, Snooks. Melikian always says about trials and juries that it's all about who can tell the best story and make it stick.''

"I've got her return address. I know who she is. I'm going to kill her. I've got your gun."

"The prisons are full of people who do it."

"First her, then you. She's masquerading as an alcohol counselor . . ."

"She just goes to AA."

". . . a sympathetic alcohol counselor. The world is full of desperate 40-year-old women. Sympathy is their ploy, the oldest one in the world. And you fell for it. I was just starved for tenderness and you were fucking this bitch, telling her everything; I just knew there was something you were hiding. I've got the Rolodex, I'm calling everyone and telling them what a smarmy fucker you are . . . You'll never work in this town again. No one would be in the same room with you." Frank hung up. The phone rang immediately. "Don't you dare hang up on me, Frank. I'll kill you."

Frank hung up. He walked to the door of the dining room and said, "Excuse me, but if there are any more calls from my wife, I won't take them. She'll be asking for Frank August. That's me."

Someone said, "I should have done that ten years ago."

The dining room went silent except for the clinking of knives and forks against plates. Frank returned to his place, but didn't eat. A few minutes later, someone said, "Phone call, Frank August."

"Is it a woman?"

"No."

Frank took the call. John Giordano. "Frank, I'm still at the office. I can't find the Perez file."

"Look in the trunk of my car. There are spare car keys taped to the underside of my middle desk drawer."

"Karen's gone crazy, man."

"Look, John, I forgot some old love letters in the files and she's found them. That's what she wanted. The letters. I told you she was running a con. She concludes I've been screwing everyone. I'm dead now anyway. Just do the best you can."

As Frank hung up, Stan Buddenhagen walked out of the dining room toward the lounge. "You okay, Frank? You look like someone just bashed you over the head."

"I'm not okay, but what the hell, I gotta live with it. I did it to myself. Isn't that what they're telling us here; we do it ourselves. I think I better leave and get back. There's too much happening."

"Yeah, it's always a mess left behind."

They were walking slowly side by side toward the lounge, where Frank, exhausted, slid into a chair, and then started telling Stan what had happened. Karen. The letters. The intervention. "I don't know if she staged it to get the keys or what. But there it is. I don't think she was really sure if I'd been having an affair or not. She has good intuitions, but she had no proof. She couldn't let it go. She just had to keep looking until she found something."

Buddenhagen nodded. "She wanted to find something. She found it." He added cautiously. "And you gave her the keys. Literally. Synergy." Buddenhagen became thoughtful. "In college, I took a course in Shakespearean tragedy. We'd been reading *Macbeth*. Macbeth and his ambitions to be king. The professor said, 'Be careful what you wish for; it might just come true.' At the time I remember thinking, yeah, so? Like, good, dude: what, I don't want my wishes to come true, what's he talking about?"

"Well, this isn't a tragedy. It's just a mess. Karen couldn't rest until she found something. I guess that's what she wished. Deal is, I'd moved past this thing with Gina—given it up four or five months ago. Another funny thing, while I was with Gina, I stopped drinking completely on my own, lost twenty pounds, was running five miles a day and Karen *liked* that. I mean, I looked good. She just didn't know where it was coming from. Maybe *that* bugged her more than my getting it together—that it wasn't coming from *her*. She says I drink *at* her. When I don't drink, she calls me a dry drunk. No win."

Buddenhagen said, "I gotta say I did get everything I wished for. Booze, pills, women, action on horses and bas-

ketball, poker. Course I lost a couple of things I didn't
plan on losing. I lost my wife and custody of my three
kids. I'm a good doctor. I could have treated someone with
my symptoms, but I couldn't do it for myself and I
couldn't stop. I was writing extra prescriptions for my patients and then filling them for my own use. Even I kinda
knew something was wrong when I started begging pain-
killers from one of my cancer patients. My associates told
me to get treatment before the medical authorities got
wise.'' He looked at his watch. ''Hey, I've gotta go for
some one on one.'' He smiled, his sardonic, sympathetic
smile. ''Maybe everyone gets his realest wish, his secret
wish, the one hidden beneath all the others.'' He stood,
put his hand on Frank's shoulder. ''I hope to see you when
I get back.''

''That's fifty-fifty. I think I'm going to wash out of this
shit and head for home.'' Frank watched Buddenhagen go
down the hall. Even after he'd joined his afternoon group,
he knew he was leaving, but hour by hour, he couldn't get
started. Maybe it was just to see Buddenhagen at dinner
and talk a little more, maybe because there was no one
anywhere else he believed in at this exact moment, and it
hardly made any difference where he was.

Frank called Kramer in L.A. Kramer answered breathless.
''Getting laid now that you've got a week away from
Snookie-Okums?''

''I've got an interview and I'm late.''

''Steve, one second. Since you're out the door, me and
Officer Trujillo have a question for you. Why didn't you
warn me Karen was going to do the intervention?''

''Frank, I told you. And anyway, last time we talked,
you ended up telling me what a loving thing it was that
Karen had done.''

''She's gone crazy. She got the keys to my office.
That's what she was after; she went through my files and
found some old love letters.''

''How old?''

"Not old enough. Remember that woman Gina who spoke at the first and only AA meeting you took me to?"

"Kind of, Yeah."

"That was the one. There were a few choice pictures in with the letters. Nothing X-rated. Maybe kinda R. Karen's concluded I've been screwing everything."

"Not good."

"Hey, this is what the intervention was really all about. Getting the keys to my office. Getting the goods on Frankie boy. Why didn't you warn me?"

"Hey, who could have known? You went on a five-day drunk. I'd never even heard of an intervention before Karen. I didn't participate."

"But you didn't warn me."

"Frank, cool off. When did you find out Karen got into your files?"

"Giordano called me this morning. She's been going through my drawers for months looking for proof of something. When she didn't find anything in the house, she couldn't let it go. She figured it had to be in the office. What a masterpiece. She orchestrated the whole thing."

Kramer said, "I don't think it's that black and white. She'd have to be some kind of weird genius if it were true."

"Why split hairs. It's true and she pulled it off."

"When she talked to me about the intervention, she was really concerned about you. She told me she loved you and wanted you back. That she was losing you to booze and who knew what all else. She said she wanted to save your marriage."

"She conned you."

"No, I don't think so. And if she did, she conned herself, too. Maybe once she got the keys she just couldn't help herself."

"Why didn't you warn me, Kramer? You're my friend, your first loyalty was to me."

"Hey, I told you, I didn't know what she'd do. You

didn't know, either, or you wouldn't have given her the keys.''

"It was love and trust on Saturday. We're putting everything behind us." Frank laughed. "She conned us, Kramer."

Kramer said, "Hey, I did what I could at the time. Why'd you give her the keys in the first place? You're not an idiot. After ten years, you know her better than any of us; didn't you know what she'd do?" Frank didn't answer. "Frank?"

"It was supposed to be love and trust."

"I'll talk to you more, but I've gotta go to this interview and I'm late."

"Trust and you get fucked. Go to your fucking interview, but don't believe what you're told." Frank slammed down the receiver.

In the morning, after breakfast, there was a small, padded envelope for him, certified mail, and going down to his room, he closed the door and opened it. Two thousand dollars in one hundred dollar bills. On top, a postcard of the famous picture of Marilyn Monroe with her skirt blowing up:

"Frank, Melikian told me the whole story. Thought you could use this now. Call it a first installment. The rest is here waiting for you when you get back. Let me know what you need. You covered things for me. I'm here a while more. Ray."

Frank riffled the bills. Melikian told Ray the whole story. He was a great lawyer, but he never could keep anything to himself. It just happened to be okay now, but how did Melikian know that? Melikian talked too much. And Kramer didn't talk at the right times. They were supposed to be friends. And Ray, say what you would about Ray, when things went in the dumper, he didn't talk. He understood and sent money. Ray was there. And this was a guy they wanted to put in prison for selling people what they wouldn't admit to themselves they wanted. Half the guys in the criminal justice system, prosecutors, public defenders went home and got stoned. . . .

Moved, Frank put the money away in a safe place and went to his group meeting. Late in the day, he dug out Ray's postcard and reread the phrase, "The rest is here waiting . . ." *The rest of it.* A few weeks ago Ray had said, "I can't get the money I lost back for you, but give me the name of the snitch, and I'll give you twenty thousand. . . ." Here it was. Frank had given him Rosenthal.

After dinner, three or four guys were bickering in the lounge over which channel they were going to watch. Frank walked to his room, but his roommate was lying on the bed staring at the ceiling and Frank backed out and walked the length of the hall before he noticed a chapel. Every hospital he'd ever visited had one of these sanctuaries. This one had an unadorned altar, a simple cross. A Star of David. Bare walls.

He ran his hand along a chairback. If this were a Catholic church, it would have the stations of the cross spaced throughout. Pieces of a prayer returned: where there is injury . . . pardon. His father's funeral. He'd stepped out of the elevator. The hospital corridor. He started walking, breaking into a trot, walking again. He double-checked the number on a door. Right room? The bed where his father had been lying. The same room he'd been in when Frank had left for school three months ago. Right? He rechecked the number. . . . When Frank glanced up, he became aware he was again circling the chapel, trailing his hand along the smooth wall as he walked. Rosenthal. He had to find Rosenthal. Find him first.

He went back down the hall to the pay phone. It was after eleven. He dialed Murray Axelrod at home. "Murray, Frank August."

"Hey, call me ten o'clock at home, why don't ya?"

"Yeah, sorry." Frank hesitated.

Murray said, "Where are you? You sound long distance."

"I'm in Texas. Dallas."

"I once got a woman's three kids for her in Dallas. A custody trip. Her ex-husband had stolen them. Almost got me killed. High-speed chase to the airport, wearing a wig, kids lying on the floor crying, all of it. I hate people. What are you doing in that shithole?"

"Murray, it's too long and boring. You'd laugh if I told you. I have a problem. I need your help." Frank hesitated. With all the weird, high-tech digging Murray did on people, and all the heavy hitters Murray exposed, Frank froze. "Murray, your line? You think it's safe?"

"Let's put it this way. I don't talk about anything life and death on this phone."

"That's comforting. Can you go to a pay phone?"

"Can this wait?"

"No. Really, man, I don't think it can wait."

There was a pause. "Give me a number, I'll call you back in ten minutes." Frank gave him the number and stood by the phone until it rang. "This better be important, Frank." Frank could hear traffic noises in the background.

"I'll pay you whatever your rate is. It's important."

"You can't afford my rate anymore. Just talk."

"There's a guy named Howard Rosenthal."

"What? Speak up."

"I can't. I'm at a public phone, there are people around."

"Where the fuck are you?"

Frank cupped his hand around the mouthpiece. "Howard Rosenthal. Got it?" Axelrod repeated it. "Right. I need you to find him."

"Who is he?"

"I can't go into detail now, but he's no one you'd particularly like unless you were big on tennis and you're not. I got Howard Rosenthal from the DMV, but I don't have any of it with me. Santa Monica's his last address. He had an alias of Jack Adams, but I'm sure he's stopped using that within the last few weeks. The thing is, I'm sure he doesn't believe anyone's onto who he really is so he may have old credit cards he's gone back to using under his original ID, Howard Rosenthal. Maybe he's been using them all along. Try all the usual places. Credit reports. I don't need to tell you. TRW. You could check with the Social Security Administration to see if anything's been coming in there. He might be getting paid by the Government."

"The Government. Fuck, is this a Fed witness you're messing with? Frank?"

"I can't talk now."

"Frank."

"Yeah, Fed."

"What kind of case?"

"Drug. I just need to find him."

"And where was he last?"

"San Francisco. Roughly two weeks ago. He was Jack Adams in the Bay Area. Mill Valley."

"When and where was he last Howard Rosenthal?"

"In Santa Monica. About thirteen months ago."

"So, what? He was Howard Rosenthal, then he was a Government witness as Jack Adams, now what? he's testified for the Feds and gone?"

"Not exactly. Look, the last I know he's in San Francisco, and pretending to jump bail."

"Where are you, Frank?"

"Murray, I'll tell you when I get back. Please. Just bill me like it's a regular case, don't talk to anyone." Murray, he knew, didn't talk to people. Say whatever you wanted about Murray, he had his good points.

"He's disappeared?"

"I don't know. I'm guessing. I think so."

"Why would you think that? Frank, there's something you're not telling me."

"You're right. It's a long story. Bottom line is I still have to find him."

"He may or may not be in California?"

"Right."

"I'll look, but it's gonna take some time. This means hooking up with other guys, databanks. You know, when it turns out a guy's really just dropped out of sight and leaves nothing behind, he's either left the country or he's dead."

"I don't know that. But we've got to start looking!"

"Okay, Frank. Easy. Maybe I'll start with the obvious."

"What's that?"

"Frank, Jesus, did you learn anything with me or were you just farting around? How about death certificates? It's all going to take time. Can I reach you at this number?"

"Yeah."

"Christ, Frank, a Government witness."

"Snitch. Someone without loyalty to anyone. Rat."

"Disappeared? What the fuck have you done now? Look, Frank, Adams, Rosenthal, whoever, goes in the dumper, you worked the case, the Feds'll come right for you, dude-san."

"Let's just stop talking about it. I said I'll pay you."

"You can't afford me," Murray repeated. Christ, what did that mean? Before Frank could make any more of it, Murray said wetly, "Fuck." Frank could see him misting the receiver with that last juicy fuck. Murray, the most paranoid man he knew, the biggest asshole, yet the last guy he'd want looking for him. As always, he'd tried to anticipate Murray's goodbye, and as always, he couldn't, and the next thing, Murray had banged down the phone and Frank was listening to a dial tone.

Early the next morning, someone screwed up, handed Frank the phone, and thinking it was Giordano, he took it. It was Karen, cursing and raging, " 'I love that tender struck look on your face!' "

"Karen, can we talk for a second? I'm sorry I hurt you. I want to say that."

"You're sorry I caught you. Fuck you, I'll kill you,"

she was crying. "How could you have written those things to her. You just poured out your heart. You didn't even know her. I haven't slept for two days."

"Karen, why don't you go to June's—I know you like her—talk to her, sleep, cool out, we can talk about this . . ."

"Don't you try to placate me. Fuck you!"

"Karen, four years ago you moved out on me for two months. It was too distracting to live with me, maybe you shouldn't be married, yes, there were a couple of guys but they were only friends, don't ask me any questions. I let you come back. I didn't throw it in your face."

"But you knew I was out."

"I knew you were out the day you moved out and I came home and found your note and it was a done deal."

"That was then. This is now."

"Well, that's what I'm trying to tell you." Frank shook his head. "Karen, I'm really sorry. The whole thing was over months ago and maybe some good even came out of it. I stopped drinking in that time on my own. I lost twenty pounds. Remember? You liked me that way. It was no big sex thing with her. I thought we were putting this behind us last Saturday. Love and trust."

" 'That struck look on your face when you come!' You gave her your tenderness! I'll kill you."

"Karen, if you really cared about me, you'd stop calling and wait until I come out to talk about it. I can't keep my mind on anything we're doing here with you calling every hour." But she went on cursing and raging and in another minute, unable to speak, he had to hang up.

Two days later, Murray called back. "Frank, you're at St. Teresa's, it's a detox place."

"Yeah, who'd you talk to?"

"No one." He sounded affronted. "You gave me the number, I ran it, what'd you think, I'm a fucking idiot?"

"No. Hey, the joke's on me this time."

"Whatever, I didn't call to talk about your personal life.

I haven't been able to find anything yet. My homeboy over at the Social Security Administration said there was money coming in regularly under the name Howard Rosenthal, and it stopped four weeks ago. There were no credit cards which lead to the Mill Valley addresses under Jack Adams. Wouldn't think there'd be. Howard Rosenthal used a Mastercard to charge some things in L.A. thirteen months ago and then there's absolutely nothing which coincides with the time he becomes Jack Adams. All what I would have expected."

"He doesn't show up on any California death certificates?"

"No, he doesn't. Not so far. Which means either he's not dead; he's left the country; he didn't die in any of the places I looked; or he died someplace where there's no medical examiner and the people don't issue death certificates. Like in the woods at night with someone holding a gun to his head."

Frank circled on the short tether of the pay phone cord. "That's the one I'm worried about."

"He's a Government informer?"

"Turned by the Feds after taking a pretty good coke bust. I'll tell you the rest some other time."

"Nice going, Frank. What'd you do?"

"I'm not quite sure. Something."

"Fuck, man, if he ratted out a major player, maybe Rosenthal's gone into the Witness Protection Program with the federal marshals. Maybe that was part of the deal up front. That's a tough one, but there's someone I might try in the Justice Department. Could take a while. Might not work."

"I'll be out of here in a few more weeks. Just do it as fast as you can. If he's alive, I've got to find him before someone else does. I think I've got to warn the rat. If you find anything at all, call me day or night. It's all going to come back on me the wrong way if I don't get to him first."

Again, Frank tried to anticipate Murray's goodbye and

hang-up, and again it was the sound in the back of Murray's throat, the bang and then the dial tone. Receiver in hand, Frank knew he had to get out of here now. He had to find Rosenthal. He had to do something—what?—with Karen. He had to save his business. Frank hung up.

After waiting a couple of more days, Frank gave in and called Murray, again at home, this time early in the morning. "Murray, Frank, sorry to call you at this hour . . ."

"Fuck, Frank, I've been looking. Now, however, I *am* sleeping!" Murray's voice was hoarse from sleep. " I've got other people looking, I told you it would take time. Shit, man, you know what's what. If I had any leads, I'd call you."

"Murray . . ."

"Come on, you're being as bad as a lawyer. Jesus, what? it's six-fifteen, we're on Pacific Daylight time here."

"Okay, you're right. Look, whatever you do, just don't tell people who you're doing it for or what it's about."

Murray made his sound of moist derision and disgust. "Smegma, dude-san." Murray banged down the phone.

When he turned, Buddenhagen had stopped on the way to breakfast and was looking at him. He said, "You still look like someone's been bashing you on the head. By the time I got here my first time, it was chaos. Course this whole thing is further complicated because we've told so many people so many different things, we no longer know what's true."

"I didn't know she'd go through my files. When she did that, it took a quantum leap." Buddenhagen's shrug implied, of course, but that's all part of it. "Did you just say your *first* time?"

"Yeah."

"This isn't your first time, Stan?"

"I did a stint here about seventeen months ago."

"Same thing? Thirty days, inpatient?"

"Same thing."

"This is your second time?"

"Yeah. And I don't want to come back again. Either I make it work now or I think I'll just have to go along until I OD, pile up in a car, have my medical license yanked, whatever."

"Christ, your second time. What are you figuring out this time around that you didn't during your last outing?"

"Maybe just what I said, that I don't want to come back here again, that I can't afford it. I wouldn't have believed it was possible last time. I thought one time would be it. Waking up the first couple of days and finding myself back here was just a nightmare. It's not just the booze and dope. Guys like you and me, Frank, we're always trying to make one plus one equal three. It's just the way we're wired. Daily stuff, *that's* the hard part. There was a guy in here last time, it was his fourth time. *That* scares me."

Frank called Kramer who was now back in San Francisco, and asked Kramer if he'd noticed what was going on back there with Karen, or if they'd talked. Kramer said that he'd seen her going into the house, but that she wouldn't look in his direction. He didn't know why.

"You didn't go to her damned intervention, Kramer! Doesn't her attitude tell you something?" Kramer went silent. "You know something else you're not telling me, Steve."

Kramer remained silent, then said, "She's been moving her things out for the last couple of days."

"What's things?"

"The red sofa, a table, some shelves, a few boxes. She takes a load, comes back a few hours later."

"She's not doing this herself."

"No."

"So who's helping her, Homes?"

"Some guy. He's got a blue Chevy pickup." Again, Kramer went silent. "Maybe six feet, brown hair, around thirty-five. He looks like he's just a friend."

"I get it all. First, she had to get the keys. Why? She

had to get something on me. The letters. You know, when she's done something and is feeling guilty, she has to make sure she justifies things. She had a boyfriend. She power-tripped me; I mean, for a few days, I actually half-believed I belonged in this gulag.''

"Frank, she loves you. She's just hurt and crazy. I think this guy's only a friend who's helping her move."

"Homes, can you do one thing for me? Next time that blue pickup comes around, write down the license plate, call Giordano or Gloria, and ask them to run it through the DMV. I better just come back there. Hey, her last words to me were, 'I'll be there for you, Frank.' No, actually, I think her last words were, 'The keys. To the office.' ''

As he hung up, Frank walked the length of the corridor to what he thought was Buddenhagen's room and knocked. He waited and tried the door. Unlocked. He pushed it open and looked inside. There were no suitcases, no books or personal articles of any kind. Both beds were neatly made. Clearly this was the wrong room. . . . Frank stepped back into the hall and double-checked the hospital room number, wrong room? . . . he ran his hand along the smooth sheet of a freshly made bed. He sank down onto the bed. His Uncle Ralph had called him on and off for several days. He's going, Frank. He keeps asking for you. He wants to see you. He knows he's going. But hour by hour, Frank had been unable to get himself into the car. He didn't know why. When he did, the car wouldn't start. He'd been meaning to check the battery, the starter; he had to keep the car running. It wouldn't start. He'd had classes, two jobs, no money to have it fixed. Three months before, he'd held his father's hand, looked down at him, the bones silently emerging in his face. He leaned over, kissed his cheek, inhaled the sour smell of his dying. I'll be back, he said, I'm here. His father nodded. He'd left for school. He stood, smoothed the sheet of the empty bed, then went down the hall to the nurses' station, but knew before the screen came up blank on his father's name that he was too late. No one had said anything about his not getting back in time, but he was aware everyone knew. Indicating his younger brothers and sisters at the funeral, his uncle had said, "You're all they're ever really going to know of your father."

Six months before, Frank had been home working as a roofer. Too exhausted to reach down and untie his laces at the end of a day, he'd just sat in a chair staring straight ahead. "Tough out there without a college education, isn't it? Hot. Dirty. People tell you what to do. It's not fun." Frank sensed his father's mood as he circled the room; he'd been furious at him since the boat smashing incident in Brother Malcolm's class. On and off, he'd had to drop out of school to work. He'd been having a tough, frag- mented time of it, holding school together. "If you'd grad- uated with your class and not had your college scholarship yanked, gone to university when you were supposed to, you wouldn't be in this spot."

Frank didn't answer. He leaned forward and started un- tying his laces. His father stood beside him. Frank looked down at his shoes. "Nothing to say, Frank?"

Frank stopped. "I've heard it. Jesus Christ! Aren't you sick of it? And you know something! Let me say it once and for all. Fuck Brother Malcolm. I'd do it again. I'm only sorry I didn't shove it up his hypocritical Jesuit ass."

His father grabbed his shirt, talk to me like that! jerked him up, and Frank instinctively shoved back hard with both hands. His father looked surprised, then winced and grabbed his chest even as he swatted at Frank. He turned pale, slowly crossed the room, fell backward into a chair. Several days later, a series of tests confirmed it hadn't been a heart attack, but the spread of cancer. At the funeral no one had said anything about Frank's not getting back in time for his father, but he was aware everyone knew.

Frank heard steps in the hall. The framed Congressional Record above his father's desk: *In Praise of Loyalty*. Con- gressman Pierce acknowledging his father's staying with him through a losing campaign while the rest of his staff had deserted. Frank had said he'd come, but he hadn't been there when his father, dying, needed him. He saw the empty hospital bed. Without being conscious of it, he'd seen the empty bed every day for sixteen years, but he had no answers. The interstate always went to the horizon, was always ahead of him, and he never got there. It was a room he had to go into; it was always waiting. He was here, now. He'd never forgiven himself. He looked up to see one of the counselors and a patient coming in. Gray. Toxic. Bled. A new patient. As he put down his bag, Frank stood up from the empty bed. Wiping his eyes and looking away, he excused himself and brushed past them into the corridor.

At dinner, Frank saw Buddenhagen. Side by side, they ate, Frank barely touching his food, finally giving up on it altogether, and afterward, as others cleared out of the dining room, neither moved; Frank stirred his coffee. Buddenhagen looked at him. "Maybe be good to see your counselor tonight, Frank." Frank nodded, but still couldn't move. Finally, he managed to say, "Yeah . . . you're right." He could hardly open his lips. His voice was thick and muffled deep in his chest and choked. "Gonna, I think. Gonna go see my counselor. Just been thinkin about my father . . . just realized it's kinda been with me every day . . . maybe fifteen years . . . more. . . . I didn't know if I had any real feelings about it . . . I did, but didn't know . . . he was dying, you know . . . I didn't want him to . . . I was going back to college. . . . He said go." Frank raised his coffee cup slowly, drank. Lowered the cup. "I told him I'd be there for him. You know, in time, Stan. . . . I'd come back in time to be with him when he died . . . we'd do it together . . . we'd always argued, fought. . . . He was a drunk. First time I'm using that word about him. . . . He was a drunk. Sometimes charming . . . very scary . . . rules always changing . . . that wasn't it, I don't think, why I didn't come back . . . that we fought. . . . Maybe I was afraid . . . I don't know . . . my car didn't start . . . one thing . . . the other. . . . When I finally got there, the hospital bed was empty. . . . It was made up and empty. He'd already died. . . . He died without me. . . . Part of me to this fucking day still hates to see a made-up empty bed. . . . I hate people who tell people one thing, do another, don't come through. . . . Strange, it's a big part of the business I'm in . . . telling people one thing, making them believe one thing . . . doin another. . . . Do it all the time. . . . I didn't set out to do it. . . . It was just kind of an accident. . . . I'm supposed to be a lawyer by now. . . . A friend of mine just got taken down by a guy who did that to him for a year. . . . A con . . . what should happen to him. . . . I thought he should die . . . but I'm not judge and jury and it's all going to come back to me if he does . . . it's a line I don't want to cross . . . sorry, I can't talk about any of this, Stan. . . . My wife keeps saying I can't trust, which is why, she says, I'm good at what I do . . . when I tried to trust, that's how I guess she got me here. . . ." He laughed hoarsely. "She can't trust, either . . . we're made for each other." Frank pushed back his chair. "I guess I'll go see my counselor."

Buddenhagen stood with him. "Wait, Frank." He unsnapped his watch. "Here."

Frank could see it was a good Movado watch. "What's this?"

"You're a good guy. I've talked to you. You listened. You've talked to me. You care about people." He held out the watch. "Sometimes people just need to give other people something. Please take it."

"Hey, that's okay."

Buddenhagen put the watch in Frank's hand. "Keep it. I want you to have it. I don't want anything in return. I'm leaving sometime tomorrow."

Frank opened his hand and looked at it. "Okay, Stan, I'll take it. It's beautiful. Really. Thanks."

"You're welcome." As they walked toward their separate counseling sessions, Buddenhagen extended his hand, "I'll probably see you before I go, but if I miss you for any reason, good luck, Frank. I hope I don't see you again.

Not in here. Go see your counselor now. You care. You can be alright.''

Though he'd been on the verge of leaving dozens of times, Frank stayed. He'd faithfully gone to step groups and done the written assignments; he'd kept a daily journal, which recorded the calamitous phone calls from Karen; he'd gone to one-on-one counseling. He talked, argued, and sympathized with the other patients. He saw guys leave and wished them well. He offered support and friendship to some, tried to stay out of the way of others. He'd been driven nuts by some people's insistent childishness, egocentricity, stupidity, and been moved by others' courage and dignity. Now as he entered the third week, his counselor started talking to him about leaving the program. People to contact for aftercare. AA meetings. Finding the right sponsor. Possible counseling.

Out of here, what was he going to find? Would his business be a shambles? He kept seeing his office filled with smoke and floating ash. Just crazy. Then Frank decided that he would take the bus home. It would offer him the decompression he needed. For the first time in his life, the thought of sitting on a Greyhound for—what would it be, Dallas-San Francisco, forty or fifty hours?—seemed right. And until then, as long as he was in St. Teresa's, he was safe. At least he didn't actually have to deal with the people behind the voices at the other end of the phone.

It was Murray. ''Frank, I haven't been able to find a trace of Rosenthal. Death certificates, passports, nothing. The place in Santa Monica was just a bungalow under lease, and Rosenthal, who paid the rent the whole last year, stopped paying about three weeks ago.'' Frank could hear the background traffic noise. Murray was at a pay phone. ''My contact in the Justice Department hasn't been able to find him in the Witness Protection Program. Maybe he hasn't made the right connections yet. So he's either left the country under a false passport or he's dead. Frank?''

"Yeah, I'm listening." Frank knew that if anyone could find Rosenthal, and Rosenthal were there to be found, it would be Murray. "You can't find him."

"I'll check out a couple of other things in the Justice Department, but that's looking pretty dim. Want me to keep looking?"

"I don't know. Yeah, of course, look."

"We're logging some hours here, Frank."

"I'll pay. Just keep score."

After a last round of goodbyes with counselors and some fellow patients, Frank was let out of the compound, the first time since he'd come in twenty-nine days ago. Halfway down the walk, he took a long look around. He'd come here in the dark and hadn't been out since. He had no idea where he'd been. Had never seen the place. It looked like a sprawling, red brick elementary school, set back on a green sweep of lawn surrounded by trees. Frank took a deep breath. The smell of morning, sprinklers, summer humidity. Fresh air. He was fifteen pounds lighter and his skin had lost its grayness. He carried the bag Karen had handed him at the airport. Several passed-around thrillers he'd swapped at the last minute for the bus trip. Inside, too, was a manila envelope bulging with his daily journal entry forms; his written step work; his detailed answers on the role booze and drugs had played in his life and the damage they'd done; and the letters from everyone who had come to the intervention. In addition, there was two thousand dollars in one hundred dollar bills which Ray had sent. He tightened his grip on the bag and walked quickly toward the taxi.

Dallas-San Francisco. The vast emptiness of Texas, traveling west into the slanting afternoon sun. Dallas to Abilene. Nose in a novel. The newspaper. Staring out the window. Abilene on to El Paso where they stopped and Frank looked south over to Ciudad Juarez and thought how he could just cross the Rio Grande and keep on going.

And a while later, passing through Las Cruces in the dark,
Las Cruces where he'd worked and gone to college until
he'd had to leave suddenly one morning before finishing;
where he'd met Kramer, years ago already . . . and then he
drifted into sleep, the darkened bus filled with the echoes
of voices, Kramer's, Buddenhagen's, Buckner's, Karen's
. . . An early sunrise throwing long shadows. In Tucson,
baking already at ten in the morning, Frank ate huevos
rancheros and drank a large coke and looked at the flat
white light in the street, and again, hearing Spanish in the
streets, he thought of Mexico, like a sleeping animal, a
dream, slumbering just out of sight to the south. Back on
the bus: Phoenix, huge, glaring, hotter still by early afternoon, 112 on the bank sign coming in off the interstate,
and then on, again into the slanting sun, now Blythe, the
Mojave Desert. All of the time, it was the sound of voices,
a face in a group meeting, a counselor. . . . Palm Springs.
San Bernadino. L.A., where there would be a bus change.
A walk through the station. Frank saw a bearded blond
guy carefully balance a laptop between his ankles and
check a timetable. Two young Chinese guys, one hanging
back, one approaching to ask for directions. Frank sensed
something coming. The blond guy pointed, the Oriental
shook his head and pointed in the other direction; as the
blond guy turned to follow his hand, and before Frank
could shout or do anything, the second Oriental dashed by,
grabbed the laptop, the first pushed the blond guy, and in
a moment, both were gone. Frank helped the man up.
Comforted him. Nothing anyone could do. It was just too
fast. In another moment, his bus was called, and he got on
and started north.

When the Greyhound pulled into the station just off Market at eight-thirty on a Wednesday morning, Frank, unshaven and stiff, stepped off, and like a tourist coming to
the city from Bakersfield or Dubuque, he walked out to
lower Market Street with his light bag in hand, looked up
and down and listened to the sound of the city: traffic, the

rumble of Munis, the racket and drama of steel work in a towering office building. Behind him, the porn arcades where runaway kids hustled ten dollar blowjobs, sometimes got beaten up or killed; he'd spent months down here, Wine Country, interviewing residents of a transient hotel in a murder involving a street kid and only after it was over did he realize he'd come to dread the smell of that hotel, Pine-Sol, hot-plate cooking and laundry hanging in the rooms. Now, like a tourist uncertain which way to go, he just strolled out into the flow of people.

It was early September, and, summer having crested, the light had muted slightly. He wasn't more than a steady twenty-five minute walk toward his office off Market, and he realized that Gloria would probably be there taking messages, paying bills, maybe nursing whatever cases might have survived. He hadn't called to let anyone know he was coming, not Karen, not Kramer, not Gloria, no one. What was there to say? He didn't know what came next. He started toward his office, but within half a block, his pace slackened and he sat down on a bench for a while, watched the flow of people. He caught BART to his stop on Mission, hiked up to Holly Park.

As he turned onto his block, the street seemed closer and dirtier than he'd remembered. He spotted his mauve Caddy. Kramer had been moving it to avoid the odd/even day street cleaning and ticketing. He walked up to his house and looked at it, the waist-high picket gate slightly askew, the sidewalk heaved up by age. It was smaller, more run-down than he'd remembered, the blue paint starting to peel and chalk in places. He'd painted the house four years ago when they'd first moved in as part of a rent reduction deal.

He pulled the gate open—it caught along the sidewalk in a familiar way, which pained him. On the porch, he cleaned out the mailbox—nothing personal for Karen; she'd obviously gone to postal forwarding. There was a yellow post office slip, an attempt to deliver a registered package to Frank with return address, a name and P.O.

Box he didn't recognize. And bills. A lot of them.

Inside, he closed the front door and looked down the hall. It was as Kramer had said. The red sofa was missing. He could tell by the flat echo of his footsteps that a lot more was gone. He stopped in the front room. Bookshelves. Books. The stereo. A throw rug. A large armoire from the next room. All gone. The kitchen table had been left, but the microwave was missing. He dropped the pile of mail on the table.

Upstairs, the mattress, stripped, and boxspring were still there under the skylight, but Karen's dresser and the TV were gone. His TV. Her pictures were gone, which pained him deeply. He walked into her closet. Empty. In his closet, things were dumped on the floor and he noticed a large box of snapshots which went back to his being a kid—himself, his father and mother, his brothers and sisters, friends—were torn up. He sorted through the box, then stood and realized that the cats hadn't come to greet him. She'd taken them, too.

Confronted with the accomplished fact of it, Frank stepped out of the closet feeling a terrible sense of emptiness and abandonment. He knew that some part of him he didn't understand had made it happen. And that he'd always deserved this. Disloyalty. Abandonment. He heard Buddenhagen saying, be careful what you wish for, it might just come true. He walked to the window, opened it, and leaning on the sill, he looked out across the rooftops.

In the morning the doorbell rang early, and checking through the front window, Frank saw a man he didn't recognize on the porch. He took out the Glock, pulled back the slide, and tucked it behind his back. He opened the front door.

"Frank August?" A guy in his late twenties, a nervous, wary expression on his face.

"Who wants to know?"

As the guy reached into his shirt, Frank slid his hand behind his waist. The guy shoved several thick pages toward him, and Frank realized he was a process server. He'd done this dozens of times himself, spent weeks trying to serve people, disguised himself as a pizza delivery boy, complete with pizza box insulator; as a meter reader; as a parcel post man; he'd had people slam the door, shove him, throw the papers on the ground, curse, threaten, point guns, try to explain and justify to him: anything to forestall the inevitable. Now Frank looked at the papers. Divorce papers and a restraining order. He looked at the server, who was already retreating off the porch and down the sidewalk. That's right, get going, you never knew what they'd do once they got served. Frank closed the door.

The next couple of days were busy. Frank took the yellow slip to the post office and picked up his registered package. In the car, he opened it. Eighteen thousand dollars and a postcard in Ray's handwriting: "The rest of it." He turned it over. It was a tourist's postcard, a picture of the Embarcadero. Embarcadero? Embark. Did that mean Ray had jumped bail, wasn't going to prison? Was already gone? He looked at the money. It could solve a lot of immediate problems. Maybe it could even pay off most of the gulag debt, which Karen had placed in his name. Drug money. Information money. Here it was. And if he refused this or gave it back to Ray or donated it to the Salvation Army, was it going to surface Rosenthal, prove he wasn't dead, or in any other way mitigate Frank's responsibility in his having given the name? Too late now. He hid some under the floorboard, pocketed some, and then went to his office and accepted a welcome-home hug from Gloria who looked better than ever.

He'd half expected to find things in the chaotic condition Giordano had described in his first frantic phone call, but except for a scorch mark up the side of his desk where Karen had burned letters and papers, things were the same. The white morning sunlight came slanting through the frosted lower windowpanes, the voices from the project drifted in from the walk. Overhead, Kramer's surfboard rested on the ducts. And then there was Gloria. *She* hadn't come to the intervention.

As the lawyers in the building passed his open door and dropped in, hey, Frankie, he could tell from their assumed casualness that each knew some version of what had happened, but was pretending not to; he didn't offer anything and no one pursued it. The moment Giordano came in, he thanked him for his help in the last few weeks and handed him a yellow pad. "Give me a run down of what I owe you, everything. Gloria, you too." He paid them. Then John and Gloria started catching him up on cases. Among other things, John had run the plates on the blue Chevy pickup—the guy who'd helped move Karen—and now Frank took the information, put the note in his shirt pocket.

He settled a few more things, went to an AA meeting, and then to the post office and got Karen's new address, which was over on Potrero. It didn't match that of the owner of the blue pickup. A relief. Late in the day, when he knew Karen would be getting home from work, he drove over to Potrero, parked a few blocks from her house, and found her duplex. She didn't have her name by the bell, but he recognized the name of a girlfriend. He crossed the street to the other side, faded half a block. After a while, Karen came quickly down the street carrying a grocery bag. Beautiful, she looked like someone who had already grown distant. She disappeared into the house. He heard Kramer's voice: "I don't think she meant to con you. And if she did, she conned herself, too. Maybe once she got the keys, she just couldn't help herself." He drove back to his neighborhood, went to another AA meeting, and then went out to his car trunk, changed into a pair of sweats—there was the loaded Remington—and started to jog. He had gone five blocks when he slowed and doubled with a stitch. He walked it off, stretched, and then started back in, jogging slowly.

*   *   *

He dialed her new number and was just going to hang up
when she answered. "Hi, Snooks, how's the new place?"

A momentary silence. "How'd you get this number?"

"God, Karen, what a question. I do this for a living.
You really want to know. First, there was your postal forwarding and that's legal up front, just check it out. Don't
do that again next time you want to disappear."

"I knew it would be just a matter of time before you
made a call like this. You got the divorce papers and restraining order. . . . Hang up now or I'll call the police.
You are not to contact me in any way; that includes phone
calls."

". . . Karen, there's a lot to say, but I won't say any of
it. You did take Sally and Joe. Joe was definitely mine.
Sandra Dominguez gave her to me before she went to the
slam three years ago. Just give me Joe. That's all." Karen
hung up and when he called back, there was a busy signal.
He knew he had to be careful now. These were exactly the
situations he'd been counseled to avoid.

Fifteen minutes later, the phone rang. "Mr. August, this
is Jane Caruso, I am representing Karen Bainbridge. You
will cease and desist in contacting Ms. Bainbridge. If you
have any questions, you can address them to me. You will
obey the restraining order or I will . . ."

Frank banged down the phone. He knew he should stay
away, and he also knew he had to be careful, but for several weeks—early morning, late in the evening—Frank
drove by Karen's, watched her place from a block away,
but there was never anyone who fit the description of the
blue Chevy pickup driver. There were no men at all. It was
just Karen who came and went alone and her roommate.

Frank called Ray's sublet by the Marina Green and got a
woman's terse message on an answering machine: Please
leave your name and number after the tone. Frank hesitated
as he felt himself being rolled up into the old fear, a dis-
tinct fear which came whenever he dealt with Ray, phones,

messages. "Frank here; I can be reached at my office."
The next morning, Ray called back.

"Frank? How you doing?"

"Let's save it all for when we can get together. Maybe later today."

"Pick a place."

"Over by the Exploratorium . . . Short stroll for you. How about the parking lot on the north side. Maybe two, three o'clock?"

"How's three?"

"Three's what it is. I'll be in the car. You'll recognize me. I'm the one who's just come home to find his wife's left him."

At three, Frank spotted Ray, pulled up. Ray looked dapper and tan, and reaching across the front seat, he shook Frank's hand. In spite of himself, Frank was happy to see him.

"You're still here."

"I'm going to prison in six days. The Feds run things on a fast track. I spent a long time talking to Melikian about it."

"Yeah, Aram can sure talk."

"I did some hard thinking. The IRS has taken my house, my cars, my art, everything they know about. Beyond that they're adding one and a half million in other taxes and penalties."

"They'll use it to keep pressuring you to give names and cooperate once you're in—and they'll try to collect. It kind of drives guys back into business. Once they get you they never let go."

"I'm not ready to become a fugitive and spend the rest of my life looking over my shoulder."

Frank saw himself sitting on his windowsill, safe deposit keys in his pocket, grating on the sidewalk, the wide, empty street waiting. Said dryly, "Yeah, I can relate. Lost her either way."

"Who?"

"Karen. Go on."

"Melikian said I'd probably get parole in eighteen months; I can figure things out while I'm inside and then do the next thing. I'm still kind of amazed at how the plea bargain worked out."

"No weapon. No priors. Good lawyer."

"Yeah, I know, but Melikian had to have had something else he's not telling me about. You know?"

Frank shook his head. "It's poker. Bluff. Hole card. Made the Prosecutor think this and that." Frank resolutely shut up. Ray looked around. Frank hadn't been paying attention and now they were funneling around onto the Golden Gate.

"Where we going?"

Frank shrugged. "Just driving."

They crossed the Bridge and Frank took an exit, another. Below, Fort Baker and the Yacht Basin. Headlands National Park. They followed the road, the red towers of the Golden Gate rising behind them. Container ships emerged from under the bridge. Across, all of San Francisco—North Beach, the Presidio, the Avenues, Ocean Beach, white in the sun. They followed the road up several narrow curving turns until they were beneath the massive World War II gun emplacements, and then, silenced by the opening vista, they descended, came to an empty turnout and stepped from the car. The crying of gulls, the surf below. A dizzying plunge down onto the rocks.

Ray turned, looked Frank up and down and said, "You okay, man?"

"Me? Yeah, I'm okay. I've been going to AA meetings. Running. Trying to get used to the idea that Karen's gone."

"The first thing that hit me, you looked like you've lost a lot of weight. You been sick?"

"I lost about fifteen pounds in the gulag. Just not eating junk. Jogging and walking. Tell me. You ever seen a happy looking jogger?"

"Come to think of it, no."

"Self-righteous, yeah. Stoical. Right. But happy. No

way. Most of my clients are being pretty understanding about my trip to the gulag. No one talks about it. Like a fatal disease. Polite avoidance. Play the game. Karen's served me with divorce papers. I know, there's been a lot of shit between Karen and me, but whatever it was, good, bad, it's your life, right? She suckered me, but I love her, maybe more than ever. Inside, I know she probably can't be happy with anyone but me—she knows it, too, but this was her payback and her grand exit. I understand. It's one thing when you think someone's been stepping out on you. It's another for her to read all the little details in letters. Anyway, it had a kind of logic for her and she had to play it out.'' Frank shrugged. ''I'm not happy to lose her.''

Ray nodded and put his hand on Frank's shoulder. He turned and looked out at the horizon. His black hair stood up in the wind, shirt whipping, slacks curling around his legs. He said, ''You and I are settled? You got the rest of the money?''

Frank nodded. ''Thanks, Ray. You've been the only guy I know who's kept his word to me.'' The wind gusted. Beyond, the horizon. Above, the infinite deep of the unclouded afternoon sky. Frank said, ''Ray, did I give you the name?''

The ease went out of Ray's posture, but he didn't turn. ''You got twenty thousand, didn't you?''

''Twenty. Exactly twenty.''

''That's what I said I'd give you.'' Ray didn't say any more.

''You were the one who taught me not to talk on phones.''

''That's right.''

''But I did.''

Ray still didn't answer. Frank turned to him. ''Okay, Ray, I'm not going to play any games. And you're too smart for me to lead you. Whatever you're doing, if it's not too late, have it called off. I know you wouldn't be doing it yourself with all the attention that's on you now.

You wouldn't do it yourself, anyway. It's just money for you. Cash goes out. A result comes back.

"You know, Ray, Karen said she wouldn't go in my files, she'd be there when I got back, but she wasn't, isn't. My friends sat me down in a room and said, you have to be this, or we're not there. Don't call late, don't argue over money, don't this or that. You never said anything like that, and you've always delivered." Frank paused, unsure of what he was trying to say.

Ray cupped a hand over his eyes and squinted at the blinding horizon.

"Hey, you read me. I'm an obsesser. Right from the start you were sure someone gave you up and you asked me to find him. You knew it would bug me until I did. That was smart. You probably didn't know if I'd give you the name. Hey, I didn't know myself." Frank watched the container ship which had come out from under the Gate bury her bow in a sea, rise in slow motion. "Look, part of me says you're right. The criminal justice system has eyes for some things, but not others. It sets things in motion, pits people against each other in ways that are often worse than the crimes they commit. People fall through the cracks. I'd be the first to say that.

"Okay, he ate with you, drank with you, got stoned with you, played tennis with you, for Christ's sake. And he handed you over to the Feds to save his ass. He shouldn't just be able to walk away from you like nothing happened." Beyond, the blown-out wakes of the freighters as they set their courses in the open ocean spread out, vectors on a compass rose.

"But you said before that you were going to prison because you didn't want to spend the rest of your life looking back over your shoulder. Okay, the Feds, the IRS will let you sit a while in prison. Six months, a year down the road, they'll come to you, give us names, help us, we'll help you. That's just their dance. That's a piece of cake. But when the FBI shows up and starts asking questions about Rosenthal, Ray, that will be a whole new ball game.'' Frank shrugged. ''I promise you, it'll come back to us. I know you've got enough cash to have him done. But if they haven't found him yet, stop it. Call it off. That's all I can say.'' He added, almost as an afterthought, ''Besides, we're not what I see in prison; we're not killers, Ray. You always said it was just business.'' He heard Karen saying, you give so many people so many different stories, you don't know what to believe yourself. He believed this now. ''Is it too late?''

Under his cupped hand, Ray squinted at the horizon. He didn't answer; it was one of the reasons Frank had always believed in him. Without looking at Frank, he got in the car. They drove back toward San Francisco without a word, and when they were just off 101 at the first red light, Ray got out without warning, leaned into the car and said, ''Seeya, Frank,'' and walked away.

In six days, Ray was to surrender to the authorities and start serving his time. Frank called to see if Ray wanted him to go up with him, but Ray never called back. That afternoon on the Headlands, the silence in the car afterward, had been a divide; they'd reached the limits of their friendship. They were on their own.

''Frank, Murray here.'' It was morning in mid-November, still gray outside, and Frank was alone at his desk with a cup of coffee. ''What the fuck you doing up so early?''

''I'm on page two hundred of a grand jury transcript. I do love grand juries. I could get your mother indicted for anything with a grand jury. What a system. Anyway, I couldn't sleep. Seems ill-advised to drink or do the other eighty-five things that go with it. Already run five miles and if I run any more this week there'll be nothing left of me but an asshole squeaking through traffic. You know that runner's high they're always talking about?''

''Fuck, no.''

''Yeah, me neither. Anyway, might as well work. Nothing else to do. Maybe make the noon AA meeting. That's something to look forward to if you like confessions, cigarettes, and coffee.''

"Frank, you're telling me more than I want to know and I've got a bunch of calls to make."

"Scuse me, Homes."

"I've got a friend who's tapped into a data bank down in Southern California. Never mind all the cha-cha little details, but he's found a checking account under the name of Howard S. Rosenthal, about six thousand dollars. It hasn't been touched in nineteen months."

Frank calculated. Nineteen months. That would be a month or so before Rosenthal was busted in L.A.

"Where is it?"

"A Bank of America branch in Leucadia, just south of L.A."

When the IRS had cleaned Rosenthal out, as they undoubtedly had, maybe they'd missed that account. Or, in return for his cooperation, they could have kind of looked the other way on a few things. Six thousand dollars was no big deal to the Feds. Leucadia. Frank tipped his easy chair. Hadn't Ray mentioned Leucadia, that Jack Adams claimed to have an ex-wife down there? Maybe Rosenthal had kept one fact—an ex-wife—to help ground him as he'd play out being Jack Adams?

"Could be the right one."

"There's no listing for a Howard Rosenthal in Leucadia."

"Wouldn't have thought so."

"So the account's sitting there untouched. Might be your guy, Frank. Might not. He might draw on it any day. He might never draw on it again."

"Yeah, that's the part that makes me nervous."

"I'll be keeping an eye on it and if it's tapped or moves, I'll let you know."

"Thanks for being you, Murray. Just keep billing me."

"You can bet on it."

*   *   *

Frank had just spotted a parking space on a side street and was slowing when a dirty white car pulled in front of him, another behind. Before he could do anything, two huge unshaven guys jumped from the car in front, dragged him out of his car, pinned his arms behind his back, and bent him over the hood of his car. Frank started to struggle, but searing pains shot up his arms and through his shoulders, almost paralyzing him. He waited for the gun. A third guy came walking up. A soft laugh. "August. August like the month. What kind of funny little houses you building now, Frankie?"

At the same time, he felt the pressure relax on his arms and hands. Frank turned. Farrell stood beside the car. He smiled at Frank, straightened his collar and jacket. "How ya doin, Frank?" Trembling, Frank could only nod. "Hadn't seen you around much lately and just thought I'd say hello. Well, you doin alright?" Farrell's over-exposed, blue-white eyes.

"I'm okay."

"See, ya gotta stay alert. All kinds of guys can get the drop on ya." Farrell pointed a finger-pistol at him. The two undercover cops stood off to one side and smirked. Farrell patted him on the shoulder. "Your businessman defendant went to the slam, huh? Boy, that taxfree money's tempting. . . ."

Farrell nodded to his guys, and the two undercover cops walked back to their car. Farrell returned to his. Catching his breath, Frank said, "What do you know, Dennis?"

Farrell smiled. "Oh, Frankie, if you only knew what I knew. Just be careful." He got in his car and drove off. Frank parked and went in to his AA meeting, but couldn't keep his mind on a thing.

On a windy afternoon in early July, Gloria handed him his morning's messages. "And this one just half an hour ago." She placed a note on the pile. Murray Axelrod. 1:15. Please call. Please. That was Gloria's ad lib. Murray had never used the word *please* in his life. Frank dialed, got put on hold. Started opening mail.

Murray came on talking. "Frank, the Leucadia Branch Bank of America account closed five days ago on Howard Rosenthal. I just picked up on it yesterday. The whole thing was transferred into the account of a Michael H. Montgomery in Reno, Nevada. Bank of Nevada. The Montgomery account is about eight thousand dollars. The only address is a P.O. Box and the only thing that ever gets written against that account are cash withdrawals. This guy never pays a phone bill, uses a credit card of any kind, nothing. Just cash. That's all I know. Except that he's not listed in information." Murray laughed. "You're on your own now, Slick."

Murray banged down the phone. Murray. The gauchest guy Frank knew. The last guy he'd want to have digging on him.

Frank walked around with it all a blank for several days and then he remembered a guy he'd been asked to serve a couple of years back. He'd run a skip trace on him, but turned up nothing. All he knew from his conversation with the lawyer was that the guy was a sheetrocker, about six three, curly reddish hair, big mustache, a hunter, and had a temper. The hunter and temper part thrilled Frank to death. Frank remembered that when he'd stayed on the move after his first outing with Ray and Jimmy Donovan and the Morris brothers, no matter where he turned up, he'd always go back to the things he could do—he was a cook, he was a house-painter, a roofer, a handyman. People changed their hair color, grew beards, shaved mustaches, but they didn't change occupations so easily. So why not look in the obvious places first? Frank had gone to the yellow pages: drywall. Gloria had started calling local contractors: Met a really nice guy, think he said he worked for you, curly reddish hair, tall, a mustache. I had a flat tire this morning and he stopped to help me, he was just so nice and courteous, I didn't get his name, but I wanted to thank him and send him something. On the twentieth call, the woman said, oh, sure, you mean . . . She'd given Gloria his name and address, his present job site. Frank had worn a pair of painter's overalls and boots, had the papers in the bib, and kept his hand on a claw hammer hanging on a belt loop. The guy'd been so astonished, he hadn't said a word, just taken the papers, and Frank had kept his hand on the hammer as he backed away, but bad temper, big game hunter, the guy had never moved.

Before he'd been busted, Rosenthal had been a tennis pro at a country club in L.A. where he'd started dealing to his wealthy clients. It had been his tennis playing that allowed the DEA to put him on a tennis court with Ray. Tennis had been his downfall; it had been his salvation. Tennis was Rosenthal's occupation. After checking the Nevada D.M.V. for Michael H. Montgomery and coming up with zero, there seemed to be nothing left to do but go to Reno.

The only thing cool in Reno were the casinos; they were freezing. The mob didn't want people falling asleep at the tables. Outside in the blinding glare, Reno was baking, desert heat, but, Frank recalled wryly, getting back into his rental car, even though it was 104, it was a dry heat.

He'd been at it several days, working his way through a list of country and tennis clubs, and he still had not found anyone named Michael H. Montgomery. Maybe Rosenthal had changed occupations, become the brain surgeon every father wished for. Maybe the Howard Rosenthal who had transferred his account to Michael Montgomery's was not the one who had played out his starring role as Jack Adams. Or maybe Ray had taken care of that Howard Rosenthal months ago—even before they'd talked out at Headlands.

Driving past a large public park, Frank passed a pool, a playground, and almost missing it, back behind a cluster of palms, he noticed a chainlink fence and saw the yellow phosphorescent glow of a tennis ball as it arced in a lob. He U-turned, parked.

He angled through the park—early afternoon, the sound of doves, the heat-muted stillness, broken by the sharp cries of kids diving and swimming in the public pool, and closer, the whump of tennis balls. He walked over toward the chainlink fence and looked through the canvas blinds, drifted down the length of courts. There were a dozen, maybe half in use. There was a low grandstand on one open side surrounded by bougainvillea, magenta and white oleander.

He walked back around the front of a brick building, which said: Reno Parks and Recreation. There was a good-looking college girl sitting on a stool at the window. She was listening to the radio and underlining some kind of chemistry text with a yellow highliter. When she sensed his presence at the counter, she looked up. "Hi. You have a tennis program?"

"We have a really good program."

"I was thinking of signing my son up for lessons. Little hot this time of day, but maybe you have other times available."

"We have lessons early in the morning, and then again, evenings, both group or individual." She handed him a schedule.

"Do you have a list of instructors?"

"All of our instructors are well-qualified."

"I'm sure; I'm looking for an old college buddy, Michael Montgomery."

She brightened. "Michael's really good. He'll be here tonight. Five to ten. He's got a group lesson, then a couple of individual lessons."

"Great. How's Michael looking these days? I haven't seen him in years. He used to have that kind of rangy, slim build, curly blond hair. Still got his hair? Keeping the weight off?"

"He looks in shape to me. He's got blond hair, but it's not curly. He's got a crew cut."

Frank shrugged. "Well, whatever, it'll be good to see him. Are you going to be here awhile?"

"Until six. Want me to leave a message, tell him you dropped by?"

"That's exactly what I don't want. I'm going to be picking up my son in a couple of hours. Michael's never met him before, and I want it to be a complete surprise."

She nodded. "How old's your son?"

"Eight."

"That'll be a terrific surprise."

"Won't it? I hope so."

Frank drove back to one of the freezing casinos and played blackjack. He won for a while, then started to lose before he realized he wasn't keeping his mind on the cards; he was just picking them up, throwing them down, losing money. He was too aware of the clinking of ice in people's drinks, of the drinks themselves, and finally, he walked from the table, a couple of hundred dollars in the hole, went to a pay phone, and found an AA meeting.

The desert heat was starting to break, the shadows from the palms and tennis nets, long and flat, were fading into the dust suffused air. The pool was quiet, but for a few adults swimming laps, and just as Frank walked across the park, the tennis court floodlights went on. Along a park path two kids, who were old enough to have gone on to other things, were riding their skateboards—de rigueur U.S. Keds, baggy shorts, hip-length lime and orange fluorescent T-shirts, haircuts with enough hair left too long and cut too short and badly in the wrong places to make an interlocking Chinese puzzle, a little from each head. Cigarettes in their mouths. He listened to the slam and thud of their skateboards as they repeatedly rode down three concrete steps and tried to climb the sloping side of a dry fountain.

He pulled the Red Sox hat brim down over the front of his face. He'd lost a lot of weight, but if this was Rosenthal, he'd met Frank with Ray, knew him, would have an eye for someone showing up from that part of his life which he'd hoped to have left behind. If Frank had wanted to take the trouble to find his apartment or bungalow and make an illicit afternoon tour inside through an open window or jimmied back door, he knew the house of Michael Montgomery would probably have no personal effects— no pictures, no yearbooks, no mementoes, no letters, no sports newspaper clippings, nothing—that every single personal effect from his life as Howard Rosenthal, anything that could give him away, had to have been left behind when he'd gone into the Witness Protection Program. If this was him.

On the far courts, beneath the lights, there were several combinations of players, and keeping his face down and shuffling along the fence, Frank walked toward them and stopped. There was a guy easily over six feet with a blond crew cut and full beard; he was playing baseline. The court was covered with dozens of yellow balls. He had someone playing net, was driving ball after ball, the student making his returns. Periodically, he'd walk or jog to the net, correct something in the swing or grip or the way the player was squaring up, and then return to the baseline. When he'd used all of the balls in the container, they both picked them up and then started a long baseline to baseline rally, Montgomery periodically calling out encouragement, "Good. Come in now. Nice shot." Frank listened, but he couldn't recognize the voice. He watched him. He was a good tennis player, he had the same coloring as Rosenthal, but with the beard and crew cut, he really couldn't be sure it was him.

He walked back toward the two skateboarders, watched them come thudding down the steps and roll toward him. "S'happenin, guys?" They kind of shrugged. "One of you guys got a cigarette?"

The tall one with the shaved temple and long black hair fumbled out a crushed pack of Kools. Frank bummed a light, thanked them. "Hey, one of you guys wanta make

ten bucks..." They looked at each other nervously.
"Hey, whoa, nothing weird, nothing weird."

Frank took a ten out of his wallet. Rocking their boards,
they listened. "See that guy teaching tennis." The black-
haired one nodded. "Okay, he's an old buddy of mine,
doesn't know I'm in town. I just want you to walk up to
the court and call him. Loud as you can. Howard Rosenthal. That's all. Couple of times. Loud. He won't say anything or ask you, but if on the off chance he does, you can
tell him it was an old buddy from Mill Valley. He'll get
it. I'm just going to walk down there under that grandstand. When you see me go under wait a minute or two,
and then you can do it. Okay?"

"Howard Rosenthal."

"That's all. Loud." Frank handed the black-haired kid
the ten. He nodded, grinned at his buddy, and pushed the
ten into his pocket.

"Nother butt?"

Frank took another Kool and walked along the fence
until he came to the end and then walked along a path
thick with oleander until he came to the grandstand. A
couple was sitting high up on the other end making out.
Frank looked back at the skateboarders, who had come to
the fence behind Montgomery. They glanced his way.
Frank stepped under the grandstand. He had a clear view
of Montgomery, who in the yellow floods, glided back and
forth across the court, making shots, returning shots, calling out encouragement.

The black-haired boy leaned on the fence and called as
he'd been asked to do. Howard Rosenthal. He called the
name once and Frank watched Montgomery. He'd been
shifting his weight and bringing his racket to a forehand
and at the sound of the name he froze, and the ball shot
by him. He looked around, looked back at the two kids,
who had retreated from the fence and were already drifting
into the park.

Frank turned toward his car. It was night now and he
could see the glow of the casinos from the middle of town.

He drove back toward the airport. He could almost feel sorry for Rosenthal; for him, the terror would always be there, right beneath the surface. It had been either rat or prison, and he'd made his choice. Today Frank had warned him he'd been found, and Rosenthal would have to find a way to live with that. Maybe it would keep him ahead of Ray. Maybe not. Frank had made a few mistakes along the way, but whatever else happened now, it was out of his hands. Frank had given him his warning.

FRANK SORTED THE last of the files into a cardboard box, peered into the empty file drawer, and then taped the box shut. As he stacked it on several others in the closet, the phone rang. Frank picked up. "Frankie, Giordano here."

"Hey! Johnnie G. How's life over in the Oakland P.D.'s office?"

"Totally out of control. Too many cases."

"I heard that. Broke their own record with 197 murders last year. Crack and blood. Volatile mix. No money. No education. Get a bellyful. It's the Pinto gas tank, you know. Cheaper to pay on the damages than fix it. Don't start me."

Giordano had passed the bar a year ago on his first outing; Sixties activist, liberal, he now had all the poor and disadvantaged and everything else he could possibly want to defend for the rest of his life. "I've got a good new murder, Frank. Drive-by. Bloods. My defendant's gonna need a lot of investigation. Maybe five or six grand worth. Want it?"

"No way I can do it, I'm just cleaning out my files, referring all my cases. I'm getting ready to study for the bar exam full time. I don't know if I'll still have a business when I come back or if I'll come back or if I even want it back, but those are all chances I'll have to take."

"Good murder. Your kind of case. And good money."

"Don't tempt me. When's the prelim?"

"Next week."

Frank laughed. "So typical. Call right before the prelim. . . . I love it. You've turned into a lawyer alright: 'Next week.'" He laughed again. "I better pass the bar. I ain't gonna miss this shit."

"Hey, I saw Melikian three weeks ago. He was happy. He'd just gotten a big check for the Valenzuela case."

"Three weeks ago?" Melikian owed Frank over four grand in that case and had promised to pay him the minute he'd been paid. Choked with anger, Frank said, "John, gotta go. Thanks for offering me the case. Good luck."

He hung up, dialed Melikian's office. This was so fucking typical of Melikian, holding his money like that. Just as Velma answered, Frank caught himself and hung up; he strolled rapidly out to the courtyard, where he turned in circles for several minutes. He was seething, but he'd just narrowly avoided a shouting match with Melikian. He knew holding his money was Melikian's power trip. Melikian had been written up big in the papers over Valenzuela, and he'd never once mentioned Frank, though it had been Frank who had turned up the witnesses who had made his case. Aram just couldn't bring himself to give Frank a little credit. Or pay him when he was supposed to. Hey, that's what it was with him. Never mind, Frank was closing his office, taking the bar. And Melikian would go on playing it like this forever. No amount of yelling at him was going to change things.

Inside, calmer, Frank made himself coffee, returned to his bare office, found that Gloria had placed the mail on his desk. He opened a letter with only a P.O. Box return address and an unfamiliar handwriting, a woman's:

Dear Frank,

   I'm sure you're surprised to hear from me. That's presumptuous. Why would you ever have even thought about me? I never imagined I'd write you, but I hated the way things got left in Pacific Grove. Knowing more now about what happened to Ray, I can understand the suspicions you had about me, though that wasn't exactly my fault, either. Finding out Ray wasn't who I thought he was—or wanted him to be—made me a little crazy. More than a little. I regret and am embarrassed by what happened that day we met in North Beach. But it's too easy to say I was crazy. Maybe it's even too easy to have regrets. Anyway, I have been writing Ray in prison. He's been writing back. I'm going up to see him in a couple of weeks. I wonder if you wouldn't like to drive down with me. I know from

his letters that something happened and you two don't
seem to be on speaking terms. Maybe I'm just afraid
to go alone. I can't leave it the way it is. I don't know
what else to say. I've come back to the city. If you're
interested, write me at this P.O. Box.

Yours,
Sarah Anne

Frank dropped the letter on the desk and then started sorting through another filing cabinet. When he was finished,
he taped the box shut and stacked it with the others in the
closet.

On a sunny May morning ten days later, Frank sipped an
espresso and waited on the curb outside his office and just
about the time she said she'd be there, Sarah Anne pulled
up. Frank looked into the car. "How ya doin?"

"Good. I'm good, Frank. How've you been?"

"You still wanna do this? Together?"

She smiled, quick, tight and nodded. "Still wanna. Why
wouldn't I?"

"Cause now I'm here for real, and, you know, people
picture it one way and then there is it and they change
their minds. And that's okay."

She shook her head no, and Frank slid into the front
seat, and handed her a lidded coffee cup, a packet of sugar
on top, and she turned to him and smiled. "Oh, thanks.
That's great. Perfect." She added the sugar, took a sip.
"You look good, Frank."

"Thanks."

The moment he was near her—it was her smell—he
felt the familiar stab of chaotic desire. It was always the
same with her. He took a deep breath and settled back and
smiled at it. Okay. So hey, okay. They wound through the
long inland valleys of 101 South—Salinas, San Luis
Obispo—stopping along the way for cokes and sandwiches
which they ate on a park bench, driving on, talking some,
falling silent. Her new job. His divorce. Sarah had a few

uncertain words about Ray, what he'd written. He was
working in the kitchen. Reading a lot. Suddenly Sarah
Anne was laughing: Ray working in the kitchen; the guy
never washed a dish or scrubbed a pot the whole time we
were together; he was helpless in the kitchen. Frank said
with his best beatific, New Age counselor intonation,
"Things even out. Whatever goes around, comes around."
They laughed again, but grew silent and thoughtful as they
took the cutoff at Santa Maria for Lompoc.

When they reached the prison, Frank felt what he always felt coming out of prisons. Fear. He got out of the
car and looked at Sarah Anne. They exchanged glances,
but didn't say anything more as they walked across the
parking lot toward the main receiving area. Just before
they reached the gate, Frank, from habit, went through his
pockets, but what would there be? "He knows we're coming?" Sarah Anne nodded. "Together?" She nodded
again. "Today?" She nodded again. "Okay."

Ray walked into the reception area, looked at them both,
no expression. Sarah Anne hesitated, walked over to him.
She smiled. "How're ya doin, Ray?"

He smiled at her. "Doin okay. Thanks for writing."

Frank walked over and held out his hand. "Ray."

Ray took his hand. "Nice to see ya, Frank. Thanks for
coming." Frank looked at him. Ray was happy to see
them, he could tell that, but his eyes gave away nothing.
Frank looked at Ray and Sarah and thought, this is ridiculous, my being here. Frank patted his pockets.

"Hey, you know, I just remembered I left my wallet
on the front seat in the car! Got the keys?" Sarah Anne
handed him the keys. "I'll be right back." Frank went
back out through security and sat on a bench in front of
the prison. Either they settled something, once and for all,
or there was nothing more to say and who cared. He
glanced at his watch. After half an hour, he figured, well,
that's enough time, either things are okay with them, or
they're not okay and she might welcome rescuing. There

was no way to choreograph these things—come together, come alone, come on Saturday, don't . . .

Inside, Sarah Anne and Ray held hands and talked quietly, their heads touching, but when Sarah Anne saw Frank reenter the reception area, she squeezed Ray's hand and stood. She walked toward him. "You didn't have to do that . . ."

He smiled. "Sure, it would have gone fine with me sitting there between you . . ."

". . . but I'm glad you did. I think Ray wants to talk to you."

She looked over at Ray, smiled, eased herself across the room, sat down. Frank sat down by Ray.

"How're ya doing, Ray. Makes me nervous just being here."

Ray smiled. "Yeah, they've got a number with your name on it waiting."

"You're in the kitchen."

"Yeah, I make a great salad. It's not fun here, but not bad." Out of habit, they spoke in lowered voices. "How's biz?"

"Closing for a while. Getting ready to take the bar."

"Sarah Anne said the divorce went through." Frank nodded. "Sorry, man."

Frank shrugged. "Happens."

"How is it?"

"Actually, it's terrible. I love her. And I know she loves me. We're the only ones impossible enough for each other." Then there seemed to be nothing more to say. The silence grew into an awkward impasse and Frank realized that he was going to have to take the next step. Frank shifted in his chair. Lowered his voice a little more. "Ray, you know, if we're going to get past whatever, I'm going to need to say something. And you know what it's about. I'm not going to take any action. You know that. And there's nothing I can do. Or will do. Just the simple truth will do. You tell it. I'll try to believe it. I know that's a tough one for both of us. Just think. If I'd wanted to hurt you, I could have done it. Hey, I could be on an island in the South Pacific today if I'd wanted. Five million buys a little. Bored, maybe, but there. Ray, what about Rosenthal?''

Ray looked at the floor a long time. "Okay, Frank. Yeah, I paid someone to find him.''

"And?"

"The first step was to find him. I did think about what you'd said to me that day up on the Headlands, that it would lead back to us pretty quick.''

"And did he find Rosenthal, your man?"

"Hadn't. Hasn't.''

"Shoulda hired me.''

"Couldn't find anybody that good.''

"And if you do find him, Ray? Do you grease him?"

"You know, Frank, most of my first year I went to sleep on that thought. Now I just want to get out of here, put it all behind me. Specially after seeing Sarah Anne today. I don't want this coming back.''

"I found Howard Rosenthal in the Witness Protection Program. It's not a camp on a lake with canoes and a roped-off swimming area.''

Neither spoke. Finally, Ray said, "I'm not asking where you found him.''

"I'm not telling where.''

They both smiled.

Frank said, "He's long gone, anyway. But I let him know he'd been made. He's gonna spend a long time looking over his shoulder. He won't have any fun. You'll get out. He won't. He's always got it. Can we leave it there?" Ray nodded. "I'm believing what you tell me, Ray.''

Ray nodded again. "Leave it there.''

There was a stirring among the prisoners and their visitors as the guards informed them the visiting hours were over. "Hey, Ray," Frank hugged him, "don't turn queer on us in here.''

Sarah Anne came up behind them. "I won't let him.''

* * *

Frank added water to the coffee filter. He sipped the coffee, circled the kitchen, looked over at the kitchen table piled high with notes, yellow pads, books, and the bar review outline. He stopped in front of the snapshot on the bulletin board. It was Kramer, fairly sleepless, more tousled than ever, holding a new baby. Beneath, the birth announcement. They had moved to L.A., where Kramer was working on a treatment based on one of his articles. Frank returned to the table and went back to work, and Joe curled up on a yellow pad nearby and purred. The phone rang.

"Hi, Frank . . . Karen. Is this a bad time to call? Am I interrupting? How're you doing?"

"I'm studying for the bar."

"I'll make it quick. How's it going?"

"It's going. I'm living on rice and beans and spaghetti and almost broke. How much can you tell someone about studying for the bar twelve hours a day. Torts are exciting?"

"I'm just finishing curating a show. Come see it after you take the exam. It's wonderful. And Camera Work is including me in their next show. I'm doing okay. . . ." She paused. "And I've been thinking about your letter, Frank. Your dinner invitation."

"Did I ask you to dinner?"

"Frank . . ."

"It's been so long, I'd almost forgotten. Not really. But I've never waited a month for someone to respond to a dinner invitation."

"This one required a lot of thought. And I've finally been able to reach a conclusion."

"Gonna tell me or are we just going to listen to static?"

"I'd love to go out to dinner with you after you take the bar exam."

"Three weeks tomorrow."

"My therapist says I'm foolish to even entertain thoughts about going out with you again."

"Just don't order oysters. Raw oysters. I have trouble

watching them slide off the shells. No, order what you want. Hey, what about me? You're a divorced woman. You know what they say about divorcees . . .''

"We're hot and dissolute."

"Yeah, I'm looking for action on the first date."

"You're impossible, Frank, and you probably always will be, and I suspect we're impossible together, but it also seems to be impossible when we're apart. Sometimes it makes me mad. I can't decide if it's love or sickness."

"I'll lobby for love. Call you back in three weeks and some change."

"I hope I can meet someone and fall in love before then, but I doubt I'll get that lucky."

"Start thinking about where you'd like to dine."

"I'll do that."

Frank hung up. Unsettled, he walked to the sink and rinsed several dishes and coffee cups, took out the trash. Then he wandered into the backyard, kneeled, and began weeding among the rows. Squash. Corn. Zucchini. Tomatoes. Sunflowers. He put the hose on low and watched it start to flood the garden; he glanced at his watch, felt a strange restlessness go through him, a hollowness in the mouth. Maybe a candy bar would be good. He swallowed hard. There was an AA meeting at six. That would be soon enough. He'd give himself five more minutes before he went in and got back to work. He circled the yard, the cat stalking behind, stopping when he stopped, walking when he walked. Frank crouched, moved the hose once more, petted the cat, who flicked his tail, and watched the water flooding the garden rows.